To Forget Palermo unfolds as a dazzling mosaic: Baron di D., cuckolded by a young tenor named Caruso; Alfio, who cannot understand what devil drives his son to Sicily's dust and poverty; little Agata's strength and courage derived from a simple faith; the miracle wrought by the Chinese Madonna of Mulberry Street. These are only a few in the long procession of unforgettably vivid characters and exquisitely poignant scenes in this novel.

In *Vogue, To Forget Palermo* is called "a very beautiful novel . . . a superb novel of our times."

TO
FORGET
PALERMO

TO
FORGET
PALERMO

by EDMONDE CHARLES-ROUX

TRANSLATED BY *Helen Eustis*

DELACORTE PRESS / NEW YORK

PART ONE

I.

*There's no such thing as America! It's a name
given to an abstract idea.*   HENRY MILLER

In New York it is startling to see a man dressed all in black sitting
on a doorstep. Even downtown, even at the corner of Mulberry
Street. So I shall always remember him, Rocco Bonavia, just as he
appeared to me that day—a dark milestone I stumbled upon. . . .

Pam and I occupied neighboring desks, and each evening I
watched her perform the complicated ritual with which she concluded all her days. In front of the whole office she would step out
of her skirt, slip off her sweater, and change her clothes from head
to foot. From a suitcase under her desk she took a necklace, white
gloves, sheer stockings; then she slid her long pale legs into a
black sheath. Ask her where was she going? What were her plans?
What would have been the use? All of her undertakings were of

equal importance to her. Her education, with its obsession for efficiency, had conditioned her totally. The framework of engage-
ments, social obligations, receptions, openings? Her career depended on it. Time and again she would begin a sentence, "My
career. . . ." The phrase filled her mouth and her existence. She
was enclosed in it as if by a shell. This was her life, and she was
completely convinced that someone like myself could only envy
her, since I had no such activities. I restrained myself, matching
her with silence, knowing how she must be worrying and wondering what on earth I could be doing when my work was over for
the day and I disappeared into limbo. Each evening I heard the
astonishment in her voice (though she tried to keep it light) as
she asked, "Well, what are you up to this evening? Where are you
going?"

At the beginning of those wandering days, before I met Rocco
Bonavia, I didn't know myself. Where was I going? Nowhere. . . .

"I'm going out for some air. It's stifling in this mausoleum."

Pam's face would freeze. Her life, her career, did not allow moments for idleness. Poor Pam! She attached such great importance
to her job as beauty editor on a big woman's magazine. She loved
her job and worked hard at it. How could I use the word mausoleum to describe this hive where she was queen bee? But I told
her I used the word quite literally.

"If some disaster befell New York, ten centuries from then
they'd find you buried under this skyscraper. You'd be just the
way you are today, the perfect seductress, intact among your samples, make-up boxes, hair sprays, powders, your complete gamut of
lipsticks, your eye shadows, your beauty creams. The archaeol-
ogists would surely make one of their usual solemn mistakes and
announce to the world that they'd found a fabulous tomb, the
tomb of an unknown queen, slender, blond, her neck laden with
pearls. They would assume that your office was the Throne Room,
the coat closet the Treasury, and your secretaries a retinue of sacred prostitutes. So you see I'm not really insulting you by calling
this a mausoleum!"

Since Pam was essentially good-natured and she liked to be agreeable, she allowed herself a quick smile. Maybe she thought it good for her to permit herself to be titillated by useless ideas from time to time. That's the way she was, always swinging between a kind of innocence and a lively scorn. After all, what was I to her? Coincidence? Chaos? Or was I simply her Aunt Rosie's lodger? No matter. I was her misfortune. But that was something she could not yet suspect.

I had come to New York in exile and seeking forgetfulness. For someone determined to think of nothing, my job as a travel writer was ideal. I worked at *Fair*, a magazine read by an enormous number of women, all hoping to acquire elegance, chic, *savoir vivre*, and above all that beauty for which Pam prescribed with an awesome confidence.

"When you smile, let all your teeth show at once. Then open your jaws just a little, allowing a glimpse of your tongue." And so on.

While Pam stage-managed smiles and puffed or flattened hair styles, I told the ladies about Europe, its cathedrals, its fortresses, its excavations, its dead cities. I also knew how to inspire our readers with restlessness and discontent. I provoked in them a desire to escape, an appetite for culture, for samples of the original, authentic past. The sirens' grottoes, the beaches Ulysses loved, balconies for serenades, cloisters for amorous nuns, castles for abductions—how can one die without having known these?

I filled my readers with folklore; I made them nostalgic for tarantellas, processions, Holy Weeks. Where did I not guide them? I promised genius to whoever drank Marsala on the terraces of our cafés. And love? I promised romantic encounters, too. I was the sales manager of happiness in foreign lands. The women I sent off, to countries that were without memories or risks for them, were easily satisfied. For them, there were no landscapes or cities to avoid. None of the constraints that I knew all too well. Thanks to me, they could go in peace. My articles were more filling than a six-course meal. They contained everything. What clothing to bring, what monuments to photograph, what souvenirs to buy, the height of the campaniles, the depth of the grottoes. Everything. I even advised the sports fans—the swimmers, the skin divers— how to study the marine maps. And to bring a discussion to a close, nothing worked better than a culinary suggestion. Sometimes I only told them about a good vintage year. But more often I titillated my readers by offering dishes on my menus that were so little known that they had to admit their ignorance. They wrote, they telephoned.

"Hello, is this Gianna Meri? . . . Tell me, just what is this *caponata?* After I visit Segeste, should I really make a forty-mile detour to go to that restaurant where they serve it?"

I would insist. I would encourage them.

"What, you mean you've never really tasted it? Why, it's the Sicilian caviar!"

At the other end of the wire, the lady would feel something new and inexplicable as I mixed the olives and ripe tomatoes for her. Then we stood together on that distant island and sliced the eggplant thin. Thinner, thinner! It can't be sliced too thin. I added basil, freshly picked, warm and sweet-smelling from the sun. Then I led her onto a terrace like a stage built out over the sea. There I seated her under a shelter with a straw roof. The water lapped the floorboards. The head drew mist from the cool sea. What a lovely terrace! Supported by its pilings, as light as a Chinese junk on the blue water. The lady gave herself up to me completely and adopted my itinerary, which was so personal and original.

"Thank you, Gianna Meri! . . . Of course. . . . I wouldn't miss it for the world! . . . I'm going to spend my whole vacation in Sicily! . . . I can't thank you enough!"

I could hear regret in her voice—regret that she was not already there.

Sometimes a reader would tell me about some disappointment or sorrow, and I took pleasure in these confidences. Not out of feminine malice or pettiness, but from necessity. One necessarily becomes curious about others when one's sanity depends on forgetting oneself.

The frequency of these reader responses began to make my foreignness indispensable to the magazine. I found what I was looking for. My days were well occupied and distracting; I plunged into them, knowing that with every hour time was passing without my thinking of myself. Only the evenings were left, and those difficult moments when your thoughts escape and run rampant. For these, I had all sorts of remedies. But there's no use trying to amputate the past completely; some stump will remain no matter how hard you try. You must come to terms with the memories which rise in your mind like bubbles from the depths of a swamp; you must beware of the hand that touches you in dreams that are more real than reality; you must fear the stranger whose smile gives some painful reminder to your heart; you must struggle against arms which no longer embrace you. You must lie to yourself, be cowardly, always expect the worst and know that if you give in even a little, the battle will have to begin all over. That is what I finally learned. The boxer who dances around the ring, feeling out the weaknesses of his adversary with his fist, applies himself to winning with no more stubbornness than I brought to my attempts to run away, to deceive myself. I was my own adversary, and I circled myself. But my dance was not limited by the ropes of the ring or the crowd outside them. The silence within me was a large arena in which I exhausted myself. I needed New York and other people; other people and New York, Pam, Aunt Rosie, the unfamiliar world of *Fair*, to still my heart. And I lived in hope of surprises which might cure me of my memories.

"I'm leaving my hotel."

"What's wrong with it?" said Pam indignantly.

"Nothing. Nothing's wrong with. Don't worry. If I could find something wrong with it I might not be leaving it. There should be at least a little something wrong. Then I'd have something to think about. It would keep me busy."

"The bathroom maybe?"

It would be that. Pam was fond of certain conversational themes: cleanliness was one of them.

"Who said anything about the bathroom, Pam? There's boiling hot water night and day. Everything is quiet and oversized. The servants are mutes; the flowers are artificial—even washable. The walls are absolutely soundproof. Everything is double: curtains, windowpanes, doors. If I look down out of my window I can see silent insects passing. Sometimes that awful cry of the police siren manages to penetrate my windows. Or the ambulance. But that's all. And each day, dawn seems to come more slowly. Do you understand that?"

Could she understand? I never tried to find out. She looked at me indignantly and said, "What you're saying is that it's too quiet to sleep."

"That's it!"

"What is it you're really after, Gianna?"

No, I cannot tell you that what I long for is the cock that cries from the invisible barnyard. . . . The cock that salutes the sun as it rises from the mists of the sea. . . . The hand on my shoulder . . . The pillows dented into white peaks like snowy mountains on a day of avalanche . . . The peasant who leads his mule through the dawn at threshing time . . . His song . . . I want to hear his song "E ditta, e ben ditta, 'n celu si trova scritta." His song, heard between waking and sleep.

"All right, Pam, I'll live with your aunt."

She smiled, satisfied. It was enough for her that I'd come to a decision—I'll stay with your aunt—without hesitation. She forgot her question—What is it you're really after?—and there was no more for us to say. So it often happens that if you speak the banal aloud, you manage to stifle the secret truth.

I moved in with Mrs. MacMannox the next day.

* * *

The day we first met, Mrs. MacMannox was ready to go out. This was evident by her hat, a froth of cherry-colored silk which plainly had been made by some well-known designer.

After I got over my surprise—she was such a tiny wisp of a thing—I was able to take in the rest of her: this sixty-year-old lady who acted like a little girl seemed to slide down from her chair rather than rise from it; she stood on one foot as if she planned to play hopscotch on the black and white tiles of the floor, and took me on a tour of the apartment with a skipping gait as if she were a schoolgirl on a holiday.

The decor reflected the taste of the late Mr. MacMannox. He had been in public relations, and business associates still remembered him as a fine figure of a man. A big eater, and one who understood foreign languages.

"I haven't changed a thing since he passed away," Aunt Rosie told me.

That was obvious. Left to herself, Mrs. MacMannox would have chosen something more feminine, more coquettish. I'm not sure just what. Perhaps the kind of Italian furniture one sees in the antique shops on Second Avenue? Let me see: a lacquered gold chest, decorated with little figures of bowing men, consoles, glass chandeliers from Murano, translucent bouquets of flowers trembling with light, and mirrors everywhere, and flowered carpets. Of course! If one had left Aunt Rosie to herself, those were just what she would have chosen. But Mr. MacMannox had decided otherwise. "That Italian stuff is gay and believe me I have nothing against it, but don't forget, baby, that only the Jews here appreciate the fake marble, the gilded mirrors and the thick trimmings. I can't help that. My clients aren't the sort that like Mediterranean bric-a-brac. I can't go in for it in my house. I've got to have something solid. Believe me, we'll be much better off with English stuff." That would be the way Mr. MacMannox laid down the law, in a firmly paternal tone. And Aunt Rosie took his advice.

A tearoom in Oxford, the smoking room of an Anglican bishop, the office of a maritime insurance company, a bank in London, an elegant haberdashery—these were the several inspirations on which Mr. MacMannox drew. On the walls, a fox hunt engraved at the turn of the century and two glass cases of silver curios were the only light touches he allowed. Everything was designed to reassure his clients. Each piece of furniture, each room, seemed full of secret promises. Here was an office in which one could sign only advantageous contracts. Next, the salon, which was not a place for dreaming. And then the library, which evoked a past, a stability, and children who would succeed in the world. There was nothing futile or frivolous in the MacMannox home. Every suggestion the interior decorator made had been refused. *French style in the bedroom? Louis XVI, gray and peaceful? You must be kidding!* Mr. MacMannox wasn't one of those people who think things are better because they're foreign. Mahogany! Everything mahogany, without exception, even the woodwork. Mahogany polished mirror-bright. *Forte, fortissimo* on the mahogany. Mahogany *ostinàto.* Mahogany *sostenùto.* Aunt Rosie's apartment was a hymn to success sung in mahogany. From room to room it breathed, rang, swelled, thundered, reminded of past successes, drew the visitor in its wake, carrying him to unknown places as hymns often do.

I feel quite sure that Mrs. MacMannox's affection for me stemmed from a crown which she noticed embroidered on my handkerchief—and to which I had no right.

After she made this discovery, I noticed that the word "Countess" had been added to my calling card which lay on the hall table, traced in Aunt Rosie's large, proud, spacious hand, with a hunchbacked *C* and two entwined *esses* marching forward with exaggerated assurance.

She began to pepper her conversation with Italian phrases, greeting me with *"Càra* Gianna," and adroitly slipping in an occasional *chi lo sa* here and there, to make me feel at home. How could I tell her that crown was an exercise for the embroidery class of the convent in Palermo where I went to school? Should

I explain it? Aunt Rose had such a peculiar idea of Europe. Much better keep quiet than run the risk of an endless discussion. *Yes, Signora MacMannox, I was a boarder in a convent. Why a boarder? . . . Because my mother died and my father couldn't bring up six children by himself. . . . Yes, I'll grant you that six children is a lot. . . . You find the Italians prolific? Prolific as rabbits. . . . That's hardly polite, Aunt Rosie. My father was a doctor. . . . Of venereal diseases? Why do you say that? . . . Oh come! Sicily has no more or less than any other place. . . . My father died of typhus, when he was a prisoner of the English in a camp in Libya. . . . No, Signora MacMannox, he was not a Fascist. Many Italians died in that war who were not Fascists. . . .* And I would have had to describe my childhood, the convent, the chapel, the refectory, the embroidery classes, the classes in music, housekeeping, deportment. *Yes, they were happy years for me. . . . No, Aunt Rosie, there were no mortifications, no severe penances. We were not cloistered, and we didn't wear black stockings. . . . Yes, I agree. Black stockings are unhealthy, but since we didn't wear them, why are we bothering about them now? . . .*

Catholicism inspired Aunt Rosie with nothing but suspicion.

"How can you place a Catholic socially?" she said to me one day. "It's practically impossible."

And as I couldn't think of what to answer, she added, "I don't trust exotic types."

This statement, added to others—"A Jew is always a Jew," or "An actor! Who on earth wants an actor in an apartment building? They're all unbalanced"—convinced me that I'd better not argue against Aunt Rosie's convictions. So I allowed her to go on congratulating herself that she'd found an Italian countess to rent a room in her apartment. Since it suited her to have a countess for a lodger, a countess whom she'd made out of whole cloth, why should I deprive her? Perhaps the whole thing sounds silly, but not if you understand the appetite for respectability that a New York widow who is past sixty and has a niece to marry off can have; not if you understand just how far she is willing to go to keep up appearances. . . .

Mrs. MacMannox's apartment was far up Park Avenue. Since her husband's death, and since Pam had moved into her own studio on the same floor, the apartment was much too large for Mrs. MacMannox. But the view was pleasant, and the neighborhood was attractively open; in winter, you met people bundled in heavy coats who were walking dogs that wore boots. I suspected that Aunt Rosie chose the place more for the excellence of the address than because it suited her otherwise.

"A good address takes the place of ancestors and family portraits," she would say.

She had a firm faith in this sort of thing.

And the lobby—a most essential room about which Aunt Rosie also held a firm opinion:

"A visitor will judge you by what he sees first."

It made good sense, and I understood how important the lobby of that apartment house was to her with its slightly Gothic woodwork, its electric fire which glowed night and day, its canopied ceiling of green billiard cloth, and behind the door, guarding the galoshes and umbrellas, a doorman with a cap trimmed in silver braid who had the air of an old family servant.

With these consolations, Aunt Rosie was able—almost able—to ignore what was happening to the neighborhood. Harlem was now just a few yards from her door, and that old Negro ghetto was seeping outward like an oil spot. Just the other day, she told me, she had installed a bulletproof peephole at the service entrance. This was in response to a warning from her insurance broker who had told her, with apologies, that his company could no longer insure her expensive mink.

Yes, things were changing fast in this section of New York, and I'd arrived just in time. For Aunt Rosie I was an embroidered handkerchief, a title added to a calling card. I was an unguent, a balm to soothe her anguish.

*   *   *

Aunt Rosie was obsessed by one single idea to which she devoted herself entirely: youth. She had an absolute horror of growing old, and for weeks at a time she would disappear into very expensive clinics. But I never heard her complain of the expense. She would emerge rather feverish, proudly offering to the world the smooth forehead of a mummy, unrecognizable, frozen: another woman. Rejuvenated? The wrinkles were certainly gone, but so was the ability to flex her mouth into a smile. She could only blink her eyes, which she did incessantly, as if to compensate for the disturbing immobility to which she was condemned; as if because of this mute pantomime, this continual play of dried tissues, one would have to believe she was still alive, alive and well, and above all, rejuvenated.

She resented my attitude. I should have shown more enthusiasm. But the change in her features frightened me. When I saw how she had changed, I felt a kind of dizziness, an irrepressible desire to cry out to her: "You aren't fooling anymore, go back to your old face!" Poor Aunt Rosie, victim of obligatory beauty and enforced youth, plumped out with paraffin, strapped up with nylon. . . .

I believe the only reason for my interest in her was in the hope of discovering the motives behind her desperate passion. When you asked her to explain, with a hard mouth and authoritarian eye she embarked on confused theories which scrambled dietary advice with literary concepts, a wild rhetoric to which I listened in silence. She permitted no interruptions. She needed complete freedom to construct her scaffold of lies. (She would spend some portion of each month in bed, hinting discreetly about her menstrual pains.) She referred to her periods in clinics as necessary retreats. Condemning my lack of enthusiasm as cowardice and using my face as a chart for her demonstrations, she threatened me with her really terrible finger. "*There.* I'd go after it there. A stitch over the temple. . . . A tiny incision. There. . . . No, lower. But any lower than that is too low." She grew angry when I contradicted her, "But Aunt Rosie, I'm only. . . ." I put my hands to my temples. I seemed to feel the icy point of the scalpel. She lost her temper. "What has your age got to do with it? You must start young!" Then she would seize me by the arms and push me to the dressing table where an embroidered cloth carried the device, "Age is vanquished." Then she would keep on talking until she believed she had overcome my doubts.

You may say that such blindness was the result of abnormality, that this old little girl hurt no one but herself. And that's true. Aunt Rosie looked worse than simply old. It was her mouth that gave her away. Her mouth was a nest of wrinkles, the Waterloo of the most famous beauty specialists, a crumpled sheet of rice paper ready to disintegrate, a disaster area. The curls that bobbed around her smooth forehead, her bangs, her ageless cheeks, her skipping walk, could only accentuate the piteous ruin of the collapsed mouth. Aunt Rosie was conscious of it. You could read it like a haunting question in her eyes.

"What would you have done about it in my place?" she asked me one day.

In every circumstance and every domain there must always be something-to-do-about-it.

"I? Nothing, really. . . ."

I think I shocked her in an irreparable way that day. She slid off her seat.

"Here, there's no prestige in being old," she announced to me in an aggressive voice that I hardly recognized, adding, "And don't you forget it!"

With that she went into the next room where I heard her viciously unwrapping her bottles and jars from their packages.

She was settling down to her work, a serious business having for its arena the mahogany-paneled room. First she turned off the two modern lamps with rose silk shades, which were souvenirs of an evening in Paris enjoyed by Mr. MacMannox. After a business dinner, the headwaiter (a sort of dandy whose suave manner, as well as his lamps, had dazzled Mr. MacMannox) offered them to him. The champagne, the orchestra, the voice of the waiter murmuring in his customer's ear each time he poured the wine, "Edward VII liked them." The lamps were wrapped for Mr. Mac-Mannox to take back to New York.

Mr. MacMannox decided that these lamps, placed on his wife's dressing table, had such a happy effect that he immediately ordered a dozen more made, distributing them through various rooms in his home.

"Rosy and soft, that's the best kind of light for doing business, also for making love."

That's how Mr. MacMannox talked about his lamps, but Aunt Rosie had just turned them off. What did she want? A brutal light that would shine directly in her face. Seated in front of her mirror, she selected a jar, any jar; it didn't matter. Moisturizers, masks, astringents, hormone creams, vitamin creams, one, two, three, a dozen jars lined up like the symbols of a cult, not to mention the half empty ones which grew delicately rancid on shelves after she decided they didn't work. For an hour, while her struggle lasted, she was going to believe in a miracle. And I was to watch her, like a fly caught in the honey of her hopes, a faithful bystander at the daily spectacle. I would follow the circular movement of her hand spreading a slightly disgusting aureole of grease around her mouth; I would watch her lipstick spread in sticky streaks, making channels, apostrophes, parentheses, ploughing through the furrows of her wrinkles, invading them one after another, coloring them bright red. I would wait for the moment when Aunt Rosie would look like those children who insist on gobbling food: the same stubborn mouth, the same sticky chin. She was such a pitiful mess that my heart bled for her. Aunt Rosie's sense of theater, of drama, fascinated me. Is that surprising? Wasn't I in New York in order to avoid my own thoughts? It was no use telling myself that I neither loved nor admired Aunt Rosie, that I saw all her ridiculousness. I also saw that I would never be able to forget her as she was at that moment, flooded with light and so plainly at the mercy of her fantasies.

Then, when Aunt Rosie had achieved the summits of her Art,

the spectacle came to an end. She looked in the mirror one last time, lightened her voice and said to me, "You know, using these products is as stupid as gambling in a lottery. My word, did I really think it would work? What a face I have! Bring us something to drink, will you, Gianna? A Scotch and soda. That'll cheer me up."

A cloud of powder, and the rosy lamps were lit again. Aunt Rosie gave up the battle with a grimace of disillusion, panting like a diver who surfaces from the depths with empty hands. What could I say to her? How could I comfort her? Face her with one of those statues of wisdom, one of those elderly personages who had dominated my childhood? Drag them out of the tunnel of forgetfulness and make them walk with long, light steps along the lighted path of words? I often wished that I could. I often imagined telling Aunt Rosie about Sundays in Palermo when I was a little girl, my grandmother's Sundays, when she took us to the beach and watched us swim. My grandmother, who always wore mourning, with her white hair, her deep bosom, her crepe dress (violet, gray, or black), thick stockings, high laced shoes, swollen legs. My God, the success she had! As soon as they saw her, far away, advancing slowly across the sand, thrusting forward with her bosom like a diva getting ready to release her high C, twenty boys would rush to meet her, their torsos naked, wearing trunks that hardly hid them, their skin bronzed, their curls plastered on their necks: "Signora Meri, may I get you an ice?" "Signora Meri, would you like me to fix your beach umbrella?" They clustered around her, looking for ways to be of service. If one of us got too far from shore when we were in the water, she rarely needed to call us. One of those charming charmers, a volunteer, would quickly make the sign of the cross, then dive into the water headfirst, kicking vigorously, blowing water out of his nostrils, spitting and making a big noise so that she could not possibly ignore his efforts, and he would rescue the foolish child and bring him back, willingly or by force, and dump him kicking on the sand, soaked and sheepish at her feet, like a living prey. Put to shame, the silly little one was forbidden to go in the water any more. Would Aunt Rosie have understood me—would she even have believed me—had I told her that the star of femininity shined on the forehead of this woman, that she was 75 years old when she sat there by the water, with no back rest, on a kitchen stool, erect as the letter *I* or a queen, her face turned toward the horizon, watching over a swarm of brats, grandchildren ranging from two to eight years—*Yes, Signora, one each year*—and that she, with those young bodies growing golden at her feet, those happy adolescents hanging on her words, made such an unforgettably beautiful tableau? Poor Aunt Rosie, had I told her that story, she could not have understood a word of it. . . . It is of no use to tell people to whom anxiety is basic, those who consider their aspirations quite reasonable even when they are monstrous, that they have made a mistake and there is another way of living, in another place. Useless. So I said nothing and a silence would fall between us, so thick and heavy that it hid us from each other. There are few things sadder than such a silence. How I would have liked to offer Aunt Rosie tranquil pictures of a land where women grew old nobly and kept their feminine power right up to the last day of their lives. But I never knew how. My words stopped short. I left these tête-à-têtes with Mrs. MacMannox filled with a discomfort that I found only too familiar: the sadness born of thoughts one cannot share.

During this period, several weeks after the day I first saw Rocco Bonavia, dressed in black, sitting on Mulberry Street, the only escape I had from Aunt Rosie—so much honest monstrosity united in a single person could make an escape essential, believe me—was the disordered review of my past.

Alone, I would go to meet my memories.

There must have been deep unconscious connections between me and my childhood to make the evocation of it suddenly seem so indispensable to me. Ah, the pleasure of those flights. Lying on my bed in a silent room, I pushed the present out of my mind, slipped away from recent times, twisted out of yesterday's clutch, fell deeper into the past to find, first, oblivion, and then like a secret hiding place, the landscape of childhood. That was the way I escaped. In New York, for the first time, I tasted that joy when each face, each person rediscovered, becomes a necessary food, a vital infusion.

There were the *Old Girls*. Why do they return to my memory, those women who were never friends of mine? Never mind. I am delighted to see them again, with their graceful mantillas. Who but they would have dared to wear such low-cut dresses and black taffeta at ten in the morning? I hear the door opening, squeaking, nobly dilapidated like everything else in our chapel. An odor? What? It's the air of Palermo invading our stuffy world: smells of warm wax and the confessional. The ladies appear in their little groups and move on with hurried steps, stopping briefly at the holy-water stoup. If I compare them to goats crowding around a fountain for a drink, I risk insulting my *Old Girls*, but that's what they look like. With the tips of their fingers they dip up as much holy water as they need, with precautionary gestures; then they go up the center aisle on tiptoe, holding their mantillas with one hand over their exposed necklines and the other holding their taffeta skirts close to their thighs against some hypothetical misfortune: a blast of ill wind, an impudent stare, a stumble which might rob them of their feminine dignity as they enter the church.

They exchange little nods, mute winks, "Good morning, good morning," "Are you still here?" with their cloistered sisters. As if *they* could be anywhere else, poor things! But these were habits of the convent, immutable as protocol. Then the veils fell discreetly; the nuns shivered like black foliage behind the gilded grills of the cloister: a tremor one hardly saw, since the grill was so thick and its openings so narrow, while the *Old Girls* continued to go forward, crossing the chapel, and while we little girls, kneeling on our prie-dieux, craned our necks so as not to miss the show they offered us. They frightened us a little. They were *old*—thirty, forty, fifty years, sixty and even more. They murmured as they looked for places. In the jargon of the boarders, only Palermans

born and bred like ourselves, raised by the Sisters of the Visitation
had a right to the title *Old Girls*. They came back every Sunday
just to dazzle us little ones, to fascinate us. For life dazzles those
who don't know it, and so our eyes followed those real women
with a past which we associated, obviously, with our ideas of love
and sin. In the confinement of our adolescence, it was easy to find
subjects for our dreams. But I'm not describing them accurately.
I'm not showing how natural our visitors were, their particular way
of clearly enjoying every instant, of expressing their gratitude by a
felicity of gesture, a warmth of expression, things which conveyed
a tenderness, a human warmth, but whose real source was a sensuality so ill concealed that it escaped and enveloped them like a
cloud. And I've left out the young males who accompanied them
everywhere. I have forgotten to mention that the *Old Girls* always
appeared with an entourage of relatives. Fourteen or fifteen years
old, sons, grandsons, or nephews, who already spoke the secret
language of seduction and all of them obviously impatient to
please. They made loverlike gestures, bustled about, pushed in
chairs, picked up slipping scarves or dropped coins, arranged the
cake for dinner under the prie-dieu, guarding the box with a watchful eye as if the precious pastry were about to run away, wiped
the noses of their younger brothers, and followed the mass with
appropriate gestures, crossed themselves broadly, silently beat their
breasts, genuflected deeply, without for a moment ceasing to keep
us little girls under surveillance, burning us with their looks, making kisses with their lips, and breathing heartbreaking sighs at us.
In short, they were seducers.

What did Gianna Meri, twelve years old, think of as she knelt
here, immobile, her eyes lowered, her hands joined in prayer?
When the mass was over, with all the solemnity due the Old
Girls' right to be waited on, we had to take their missals to the
sacristy and place them correctly in the big walnut cabinet with
its cracked woodwork: missals with coats of arms on the right,
missals with initials only on the left, and missals wrapped in rosa-
ries with medallions in the locked drawer. And then we had to run,

though I always found time to make a few deep curtsies to my favorites so as to receive a few compliments on the wing: "There's little Gianna. Her father is a remarkable man. . . . There's no doctor to compare with Meri, even in Rome!" He took care of them all, knew them all, my father. . . . Then run, run to the refectory for refreshments—orgeat syrup in summer, marsala in winter—and bitter almond biscuits which we served them in the garden. During this hour of reunion, the males were excluded. I would watch them leave the chapel one by one as the *Laudamus* burst forth in loud organ peals, very loud, in fact, lest during the time when the doors were opening and closing the sound of the "Brilliantine Polka" might enter the chapel (a popular song played by the Sunday orchestra on the terrace of the café just across the street where our seducers were going to stuff themselves with sherbet while waiting for their mothers).

"Run. Don't keep them waiting. The Old Girls are in the garden." Those words, repeated every Sunday, how often have I heard them? I see again our walled garden, planted to the clipped border of magnolias and wisteria, filled with perfumes and freedom, rare pleasures to which we seldom had easy access. In the center of a bed of zinnias and fuchsias stood the statue of our founder, Marie-Adelaide, her fervor as disturbing as the disorder of a Leda. Head thrown back, eyes cast heavenward, lips half open, hands pressed to her breast, she awed us. I wondered what strange state of mind the sculptor must have been in when he executed this statue of a woman whose reputation was so chaste. She used to inspire our history professor to heights of eloquence. "Luminous example of the feminine virtues. . . ." Our preceptors counted on that brave Savoy princess to give us a taste for moral values. "In spite of the splendors of the throne, she kept faith with the humblest Christian virtues, the humblest. Repeat after me. . . ." And we would repeat, in French, because the mistress in charge of this course had been born in Paris, of a family ruined "by the Revolution," she used to say, without further details.

And I can see once again Gianna Meri, passing flat marsala,

warm orgeat, and biscuits with a medicinal taste, a conscientious child in a serge skirt, gripped by the fear of upsetting something. And is that anything to be surprised at? Would our pious mistresses have guessed that a cyclone was going to obliterate that way of life they believed in so firmly? One could hardly have expected them to imagine the future. How could they? One does not prepare for the shattering realities of war behind the walls of a cloister. But even if it didn't account for the changing world, this system of education at least exempted us from its tyranny. Nothing was forced on us, unless it was the belief that God took part in our deeds, and it was for us to adapt ourselves to that collaboration as best we could. No one explained this reality to us lest it be distorted in the telling. God existed. And having accepted this, we were free. Free to choose a paradise inhabited by the interlocutor of our choice, or free to choose none and find paradise all around us, free to live our golden age thoughtlessly.

Aside from that, we were endowed with several accomplishments of no particular utility, but which were nonetheless gifts that were not to be scorned, like provisions slipped into the baggage of a traveler setting off on a long journey. There were twenty-two pianos and seven harps at the Marie-Adelaide Institute, and they were silent only at night. But we were all free; yes, it's true, a thousand times more free within our crumbling walls, under our eiderdown of rules, than all the Pams obsessed by their careers and their need for success.

So. Once I was that child who on Wednesdays attended a class in minuet, accompanied by a deafening battle fought on the piano between la signora and Jean-Baptiste Lulli. No way of escaping it. "Why the minuet? Who does that dance nowadays?" These questions were never asked. "Because the grownups say so." Period. That's all.

Once I was the twelve-year-old guide who showed the mosaic-paved floor of the church to foreign tourists in the cool hours of the day and was not surprised by variations in the lecture, depending upon who delivered it; whether it was the Mother Superior, hidden behind her grill, or Sister Rita who was permitted to emerge and walk with long steps about the church, or even by Father Saverio, our confessor, a Piedmontese whom none of us could abide. To know at twelve that truth is not single, that it changes according to the tongue that pronounces it, that it is at the mercy of language, of tone, of gesture, of passing invention, this indeed is the beginning of wisdom.

In the center aisle certain slabs of the majolica paving had come loose; I could still show you which ones. Just beside the head of the Child, it squeaked when you set your heel on it. A two-hundred-year-old pavement has the right to squeak in places, doesn't it? Ours did, and it was a beautiful one made by Vietri as a gigantic picture. A Madonna extended across the entire floor. Not that she was awe inspiring. In fact, with all the area that she covered, she was a very slight Madonna; merely a young girl with a stubborn forehead. But she was seated on a throne, a great armchair so long that it reached the altar steps, and her cape, the color of the sea, stretched across the church like a sail under which knelt (as if to keep warm) a half dozen gentlemen dressed in doublets and boots. "The donors of the pavement," according to the Mother Superior, who always added in a distant voice, "Palerman nobles who were more generous in those days than they are today," and she paused significantly until some tourist, taking the hint, dropped a coin into the box I held. But were those gentlemen really the donors of the pavement? Sometimes a tourist would wonder. Our Mother Superior, still invisible, was emphatic. "They are all donors." Those who were represented in the pavement as well as those who were buried in the church whose effigies could be seen. She knew them by name, and their names were magnificent. She recited them in rapid cadence, a litany that went straight to one's heart. "We have a Duke of Verdure, and a Duke of the White Mystery. We have also a Prince of the Flowery Dawn, a Baron of the Rock of the Doves and a Marquis, Vincent of the Moon, spouse of Agatha of Saint Colombe. We . . . We have. . . ." The Mother Superior had a special voice for chanting these names.

I often found it difficult to know when the moment of silence would come, the space into which I could stuff my sentence, "We had plenty of donors in those olden days," which always produced the desired effect if I said it to the tourists with my voice full of regret. Then the coins would pour into the box which I shook loudly, very loudly, so that our Mother would know behind her grill that all was going well. She could then list gaily those lords of lesser importance. No, not the deplorable Antonius de Casa Pipi who lay in plain view—too much in view—and whose tombstone mortified us. But modest knights, with decent names like Modeste. Yes really modest: Modeste the Short Legged, Vespasian the Fiery-Mouthed, Louis of Grain and Song, Knight of Saint James of the Sword, a name which always pleased the tourists so much that they wanted to hear it again. But our Mother didn't entirely approve of him; she never adopted for him that voice of hallelujah reserved only for dukes and princes.

To make myself clear, I should say that our Mother was of high birth and that she could even recognize an ancestor of hers among the gentlemen on the pavement, a lord with a severe face wearing a purple doublet. Part of my task was to point him out with an insistent finger for the admiration of the visitors: "No, sir, the donor to whom our Mother refers is not that gentleman in pink; it's that one—see him? Dressed in violet. No, a bit lower. . . . There, you've got him now, directly under the Madonna's big toe. . . . Yes, it's that frizzy fellow, with the swarthy skin and thick lips."

Sister Rita's story was different, perhaps because she had studied in Rome? And was history subject to the same variations as truth? Would it change depending upon the sky under which it was taught? In any event, Sister Rita was convinced that the lords who knelt at the feet of the Madonna were not donors but Crusaders: "On their way to the Holy Land, the Crusaders stopped in Palermo in order to beg the protection of the Virgin." When she guided the tour, my role consisted of simply repeating to the latecomers: "The Crusaders stopped at Palermo. . . . The Crusaders stopped at Palermo. . . ." I had only that to say. Sister Rita took charge of the rest. A helmet placed at the feet of the Madonna, an iron gauntlet thrown on the ground left no doubts as to the truth of her thesis—"The Crusaders stopped at Palermo." I helped her as best I could. She knew how to construct an argument, nor did she lack imagination. From the helmet and the gauntlet, she passed vigorously to bloody knights, to impassable deserts; she evoked for the tourists those fortified cities and distant citadels where our paladins, after terrible combats, fell beneath the blows of the Unbeliever.

Sister Rita's voice was lofted across the church. Resistance was vain. "Unbeliever": a word that she threw at the heads of the visitors. That was the moment for me to go among them, to seek out especially the occasional Lutheran who, feeling the weight of this attack, would seek to redeem himself with some gift. Sister Rita, I hear you today. You are the first of my travels, my adventures, my violence. I believe in your Crusaders. But it's possible to make a mistake. If there is your truth, there is also Father Saverio's interpretation. "Make these gentlemen into Crusaders with no more reason than a helmet and a glove? What next? Why not Saints? Crusaders—them? Come now. What nonsense. How can costume prove anything in a country where the statues of the Beatified are shown with naked breasts? And Saint Alfio, the brave Gascon, haven't certain popular painters represented him as one of the Muses, floating on a cloud surrounded by his long hair? Haven't they?" Father Saverio was our confessor. He was the one who ordered that they remove from the church any picture of Saint Alfio, a saint of indeterminate sex, flying over the world dressed in a sleeveless tunic, with white round shoulders, a full bust, and large haunches.

Poor Saint Alfio, an enigmatic figure, a hybrid who never did any harm to anyone. We liked him very much that way. . . . But Father Saverio was a stubborn Piedmontese and so he insisted that the twelve personages kneeling at the feet of the Madonna were neither donors nor Crusaders, but Magian kings. How did he know? "That coppery complexion, the kinky hair, those broad nostrils. Unquestionably: Balthazar!" So much for Mother Superior's noble ancestor. To Father Saverio he was a Negro, and the whole convent despaired. But Sister Rita was tenacious. "You never see Balthazar without a turban." She was right. The lord in question, although his skin was a bit dark, was not wearing anything even slightly suggesting a turban, and therefore, he could not be Balthazar. "He's taken it off in respect to Our Lady." That really made Sister Rita angry. "When have you ever seen six Magian Kings, may I ask? Six Magian Kings at the Madonna's feet! I'll die laughing!" The priest grew red in the face. "And you, Sister Rita, do you know any kings who travel alone? If there are six figures at the feet of the Madonna, that's because there are three Kings and their entourage. Is that clear enough for you?" Father Saverio always had an answer, but nobody liked him for it. He irritated everyone: the Mother Superior, Sister Rita, and even us little ones. Father Saverio said we smelled of garlic. He let us know that in the last convent he was in, somewhere in Milan, the cooking was infinitely better. "They didn't stuff the students with *caponata*." That was possible. But in Palermo, economy and its handmaidens bought what they could. So we smelled of garlic. Father Saverio said that in the confessional it was more than he could stand, that we suffocated him, that we were a plague. That was the reason why he heard confessions without drawing the violet curtain. So everybody could hear the penances he gave, the scoldings, everything. He had a voice that carried and a most precise diction. The Old Girls wanted no part of Father Saverio. Understandably, they took their confession elsewhere. After all they were real women and had more to divulge than we did: husbands, troubles, desertions, sorrows, children. . . . Life. As for myself, I never had much to reveal except those accursed distractions during mass. "If you aren't praying, what are you doing?" Father Saverio would ask in his piercing voice. I answered through clenched teeth and tight lips. "Speak up." Many thanks, so he'd say again that I smelled of garlic. At my age one has a big appetite. "Well then, if you aren't praying during mass, what are you doing? Sleeping?" "I look at the pavement." No danger of the good Father getting rid of our pavement; it was registered as one of our works of art; people came from all over to admire it. It was one of the wonders of Palermo. "I look at the pavement, that's not a sin." Then Father Saverio took up arms against the style of our churches. "Like theaters!" he said. "Impossible to pray in a place with such decorations. That's what happens when you offer such distractions to light minds. That's religion in Sicily. Who would dare maintain that anyone needs marbles, stuccos, and mosaics to find God?" He held forth on the soothing power of walls without ornaments and stone pavings. He grew indignant: "Barbaric practices!" Breasts, noses, feet, eyes, stomachs, and other equivocally formed objects, all those votaries, all those silver or wax plaques which are hung like grapes around our statues in gratitude for the accomplished miracles and healings filled him with fury. "It's worse than Mexico here! I'm serving savages!" Tell him? What would have been the use? Northerners are such prudes. And then I liked my seat, why risk losing it? My bench was placed over the belly of the infant king, the naked child. I said nothing to Father Saverio. I never told anyone that when I lowered my eyes I could see three rolls of flesh contained by a narrow belt on which was written, "My name is Jesus." But below that I saw that mysterious appendage shaded in such a delicate pink, that sex, the color of a shrimp, or a sugar plum, at which I couldn't stop staring. At times when the church was empty and the benches pushed back, it was there that women knelt to recite a rosary or to ask a favor. I have seen them rubbing their holy pictures against it, then putting them back in their handbags; I have seen them bringing their handkerchiefs from that special spot to their lips; I have seen them fervently kissing the pavement there.

Gianna Meri, eyes lowered modestly, had no one in whom she could confide that this cult of the child divinity did not frighten her. And the secrecy of her feeling, now as then, isolates her.

To whom could she confide it now? To Aunt Rosie, to Pam, to

any of the high priestesses of beauty? Which of those puritan ladies would not have cried scandal louder and stronger than the most austere nun?

Pam most of all. I can hear her now. . . .

II.

*The curriculum obliged her to take courses
which taught her that the devil no longer
existed and that the supernatural was only
the natural which had not yet been explained.*

PAUL MORAND

Pam—let me try to describe her. She was tall, blonde, and abstract.
To me she always seemed to be waiting for some surprise. A mirage. . . . A sleepwalker. I tried hard to find in her face some trace
of fantasy, of humor, or else of some emotion—joy, sorrow, disillusion—some battle lost or won, a wrinkle at the corner of her
mouth, I don't know, a wandering look. Nothing. Neither defeat
nor victory. At twenty-five, at an age when women's faces already
show the geography of their past, Pam bore evidence on the surface
of her skin of a success without any history. Her porcelain blue
eyes were impersonally nice. Sometimes—rarely, briefly, but unmis-
takably—a doubt would assail her, about her image, about the

price of refinement, about being the flawless woman, indefatigable and unrufflable, with whom she was identified once and for all. A fear to be quickly dismissed. All she had to do was make a series of elegant gestures. She would play with some of her convincing props: powder box, mascara brush, the panoply of the amateur smoker, all precious equipment, an assortment she knew how to extract from her bag with a joyous jingling of bracelets and charms —each gesture calculated to express the certainty that she was no cheap imitation of the elegant woman, but the woman herself— and let's not forget the cloud of perfume atomized in little puffs just under her earlobes. Then, reassured, Pam was back on familiar territory, safe and dry on the river bank of her convictions.

Sometimes I joined her for lunch. She ate in her office, where a secretary brought her a paper plate filled with frugal fare. Grated raw vegetables, a slice of cold meat, a bowl of yogurt, and a cup of black coffee, all of it gulped down in a hurry. There was time afterward for us to talk. But anything I had to say could not interest her for the whole thirty minutes that was left of our lunch hour. She began by taking off her shoes, stretching her legs, and doing some stretching exercises, an expert rotation of the toes and ankles; there were five minutes left for a check-up. "A run in a stocking? A twisted seam?" You never know. Then she strode to the window to lower the blinds and produce what she called her "Lautrec" light.

Lautrec? A glaucous light filtered through the greenish slats, slid across the carpet, exaggerated the uncompromisingly harmonious green of the walls. Everything was gooseberry colored in Pam's office. But Lautrec? What had he to do with it? Pam, ever the alert journalist, simply used his name as the seal of her own originality and inventiveness. This was a way of being impressive one soon got used to, and high-priced painters spawned all sorts of unlikely offspring. In my early works, I sometimes tried to embellish certain descriptions with the names of da Vinci or Michelangelo, but that only exasperated our editorial secretary, Miss Lynn, an employee of thirty years standing, and an overpowering person.

"That's enough, Gianna, let's forget the Renaissance," she told me. "It's a bad period and will recall unpleasant stories to our readers' minds. Poison, orgies, married popes. Stick to the Impressionists and the Cubists. Renoir and Picasso are quite all right. Stay away from Modigliani, though. Pregnant mistress, delirium tremens. People are beginning to know about those things here. And after all that, he died in a hospital ward. Too much misery, too much despair."

"Doesn't Lautrec's misery bother you? He was a cripple."

"Quite all right. Old line nobility, tainted ancestry. Mustn't be afraid of pathos. Women like that. Maternal instinct, don't you know?"

So originated Pam's Lautrec green, a bilious color of absinthe or bad digestion. So much for Lautrec. But Pam's office depressed me.

"Do you really like these aquarium colors?"

"It's very soothing," she answered. "You don't know how to relax, Gianna. Do what I do."

She settled herself on two armchairs placed together. Then, with the impenetrable look of a physical education instructor executing a difficult movement, she slowly pressed her two open hands into the hollow of her stomach. An infallible performance, which, according to a Tibetan or Chinese method (I always confuse them), helped her to shamelessly belch up the superfluous air which collected there, no one knows why.

"Are you shocked, Gianna? You people always disapprove of anything that surprises you."

That terrible "you people" was insurmountable. A wall of China, "you people."

"You? What do you mean by you people?"

"You, you Europeans. One day when I was explaining my method to a Greek friend she positively jumped with indignation. She left right in the middle of a poker game!"

"And didn't it strike you that she might find your method of relaxation a little unattractive?"

Pam let her big eyes roam about the half-lit room and lowered her eyelids for a moment to show me she wasn't listening any more.

"You ask so many questions!"

We were silent.

That was how we spent our lunch hours.

The discovery of a family photograph changed our relationship a good deal. Pure chance. It was no retouched enlargement framed in silver, one of those works of art you see placed at an angle on the dresser top. It was a yellowed snapshot, a little dog-eared, acting as a bookmark in a dietetic dictionary.

"I can't decide," Pam was saying to me that day. "What should I advise for the complexion? I should begin by showing our readers how they all have bad complexions, and how their future, their career, their love life will suffer from it. That will take me ten lines. Get them worried. That's my technique. But after that, I need a discovery, something that will give them great hope."

I suggested carrots.

"At home, they say that if you want the skin of a peach, you should eat—"

"Impossible," she cut me short in a tone that stopped all objections. "In our business a truth that's too obvious is suspect. Take my word for it. I need something unexpected, mysterious, wise. Look up the word *carotene*, will you? There."

With an imperious finger she pointed to the dictionary of dietetics without leaving her chair or changing her languid position, as if she were imposing the task upon me for my sins. I must look for the definition of the word *carotene* because I ridiculed her system of relaxation and also because I asked too many questions.

"Did you find it?"

Because I was slow, she got up.

"Read it, for heavens sake. The page is marked. There. 'Carotene, the pigment which causes the brilliant color of the carrot and also its purifying action.' "

I wasn't listening any more. There was the photograph. Were

these Pam's parents? This man and this woman? A man of fifty, cotton gloved, taller than his wife, with a timid look, a boyish haircut, and square hands. Wrinkles! Pam's mother and father had the deep wrinkles of peasants.

"Are these your parents, Pam?"

"They were missionaries in Korea. That picture was taken the year they went away. I was twelve."

"And you stayed behind?"

"Aunt Rosie told her brother that it wasn't enough to believe in God and to want to open the doors of Heaven to men if you wanted to educate a daughter properly. So she kept me. My mother died afterwards. My father comes back every six years or so. But we're strangers now. We haven't a thing in common. Nothing."

I don't know why the discovery of a father who was a missionary in Korea should have changed our relationship. Pam, who up to that time had had little appeal to my curiosity, seemed different. I needed that photograph and that missionary couple to believe in her reality.

I tried to reconstruct the way things would have been had Aunt Rosie not intervened. I visualized Pam raised by an earnest clergyman who watched over the purity of her soul; Pam growing up at a Mission among converted Baptists and Koreans, spending her rest hours in embroidery, stretched out beside a window as she stretched out here in her office, the same pose, the same pleasant look, I imagined her helping her mother, teaching school, addressing God's forgotten in a high imperious voice—her voice. I heard her: ". . . The unchaste shall never pass through the gates of the Kingdom." I heard her, there, spreading the good word and distributing Bibles with the same energy that she devoted to preaching the gospel of seduction. Her true nature? An overwhelming seriousness, frankness, the uncompromising rigidity of an expert in difficult conversions. Gallant little salvationist! If you should one day stop struggling with strokes of the buffer against the square fingers and the solid hand which are your mother's legacy. . . . If you should forget Aunt Rosie's ideal of respectabil-

ity. . . . If you should renounce those smiles you practice in the
mirror and that model's walk. . . . Then the truth of you would
appear. We could see your round cheeks—yes, round. You would
have stopped sucking them in, hiding them with clever tricks. And
your round, healthy goosegirl's calves, we'd see those, too. We'd
find out who you are. It's bound to happen. . . .

"Gianna! What are you thinking about?"

It was more than she could bear. When Pam was with someone
who said nothing, she was seized with anxiety.

"What are you thinking, Gianna? Are you going to sit here the
rest of the afternoon looking at me without saying a word?"

I listened to the punctuations of our silence: to the coming and
going of the elevators, their sliding doors that opened and closed
on employees coming back from their "snack," a soft noise, regular
as the ebb and flow of the sea, ten elevators sighing one by one,
ten distant voices, the elevator men announcing the floor with
fierce elegance, crying the name of the magazine—*Fair*—as if they
were saying "Fire!" in a war movie, except for the Negro who
made a tender song of his work, a sort of blues: "*Fair . . . Fair . . .
Fair,*" a counting rhyme he hummed to himself all the way up
and down in his cage. I heard the personnel breaking like waves
and the "tac, tac, tac" of high heels on the linoleum of the corridor, the hygienic copy of an Aubusson carpet. I was hardly thinking of anything then, or rather, yes, I was thinking: "Pam exists.
She's real. All I have to do is wait."

Then there came the death of Miss Lynn, the editorial secretary. Miss Lynn, thirty years of type measures and squared cap-
tions, dead of cancer of the breast.

The funeral home had only one story, a handsomely varnished
door, and a pink façade. Its roof, of lacy metal, was an imitation of
a Gothic chapel. There was no doubt about its intentions, but
several television antennas, grouped in a bouquet, destroyed the
desired dome which, placed between the façade of a cinema and
a cafeteria with a window filled with gigantic cakes drowned in

cream and sad pale chickens, had something of the burlesque about it, as if Louis II had built one of his Bavarian follies on the sidewalks of Madison Avenue.

The good Lynn was dead, and Pam asked me to go with her to the funeral.

"She was a member of the Eternal Assembly. One of those religions, something like the spiritualists," said Pam. "They don't have any sermon or service. All you have to do is sign the register, look at her, and leave."

Look at her! Look at Miss Lynn exposed in a plastic-lined hall, under a cream silk eiderdown, that was what I least looked forward to. She wore a dress I'd never seen her in, a tightly fitted one which left one shoulder bare. The color with which she had been painted did not succeed in reproducing her country freshness. A few bones in dessicated tissue: that was what we had to look at. And an Underwood typewriter—resting on her stomach.

I'd hardly sat down beside Pam when I wanted to leave. But how could I? The members of the editorial staff filed into the room, sat in the ranks of empty chairs, and talked about poor Miss Lynn.

"Doesn't she look lovely?" my neighbor murmured.

It was our office nurse, a specialist in migraines and heartaches, in charge of the nervous upsets of covergirls, faintings in the studio, a sort of stage manager, her pockets always full of powders, tranquilizers, and also with messages which she had been asked to deliver to these ladies.

"We're going to miss Miss Lynn," she said again.

I shook my head yes.

"That set is becoming. She's never had a nicer hairdo."

I saw the editor-in-chief. Her name was Daisy, Daisy Lee, a pretty name. Scarcely a yard separated her from poor Miss Lynn in her silken eiderdown. Daisy sat in the front row. Behind her were empty chairs. Accountants, designers, secretaries, production men, laboratory assistants, and the little people—office boys, messengers, telephone operators, the shoeshine man who strode up and down our corridors every morning with his box in his hand, and even the black elevator man (Lynn was a member of a civil rights group)—stood at the rear of the chapel, as if the empty chairs marked an impenetrable frontier beyond which they dared not venture.

"Move up, move up," Daisy Lee seemed to be saying to them, her body slightly turned, holding out her white-gloved hands. She thought she was being encouraging and friendly, but her theatrical gesture was more like that of a prima ballerina in the last act of *Romeo and Juliet*, when she gestures to the audience to share her unhappiness, standing on her points. "Look, look what I've come to, separated from my Romeo, alone, so desperately alone." Daisy Lee managed to be at least as pathetic in her rendition, but to no avail: the employees did not come forward. Then she gave up her Juliet-at-death's-door manner and returned to her habitual mien of the superior woman who intends to be obeyed. She even tossed her head in exasperation.

"The boss is upset," said the nurse.

I agreed vaguely.

"She doesn't like anybody to resist her. Say, are you all right?"

"You look funny," whispered Pam.

"I feel dizzy. Don't you think it's disgusting to see our Lynn, our good Lynn, with one shoulder bare and an Underwood on her stomach?"

"What's disgusting about it?"

Pam seemed morally offended.

"You should have filled your purse with rubber bands, pencil ends, paper clips, staples, scraps from wastepaper baskets. We could have thrown them on the bier in handfuls, like confetti. That would have made the masquerade complete. Anyway, I'm leaving."

Pam knit her brows and pinched her lips.

"You're crazy," she said.

Then, feeling that her indignation was lacking in amiability or nonchalance, she granted me her all-teeth-at-once smile with the pink tip of her tongue protruding between her lips: her classic attempt at seduction.

There was a general movement. An object was pushed in, a sort of juke box on wheels to which no one paid any attention.

Pam was involved in a low-pitched conversation with the nurse about a recent liquid invention designed to facilitate hair setting.

"You stay a half hour less under the drier, and the wave holds a week longer. The shops that use it will make a fortune."

Pam interrupted her. She was excited by the discovery: "We'll recommend it to new mothers, to people down with flu, to people who've just had operations."

The nurse made a gesture with her chin toward the undertaker's assistants who were looking for a place to plug in the juke box. One of them took off his cap and wiped his forehead.

"And those people? Don't you think they'd be interested? It isn't every day they get one like Lynn, well groomed and with a nice hair style. And it's always the families that neglect a sick person, the ones that desert her when she's dying, those are always the ones that want to show their friends a beautiful corpse. You know what I mean. Well, if there were some product. . . . You should write about that in the magazine. Everybody would be interested."

Pam maintained her lofty manner and said nothing. That was her way. When she had found a companion in whom she could try out the subject of an article, she squeezed her like a lemon, then acted as if she'd never met her. But I knew she hadn't lost a word the nurse had said, and that the product they'd been discussing would be the subject of an article next week.

To get out! Not to have to look at Lynn. Lynn, rotting under her silk comforter. It was just then, I remember, that the need to leave came over me like nausea. I can still feel the coarse hand the nurse put on my knee in a comforting gesture.

"I know what you need. Come on, swallow this. It's a tranquilizer. I never go out without a supply. I know how you Italians are. We've got a houseful of them these days; that's all we photograph:

Italian cover girls. Nothing else. One of the boss's fads. One day she only wants English girls, the next thing she swears by Italians. At the moment she likes swarthy skins. Know what I mean? And are those Italian girls nervous! And crazy. Oh, I know them! All I needed was to sit next to you the day we come to say good-by to our dear Lynn!"

Shafts of light shone behind the windows. The lighting was a perfect imitation of a sudden burst of sunlight. At that moment Aunt Rosie appeared, a wet umbrella dripping in her hand; rubber-booted, her hair protected by a plastic triangle, she walked down the center aisle. Looking tiny in her skating costume, she distributed charming deferential smiles in the direction of the first rows and then, seeing the employees grouped around the entrance, still hesitating, with fresh smiles even more engaging than the first, though less deferential, she managed to draw them after her and, very much at her ease, very conscious of her importance, she came to join us. Daisy Lee threw her silent bravos with her fingertips, which Aunt Rosie pretended to catch in midair, always the little girl, while the editorial staff came forward to take seats.

"Aren't we one big happy family?" she asked, sitting down beside me. "Why were those poor people standing up? Shocking, don't you think so? Anyway, that's that."

Then she added in a low voice:

"Every time I have a chance to help Pam's career, one way or another, I grab it."

The nurse complimented her on her appearance.

"Mrs. MacMannox, I wouldn't take you for a day over. . . ."

They had succeeded in connecting up the juke box, and its dial was lighted up. From my seat I could read the names of the songs we would be hearing. But nobody thought of starting it. There was a moment of irresolution during which we could hear the sound of the rain. Then the shafts of light suddenly went out. The juke box, too.

"The big lights are reserved for ceremonies with music," the nurse explained, taking my arm. I'm telling you this as an interesting piece of information. In your country things are probably quite different. . . ."

The workmen in caps took away the juke box. They pushed it out of the room with tired nods, while Aunt Rosie craned her neck so as to get a better view of poor Lynn under her eiderdown.

The absurdity of it. What a mixed-up ceremony, a blasphemous carnival. Get out! But I couldn't. Tell Pam I felt faint? I felt a terrible shame and confused everything—Pam's face with Aunt Rosie's. No, it wasn't Lynn's rouge that was running, not she with that mouth of a child being fed; she smiled a subtle smile, traced with a pencil, a real horror. And then what was that odor which permeated everything? A perfume.

"You smell delicious, Aunt Rosie."

"Oh no. Mr. MacMannox always thought a woman who put on perfume to go to chapel would reflect badly on the careers of her loved ones. You can be sure it isn't I."

Then it must have been the perfume they sprayed on Lynn. And I could no longer take my eyes off the dead woman who was so insistently, so carnally present, with her painted mouth, her naked shoulder, and that abrasive perfume.

Now a man came forward wearing a black jacket and striped trousers. He had bad teeth; his smile was gray.

"Is there one among the faithful united here who is a member of the Eternal Assembly?" he asked in a weary voice.

How ridiculous. No one moved. No one in the congregation belonged. In the first row, Daisy Lee shrugged her shoulders discreetly.

"That would have hurt Lynn very much," Aunt Rosie said to me. "What an impossible religion."

Then the man in the jacket who looked as if he were in a hurry to finish asked in a loud voice,

"Who will say the elegy for the deceased?"

Daisy Lee took some papers out of her handbag. But she did not get a chance to rise. A big dark haired girl, with a handkerchief pressed under her nose, stood up in response.

"That's Lynn's secretary," Pam said to me. "Poor Inez. She looks sick with grief."

The man in the jacket went to meet her. Inez's cheeks were red and she kept twisting her handkerchief.

"Have you prepared something, Miss? Come up here. No, come further."

He supported her.

"Don't cry that way. Try to control yourself."

"Really! She's having a hard time of it," murmured the nurse, who seemed ready to intervene.

Inez sobbed. In the front row they were shocked. A tremor of disapproval went through the teased hairdos and the mink stoles. Yes, they were shocked.

"Grief is one thing, but hysteria—! Unbelievable!"

"They say her mother is Puerto Rican," said Aunt Rosie, as if to herself.

The gray-toothed man no longer knew how to soothe Inez's grief. She sobbed on his shoulder, repeating in a mechanical voice, "The fastest shorthand. . . . Lynn could do one hundred and twenty-five a minute. . . ." He answered, "Yes, yes," wiping her face and rocking her like a child. To see them together, the girl crouched against him, disjointed, as if her legs were collapsing, while he remained sprightly erect in his jacket and striped trousers, you would have thought they were a ventriloquist and his dummy: a shoddy doll with cotton hair on a papier-mâché head.

"Now, now, calm down and say what you want to say."

But Inez was gripped with a convulsive trembling which made her shake all over. She grew pale, leaning against the man's vest, then on his shirt front, she took his arm and pulled it towards her violently in a possessive gesture, finally collapsing at his feet and groaning, "Oh, kiss me. I loved her so much!"

"Overwork," said the nurse, getting up suddenly.

On the sidewalk of Madison Avenue the cinema's blue façade bore the poster of a monumental Kirk Douglas, all hair and muscle, a beautiful bundle of rosy flesh. His picture soon drove the

image of Lynn and her eiderdown from my memory. A little farther on, in the cafeteria window, were the cold chickens under
their cellophane covers. They looked sad, but at least they weren't
smiling. A few more yards and I thought no more of Lynn. Her
memory was nothing to me. I lost it turning the first corner. Was
it even a memory? No. A memory sticks to the inside of your skin,
belongs to you, like childhood. But nothing that I had seen there
could belong to me, nothing could remain in me without provok-
ing an overwhelming urge to give it all back, there, never mind
where, in front of the movie, on the doorstep of a cafeteria. It
may seem strange that I wanted so little part of it. But these are
the signs by which one recognizes the exile.

Several weeks went by after my arrival in New York without
any success either in cutting off my past or of curing my desire to
look backward. It would have been wise to be more careful, to live
in a state of alertness, like a sick man to whom the slightest move
may prove fatal. But I was inexperienced. So, on certain days, the
sight of a telephone was enough to touch off associations of ideas,
of sounds, of pictures, with lightning speed. I heard a voice breathing reassurances to me. As if love could come back from the dead.
I dreamed.

During these relapses, Pam regarded me with a stupefaction
that was understandable because she did not know what was the
matter with me.

"What's gotten into you?" she asked.

"Nothing. I'm going to call Palermo."

"Well, go ahead and do it, but stop looking at your watch every
minute."

"I'm blocked on my article. I can't get into the tourist spirit."

Pam was accustomed to my sudden moods; she went back to
her work without answering and I left the office, saying I needed
the quiet of some empty room so that I could hear every word of
the long distance call. Alone, my inner voice changed its tone, or
rather, perhaps I simply stopped believing what it said. I remem-

bered. . . . The telephone fell from my hands. Then I went out, my sovereign remedy. For New York acted upon me like the blaze which consumes the first spark. I saw Sicily everywhere and this exercise kept me in balance. Whether my walk lasted for an hour, a morning, or a whole day, I would almost always finish it in aimless wandering, wrapped in my vision as if in a happy fog.

It was at about that time, I think, that I pretended to not be able to find a subject for my column if I stayed shut up in the office. When she heard about my frequent absences, Daisy Lee decided that she would allow them so long as my method was effective. She assumed her elevated tone to lecture on the mysterious ways which can lead to success. She was sure the magazine would profit by this new way of doing things. Then she alluded to what she called my "professional *laiser-aller*," my oddities, and the crazy way I spent my time. She paused, awaiting some confirmation from me.

I could not answer her. Daisy Lee was not the woman to understand how one can keep on living, for long periods, poisoned by the dregs of hope.

Wander in a city where dreams are coherent, where anxiety has only the shadow of power. Follow Fifth Avenue like an escaped prisoner. With a troubled mind, say to yourself: "What I want is useless, beyond me. I want marble busts on leprous façades, I want streets in which one can get lost, a labyrinth, a maze, and the loud songs from my part of town, and the bars wide open. I want three-faced gods and allegories at the crossroads; I want the tinkling fountains of countries where water is scarce. I want the inexplicable, the legend of dragons; I want great gardens and sheaves of stars, I want Palermo." And what do you see? A building site with a cloud of dust floating from it. A taxi driver stops and looks too.

"Yesterday there was a house there," he says in a happy voice. "Today it's gone. All gone. That's something, isn't it?"

He is friendly. The sudden disappearance entertains him. If I

said to him: "Where we live, everything was three quarters destroyed. So people take care of what is left, they prop it up, they
restore it, and if they can't afford that, they live humbly in the
ruin." But you can't interest such a man. You think how indifferent he would be to this story of crumbling houses in Sicily. So
you must rid your mind of this thought which is no help to you.
What are you looking for? A travel subject for *Fair* readers. Nothing else should be in your mind. Daisy Lee did not mince words:
"Satisfying unknown people, that's what you're paid for. Look
around you when you're in the streets. Anybody you pass may be
one of your readers." And she added, "Above all, let's not have
any poetry. Be direct. Be specific. *Fair* is not a magazine of ab-
stractions," a statement punctuated by a blow of her clenched fist
at the air, with all the force of her arm. "What *Fair* needs is
zzzang, you understand. Vigor, that's what." I understand. But
what escape can I offer to these architects of transparency? They
give themselves to glass as to some forbidden pleasure. They present themselves with houses of smoked crystal, they demand that
their walls reflect changing forms of a city with no past. How can
anyone get away from that? From the depths of blue days, from
the depth of yourself comes a memory. All of a sudden it carries
you away. It is as if a living spring is suddenly released, a torrent
too long dammed behind the closed sluice gate of your memory.
For how long has it lain in wait, this wall of stones you see so
clearly with its tufts of wild jasmine and its spills of honeysuckle?
Swarming with insects. A kiss on your eyes, then another on your
lips. The first kiss was there, lying prone in the grass. And there,
several years later, hands full of earth, mouth full of prayers, there
again, when the planes came, was where you lost—as one loses
innocence—the childish belief that life never ends. Can you forget
that wall? Is it possible that people don't know what they can expect from stone? Full of holes, sounding with emptiness, it shelters,
it protects, it resists sturdily, and for a long time it remains as one
of those dreadful ruins, a refuge of our dead loves, the wash line
of the homeless. How could I tell the readers of *Fair* about that?

About the raid on Palermo? Would that be direct and specific enough for them? Three days after Saint Rosalie's day, a blast of light like the end of the world, an explosion to blow you from the earth, and at the striking of every hour, bombs fell with fantastic crashings and destruction, sounding the signal for annihilation, blowing the perfume of the trees and the pink snow of the laurel trees across the city. Could you tell the readers of *Fair* about that night, that night when death ran its gamut in the sky and fell with the noise of thunder, when bleeding marionettes left on the sidewalks groaned, *"Ambulànza, ambulànza,"* trembling voices calling the old jalopy that was busy elsewhere, lost, hiding, how should I know? . . . And the tramping about of the police? A dark circle of strong-arm men, Fascists advancing with gymnast's tread, pushing back the furious crowd which was out of control, prepared to kill, to pillage, to rob. And then the cry of women rising among ruins under which all life was extinguished. Oh, my city, my poor city. . . . And the only answer was the bewildered flight of swallows in the sky.

But no sadness for *Fair*. Such was Daisy Lee's command. We were a magazine of happy lives, bright futures, and successful women. Have you forgotten the message I sent you yesterday? A memo from the administration. That was how she referred to written instructions which were always bad news. "Your job is not to tell your memories to the readers. You are paid to amuse them. Give them local color." Very well.

What would Daisy Lee say about Signor Giuseppe? Was Signor Giuseppe a subject for *Fair*? Would a business agent be considered a subject? His was a rough trade, always on his feet in mayor's offices, standing in line for the rich. From morning until night in waiting rooms, repeating "Of course, your Excellency. . . ." Busily convincing functionaries, while inobtrusively slipping them a bonus: "It's just a small thing, your Honor. . . ." And his particular way of presenting himself: "Here is Signor Giuseppe, at your service," bowing. Always correct, always in white shirt and necktie, champion of getting access to family records in record

time, an eminent expert at notarizations, draft deferments issued
with the force of a blow. Draft deferments are not so easy. "Your
Excellency can take my word for it when I tell you that my client
has a serious illness, an illness no doctor can cure, and besides
that, he has flat feet. Flat feet." Fifty lire, one hundred to be
quite correct, for Signor Giuseppe if he got the deferment, stamp
and all. . . . Was our neighbor a fit subject for *Fair?* The best
business agent in Palermo, always wearing a jacket, even when it
was very hot, and then, here he was in his shirtsleeves running
over the ruins, searching, howling, hunting for his wife, "Agatha,
my Agatha!" staggering, his clothes torn all over with only one
leg of his trousers left, and on the bare calf that varicose vein
earned waiting so long in so many lines, that ugly vein which bled,
"*Agatha, my Agatha,* my darling, my sweetheart, my dove, my
honey. . . ." All he found was his coffee pot, which he hugged to
him, a precious treasure trademarked *Vesuvian,* holding just two
cups.

No, Signor Giuseppe would not do for *Fair.* Daisy Lee wanted
none of that. It was her view that in a democracy one wouldn't
require such men. "We have no business agents here. Everyone
stands in line. Please, Gianna, leave Giuseppe in Sicily and let's
not talk about him any more." I must find another subject. I must
walk farther. Walk between these colossal dwellings, walk among
these towers which stifle you, which proliferate with crazy speed,
this crowded army, these masses which bury themselves in the
sky, make holes in it, violate it, that are polished, washed, cleaned
with the gestures of dishwashers by little men lashed to a scaffolding anchored at airplane height. No benches, no squares. But
building sites at every corner which almost crumbled under your
feet, as in nightmares. Serious-faced men supervised the steam
shovels. They checked arrivals and departures, they made columns
of figures. One of them—the Contractor, with a capital C—
watched particularly closely. This machine which turned ceaselessly needed him to open its fierce jaw, pick up a translucent slab,
and leave again, carrying its prey. Without him, plainly, it would

be immobilized, paralyzed, a powerful silhouette against the New
York sky. But the Contractor is there, watching it under the
broad brim of his hat. In Palermo, when night falls, there are men
who, like him, as still as statues, watch a discreet movement. The
comparison is striking. There, too, it is a matter of adding columns
of figures while a walking doll perched on high heels picks up a
client, follows him, tries to convince him. "Love, come on, shit
or get off the pot! I never saw anything like these guys. They're
regular Red Indians. *One dollar.* Do you understand?" How she
clings to him, nuzzles him, clutches him, how she pushes him
into any hovel she can find, an abandoned apartment, a cellar, a
basement, no matter what. Those cries! You'd have to hear them.
Then nothing. We robbed our liberators of everything: wallets,
papers, money, family snapshots, anything. They came out raging.
They shouted their name, rank and serial number as if they were
proofs of honor. They yelled for the Commander of the area. The
answer was always *Si signore! Cèrto! Súbito!* But nobody moved.
Nobody had seen anything. You should have seen our conquer-
ors' faces then. . . .

The Contractor has a satisfied look. The most beautiful child
of the Kalsa district all dressed up, crouched down so that you
wondered if she had a backbone, all the girls of Catania and Messina together with their skirts tight over their buttocks, a pretty
chain around the neck and a holy medal swinging between their
breasts, a girl to drive a man crazy, to make him lose his words,
his breath, his appetite, and all—even such a girl—would not have
succeeded in distracting the Contractor from his work. All that
interests him is the machine and the notebook in his hand. He
fills a sheet of paper without taking his eyes from the crane.

"Nothing like it. There's nothing like it in the world!"

He wants to explain its merits to me, its performance, he insists
on it. He talks and talks, he can't stop. He seems so sure of himself, so full of conviction, so superior, so condescending. How irritating he is! He insists:

"Thirty stories. We'll be finished soon. Because this can do miracles," he said, giving his machine a tender look.

"Miracles?"

He is worried.

"Have you ever seen a bigger one? Maybe you saw a bigger one some place else. Where was that?"

Yes, better ones by far, at the end of the road which led to the very edge of the cliff. There Polyphemus threw somber blocks pierced with grottoes into the sea where one can go in boats to find shade. Yes, with a single arm, balancing them on top of a rock. Your machine will never be able to do so much. Tell him that and he won't believe it. This man is not allowed to believe that the outline of a coast was destroyed by the bad temper of a Cyclops. To pay attention to such cock and bull stories would be against his principles. But you have your reasons. "I will wait on Polyphemus' rock." Can anyone forget such a meeting place? The passage by boat, the fear of getting lost, the calls—where are you?—drowned out by the slapping of waves, and then the rock of Polyphemus, just which one is it? There are at least three. It's clear that such rendezvous secretly transformed the adolescent girl who kept them into a grown woman.

Come now, these are thoughts which get you nowhere. Argue with this unknown man? What's the use? But he insists. He wants to be reassured.

"If you've seen better ones, tell me about it."

Yes, better, much better at Valverde, where the columns of the mother church were painted in a single night by a heavenly hand. By a celestial hand, do you understand? A self-portrait of the Madonna . . . are you surprised? There is no other way to explain how a picture could have appeared so suddenly in a little lost village in the Valley of the Demon as to distract the villagers from the volcano which threatens them and their quaking earth. If you said that to the Contractor—he would really look at you. He is still cordial. What does he expect of you? Approval, of course, and comfort. Americans seem to want nothing so badly as these, and their glass houses built in the century of aerial menace play a part in the New York landscape similar to that of the tranquilizers they take so often. These too encourage optimism.

"See if you can think of a better one."

"A fortress built without the help of any machine, built overhanging a precipice at such an angle that you get dizzy looking at it."

"Very interesting. Where is that?"

"In Sicily, on an inaccessible rock."

"Who is the architect who? . . ."

"Oh, the architect, you know. . . ."

"There is one. There must be one, whether there are machines or not."

"The country people say it is Saturn. . . . No, I'm not making it up. Arx Saturnia, that's its name. There's no other explanation. . . ."

What have you done? Suddenly everything is spoiled between yourself and this unknown man. You might have guessed. Daisy Lee's instructions, why did you forget them? "We've been publishing this magazine for thirty years and we think we know our readers. One principle to remember is: never contradict them. They expect you to respect their convictions. So limit yourself to the picturesque, the exotic. Escape, that's their great dream." What have you done? He throws you out.

"Every man to his own opinion. Now out, out of here. This site is off limits to the public. We don't want foreigners hanging around, picking our brains."

He was close to talking like the memos from the administration: "You're a foreigner, don't forget it."

You've really upset him with your blunders and your comments. He complains:

"There are too many like you around here. We let anything in, anyone."

He hates them all, wherever they come from, whoever they are, with their past spent on the roads, in the brambles, in the dust.

Let them go back where they came from. Parasites, all of them. And since he's got you at hand, you may as well suffer for them. Probably your interlocutor can't look at the Statue of Liberty, that symbol of a welcoming wide open fatherland, without tears filling his eyes. He loves her. She has everything to please him: a mother's breasts and belly, respectability, the look of a good girl. She turns her face towards those ungrateful countries whose shores she lights from afar.

The torch she brandishes would make a fine bludgeon. He goes to visit her on Sunday with his family. But today isn't Sunday. You're trespassing on the time he owes to his machine. He's had enough of you here. Then he spits on the ground, he fires a bullet of chewing gum to be crushed under your shoe: "Moslem, get out!" is what that would mean in Palermo, but in Palermo it is said without malice. We would call this coarse man a Moslem like that because that's what we've been saying for five centuries. "Up yours, Moslem!" is a turn of phrase which might have sped you on your way from the time when the invaders, come from Barbary, sowed terror on the Sicilian coasts. Black keels and red sails. The pillagers took the city by storm, abducted the women, and left only corpses behind them. An epoch long gone, but one which serves well if one evokes it to perpetuate fear. "Begone, Moslem!" Not the slightest spirit of insult. Just a familiar oath and you can add: "Go let the devil wipe your nose!" Why do we keep it? Bluster never hurt anyone. There's no real hatred in any of it. It's a matter of getting rid of the first thought of violence, that passing demon, and of choosing the best way of being rid of him. "Begone, Moslem!" Say it over a while to recall youth, embroider it, improvise on it, be imaginative, have a flight of fancy: "Your face is so ugly I don't want to slap it!" You feel stronger, more manly, but who's talking about being angry? It's well known that insults grow old with the men who invent them, they get wrinkles, they become empty of substance, grow dusty and fade away, but that's no reason for changing them. Come on, let yourself go. . . .

"Begone, Moslem!"
That settles the business.

Today *Fair*, magazine of great successes, great dresses, great
apartments, and great fortunes, waits for you. You arrive at least
two hours late. You are welcomed with a gentle solemnity and
hypocritical smiles born of all the unexpressed doubts which you
rouse.

"Well, how goes it?"

Pam has the smile she wears for catastrophes, a way of looking
at you which tells you clearly that you are a walking disaster area,
a bad example, and that you'll manage to get yourself fired in the
end.

"You aren't exactly early, and your copy isn't in either."

The peddlers of promptness assail you and the secretaries address their grumbling to you, the editors shrug their shoulders at
you, the telephone operator hands you your pile of messages with
a disgusted gesture. You must have been lost. That's the only
possible explanation. Not at all. The discussion goes on and on.
Now look here. . . . And with whom? You may imagine how
stifling it always is in an editorial office between women on the
downhill slope with young ones ready to step into their shoes. You
arrive like a fresh breeze. Then they try to involve you, with a
tone of false curiosity or simple amusement, in one of those tales
which has been salted, peppered, and well-stewed. Europeans, my
God! A pick-up, maybe? Don't let go of yourself. Better shut up.
It would look very odd, that conversation with an unknown man
on the street and that exchange of coarse words. You know instinctively that your story won't be appreciated; it could even, as
Aunt Rosie would say, be "harmful to your career." But your silence is scarcely more successful. All the editorial eyes are trained
on you. There are eyes behind the telephones, behind the desks,
behind the typewriters, and then suddenly there are those of the
editor-in-chief, who makes a rather solemn entrance.

"All our acts, all our thoughts should be suitable for offering to our readers as material. All our ideas, our smallest enterprises should have potential for our articles."

"I know . . . I know."

You know that old refrain by heart and the piercing voice of Daisy Lee nauseates you. Although it is her ordinary voice, it seems to you higher, more strident than usual. She must have had a drink. That often happens on the days of emergencies, when the magazine is late, or the circulation drops.

"The trouble with you, Gianna, is that your originality isn't always digestible. You're too likely to forget our readers' hunger for honest, creditable emotions, do you understand? That's what travel means to them: creditable emotion, a subject for conversation with their friends. Nothing more. So give them what they expect."

You are tired to death. Grief lies in wait for you. No doubt that explains why, while Daisy Lee continues to talk, you feel yourself drowning in a wave of confused thoughts—a vague, very vague intuition that life and its chances will offer you, in some distant future, the chance of throwing confusion into the hearts if not of all these women—models of energy and efficiency—then at least of one of them (and unconsciously you anticipate your meeting with Rocco Bonavia and its consequences); a feeling that one day Sólanto will show itself and that a word pronounced before you, a name, will revive in New York the lost continent, with its vast spaces, its perfumes, its rocks; a dead world, *your* world, and then also along with a desire to be elsewhere, a desire for a boat, for oars gliding on the water, for humid earth at the hour of watering, a desire for the sun falling abruptly behind purple rocks: "You'll get your article. It's coming," you say in a tone which is not your own and which you hardly recognize.

"You got out of that well."

Pam approved of me. I've read her my chronicle. She followed me up to the villa with its sculptures crumbling in the grass, and she liked it. I had made her appreciate the beauty of the place.

I had described to her the retaining wall with its procession of gesticulating statues, leaving nothing out: Tarascon monsters, cripples, they all passed by there. She followed me right up to the demoniac crowd of werewolves and manticores, bearded sphynxes, two-headed serpents, hippogriffs, of turbaned men-dogs playing unknown instruments to the ballet of fat, squatting Turks with little ones baring their behinds in the faces of visitors. I had even remembered the strange silhouette of a giant, wearing a high wig, a sort of moonlike fan, a nightmare marquis who surveyed the abandoned garden proudly.

She had listened to me with what seemed to be sincere interest.

"That's really interesting, you know? It makes you want to see that house."

"Why?"

"Because it's a fairy tale house. An eighteenth-century Disneyland. Temples, you know, Segestum, Agrigentum. They all look alike at first, and then, rightly or wrongly, you always have the feeling you've already seen them, at least one of them. Columns, pediments, Washington is full of them. But your gnomes. . . ."

"You think so?"

"I'm sure of it. Anyway, if you explain the significance of the ornaments, or if there isn't a plausible explanation, present them as a puzzle that baffles the greatest archaelogists. There's nothing in between. Readers hate to be left hanging."

"Don't worry."

"Well, what do the statues mean?"

"They are a protection. . . ."

"From what?"

Pam pretended not to understand.

"Ornaments for guarding against the evil eye," I repeated quietly. "Magic battlements, if you prefer."

"You're not going to tell me you take that nonsense seriously?"

"What do you find nonsensical about it? Don't you believe in the supernatural? There's nothing more serious."

Pam could only shake her bracelets without speaking. A total blank. Her expression was frozen, and for an instant I thought she might burst into tears. One would have thought a support had suddenly collapsed beneath her. But which one? Aunt Rosie, perhaps, as a mirror in which she had a habit of finding her own thoughts reflected. Faced with an idea which changed her mind, which she had hoped to have banished among the scattered products of an archaic world, Pam felt lost. I insisted.

"It's not hard to see that certain things are beyond human control, you know. . . ."

"I hate that kind of talk."

"You started it."

"The inexplicable depresses me."

"That's not enough reason for the look on your face."

Pam looked at me anxiously. She had tears in her eyes.

"But, Gianna, I'm just waiting to be convinced," she said. "Why don't you believe me? If there are such things, let's talk about them. Tell me, how do you recognize the evil eye?"

"There is no way."

"Why?"

"The more malevolent it is, the less one suspects. . . ."

"I can't stand people who hide things," she said, sounding self-assured again. "They're hypocrites."

"I can't see what hypocrisy has to do with this."

And once more there was an edge of anger in my voice. How could Pam have suspected the kind of adversary she was confronting? Nothing I had said was premeditated. The words welled up like an unsuspected memory and the moment they were pronounced were converted into an irresistible pleasure, like songs which spring to one's lips, bringing all sorts of memories with them, some forgotten air which one whistles, then which one hums, asking oneself what, but what on earth, made me think of that? So I let myself relive the fears of my childhood. Was it my fault if they appeared to me more troubling now than when I first discovered them? An English governess all starchy with Victorian traditions; that's probably what I should have had. But there was

no such creature in Sicily where we were left in the care of a wet
nurse until we were old enough for the convent. Is it my fault if,
having passed the age for the breast, until I was ten years old I
was crammed with stories in which sallow young men, always only
sons, sometimes noble, died from the glance shot them by a hated
neighbor; in which charms muttered between clenched teeth were
enough to send a boat to the bottom of the ocean, make a brother
fall in love with his sister, or provoke a series of suicides? And
how could I help it if such tales appealed to me? To what Orient,
to what Asia, to what drop of unknown blood did I owe my superstitious nature?

No doubt Pam wondered how to treat me. She looked at me
with alarm. Why not tell her that she annoyed me? But I forced
myself to remain calm.

"Hypocrisy has nothing to do with it. The worst lady-killer in
Sicily, a man whose evil power had manifested itself for over a half
century in the cruellest way, had no idea that he had the evil eye.
So unaware was he, that he laid a spell on himself while looking
in the mirror. I don't know how such things happen. The mirror
may have fallen from the wall and fractured his skull, or perhaps
it sent his own glance back in a burning ray which disintegrated
him."

"Oh my God!"

Pam made an instinctive gesture to protect her eyes. For an instant I was unable to say any more. She rejected her own image
of herself: no longer the worldly journalist. I don't know if she
saw herself changing, but I saw it. There she was, listening to a
story of no possible use to her. We talked. And we were no longer
talking to exchange opinions on a title, or the "shock effect," or
even effectiveness. She ceased to share with me her ambitions as
a penniless journalist living on her wits in a world of money. She
spoke to me no more of that house she would have one day, like
those citadels of the good life which she had so often visited, photographed, described, praised, with real ancestors grouped on the
walls and "intolerably beautiful" Picassos—all those Picassos, blue

period Picassos matched to the silk of the armchairs, all those manifestations of troubled minds and authentic miseries—"cut off his ear, you know. . . ." She forgot them. She detached herself from the gloomy geniuses who always led impossible lives, ruining their livers, drowning themselves in absinthe without suspecting that this would raise their prices in New York. These beloved damned whose canvases made such a good effect on one's drawing room walls. She gave herself up.

No, no, my conversation didn't bother her. She recognized her faults, of course. She was too absorbed in her work. It got tiresome finally to hear the same things over and over. Yes. . . . Yes. . . . She was perfectly aware of it and it shouldn't be held against her. I either had to shut her up or else force her to listen to me as I did at that moment. She wanted to hear more of these stories about "waking dreams."

"But, Pam, that's not possible. We were talking about a method of protection, a way of security, a very ancient one, and you call it waking dreams. It's obvious we'll never understand each other."

I still hear myself talking to her this way, and I still hear her reply:

"I know, I know, Gianna," she said humbly as if trying to excuse herself. "Explain it to me, please."

"What's the use? The evil eye? Is it the expression that frightens you? You meet with an unknown expression and instead of trying to understand it you stand there wide eyed in the dark calling on the solid principles of Aunt Rosie for help. And you call in vain. The idea of the evil eye isn't on your list. So you conclude with a shrug of the shoulders that such a thing doesn't exist and you're shocked by it, you make a face. You don't see that what we're dealing with is a figure of speech, nothing more. An image for the threat which hovers over those rare moments when man calls himself happy. But do you even know what happiness is, Pam? I'm not talking about those little pantomimes which keep us going, a bath just the right temperature, or the bed where one satisfies a brief desire for love. No, Pam, the evil eye doesn't deign to

threaten such little pleasures. It only attacks those which are immense, ambitious, irrational. The evil eye threatens those who
dream of the impossible."

"What does it look like?"

"Like the builder of that villa we were speaking of a moment
ago. That man, if you like, must have pursued a dream. I don't
know what it was, but I know that's what counts, and that alone.
A dream to which he must have devoted all his leisure, all his
imagination, all his strength, and more. A dream to which he gave
the rounded and enclosed form of that garden."

"Are there really such dream gardens, Gianna?"

"I know some, and some houses, too. They are built like balconies open to—I don't know—to everything that makes a certain
kind of night: its faceless noises, stifled, scarcely audible, dry twigs
cracking, restless flutter of moths around a forgotten light, mur-
murs, confused questions which would ordinarily command attention and provoke worry: What is that step? Did I leave a lamp
burning? But they are scarcely felt in this happiness. Nothing is
hurried, nothing is delayed, everything belongs to the night. The
sky is seeded with stars like a puzzle to be solved; far away the
song of a fisherman who went to cast his nets when the moon
rose, and on the sea that miracle one cannot stop looking at, that
dancing furrow cast by a beacon in the water. . . . You must understand, Pam, that there's a great danger that all this will suddenly lose its special light and fade into banality, boredom, dis-
affection. It doesn't take much, just a gesture or a look suggesting
weariness. It's just that unforeseen flick, that sudden lurch that
rocks us when we least suspect tragedy in our happiness, that is
what is called the evil eye. You must admit that it would be a
mistake not to be prepared for it."

Pam rewarded me with a smile in several stages, a very successful
one in which her lips, barely moist, slowly revealed her teeth;
then, at the end of a surprise operation as studied as the flourish
of a strip-teaser, it let the tip of her tongue appear, as appetizing
and delicate as a bite of ham. I was beginning to know Pam's

smile by heart. I was getting some sort of indigestion from seeing it not only on her mouth but also on those of all the stars photographed by *Fair*. No doubt about it. But the expression on her face was different. Maybe it was that she looked less virginal than usual. As she repeated, "Be prepared for it, yes. But how?" she crossed her arms, put her hands inside her kimono sleeves and mechanically stroked her shoulders.

"Yes indeed, how? How can we be assured of our happiness, and when we have it, how can we keep it from leaving. How? Everyone does the best he can. By staying on the defensive. If you need to, you make horns, which is just another way of expressing one's protective spirit."

I showed Pam how to make this sign and it seemed to amuse her, for she twice rehearsed the gesture of throwing her arms wide and pointing at the ceiling with both hands, her index and ring fingers childishly stuck out, with a long sensual cooing laugh, and I didn't dare tell her any more, nor warn her of the real meaning of "horns," for fear of shocking her. Then, laughing again and shuddering happily, she asked me, as I stood there staring at her in surprise, if I knew any other conjuring signs. "Those old customs are absolutely enchanting!"

She insisted. "There must be others." What could I answer? I could hardly see myself describing the Mediterrean burial custom which obliges a man to grope for what is at the bottom of his pocket, nor that gesture which is made every day in sight of everyone, with everyone's knowledge, thumb pointing bravely into a closed hand, nor those grimaces, spitting out such crude obscenities that even Pam in her innocence could not have mistaken what they meant. I said nothing and she continued to stare at me sharply.

"Tell me, Gianna, that can't be all you have to tell our readers. Horns? That doesn't really tell enough."

My God, I thought, she is really made in the image of her audience. More, they always want more. And deep inside myself I heard Daisy Lee's voice repeating: "You forget how hungry they are. Don't forget that hunger."

"I'll tell them about it. Don't worry, they'll get their money's worth. I'll tell them about the shops in Palermo where they can buy talismans of all sizes. They can find horns for the grown-up, for the child, for the newborn, the right size for a cart, for a car, for a Lambretta, for a cradle, others to hang around their necks, on their blouses. You'll see, horns from Palermo will become the rage. They'll be copied and sold for a dollar here in two months. Daisy Lee will crown me with garlands and congratulate herself on the way our publication has influenced the amulet market. She'll be able to say of Sicily what she told me about Greece: 'We were the ones who put it on the map. Nobody talked about it before our Greek issue came out!' I guarantee she'll be satisfied. 'If our readers don't buy or copy the things they like abroad, they feel frustrated. The trouble with your temples is that there's nothing you can do with them.' All right, we'll give them horns! You can buy coral horns, silver horns, even wooden horns. For those who seek the wisdom of the ages, there's something for them too, believe me. I'll give them that old house with its idols forever embracing. I'll give it to them all wrapped up in its crenelated wall, hideous and superb at the same time, massive and crumbling, wearing a name with claws, the name of a carnivorous beast or a black goddess: Bagheria. Besides which, our readers will be able to read about the memory of a legendary prince who built a house for his amours. They'll have a busy time figuring out those architectural aberrations. Enough to take up a whole afternoon. I can see them now, in their striped dresses and flat heels and rosy cheeks, moving back and forth with guide books in their hands. The prince of Palagonia himself would not be offended by their astonishment. You see this man, who knew how ugly he was, loved a beautiful woman. That's not important. A threat to one's happiness arouses the same anxiety whether one is handsome or ugly. But the prince was ugly. One day, then, when he was walking arm in arm with the one who filled his every thought, he saw, on the balcony of a nearby house, a silhouette which quickly withdrew, and a blind which was drawn after it. He felt his love endangered. Nothing more was necessary. To banish his obsession, he applied customs which came from who knows where, perhaps from the valley of the Nile, according to which one guards against unhappiness by the protecting virtues of laughter. Laughter, do you understand? Under certain conditions, it can save you. That was the weapon the prince used first, and he set grotesque statues, hunchbacks and dwarves as sentinels on the walls of his garden. But undoubtedly he feared these were not enough. Something within him still trembled and tired of pretending, he placed, between these comic specters, cariatids contorted with passion to do battle for him, some making great gestures of love to the heavens, some prostrate, forming a circle of mad hope. Remember that the demand for eternal love is an urgent one."

"Eternal love," Pam repeated, "that's something I've never thought of."

"Who does think of it? We love where we can and how we can until we can love no more."

"Oh, I'm much simpler than that. I've never been in love."

"Oh, come now!"

I began to laugh, and so did Pam.

"If you think I mean I've never made love, you ought to know better," she said. "That's not what I mean. Anyway, I'm not a virgin, if you're interested."

Pam found her smile again, smoothed her hair, retied the belt of her kimono, losing a bit of truth with each gesture. Perhaps they only served to hide her uneasiness. Her story was going to be harder to tell than she had imagined. . . .

"We've talked a long time this morning," she said. "Ethel is late."

Pam was trying to gain time, and I would have been glad to help her. But how? Her last statement put an end to questions.

It was Sunday. Outside there was frost in the air. You could see it in the numb look of the sweepers in their helmets who had come down from Harlem under the eye of the policeman who, club in hand, patrolled Park Avenue with a quicker step than usual.

We were seated side by side in Aunt Rosie's dining room as we always were on the day of a party, while Pam, barely awake, checked on preparations and issued orders. No lazy mornings on those days. No prolonged baths. No magazines in bed while the radio played softly. No rubbing with pumice, with lily water, with almond oil. No masks. Pam renounced her Sunday customs. Up early, she crossed the landing dressed in her long kimono of brown silk, her feet bare, her hair rumpled, smiling her beautiful smile—the first of the day—as a dress rehearsal for all those smiles she would later bestow upon her guests.

Aunt Rosie, already seated at her dressing table, was much too busy to join our conversation. She participated actively in these receptions of Pam, so she must get ready. Leaning towards her mirror, addressing encouragements and criticisms to herself aloud, sniffing, digging, searching among the vast assortment of products accumulated before her for just that one which seemed to her worthy for such a special occasion, Mrs. MacMannox limited herself to tossing short sentences at us through the half open door. They reached us sharp as machine gun fire: "I really can't see what anyone has to talk about at nine o'clock in the morning. . . . What a horrible hour for conversation. . . . If you want to keep your figure, Pam, and you should keep it, don't touch those rolls of Gianna's. Not even toasted. . . . You have no idea. . . . Do you hear me, Gianna? . . . You hear what I'm saying about you? . . . Bread in the morning! Why not spaghetti while you're at it? In underdeveloped countries it's understandable. . . . They fill up on bread. . . . But here. . . . Oh, I . . . it's very simple, I eat nothing. . . . Not one thing in the morning. . . ."

There was a mixture of assurance and foolishness in her way of speaking—a foolishness that was her very own—such an assurance in her prejudices that one couldn't help wondering about Aunt

Rosie's past. By what steps had she arrived at this point? Had Aunt Rosie ever said things that were light or irrelevant? Did she laugh in the time of "Mister Mac"? (Nobody used this diminutive except people in the know who had really been intimate with that great expert in persuasion.) Surely in Mister Mac's time she did not have this tense, serious air. But he was dead and her reasons for being gentle or laughing had disappeared with him. Pam was now the only subject which occupied her, and Aunt Rosie was forever announcing how she had transferred all her ambitions to her niece. "When you begin to understand what fatigue means. . . . And too much coffee, so idiotic. . . . Three cups in the morning. . . . Keep that up, Pam, and I wouldn't give much for your skin. . . . Gianna has less to lose. . . . Latins all have sallow skins, everybody knows. . . ."

Was Pam submissive? The word is too strong. Let's say that in her aunt's presence she let her decide and solve things for her. She gave way willingly, acquiesced, welcomed it, like a healthy gust of wind. Dry little sentences continually crackled in Aunt Rosie's room. Pam rarely replied. She hunched her back like a cat one strokes with a hair brush. But if that voice had not been there, if the rosy lamps had suddenly gone out, Pam would have felt deserted. Aunt Rosie was a necessary counterpoint.

Of those two voices I listened only to one, Pam's, which drew me through her childhood in the hope that we would find the causes for everything there and, to be sure, she was right. I saw her accepting the imperious domination of Aunt Rosie, at thirteen under a cloche hat posing for her photograph as a Girl Scout; at fifteen, going to a good dancing class. I lost her for a little during her studies, for she was not talkative about her college years. Her debut in New York made her more expansive.

I found her again after a few years participating in charity parties with girls richer than she, then invited to the same balls, to the same clubs. "You've got to have rich friends. . . . There's no better capital. . . . However charming they are, poor ones can become embarrassing. . . . Especially when you're more successful than they are." Aunt Rosie! There she was, always overflowing with experience . . . always her voice . . . always heard and obeyed.

I listened to Pam telling me how she had learned to run her finger over an invitation, to hold it up to the light to judge the quality of the stationery, to rub her thumb over it to make sure it was engraved. And Aunt Rosie insisted on a pitiless refusal to any which seemed to her to come from some dubious sphere of society: "I don't want you seeing those people. . . . Where do they come from? . . . The address is in green ink. . . . That's a bad sign. . . . And the card was engraved out of town. . . . Where is the party? . . . One simply doesn't give a ball at the Barbizon Plaza!" Into the wastebasket with it!

"But, Pam, how on earth does Aunt Rosie know all these things?"

"From my uncle. She inherited all his secret tactics."

Mister Mac. I might have guessed. Above us his portrait was enthroned against the mahogany. He watched us, he observed us while we talked, and Pam and I could consider the resources of this figure that some vaguely Spanish painter, anxious to please, had succeeded in making unforgettable. Something to dream about. First that drooping moustache that made Mr. MacMannox into a sort of Taras Bulba old-fashioned milord. The British note came from his shirt with a high starched collar and the vest buttoned almost to the knot of his cravat, and his high-topped shoes.

"Did he always dress that way?"

My question seemed to surprise Pam.

"You didn't know?"

"No. I thought he just wore that costume to pose for the painter. The way kings wore armor."

"My uncle never wore anything else. But there was nothing funny about it. He was only trying to impress his clients."

And, looking at that portrait, one could easily see that he was a past master at the art of dazzling his world. So slicked up and agreeable.

"He was very attractive."

Pam's voice became dreamy: "If he were alive, would I still be here?"

"What do you mean?"

"My life would have been different. . . ."

Apparently Mr. MacMannox had a rare pastime for a business-man. Impressing the nation with brands of stockings, cigarettes, or pills was not enough for him: he also went in for young girls. And his achievements in the market of social success were so re-sounding that a sort of understanding was established between MacMannox and his rich clients. They entrusted their daughters to him. They couldn't do without him.

"He did it for fun, and out of the goodness of his heart. It was his way of amusing himself."

Aunt Rosie must have been very proud. A man without equal. He had played and won on two scenes simultaneously without one damaging the other. With serious products—stockings, cigarettes—the success was financial. With girls, the success was social. And he knew how to extract more and more power from this business. By comparison, his competitors seemed impoverished.

Pam explained to me how he set out to make any unknown girl into the debutante of the year. He planned it like a military campaign. His first challenge? Decorating her. He took her to a good hairdresser, and sometimes he had her teeth capped. He then selected several intimate friends for her, and arranged for her to be listed in the social register. He wasn't in the least ashamed to busy himself with such trifles. Even Aunt Rosie would become involved in all this, and she did her best to help the girl.

But the battle, properly speaking, did not begin until Mr. Mac-Mannox went into action. The strategy allowed the young lady in question to go to fashionable nightclubs or elegant restaurants only after the match was virtually won—that is to say from the moment when the gossip columnists could put a name to her young face: "Seen at the table of Mr. X, Miss So-and-so, who was elegantly dressed in. . . ." Mr. MacMannox launched her—always in the same rented limousine (chauffeur with cap and in winter a fur

lap robe)—in her assault on the season's big events, by alternating
prudently between classic spectacles and avant-garde occasions, important concerts, and openings of exhibitions of abstract paintings.
No one could miss them. Such a moustache as Mister Mac's was
seen and noticed. And the cut of his vest and the tops of his shoes.
Details of which the dailies never tired. People crowded around
Mr. MacMannox with questions, "Tell us who's with you." He
would act mysterious, "I'm not here to do your job for you. Come
now, my friend, look for yourself." But he always ended by letting
slip the name. "Know who I mean? . . . No? . . . Well, she's So-
and-so's daughter." Sometimes that was enough. Sometimes success was more difficult. A face didn't catch on. But the harder the
task, the more he enjoyed it. He enjoyed little passing defeats: a
photographer who passes without recognizing you, sightseers who
don't turn around, invitations which don't arrive. Then he added
to the list of habitual enjoyments more subtle pleasures: short appearances with intellectuals of Greenwich Village; dances in the
salons of the moguls of high finance. He took the young lady to a
baseball game or a jazz concert, never let her go until she achieved
all he had promised her: an imminent marriage, her photograph in
the Sunday edition of the *New York Times*, and finally, when no
star was missing from her firmament of success, a page in *Fair*.

And then the name of Mr. MacMannox had its turn on the first
page of these same journals, on the occasion of his death—one
glass too many, a foolishness, a crazy audacity in trying a dance
which had a rhythm which was not for a man of his age. They
carried him off hiccoughing, his mouth twisted. That dance had
cut him down as a live shell finishes a soldier. Aunt Rosie took
great care of her niece, so that Pam had only to let go once she
finished her studies. Mrs. MacMannox took care of everything. But
as the material circumstances of her life no longer permitted her
to offer Pam all the necessary show, she demanded of her niece
much more effort than would have been necessary had there not
been a regrettable loss of pomp. No chauffeur in a cap to open
doors for her. No fur lap robe, social symbol which the dear de-

ceased had known so well how to use. Often no limousine. Aunt Rosie preached flirtatiousness, grace, and a great enthusiasm for wealth. At the end of a year things were looking up. Pam, according to Aunt Rosie, was a "really popular" girl. She had no intimate friends, but she was asked out a lot. It was plain that she was the very soul of seriousness, and that her ambition left little place for sentiment. Aunt Rosie could call herself satisfied.

However, something hung over her enterprise like the threat of failure. Aunt Rosie spent long hours trying to imagine what would be the face, the voice, the tone, the occupation of the unknown young man who would come one day, overcome, worried to the point of suffering, drunk with happiness, and who knows what else—she had a romantic notion of love—to seek her approval, and after various embarrassed false starts would end by asking for the hand of her niece. But that stranger, she was forced to admit, was not materializing. Perhaps Pam lacked some casual quality, a fancy or gaiety, some generosity, some sense of intimacy that is so pleasing to men. What could it be? Ease? No. . . . She had that. . . . Oh, if only Mr. MacMannox had still been in this world! With his critical mind, he who was never wrong would quickly have found what was missing. He was light, witty, full of enthusiasm, he was . . . alas. . . . Everything added to Aunt Rosie's perplexity until at last she came fearfully to the conclusion that her husband's methods, perhaps, were only infallible when he himself applied them.

It was by means of a symposium, organized and presided over by Daisy Lee, a meeting at which Pam was the prize-winner, chosen unanimously, that a new idea possessed Mrs. MacMannox. A job on *Fair* was the new goal. Pam got it. Aunt Rosie rejoiced. The bitterness left by her other failure was erased: Pam and *Fair*, it was the best of marriages: an alliance with the haughty and mysterious power of the press, a force which consecrated or killed. Pam was finally going to occupy that important position that Aunt Rosie had dreamed about so long. "Called to a great future in our publications," said the article devoted to her in *Fair*. A great fu-

ture, what better could be hoped for? Marriage? The two were not
mutually exclusive. Everything was going to be all right and soon
they would again be able, as they did when Mister Mac was alive,
to associate with high society. Aunt Rosie's worries suddenly
seemed unwarranted.

"But you, Pam. . . . How did you feel about this change of direction? Were you happy about it?"

"Me? I felt I would be wrong to go on the way it was before. . . ."

"The way it was before what?"

Pam looked at me with embarrassment.

"Before what I was just telling you. Give me time to. . . ." As
if in the hope of being interrupted, she turned toward the room
where, through the open door, we could see Aunt Rosie preparing
to go out. But Mrs. MacMannox appeared to be as far away and
detached as possible. Her detachment was feigned. She was listening to every word we said.

"You two talk too much," Aunt Rosie said. "And for what?
Well, better to talk than eat. . . . It's just as useless but less unhealthy. . . . But then what else can you do. . . . Ethel is late
again. Colored people have no sense of time. None. . . ."

Pam was upset.

"Give her time to get here, Aunt Rosie. It's cold and it's Sunday."

"Sunday . . . Sunday. She's late and that's it. . . . She's probably in that church I went to once to please her. . . . On Lenox
Avenue if I remember rightly. . . . I thought I was in a dance
hall. . . . A panting woman came to meet me. Then she took me
to my seat and called me 'honey . . . baby' as if we were old
friends. After that, as if she were introducing me, she said, 'A soul
for salvation!' and a hundred people began to stare at me. While
they intoned hymns for my sake a child began to dance right in
front of the altar. His mother had given him a tambourine. He
played it in time to the hymns and nobody seemed in the least
surprised. Two or three times the child tried to pull me up there.

I didn't know what to do: he wanted me to dance with him. Never . . . I'll never forget that incredible scene. Right here in New York. . . . Just a few minutes from here. A black child with his arms out dancing in a church with a blue paper star pasted in the middle of his forehead."

"Ethel explained about that. It's the star of Bethlehem."

"What has that to do with me? Bethlehem or anywhere else. . . . The only thing that's clear in the whole story is that you'll never change them. And Ethel's just like the rest. . . . Late again. . . . You'll never teach them to use a watch. . . . You can't tell me anything else, Gianna. . . . The Latins aren't exactly punctual themselves, but, I find it shocking. . . ."

After a final appraisal in the mirror, she left the apartment.

"I don't think your aunt trusts me."

"That's not what's the matter."

Pam had answered with impatience. Now it was she who wanted to go on.

"Good. What were we talking about?"

She answered at once, "About me. . . ."

She hesitated a moment, then cried: "That's enough! I've had enough of it, you understand? *Fair* freed me. But it was only a pretext. . . ."

"To what?"

"To change my life. I was finally going to get rid of my following of beaux who had gone to the best schools. Of the things they took me to. The movies every Saturday, holding hands. Yes, the movies *every* Saturday, *every* week with a different boy."

Having heard Aunt Rosie recite her principles of education, I could sympathize with Pam.

"I know, I know," Pam continued. "I know the cliché: 'One lover is hateful. Two is open to criticism. But when three or four young men of good family ring a young lady's doorbell regularly, that's just right.' I know. I heard it all day long. Then, when you went out three times running with the same boy you felt as if you'd done something wrong."

I made her task easier. I encouraged her, I became docile. I was becoming interested, without irony. And Pam, sensing my sympathy, showed tremendous gratitude. She took my hand.

"Suppose Aunt Rosie. . . ."

I interrupted.

"Don't talk any more about her, Pam, please. Talk about yourself. Anyway, I know what you're going to say to me: suppose Aunt Rosie was wrong. That is what you are thinking, isn't it?"

Suddenly Pam seemed to decide to tell me everything. Hesitating at first, then more and more resolutely.

"I think especially about the morning of that party when she began to sell her idea of vertigo: 'To be attractive you must make them dizzy. . . . How do you do it? You are so reasonable. Hide your sense of balance a little,' she told me. 'Try to, anyway.' I can see what she meant now. She was probably thinking of my uncle and that way he had of putting on an apparent lightness, even though he was seriousness itself. But at seventeen how could I understand? It was at that party that everything began. A long dress, white gloves. A ball. One of these enormous affairs we give here. Always for the benefit of some charity and always in a hotel where several mothers, just a few, and hundreds of girls meet and dance and are sometimes bored.

"I had a date who managed to convince Aunt Rosie at three in the morning that she could go home without waiting for me: 'We'll stay until the wee hours.' He took me back. She'd known him more than ten months. She considered him a nice boy. A boy of good family, eighteen or nineteen years old. And his father had lent him his car for the evening. So she left. And he drank.

"As soon as we left the ball he suggested going through Central Park and driving around a little with the windows open since a little fresh air wouldn't hurt either of us. It wasn't a bad idea. My head was spinning. I had drunk, too. All this, as you can see, was perfectly ordinary. Cars are used for everything here.

"Once we were in the park I was the one who suggested stopping near the lake where people go boating on Sundays. Trees, nothing but trees and night. Central Park, that green pocket that the city wears as proudly as a kangaroo, that poor moth-eaten thing, faded, chewed, became a real forest again. Silent, dark.

"What did he think? That I was leading him on? I had only one idea in my head, to get rid of what was in my stomach as soon as I could, to vomit. I opened the door and leaned out of the car. Something crackled in the underbrush. A cat or dog on the prowl. At least I thought so.

"He didn't seem worried. He even laughed, trying to put me at ease. I trembled. That was natural, it seemed. The first few times one gets drunk one must expect to have a chill. Then he got out to find a blanket in the trunk of the car, and he stayed out a long time without my understanding what he was doing. When he came back, I began to regret stopping there, and as my teeth continued to chatter, he put the windows up, wrapped me in the blanket, turned on the heater, and tipped the seats back saying: 'It isn't very romantic with you. . . .' Then he turned on the radio as if the music could make everything right.

"Since I didn't move, he put his hand on my forehead.

" 'Listen,' he said, 'you mustn't be afraid. I've taken care of everything.'

" 'What do you mean?'

"He looked at me suspiciously, then began to struggle with the lock of the glove compartment. I congratulated myself that his activity would distract him from me. It went on for a few minutes while he cursed his father's mania for locking everything.

"When the compartment finally opened he said, 'See, we've got just the thing for you.'

"I didn't know what he meant by that. I hated the way he was talking. Then he put on a scientific manner and said, 'I believe you are completely frigid or a total idiot.'

"I was trying to think of a way to get him to start the car when he took a flask of whisky from his pocket and began to drink.

There was really no way of stopping him. He drank with his eyes
closed; so pale that I really wondered if he wasn't going to be
sick. A few seconds later he went into a kind of delirium. A crazy
drunkenness, rambling, all about the stupidity of girls. I made him
furious. Happily he'd known a great many who were used to cars
and knew what they could do in them. I told him I wanted to go
home right away, and then he said, 'You're a blockhead. You ask
me to stop and all you can think of is yourself. What about me?
I need somebody to fix me up. I'm tied in a knot. Do you understand? I need you.' He squeezed my fingers so they hurt. You can
imagine the rest. He fell on me, his face against my face, collapsed,
sweating, his hands clasped around my neck. I struggled, then
collapsed. He babbled incoherent words, 'I'm unhappy. . . . I need
you. . . .' I could hardly keep from crying out, not from pain—not
from pain nor from the slightest pleasure—but from fear. When
I saw him straighten up, his nostrils pinched and his face gray, all
the fever had disappeared from him. Soon he fell down beside me
and I heard him crying. A miserable kid. That was really all he
was. Then he began to shout, 'It's your fault, too. You shouldn't
have led me on.' I was so surprised that I couldn't think of anything to say. But from that moment I knew I hated him. I was
sure of it. Day began to break with a white light on my soiled
dress. He began to groan again, 'What can we do now?' But he
said no more than that. A man was spying on us through the door.
How long had he been there? A long time surely. Maybe from the
beginning. A man with a hungry look. Eyes of a peeping pig, a
rodent. Disgusting. A bum with a four-day beard. I cried out.
Then the man moved to open the door and I heard something
like, 'You don't seem to be having a very good time in there. . . .
You want a little help, mister?' I pushed down the lock so quickly
that he stood still, his hand on the handle, his mouth against the
glass, then he said: 'You know what I want, don't you? Are you
going to open this damn door? If you open it, you won't be sorry.'
I thought he would break it down. The boy looked at him, riveted
in his place, too frightened to move. It was I who turned the key

in the ignition; I who put his hands on the wheel; I who released the brake. Finally he understood. We began to roll with that orangutan of a man crouched by our door, that nightmare man crying out, howling, 'Thanks for the show, anyway,' following us in leaps. It was horrible. And the boy was in no state to drive. I tried to help him. I tried to shift gears for him. At first he couldn't even manage the clutch. Finally, when he did, the man stopped following us. I heard him one last time: 'Never even offered me a fuckin' shot. Your goddam bottle of Scotch, you can stick it up your ass, hear me? Up your ass. . . .' and more threats, 'Lousy mothers. . . . Louses. . . . Halfbaked whore. . . .' A thicket hid him from us.

"After a few yards my driver got sick and vomited between his knees while I held the wheel. He spewed it all over, on himself, and me. And I almost thanked him for this additional horror.

"I knew that this was the only explanation I could offer at home for the spots, for my ruined dress, and for our return at dawn. The state of my suitor, this young man who had such nice manners, his drunkenness—'An unfortunate accident, but one which can happen to the best people'—I think that's what Aunt Rosie said. She didn't ask for any more details. I didn't have the courage to offer them.

"The next week I pretended to have a sore throat so I could wear a dressing gown and a scarf around my neck. I was covered with bruises on my arms and wrists.

"And then his father came to see Aunt Rosie. To my great surprise she welcomed the announcement of this with enthusiasm, and dressed up as if she were having a reception. Poor thing. What did she imagine? He had come to demand an explanation. First, the car. A mess. He'd never seen a car in such a state. The glove compartment forced open. What happened? Since that evening his son had never recovered from a most upsetting state: semiprostration and weeping. They were afraid of a nervous breakdown. I listened behind the door, terrified. It seemed to me that I was the one with more right than anyone to be complaining and sick, but he was the one having the nervous breakdown. I think I cried. In all my life I had never felt so alone, so wretched as I did that day. His father kept asking, 'What happened?' He wanted me to tell. I listened, terrified at the thought that this imbecile had blurted out the whole story. But Aunt Rosie refused to let me appear. She told him in a tone which brooked no reply that young people should be taught to drink decently before they were allowed to go into the world. That his son had been too drunk to walk or to drive. That the doorman had found him dead drunk, passed out on the sofa in the entrance hall without tie or shoes. That he had to dress him, put him in a taxi, and clean the carpet and the cushions. A scandal. And, for the rest, that she had said enough about it, seen enough, heard enough, that she really didn't know whom to trust these days, and that she must ask her visitor to leave.

"I was safe.

"Sometimes I feel the memory of that night coming back to me. I imagine the worst. The man is armed. Ready for anything. Nothing can save us from him. The car gets stuck. They find us the next day. One on top of the other. One body, two victims.

"At other times I forget all about it for months at a time and think of nothing but my work."

I listened. I listened to these words, these words that escaped Pam, fleeing from her and filling the room with their strangeness. They floated like a mist; they clung to the furniture, to the walls; they penetrated everywhere; they poured a sort of pathetic jelly on the corners of Mr. MacMannox's lips—clowns have that false smile. They followed Pam around the table, for she had risen and was walking with hurried steps, pulling her kimono about her hips as if, suddenly, she had lost her nonchalant mannequin's manner. If I tell you everything was changed, yes, everything about her was changed: her perfume, the fresh odor of eau de toilette she'd sprayed on herself, the odor of the coffee which cooled in our cups, and even the outlines of the trees in Central Park with their poor twisted naked branches which seemed to address wordless supplications to the sky.

"Well, you see, that's how things went. . . ."

"I see."

I thought I heard her murmur: "I wonder what I should have. . . ."

Then on the off chance and making an effort, I remember having answered:

"A little love might have helped, maybe; or even a little anger. And then some drama and revenge."

But my voice lacked warmth. And anyway, was she listening? I looked at her, my pathetic friend. She needed to move about, driven by her own words. She walked around the table the way one looks for a cool place in the bed when one has a fever. She repeated vainly, "It would be wrong to make a tragedy of this story. There's always a first man, then another and another. What bothers me is that the last two hadn't any importance either." She was thinking of something else. Just those words and the terrible distance between her and me. I looked at her—new, unknown, a little tired, a little bent under the burden of words. Pam, her armor down, faced her truth. Pam finally admitting her wound and its pain, the wound of a woman deceived by life.

We left each other that morning as if we had not spoken at all. She would never again let those long questioning looks escape her. We spent the rest of the day preparing for the party. She behaved serenely, convinced that she was doing a job that was an integral part of herself, her reputation, her career.

III.

You meet all kinds of people there. . . . There
are even merchants who sell wind.

URI TYNIANOV

The guests were arriving in buzzing swarms—an incredible farce composed of the two hundred people indispensable to the life of a woman's magazine. Their mixed noises sounded like an unknown tongue; an uninterrupted brouhaha pierced by occasional laughter. That hour called cocktail—the one when the struggle against loneliness takes on its most singular aspect in New York—had struck.

Everyone who could serve as food or spice for *Fair* was there; everyone who counted in New York as big, wonderful, successful; everyone who could be bought in the market place, in the book store, or who was applauded (always on the condition that the audience, readers, spectators could be counted in the hundreds of thousands), came. Those who were likely to buy full-page adver-

tisements and those whose business it was to infect women with a
fever for change, a need for something new bought on credit, all
the technicians of spreading dissatisfaction through pictures, all
the merchants of illusion—"Buy the carpeting and the house will
come later." "Here is your soap, the bath will come after."—all
the masters, all the champions of obligatory luxury, all the big
shots were there. Everyone was kissing each other, hailing each
other, looking for each other, measuring each other in terms of
big circulation, famous labels, registered trademarks.

All the same, there was a kind of unspoken uneasiness in the
gestures, in the odd glances; in fact, the true nature of this gathering could be seen in the inexplicable traffic. Groups were constantly forming, breaking up, melting, re-forming moments later
only to dissolve again. There seemed to be a general distaste for
conversation, as though they were not here to talk to each other.
All that was really expected was a *hello* between entrance and
exit, between two drinks. The old aristocracy of the garment business, the feudal lords of cosmetics and hairdressing, gravitated as
if by instinct toward Mrs. MacMannox's respectable salon, with
its mahogany woodwork and rosy lamps. The debutantes, the hope-
fuls of high fashion, the tenors of the press and the theater, several international beauties who regularly toured the elegant
beaches, the great sportsmen of Long Island and the Côte d'Azur,
the titled habitués of yachts, casinos, and Bentleys, all crowded
together among the low benches, the black walls, and the Japanese lanterns in Pam's studio. Finally there was the overflow of
unknowns of both sexes, young and unemployed, who had come
with the intention of getting into a picture or an article. They
formed an indeterminate crowd in the corridors and on the landing.

To sell one's name was a privilege reserved for Europeans of
high society, and there were many of these among the publicity-
seeking women at Mrs. MacMannox's that day. Thanks to these
foreigners, creams or perfumes bore ostentatious titles, and the
crowns on their labels in relief were irreproachably legitimate. By

such barter the ladies who bestowed them earned both an income and a reputation. Everyone bragged about the honor of knowing them. "Princess Farnese, you know, like the cold cream. . . ."

A redheaded girl with a fragile look who had posed nude for one of the *Fair* photographers in order to promote her modeling career made a great impression on the company. When she entered a loud "Ah-h-h" echoed. A dozen men, all executives or assistants in publicity enterprises, surrounded her at once. She was congratulated. She received their compliments in silence, eyes half closed, mouth half open, like an ecstatic nun, an expression she had worked a long time to perfect.

"She's adorable. . . ."

"Fearfully distinguished. . . ."

"You'd never believe. . . ."

"What a marvelous vitality that girl has. . . ."

"And she comes from a really good family."

The ovation mounted as the new celebrity, rounding her mouth and wetting her lips to smile more effectively, declared that her arrival in New York was really more exciting than a love affair. She concluded this confidence on an even more intimate note, telling a persistent journalist who was going from group to group with his notebook in his hand:

"Let's talk about my temperament. That's the secret of my success. My terrible temper. And don't believe it's an easy thing to live with the kind of fire I have in me. And please, call me Sunny. That's my professional name. My real name is impossible. I was born in Venice. . . . You can't get to the top with a name like Faustina. Don't forget, now, call me Sunny. . . ."

Her voice broke and a shiver spread out among the public relations men. One of them, the most powerful of all, Carl Pach, a nabob, a virtuoso, a witch doctor, who had been staring at her fixedly for some time, murmured in her ear, "Let's split this scene, how about it?"

There was nothing attractive about this man. He was enormously fat. One of those men who profit by the fact that fifteen are crowded into a space that would barely hold six, who used the advantage to nudge with their knees, to slide their thighs between their neighbor's. And the bestiality of that face, the thickness of the neck, the deep self-satisfaction which showed in his expression. But the new celebrity did not examine him so closely. She made another movement of the lips and another moist smile:

"You mean now? Right away?"

"Why not?"

In an instant they were gone. A tart. When *Fair* published the photograph which had made famous her graceful form, her pale flesh, the almost curveless contours of a belly painted by Cranach, the accompanying text explained that this delicate beauty with the winning personality worked because she liked to, not because she needed to; as if this fact would win her the warm sympathy of the reader. Then the text added interesting biographical details: descendant of a famous family, her ancestors had provided the most Serene Republic with several islands, some doges, a naval victory over the Turks, and too many other distinctions to list. But they managed to cite the names of her properties, to describe them, and tell how many servants she employed. All this permitted the reader to appreciate just how extraordinary her nakedness was, and to appreciate it with a more refined detachment.

Apparently there was no room to protest against this aspect of journalism, nor to question this kind of an appeal to a blatantly flesh-and-smiles market. But in my isolation, and perhaps because of the phantoms on which I nourished myself, it seemed to me the worst possible insult to invoke the spirit of beauty, to speak of art and culture, with the sole object of disguising the most vulgar materialism. All the means she might have found in Europe of being unfaithful to herself, all the occasions for offering the most degenerate part of herself for applause and celebration, all the occasions for selling the value of the past for money, all these were spread out in the salons of Mrs. MacMannox, and if there was one missing, we may be sure that some specialist, glass in hand, but with a wandering eye, was busy searching it out. Enormous, proliferating chicanery. Everywhere offers to degrade oneself. And the grip of money on every face. It was *that* which seared me, *that* which wakened a suffocating anguish in me. I saw and heard nothing more: crumbling Sicily, evicted from the world, weighed in all her mystery against all these beauties of high debauchery and against these chieftains of consumption. She was there. She hovered over us and a blind rage consumed me. I would have liked to shriek, "You are nothing. You are a gaggle of shopkeepers giving yourselves airs! The dollar is your disease!" But I was silent. Because I kept on hoping. I imagined still that there must be exceptions, some few who were more persistent than the rest and who refused to let themselves be corrupted. Corrupted they all were, and to the bone. There were bunches and heaps of them there at Aunt Rosie's, hung one upon another, stuck together in species, the French with the French, pretty empty rogues and degenerates, men who had never fought, young people whom the war had surprised in New York and who found themselves very well off there, who had developed a taste for golf and rich women. Russians with Russians, entrenched in the hotel business, flag bearers for deluxe suites and air-conditioned apartments, making money out of their past, out of an accident that they threw at their interlocutors like a lie they had patented, and always the massacre at Ekaterinburg worn on the sleeve, as if having once been a part of Mother Russia's misfortunes gave them the right to wear carnations in their buttonholes and double-breasted vests forever. Photographers with photographers; designers with designers. But whatever they were doing, the fear was always with them that somehow they were not doing enough of it; the fear, the huge fear that a new age could dawn from which they would be excluded, the fear that the wave called revolution might really exist. . . . Antonio, it is you who fill my mind, you who are dead because you refused to corrupt anything. What would you have thought of all this? You used to say, "Nothing bothers me," and you believed you were freer than the birds in the sky, but you cherished the red and secret flower of pity. You pretended indifference but the past lived in you, our past of violence and adventure. It is of you I write, you know it well, when you used to say: "We are the China of Europe, and the Negroes of Italy. All men are powerless before our blazing wretchedness." Yes, you were the most wholesome of our race. What would you have thought of this gathering of false nobility?

From my half-dream, which permitted me to be at Pam's party and somewhere else at the same time, I saw the illusion which had drawn me so far from the barren shores of my own country going up in smoke.

I must look elsewhere for the youth of the world.

Leaning on one another like blond mares in a meadow, the apprentice cover girls delayed leaving Pam's studio. What else was there to do? They were waiting. When one is used to waiting. . . . To wait for the sun on rainy days, to wait in studios, to wait in dressing rooms, to wait, talking in low voices, chewing gum, fixing one's hair, making up one's face, swallowing vitamin pills. In that way one made friends of those one knew nothing about but whom one met over and over. They had met each other once more here, at the door of Pam's studio, and once more, while they waited, they exchanged addresses, gossip, and drank Scotch in gulps to give themselves courage.

Two Botticelli figures arrived in black fur with odd necklaces, long chains from which hung, like charms, padlocks. These objects, dangling to the pelvis, were as surprising as chastity belts laid on a kitchen table, and one couldn't help staring at them. The girls were young. They talked with animation, and to hear them one would guess that they were scheming how to get the goodwill of a famous photographer.

"Never talk to him about photos."

"What should I talk to him about?"

"Well, not pictures."

"But that's his business."

"He's ashamed of it. Act like he's an artist. Talk painting."

"I don't know anything about it."

"That doesn't matter."

"But what should I say to him?"

"Pretend you saw some of his canvasses in a show. He'll never know the difference."

"Why not?"

"He always paints the same picture, just one color, as shiny as a new car. And he always puts a little white spot in one corner. Tiny. A pinhead. Those are the only designs he makes. So you see. . . ."

After a half hour of conversation completely dominated by the obsession with success—what this fashion editor, to whom one should only talk politics, or that agent ("the best in New York, the only woman who can really put a model over") whom you could offend forever if you didn't know she was a poet and mother of six illegitimate children born and reared in Europe—the two Botticelli beauties floated into the corridor for a moment, managed to pluck a glass from a passing tray, then decided to cruise to the front of Mrs. MacMannox's salon.

There were more and more girls on the landing. The party was at its height. The elevator emptied out beauties by the dozen. They were all alike: twenty-five years old, with a famished look, a vague gaze, and skin like cream. The most striking of them hugged tiny dogs in their arms, dogs that had long since lost the look of being dogs at all, having been carried into offices, into studios, forgotten in cloak rooms, baked under hair driers. They smelled of perfume and stale smoke, they opened their eyes with difficulty, they dangled moist tongues, and it was funny to see how they staggered when set on their feet. But they were useful. They were useful for making pick-ups. It was a poor show if you couldn't succeed in getting a few words out of those girls by complimenting them on their friendly little companions.

Yes, any means that gave you a personality was a good one, anything to rise above the crowd. In this crowd you hardly noticed women who make childish mouths and speak meowingly, or in

tender mooings. Accents were in this season. Others wore discreet
bandages on the wrists waiting impatiently to be asked about their
suicide attempts. Still others, who wore wool stockings, told about
how they moved to a new hotel every day because they liked the
gypsy life and that the bags of extravagant proportions, the deep
pouches that hung from their shoulders, held everything they
owned. But there were others who were odder still, languishing
eccentrics who wore old elastic bands wound around one finger
like a ring. Sign of belonging to a secret society which it was necessary to join, they said, if you wanted to succeed in the magazines.

They were all waiting for the same thing, for Daisy Lee to notice them once, just once. Should she stop one of these unknowns
in passing, should she speak to her of charm, elegance, photo-
genicity, then all hopes were permitted. If no sign were made to
them, all that was left was to wait for a big shot from Aunt Rosie's
salon to take notice of them. But that didn't happen often.

They were all alike, the big shots, triumphantly American with
a faculty for forgetting their origins, erasing them, making it impossible to imagine their unimaginable fathers or grandfathers—
the Jew from Warsaw, the Czech with strong breath—a great de-
vourer of cabbage and herring soup, the fat German—the fathers
or grandfathers who, in some far-off suburbs had them to Sunday
dinner; all alike, with the same prestige, the same power, the same
jovial condescension, the same finely etched complexion of men
able to spend weekends in the country; money men, speaking
brusquely and crisply, going about with their jackets unbuttoned
over loosely belted trousers, not over paunches, to be sure, but
their own way of swelling the torso so that at stomach-level they
had to suck in the swelling caused by excess of alcohol and a sedentary life. Typical Americans, speaking only their own language,
but with the experienced air that comes of frequenting foreign
capitals.

Aunt Rosie treated them like old uncles who once a week permitted themselves to leave their wives at home and get drunk in
peace. She played little girl, clapping her hands at the least joke,

popped up beside them for a surprise, posed boldly on the arms
of chairs, ran, hopped from group to group, lighter than a firefly,
or else, even more provocatively, sat on the floor crossing her legs,
played at being the flower of the harem in her long hostess pajamas, cuddled up to one of those Nusselbaums or Frühling-
scheins, turned into a sheep dog herding her rich flock, pulled a
moustache, gave affectionate nips, saw that the glasses were never
empty, gave a good example by drinking a great deal herself, and
often, bending an elbow to the memory of Mister Mac each time
she passed under his portrait, offering to her guests such a polished comedy that she exacted cries of admiration from them.

"She's a darling old girl," they said, watching her. And there
was no doubt, she was behaving beautifully this evening and no
one dreamed of mocking her. Not even Daisy Lee who, wavering
on her high heels, became more and more expansive and little by
little gave up talking about figures, business, budgets, or renewal
of contracts. Her voice went up a note. She passed from one subject to another without transition, forgot the name of the person
she was talking to, frequently asked that someone accompany her
to the bathroom, and continued to talk through the door while
she relieved herself. Aunt Rosie put on a loud record to mask
Daisy's disappearance. Then she made the rounds of her guests,
encouraging them to eat, to drink, to dance, citing the precepts
of dear Uncle Mac to urge them on, "Nothing's better than a little dance to get business going," or else, "When you're dancing
you say things you'd never say behind a desk," and when Daisy
Lee reappeared the music was filling the salon with its beat. She
had to shout to make herself heard:

"Here's a little girl who wants to dance. Do you hear me, dar-
lings, I want to dance. I want to dance."

Who could resist such an appeal? There was a general movement towards her dictated less by real desire to dance with her—
for she was singularly unattractive, leaning on the door frame, her
double whisky and soda in her hand—than by a wholly calculated
force which was instinctively loosed at her cry. A rough pell-mell.

Kaplenberg, a world-famous furrier, got a bump on his forehead which made him roar with pain, while a Parisian restaurateur, here in the hope of improving his clientele—a peaceful man whose profile, sharp as a fork, often appeared in the worldly pages of *Fair*—was knocked down suddenly and jostled from right to left, shouted that one might as well have been in a madhouse. He repeated it three times: "A psychiatric hospital at recreation time!"

Then he turned on his heel furiously and left.

Aunt Rosie, who was busy putting ice on Kaplenberg's bump, arrived too late to stop him. The mischief was done. Daisy Lee didn't care. She laughed wildly and let herself be carried by the crowd as a star lets herself be lifted by her admirers. A guest who had been flung against her almost involuntarily succeeded in grabbing her and pushing her before him, cheek to cheek, in a slow rhythm. But evidently she did not care for his dancing for she recoiled so abruptly that she lost her balance.

"I'll take care of her."

The man who caught Daisy Lee like a ball at the end of a throw seemed to have been placed there for that sole purpose. He was a dark man, well built, who had an air of being too well groomed; it was difficult to define, as if his elegance should not characterize the man himself, but testify only to his regard for neatness.

When he had first appeared in Aunt Rosie's apartment, I was sure from her expression that she was put out by his presence. And it was certainly about him that she had asked Pam, "What's that fellow doing here?"

She must have added more violent protests or even some definite prohibition, for the aside with her niece was prolonged for a moment and I heard Pam answer her, "You know he's invited everywhere."

Aunt Rosie's laugh sounded more nervous than amused. And now he was dancing with Daisy Lee and everybody seemed to find him a good and conscientious fellow. Each time he tried to calm the passionate exuberance of his partner, she clasped his neck, pulling his face against hers brutally and asking him, "Well, Rocco? What's wrong? Emotional short circuit or what?"

"It's time for you to go take a rest, Daisy."

She began to groan in a dying voice:

"You know what I need is loving!"

I had never seen a woman so drunk. When she kissed him on the mouth and he hesitated for a moment before pushing her away, surprised and embarrassed by that open mouth, by that tongue, and by the saliva running down the chin, everyone felt upset. This was followed by shock when Daisy began to insult Aunt Rosie's guests in her most strident voice.

"Nobody here dances like him," she yelled. "Nobody. You can say it and say it again. Nobody."

There was nothing funny about it, and we were ashamed for her. But if the man who received such homage from her was disturbed by it, he hid it well. Was it the deliberation of his movements which made him so different from the others? Was it his excessive correctness, or the fact that he wasn't drinking?

"Who is he?" I asked Pam.

"A man named Rocco Bonavia."

"Who is he?"

"He has a future."

"In what?"

"Politics—or something like that. He's one of the bosses of the Democratic Party. Attractive, isn't he?"

"Very. They seem very intimate, he and Daisy Lee."

Pam looked at me as if she didn't understand what I said.

"But she's like me," she cried. "This is the first time she's seen him. Aunt Rosie is the only one here who's met him, and that was a long time ago, in Uncle Mac's office. But she never forgets anything, and if you take her word for it, Bonavia was pretty shabby in those days."

"He must have changed since then."

Pam turned and looked for Daisy Lee. She was still dancing, if you could call that drunken performance dancing. She had managed to get her hands under Rocco's jacket, and she continued to undulate, her eyes hermetically sealed, holding onto his belt.

"She's been drinking terribly for quite a while," Pam confided to me in her most serious voice.

"I can see that."

Rocco freed himself of Daisy Lee's hands, but as soon as her grip was broken, she knocked against a piece of furniture, a collision which seemed to amuse her enormously, for she immediately began to laugh wildly.

Pam looked around as if to see the effect of this exhibition. But nobody noticed much of anything at Aunt Rosie's house. The kidding, the dancing, the flirting went on surrounded by mahogany woodwork while Ethel, unflappable as ever, continued to pass her trays. Everything was under control and the worried light went out of Pam's eyes after a few moments.

She added for my benefit:

"You know, the real professionals know just what it is that really matters."

"Even today?"

"Yes, they know—" she paused to search for the word—"that Daisy's outbursts don't affect her professional capacity. With a few martinis too many she's been known to nod off while someone was showing her models. To go to sleep right in the middle of a collection and to wake up for a second, just long enough to applaud the dress going past her. Always the best one, too. Just in time to make it a best seller. There's nobody like Daisy in the fashion world. That's why people accept the way she is. And then, what can you do about it? I've nearly killed myself trying to persuade her to take a cure. She says she hasn't the time. Her nerves are jangled, you know. Jangled. So at the end of a day one glass is enough and pfft! Daisy Lee is out. But she must have had a run-in with someone this evening to be in such a state."

Daisy Lee still held Rocco Bonavia around the waist, her eyes closed, her head nodding. She was now laughing a continuous, hysterical laugh. When there was a pause in the music, Rocco took advantage of it to prop her against the wall with a firm hand. Daisy Lee stopped laughing.

"You're going to stop that. You're going to calm down and go home," he told her, and he punctuated his sentence by pointing to the elevator door.

"Go!" she cried in such a piercing voice that everyone stopped to stare at her. "Who do you think you are? Anyway, I'm thirsty."

She tried to get away from him, but he had his arm under hers and he held her flattened against the wall.

"Leave me alone, you hear me? Leave me alone!"

Daisy Lee was shouting. Rocco tried to persuade her in a low, warm voice. He kept calm, but from time to time bits of typically Mediterranean gesture escaped him. His absolute assurance that he would make his point was enough to give away his place of origin.

"Listen to me, Daisy Lee, what good does it do you to drink this way? You're going home now while you still can, and I'm going to help you."

"That's too much!" she answered. "Do you think I need your advice? I'm drunk. Good, that's understood. But you? You? Who are you? I'm going to tell you what you are. A nobody. That's what you are. A guttersnipe. A guttersnipe, you hear me? A guttersnipe without any education. I know it and I'm not the only one."

Rocco hesitated a moment, then took his hand away from Daisy, who crumpled to her knees. There were people who laughed, but they could see Rocco did not like it. The laughter stopped. He helped Daisy up when the door of the elevator opened. A young man got out. Almost all I could see of him at that moment was that he was dark with cold violent eyes and a weathered complexion.

"You came at the right moment," Rocco said, tapping him on the shoulder.

As if he'd known for a long time that this young man would come. As if he had organized this diversion never doubting the effect it would produce on Daisy Lee. He looked at her. Something had broken in her and tears were running down her cheeks. What she was saying between her sobs no longer contained threat or defiance. She was begging for help.

"Yes, thank you. Help me. Help me. I want to go home."

Rocco was compassionate. He spoke as if he had known her a long time. And in his gestures too there was a special thing: a strength able to reassure her.

"Here's the man you need, Daisy. Exactly the man to take you home. This is my nephew, Theo."

Rocco was before her, very handsome, very dark, with the face of an avenging angel. There really was no more reason to worry about Daisy. Rocco gave off something so fresh, so determined, so strong, so dark. He might have been an athlete before some great contest.

"Go on, Theo," he said with a visible effort. "I'll wait for you here."

Then he added in a lower voice, "Make it fast. And thanks. It's like a nightmare starting over. I'll never get used to it."

Daisy Lee let Theo lead her along in jerks, then push her into the elevator like a groaning bundle. It was past midnight. Mr. MacMannox's moustache continued to mount guard on the mahogany wall, but it had become difficult to see him, the air was so full of smoke. The cover girls were bickering about some waterproof makeup, but they changed the subject abruptly when the record player began again, as if it were no longer possible to talk of the coloring. With the same intensity they began to chatter about a reducing diet.

A hundred guests still played for several hours at the game of who would be the last to leave.

When the door closed on the winner of this contest, Aunt Rosie, stretched on the salon sofa, was not even able to raise her glass in a last toast to Mister Mac.

We had to call Ethel to help us put her to bed.

No one knew Rocco Bonavia at Mrs. MacMannox's and no one wanted to know him. He was only an attraction offered on the

bill, a rather daring number added to the usual program, a wind-
fall, an occasion by which everyone would profit the next day
when they invented stories according to what they had made of
him. Yes, nothing more. Like watching (with excitement) a lion
tamer, a juggler, a tightrope walker. But who, for heaven's sake,
would ever think of shaking hands with him?

For Pam, it was more complicated: she played with a day-
dream. She was receiving a notorious man. "Rocco the hurricane."
To some newspapers, he was "the great Rocco." These were the
ones which praised him to the skies. For others he was "the troublesome Signore B—the man with the white tie." Some openly
called him a pirate, a corruptor. Others more prudently admitted
that "nothing, absolutely nothing is known about him," and unconsciously contributed to the further enrichment of his legend.

The stories about him always began with, "They assume," or,
"People say," since, I repeat, no one knew him. In this society
where every confidence was seized with interest, anyone's past,
present, or future belonged by right to whoever could grasp them.
Rocco's silence about himself made him suspect. Since he said
nothing, he must have something to be ashamed of. They forgot
the simple fact that he belonged to a race in which silence takes
the place of morals and law. I knew that, and I was not surprised
by how little we spoke while we waited for Theo's return. I don't
think I was even much struck by this meeting. When I saw him
several weeks later, sitting on the sidewalk on Mulberry Street, it
took me a moment to realize it was the same man.

There were several reasons for this. On Mulberry Street, in his
black suit, he was all you saw. He ruled the street. At Aunt Rosie's
he seemed unaware of the people who surrounded him. Perhaps
the essential part of his charm was that air of always thinking of
something else. Was he even listening to the answers to the questions he asked me?

"Do you often come to these parties?"

"I'm here professionally."

This explanation scarcely interested him at the moment. He let his eyes wander over the company and said in a mournful voice, "What a racket. I hate this kind of thing."

"I do too, as a matter of fact."

I hesitated to say any more. For a moment I thought of thanking him for having helped Daisy Lee. Then I said nothing. He was not a man to accept compliments from a stranger.

"You say you're here professionally," he said, as if suddenly remembering my remark. "Me too. But what is your profession?"

"If I tell you, will you tell me yours?"

"Oh me. I'm chief of the tribe."

And he burst out laughing. I laughed too.

It was clear that my personal occupation didn't interest him. He felt in his pocket, pulled out a notebook which he opened to that date and showed me what a tribal chief's evening consisted of. There was enough to consume the whole night: a contest to elect Miss Beatnik in Greenwich Village; an appearance at a commemorative concert for Caruso's first record; a few words to deliver at the annual banquet of the League of Voters—and he was too late for any of the rest. The symposium on the sainthood of Mother Cabrini was certainly over by now. And the Lodge of the Sons of Italy, with three stars beside it in the margin of his notebook, had closed its doors long ago.

Because of this collection of appointments, he hadn't a moment to lose. Theo's appearance made him jump to his feet. He was almost at the door before he stopped short.

"And you?" he said. "You still haven't told me what you're doing here."

I told him in a few words. He seemed surprised.

"You don't look the type. I'd expect to find that Gianna Meri was a woman from this country. You know, some rich woman traveling on an expense account and using a pen name. So you come from Palermo! I hadn't made the connection. From Palermo."

His voice trembled a little when he said "Palermo," as though that word set a long story in motion, so long that it could not be told. But perhaps that was just my imagination. Rocco's voice was calm when he said to me:

"That gives me an advantage, because we'll surely see each other again. You can't be what I am without being in some sense connected with these people."

He looked at the company for the last time.

"Meantime, I'll take you under my protection," he added.

The Sun God addressing a lost planet and offering it a star to turn circles around: so Rocco appeared, with his unexplored novelty, with that kind of melancholy which the southern light always radiates.

When he bowed before Aunt Rosie to say good-by, with a slightly exaggerated politeness, she acted as if she neither saw nor heard him, as if the conversation around her had her complete attention. All the same, she had seen him. Her eyes followed him until he disappeared.

It was plain she did not like him.

PART TWO

I.

We are uneasy people who feel at home anywhere except in our own country.

CESARE PAVESE

Rocco Bonavia was born in New York. His father was a Sicilian who had tilled the soil for a baron up to the day when a tidal wave convinced him that Sicily no longer wanted him. This was at Sólanto. Alfio Bonavia was neither the first nor the last to want to leave his native land. But those who had preceded him, the Bonavias of the past century, who were tempted by liberty, only had to jump into a boat to leave. Jump into one or steal one. Either way, their consciences were clear. They had not asked to leave; they had been driven into exile by some generally acknowledged injustice: the unification with Italy in 1860; military conscription in 1861. "You go to die for your fatherland. . . ." But it was a fatherland they did not recognize as their own. And those taxes, and those famines, and those droughts. Cholera in 1887. The earthquake in 1908. The history of the Bonavias was entwined with a history of such misfortunes that the saints never interceded, even though the saints of Sólanto were among the most pampered in Sicily. Any occasion was a good one for taking them from their niches, showing them off, parading them on men's shoulders, following them with bare feet. So many processions, so many parades, so many offerings, so many sacrifices. There was not a Bonavia worthy of the name who would not have cut off his right arm in order to offer them paper flowers, fireworks. But the saints remained deaf. Finally, tired of waiting, Bonavia decided to leave. Immediately, the stern shadow of Authority loomed threateningly over this man who had chosen to become a foreigner. Things had changed terribly in Sicily. Under a pretext of order and progress, the mainland invented numerous ways of binding men to their misery. Visas, passports, emigration permits, how could you get such things when you hardly had enough to eat? Early in the century such things were possible. The coast guard was not very vigilant. Floating idly at the state's expense—could you call that work? They knew they were scorned. And from Catania to Messina, from Palermo to Trapani, those who hunted down defaulting recruits, those who traced missing persons, those who hailed suspicious vessels, whether out of laziness, distraction, or perhaps pity, knew how to look the other way. They observed the siesta hour; they returned to port to eat and to sleep. Well then, at night the sea belonged to no one. That was how, from one end of the island to the other, the Bonavias succeeded in beaching their boats on the shores of their choice. But that was long ago. Now it was dangerous to sneak out of Sicily without permission. The sea was too well guarded.

And now, on one black day, misfortune visited the house of Alfio Bonavia in the form of an enormous wave which carried away his house and all he possessed. A wave? What kind of a wave? The municipality of Sólanto heard the arguments, weighed the evidence, and issued a verdict. Let Alfio Bonavia labor under no illusions: it was simply *a wave*, and not the *tidal wave* he pretended. He should not confuse that single modest wave with one of those huge marine tremors, one of those monstrous eruptions that flushed houses of their inhabitants, inhaled them and spat them out to sea to create a tragic fleet of beds and cradles. No, my good man, no use protesting. It was only a wave. Waves don't give a man the right to collect damages. If your house collapses because it was badly built, *you* have to take the consequences.

The State certainly had no responsibility.

"The State? What has the State to do with such things? To hell with your State!"

"*Basta*, Bonavia. Try to behave like a Christian for a change."

That was how the mayor of Sólanto dismissed Alfio Bonavia, and Alfio turned to the priest. Fine fellow. More than anyone, the pastor was a fine fellow. He sensed the danger of being stubborn. Why insist that the wave was a tidal wave? Change tactics. Better convince the Authorities that it was a water spout. The priest had heard tell of such things; he was even sure that water spouts were grounds for collecting damages. Come, courage, my son! What can you lose? Take a last try at it.

But to do this, Alfio had to journey to Palermo. At his own expense, he took with him twelve witnesses ready to testify before competent authorities that the devastating flow, the infernal cataract, had been ten meters—more than thirty feet—high. Yes, your Excellency. And that if such a fearful thing had carried away neither boat nor child, that was something for which to thank God on one's knees. A few minutes later—when the boats would have been back from the day's fishing and the children out of school—and Sólanto would have suffered one of those disasters which make covers for the illustrated journals. His Excellency listened to the testimony of the witnesses, and then murmured:

"Such things *can* be. . . ."

But at no time did His Excellency agree that there *had* been—indisputably—a water spout. Things dragged out so long that Alfio was obliged to spend three days in Palermo.

Those three days in Palermo! Days of humiliation! Alfio Bonavia would never forget them! He was still talking about them a quarter of a century later. In New York the story had become a classic in the family repertory, a great aria which Rocco, scarcely four years old, already knew by heart.

Those humid, hot Palermo days, Rocco hated each moment of them as his father did. All these men had to eat was the bread they had brought from the village. Three days of weary shoulder-shrugging functionaries. Three days of filling out forms. All to satisfy some morbidly curious Authority—"Who is your mother?" "Where were you born?" Three days of squirming under the scornful eyes of functionaries to whom he was forced to admit, point blank, that he did not know how to fill out those forms. For that was the worst of his humiliations: asking help from strangers, confessing to the first townsman who came along that he was ignorant, illiterate. And then, once again out in the street, all the pleasures he had to pass up because he had no money: all those women, all those inviting odors of flesh beyond his means. Humiliation! That was all Alfio Bonavia had to show for his three days in Palermo.

But still he would have continued to struggle. Perhaps he would have succeeded in rebuilding his house, perhaps he would never have left the rocky cape on which he had been born had he not insulted a considerable personage, the man on whom almost all the inhabitants of Sólanto depended: Baron di D. The quarrel began with the Baron's son, with Don Fofò, whose games Alfio had shared since childhood, and against whom he had no grudge at all.

Many years later, recalling the memory of the young lord of Sólanto, Alfio Bonavia admitted that he wasn't a bad sort. Wildly easy to anger, yes. But too well bred, too tall, too thin to be frightening. And the gun he'd carried on his shoulder since he was eleven was only one more mark of distinction, like his broad-brimmed panama, his white tussor vest, and the black buggy he drove so fast among the peasants. And Don Fofò was fond of

Alfio, there was no doubt of that. He liked him so much that he preferred seeing him working in his fields to having him waiting in line in Palermo offices. The conclusion had always been obvious to Don Fofò: Alfio had lost that house. When Alfio tried to talk about it to Don Fofò, he acted as if he didn't understand. And the effort to seem indifferent made Don Fofò even more nervous than before.

It was this uneasiness which caused the incident. Abruptly Don Fofò had begun to reproach Alfio with arguments like these: "Bonavia, I ask you, what are you thinking of? How can anyone believe someone who's depriving his employer of two indispensible arms, who's left orange groves, flocks, and pastures for three days? Is anyone going to trust a field hand who spends three days in Palermo discussing how high a wave was with the Authorities? What are you trying to prove, Bonavia, with all these comings and goings?" Alfio tried to get his request in edgewise: an advance of funds, just enough to buy materials for rebuilding: "If your lordship wished. . . ."

But his lordship wasn't a bank and Bonavia would have to make an effort to control himself, to stop annoying people with the story of his house. If he wanted help, he'd have to work harder. "Either you measure waves, Alfio, or you work on my land. You cannot do both." At that, Alfio exploded.

How a discussion in an open field, with no witnesses, became known to the whole village is a mystery. But there wasn't an inhabitant of Sólanto who couldn't recite every word of it. No one had any doubt that shaking his carbine under his field worker's nose, the young Baron had given Alfio to understand that he wouldn't hire him anymore. And by getting so angry that he called a nobleman's son a son of a bitch, Bonavia had openly invited his dismissal.

It was at about that time that Rocco's father received a letter, the Palermo Letter, a document which he kept at hand for ever after. It was brought to the cave in the rocks where he had taken refuge. He gave it to the priest to read. While the father was running through the text in a low voice in order to get a grasp of the contents and, as he said, in order to be able to read it to the interested party in the proper tone of voice, Bonavia—by the way in which the good Father mopped his forehead, knit his brows, and expressed his torment by all sorts of expressions—understood that some new disaster was threatening him. But what? Finally, unable to wait any longer, he asked, "Reverend Father, is it about the damages?" And instead of answering the priest howled: "Bastards. . . . Criminals. . . . Bedouins. . . . They'll make a murderer of him . . . an outlaw. . . ." Did he mean the Authorities? Because that was still what it was all about.

Alfio Bonavia was being notified that his house had been destroyed by a wave because it was built in a place where it shouldn't have been in the first place. The inquiry had shown that the error was the plaintiff's, who, without permission, had made his home on a piece of land unsuitable for building. He was therefore liable to a fine, the sum of which would be specified later.

And so, once again, a Bonavia decided to leave. That which had driven distant ancestors towards the shore of Africa, that which had for generations drawn Bonavias to dusty, poor, wretched places, that which forced them and their families to be among the first settlers wherever someone announced there was to be a road, a town, a port—that same threatening Authority, strong in its arms, its fines, its prisons, drove Rocco's father to America, which was then still open to emigrants.

After Bonavia had said and said again that he wasn't a doormat for Authority, that he would carve up any policeman who tried to collect such a fine and that he'd rather leave forever than ever set foot on this bitch of a motherland again, he needed to find money. The odd thing was that it was Don Fofò who gave it to him. Not from generosity, but from prudence. It was enough for him to consider what it would be like if his former field hand, with his knowledge of the Baron's fields, farms and cattle, were on the side of the Mafia. Safer to buy him a passport. No villager of Sólanto doubted that if Don Fofò hadn't helped him leave, Alfio would soon have been found behind a hedge, ready to use his gun.

But what a prodigious offering this passport was. To live somewhere else, to love somewhere else, to work somewhere else. Freedom! Rocco's father, after he had contemplated the precious document for a long time, sewed it into the lining of his coat and decided not to take it from its hiding place until he had gone through the Strait of Messina. He was the kind who always expects the worst. Someone could steal a passport, someone could fake it, someone could deface it. You could be waylaid on the road for less, and he'd be crazy to let anyone know that he possessed a document that others waited years to get. "Under certain circumstances, it wasn't for talking that the Lord gave us a mouth." The priest agreed. Not a policeman, not a *carabiniere*, not a toll collector, not a coast guardsman, above all not a customs inspector—Bonavia didn't want to show it to anyone, this passport. One of those uniformed bums might take it into his head to grow zealous. "He might hold it against me, *reverendo*. He might ask me: 'A passport? Let's see this passport. Show it to me. How did you get it? At the emigration office? And how did you pay for your visa? Where did you get the money?' Not to mention last minute surprises when everything seems in order, and suddenly a hand falls on the traveler's shoulder, the hand of one of those whoresons, a well-fed hand, washed, gloved at State expense, the hand of one of those damned dirty skunks with their 'Just a minute there. No arrears? No debts? No unpaid taxes? No fines you've forgotten? Show me the receipts.' And little by little, what with one thing and another, they can send anybody on earth to end his life in prison, those turds."

As it happened, that summer Sicily was suffering a heat wave the like of which the Lord alone remembered. Deathly. And Don Fofò, who had a flock of a hundred head to send to the highlands of Civitavecchia, agreed—somewhat in obedience to the Reverend Father who never stopped telling him, "Let's leave off the insults, your Excellency, let your heart speak," and even more to get rid of that crazy Bonavia—agreed to entrust Alfio with the cattle. For once Don Fofò's curtness worked to Bonavia's advantage.

"I'd rather die than say a word to him. If I were to meet him, he'd soon know what it costs to call my father a cuckold."

At that point the young Baron lowered his voice a little and struck the flat of his hand on his gun belt to make the priest understand clearly that nothing could stop him from putting his deadly intention into action.

"But I know my duty," he added, "and I couldn't forgive myself for letting him starve to death."

When he learned of the job he'd been given, Alfio Bonavia answered that the little Baron made him so sick he couldn't even stand to see his name written on a wall, but he added: "His sheep will arrive safe and sound on the peninsula."

The priest sighed with relief. All was in order; everything was going as he had hoped. The two men hated each other; had they met, they would have killed each other. But Alfio was leaving the next day, so the pastor wouldn't have to accompany anyone to the cemetery. Both men would continue to live as they wished, sole judges of their own honor, Alfio as an emigrant and the young Baron in Sicily. Things could have turned out worse—to tell the truth, much worse.

So at sundown Rocco's father started towards Palermo. The dust of the road, raised by the trampling of the flock, hung in the warm air and floated like a concealing fog. Alfio Bonavia saw his village disappear. Here, the square where nocturnal discussions were held and the wall against which he used to sit between the others waiting to be hired; there, the roofs, the terraces, the open windows, like stages where women would make their furtive appearances, farther on, the dry fields, the hollow roads bordered by hedges, all alike, always those Barbary fig trees, sharp, fierce, thorny; still farther, sheltered from view, the crossroads where, under a tree, the itinerant prostitutes who came in carts from Palermo sometimes stood; and the farthest yet, out of sight, all those familiar landscapes now blotted out by the glare. As the dust rose around the shepherd Bonavia driving his animals, walking with his yellow dog before him, behind him followed another Bonavia, Calò, his youngest brother who would return alone with the flock. As that cloud of dust grew higher, rounder, thicker, what was growing in the hearts of the two men, what burned within them, was the knowledge that one of them, the older, the father of Rocco, was leaving Sicily for good.

Alfio was strong and accustomed to misery, so he arrived in New York safe and sound. The young Baron di D., frail and gently bred, could never have withstood so much.

He was rarely called Baron di D. in Sólanto, but more often Don Fofò, or Signor Don Fofò, or even "our little Baron," and this last was neither because of his height which was commanding, nor his age which was the same as Alfio's at the time of his departure, that is to say nearly twenty. Sicilian custom bestows the blessing of eternal childhood on all the male descendants of any man of importance. And nobody in Sólanto was more important than Don Fofò's father, the real Baron di D., the head of the family, he who—as owner of the fields, the farms, the boats in the harbor and even the fishing nets—gave work to the whole countryside. And even that doesn't indicate the measure of his real importance which stemmed from something else entirely, and did not depend solely on his rank or fortune, but on his particular sort of misfortune. In Sicily, misfortune has not the same effect as elsewhere. It might be said that the doom which hovers over spirits and weighs on them like so many incipient dramas is there to give witness that abundance exists, at least in such matters, and that if one has no other provisions, one can feed on and live from tragedy itself. Then, too, it is evidence of the equality of the human condition, since there is no man powerful enough to escape it. It was in this manner that misfortune magnified Baron di D.'s importance: the trouble which had wrapped itself round his fate was a share of common wretchedness, familiar to all, one to which each inhabitant of Sólanto could have given a name.

The D. family had been known for its liberal ideas for several generations. Don Fofò's grandfather had been among the few Sicilian aristocrats who had borne arms with Garibaldi instead of cowering in the depths of his estate like so many other gentlemen of that period. At the time of the plebescite which joined Sicily to Italy, bonfires of celebration, by order of the Baron, were lighted on the top of Mount Catalfano and on the high towers from Cape Mongerbino to Sant' Elia and even to San Nicola which dated from the time of Charles V and were owned by the Baron. In the castle at Sólanto, chandeliers were lit in broad daylight and windows were left open so that the people could join in the family celebration. So much enthusiastic patriotic sentiment aroused in the members of his family corresponding bursts of enthusiasm. No doubt this explained his son's decision, several years later, to show equal devotion to the idea of Italian unity by deciding to do his military service on the continent. People in the countryside were very much surprised. The fatherland, the fatherland. . . . Well, that remained to be seen. But one could believe in the idea of the fatherland without feeling obliged to do one's military service on the mainland. What was eating the boy? A man like him. Couldn't they afford to pay for a substitute? Thus it was that the father of Don Fofò became a lieutenant in the 13th Artillery at Rieti, then in Rome, to the immense astonishment of the people of Sólanto, who could imagine nothing more bizarre than voluntarily submitting to such discipline when one was in a position to avoid it. But the folly was forgiven him when news arrived of his engagement to a very beautiful girl (so they said) of an old and noble Florentine family, which would connect him with people of high position and earn him the respectful homage of several ministers—all useful things.

When the Garibaldian gentleman died, a nonagenarian, he was carried to the cemetery by four horses with black plumes, preceded by a double line of orphans, all born in the neighborhood and fed and dowered by the dead man, who was also followed by a considerable procession of carriages decorated with crowns and bearing disconsolate relatives. The lieutenant of artillery tore himself away from the joys of the capital, and from the pomp of the circles which he frequented in his dual capacity of nobleman and officer, and returned to Sólanto in order to assume his role as Baron di D., and lord of the land.

He was accompanied by his young wife, who displayed a disconcerting independence of mind and odd tastes, like sitting in the sun or walking by herself to the Roman ruins of Sólanto, piles of old stones mentioned in no guidebook and in which it was considered abnormal to show interest. Or worse: she decided to go with the fishermen to catch tuna at the mating season, to wait near the trap stretched in their path, and she was seen leaning for hours over the nets. What kind of a place was that for a woman to be? Wasn't it really a strange obsession to want to follow fish to their death? And why did she listen with such attention to the raucous voice of the rais, standing alone in a boat in the middle of the fatal quadrilateral like an omnipotent executioner. It was no use her saying that she was only interested in his ritual incantations, his prayers to Saint Peter for success in fishing. Wasn't it more likely that she had become infatuated with the leader, that rais who gave the hex sign and the right cadence to the work of the killers? Yes, infatuated! It seemed obvious, watching her there, submitting to the noises, the cries, the silent blows of the knives which finished the victims in the bottom of the boats. She succumbed to the violence of the scene and was carried away, entranced by it. She filled her new family with all sorts of apprehensions.

Baron di D. and his wife no longer belonged to that nobility of the past among whom only the men had any rights, were allowed to go about, live, speak, and with whom no women were permitted to voice disagreement. But their household seemed a happy one, and their occasional arguments sounded like lovers' quarrels. This was hardly evidence of dissoluteness. They lived according to the new freedom; they left their lands, they traveled. All the same, the young couple's dignity suffered as they followed certain singers from engagement to engagement and even asked them to the house. One might as well invite mountebanks to the castle. It was one thing to go to the opera once a year and sit yawning in the family group, and another to make a long journey simply to judge the good and bad points of a tenor, and to allow enthusiasm to outweigh propriety.

There was one name in particular, that of a soldier of the 13th Artillery Regiment in whom Baron di D., when he was with that unit, had discovered exceptional gifts—"An unequalled voice," he said. "Still some weakness in the high register, golden all the same. A voice of pure gold." And the young Baroness, she too never tired of eulogizing this singer. Eulogizing hardly begins to describe her enthusiasm, for she declared herself ready to walk to the end of the world if, once there, that young soldier would be singing. Times had indeed changed.

It was during Easter, in Rieti, at a reunion dinner for officers and soldiers that the Baron di D. had met the young artilleryman. After dessert was served, a new recruit, dark and painfully thin, had risen, his glass in his hand. He knew how to sing, he said. Around the table a roar of laughter arose. Singer! That black-faced bundle of sticks would have to prove it. A good boy, no doubt, but he'll sound like a squeaky hinge. Where was he from, anyway? Naples. Not surprising that he was so thin you could hardly see him. The upstart had paid his respects to the Colonel and was announcing that he would sing the *brindisi* of *Cavalleria Rusticana* because that was the only aria he knew. And he sang. Baron di D. leaned his head against the back of his chair, closed his eyes, and knew an unspeakable happiness, akin to drunkenness, the winged drunkenness on which one soars to heaven. A true ecstasy. Nothing, not the difficulties he encountered, or the general apathy, or the Colonel's inept judgment: "Lieutenant, where do you expect to take such a scarecrow? He has a Venetian glass voice just about to break." Nothing could discourage the Baron di D. from asserting that a little training would transform this poor fellow into the greatest singer of all time.

"You could sit him at the table of the Eternal Father, hand him over to Saint Peter's cook, stuff him with sardines until he burst, and I tell you he'd stay thin, flat, and voiceless to the end of his life," the Colonel insisted. But nothing, nothing could ever make Baron di D. forget the sublime moment when he had heard a soldier named Caruso sing before him that first time.

Caruso owed everything to him. Without the intervention of Baron di D. with the Authorities in the capital the singer never would have been released, and they would never have accepted a replacement for him in the 13th Artillery who was as thin and wretched as the first Caruso, his youngest brother.

Ah, the beautiful days, the happy days of Rieti, when Caruso, finally free, could give his life to singing! Less than a week, it had taken him less than a week to learn the role of Turridú from start to finish! Baron di D. had been granted a leave to devote himself entirely to his protegé. He accompanied him on the piano, vigilantly watching over his style and his voice:

"Careful of the tempo! Careful of the tempo! . . . You're dragging. . . . Come on. . . . One, two, take it over. . . . And pay attention to the beat this time." Seven unforgettable days!

"You will be an incomparable Turridú, my dear Errico." In those days he was called Errico, with a trilling Neapolitan r, Errico and not Enrico as it is pronounced in Italian. That name would not be his by right until later, along with fame, wide-brimmed artists' hats, tailor-made suits, white pianos, and huge posters in front of the Metropolitan. In Rieti, Caruso was still just little Errico, as he had been in Naples where he was born, as he had been in the echoing alley, where, under the awning of laundry a crowd of brats sweated and yelled. . . . Errico of the *via San Giovannelli agli Otto-calli*, Errico, son of the fellow with the beard, of Marcellino who was a worker in the oil factory—"You know the one I mean"—the kid Father Bronzetti took into the choir because he's got a voice, our Errico, a voice like nobody ever heard in this neighborhood. The night of the feast of the Corpus Domini he made the worshippers cry. . . . That was the night Anna died.

. . . Anna, you know the one? The mother of our Carusiello, of our little golden-voice, the mother of our Errico who was crying that night, crying his eyes out. . . .

"A little too tearful, your Turridú, my dear Errico. The notes, dear boy. Just sing the notes. Let's leave out a few of those sobs, eh? And fewer sighs, too. Let's leave those to Santuzza. She's the one who should be crying, not you. You are Turridú, an unscrupulous fellow who tempts a pure woman from the straight and narrow path, compromises her, dishonors her. Don't forget. . . . Well? . . . Watch your tempo this time. Let's go."

And the Baron whistled Santuzza's answers through his teeth, or, letting himself go, he sang them aloud, and his "Ah, Lord!" would have brought tears to your eyes, and then forgetting where he was, believing himself in some theater during a rehearsal, he imagined himself with fifty violins singing at his fingertips, fifty violins playing a music which would be played by every dance hall in the world, music that café orchestras would scratch out until they were parched, but which, played by the Baron, took on style and soul. He loved this music. He acted out all the roles: the harp, the mandolin, the cymbals; here and there he cheated a bit, since Mascagni is hardly Bach—but always out of sincerity, and when he came to big moments he left nothing out. One by one he plucked the pizzicati, sang those sobbing Easter hymns at the top of his voice, and felt himself so exalted that he ended in tears, crying, "S'pedi! Avanti!" without taking his hands from the keyboard. Such moments unsettled the young singer who stood, crowded between the piano and the dressing table, wondering what the devil was expected of him. But Baron di D. was addressing a crowd of extras when he cried, "Forward, for God's sake, forward! You have to treat these people like cattle. . . ." And a hallelujah burst forth while a procession crossed the room, all candles lighted, choir boys without end, a baldachin for the Holy Sacrament, and monks, monks, and more monks. . . . Ah, the beautiful beautiful days at Rieti, hallowed by a love for *bel canto*.

As the years passed, Rieti and the lieutenant's modest apartment faded from memory. Then, after all, the Baron had no choice. It was that narrow room in a two-room flat or nothing. And the upright piano which had been squeezed, with some difficulty, between the bed and the dresser to leave space for that table where the young bride, each evening, silently served dinner. How beautiful she was. God in heaven! Beautiful, beautiful, so beautiful. The young singer would lose his place as soon as she came into the room. She lay down on the bed to listen. And where would she have been able to sit? There wasn't another seat. She lay down and it was impossible not to look at her, blonde and slim beyond belief, with such legs! And how could he not listen when she said: "Beautiful, beautiful. . . ."

And the Baron would respond to her, "You are a musician's musician. You are my music." And it was true. You could feel it in her voice, in the rhythm of her sentences, in each intonation. And Caruso would enjoin her: "Stay. When you are here, my voice flies on wings." Then the lesson would continue, time and food forgotten. Oh, that Florentine! There was exaggeration in everything she did, in the way she had of letting the hour slip by and opening her too big eyes, dilating her pupils.

At the table, when finally they sat down to eat, she touched nothing. What was she dreaming of? And what did those eyes signify, impossibly green, moving from her husband to the singer? Was it the dustiness, the continual shimmer of Caruso's voice that absorbed her, that miraculous voice extending like a golden sky over a gray landscape, was that it?

Neither the Baron di D. nor his wife were present at the great singer's debut in 1895 at the Massimo Theater in Palermo; because that night a son was born to them. The names he received were all given to him by his mother, against the wishes of her family. She wanted to call him Rodolfo, like the poet in La Vie de Bohème—that French novel that Signor Puccini had read so enthusiastically—and then Ladislas, after a distant Polish relative, and finally Franz, no one knew just why. After Liszt, perhaps.

Rodolfo Ladislas Franz di D.: what gibberish! No one was all

that proud in Sólanto where this string of foreign names grated
on the ears. At the time of the baptism, which was celebrated by
the Cardinal Archbishop of Palermo, the dignified old man, in
an effort to pronounce such unnatural syllables, released a rumbling belch followed by "Let's get on with it. . . . You know what
I mean," but not without remarking after the service that it would
have been preferable to call the child Antonio like his father and
grandfather—which would have made it possible for the people of
the countryside to nickname the young Baron Ninuzzo and not
Don Fofò.

The letter was sent from Trapani, thereby making the proximity
more offensive than the treason. The intolerable wantonness of
that proximity. In Trapani, of all places. Baron di D. could have
had the informer found and interrogated. He could also have ordered an inquiry to verify whether or not his wife had stayed in
that city when she was supposed to have been in Florence. But
he anticipated the evasive answers, the impassive faces. No one
would have seen or heard anything. That white immobile city,
folded in upon itself, with its empty quais, its shutters, its lonely
alleys stretched like swords is like a fortress against truth. No one
has ever pried a secret from its unyielding silence. And yet, from
Trapani, from that gloomy promontory where the tramontane
wind never stops blowing, from this soulless city over which hangs
the heavy odor of salt marshes, came a letter that darkened the
Baron's universe. "At Trapani . . . At Trapani." How had she
got there, in the company of that mountebank, amidst the disorder of a tour, with all that shouting, confusion, fatigue, baskets
dragging behind, rumpled costumes, lost wigs? How could she,
she, in Trapani, only a few kilometers from his ancestral lands.
Strangers—oh, not a big crowd, just a handful of spectators—met
at the entrance of the theater to watch for the one who would
sing Edgar in *Lucia di Lammermoor*, to see what he looked like,
that Neapolitan of whom such marvelous things were said. That
woman passing, the blonde over there, that's his mistress, it

seems. . . . A foreigner from the mainland. . . . And perhaps the name of Baron di D. had even been passed among these peeping Toms. . . . Why bother? It wasn't everyday they had reason to celebrate in Trapani, where scandal was welcomed, like rain after an endless drought, to break the boredom of the town. How they must have circulated little notes, obscene drawings, smutty stories in the dress circle. And the exhibitionism of that tenor, his taste for ostentation. . . . He'd been obliged to call attention to himself on the terrace of a café "with a lady whom Your Excellency would have done better not to have allowed to travel in such company" the informer wrote him, adding that the foreigner talked loudly, gave out autographs, and finally, behaved in such an exuberant manner that one had to conclude he was spilling over with wine.

What kind of love was that? Was it love at all, that craving to display oneself? In the silence of his heart Baron di D. had begun to hold long conversations with the departed one that she would never hear, and never answer. "When I was the one whom you took for your law, when I was the one who occupied your thoughts, I never took you to café terraces. I loved you in our secrecy and our solitude. I loved you and longed for no one else, no one but you. And you loved me too, my Florentine. Real love is what you knew with me, whether you admit it or not." Such thoughts soothed him for a while. He lingered over them. True love. . . . It wasn't possible that she would not return. She would come back, wouldn't she? But the certainty that she was deceiving him soon gripped him again. He imagined her intimacy with the other. A fearful jealousy rose from his belly, overcame him, took him by the throat and made him cry out with pain, would have choked his life from him if he had not rid himself of the sources of his despair. Little by little he educated himself to scorn. Caruso was no longer the humble genius of Rieti whom he had discovered and loved, but a ridiculous, puffed-up fool who counted his admirers at backstage entrances and dispensed autographs with the solemnity of a pope applying the bulla to a new proclamation. He was a numbskull wallowing about in his successes. And to that she had attached herself. A fine conquest! A fool whose memory was so fuddled by the Sicilian wine that he missed three cues. And it was in Trapani, in that wretched hole, that he was booed. How quickly a man can become too sure of himself. Talent and stupidity, a mixture often found in tenors. Incredible fatuousness. The fellow thought himself a Don Juan. Could anyone be jealous of a man who allowed himself to be photographed in such ridiculous poses? Jealous? No, the Baron was not! Jealous of a jackass! High notes, head tones, finally must have affected his mind. He wasn't the same man any more. He believed he could get away with anything. Imagine! Singing in a kilt! That was the last straw. Gambolling with bare knees, uncovering his thighs with every move, shamelessly exhibiting himself like that in Trapani before men who would not dare take off their jackets in public for fear of compromising the lady in the next seat. That might be fine at La Scala, but not at Trapani. The audience was outraged. One man, his face white with rage, rose and shouted:

"I say. . . . I say, you! Are you waiting to have your face smashed before you get off the stage?"

It had been necessary to stop the performance to keep the audience from tearing the theater apart.

And what did she do then? Where had she fled? The Baron imagined his wife witnessing such obscenity, shaking as if she had been drenched in some foulness. He shuddered.

Scandal and ridicule were what Baron di D. dreaded above all things. It was extraordinary how the palaces of Palermo, its salons, the villas around it were full of people who seemed to know everything. How could one show oneself after such a thing? How could one pardon the unpardonable?

There are dreams which, once disturbed, leave no room for hope. She had wanted to wound him, to hurt him. She would not come back. That was obvious. Baron di D. looked back upon Rieti and the first days of his love for her, the perfect days in the attic room. He saw the upright piano and her immense eyes looking from one to the other. God, she was. . . . And then? Had she chosen the other? Was it he she had followed from city to city like a shadow? Our past, my Florentine. . . . The great orchestra of our heart, those violins which for four years sang for us alone, you have ruined it with one blow. Have you ruined it all? And our nights, my delicate one, the fire and the madness and the harmony and the lunacy of our shared bodies. Yes, you no longer think of that. But the rest? That too was nothing? Did nothing happen within you when you put your hand on your heart to quiet its beating; when you wore the look of a lost little girl, oh my music. . . . Did you know that under the gilded ceilings where we used to run together, in the plush grottoes where we sat in silence before the slow rise of the faded curtains and the dimming lights and the tentative scratching of the instruments tuning up, did you know that pleasure was as great as the other and that I was at your mercy? No more bassos in false beards, no more Gauls in rabbit skins, no more gouty spear carriers, ridiculous legions who made your lips tremble and wrested from you, between two ecstasies, something like a smile. You sometimes laughed at the opera. But no more. No more Lucia trembling in the yellow mists of Scotland, no more Mute in Portici, no more Italian girl in Algiers, no more Florentine in my heart. No use pretending. I only listened to what you heard. To me, the sounds were a road we traveled together. But from now on, there is only your absence.

Caruso. The word made the Baron sick. If only the other had sung better, perhaps the misery would be more endurable. If only that golden voice had been worthy of the Baron's memory. But why continue to speak of this man? This name would come to his lips no more. As for her, they would never see each other again. Completely cut off from everyone. See no one. Never.

The future stretched ahead like an endless desert.

A few lines from Stendhal, concerning "those public slights which make it impossible ever to see people again," served as a point of the very short letter in which Baron di D. asked his wife never to appear in Sólanto again.

In Sicily they say, "Things left, things lost," a chilling comment on the limitations of sentiment. Baron di D. scorned to appear unhappy. He preferred the look of disillusion rather than that of pain. But solicitous attentions were heaped upon him, nevertheless. His intimates missed no opportunity to remind him of his catastrophe. The way they constantly referred to "poor this one" or "poor that one" with an almost physical pleasure, their humiliatingly tender gestures—someone was always pressing his hand, or murmuring consolations in his ear, or worrying whether he was wearing the underwear without which—winter or summer—a Sicilian considers himself doomed to the worst illnesses. Holy images mysteriously appeared under his pillows. Even the expressions appropriate to the servants, everything conspired to suffocate his suffering in a pillow of hush. What were they trying to do, this family, with its bigotry, its nonsense, and its bits of blessed boxwood? One day there was a great plan to leave him alone with a monsignor who had come from Palermo and who, after a thousand circumlocutions and "Let us speak as Christians"—issued like threats—proposed lawyers to him, a trial, the Holy Rota, an annulment. Baron di D. was curt.

"One word more," he said to the visitor, "and I shall ask you to leave the room."

The Canon had the good sense to retreat immediately.

Baron di D. had no wish to violate the Christian principle. This was his own code. As for the people around him, his intimates, his uncles, his cousins, these were people of his own rank and he would very much have liked to respect them all. "Every one of them," he repeated, giving these words all the urgency one could imagine. As for the monsignor, he too was a man of whom the Baron could not think without anger. No, it was not in the Baron's nature to break with his equals, but when the idea came to him he was amazed that he had not thought of it sooner.

In Palermo society, people spoke of black moods and madness:

Sólanto was padlocked, Baron di D. no longer went visiting, no longer received callers, and his son played only with the children of the countryside. Sometimes visitors coming from or returning to Palermo tried their luck on one pretext or another, out of curiosity. They wanted a look at this twenty-five-year-old man who had disappeared into silence. Amid the cackle of ladies in black in the salons of Palermo, they imagined how his confinement might have affected him. Would they have reacted differently in another country? Did families exist, did societies exist, which could have accepted the idea that someone could do without them? Come, come, must not a young man be a bit mad to live apart from neighbors? So they tried to penetrate the forbidden door. They laid seige to the castle, where the sea mirrored the sky on three sides and where, to the south, its orange grove, boxwood, trellises, statues, nooks, and narrow paths spread a carpet of shade. Only the windows facing the sea remained open. The tower in the middle, the particular shapes of its three rising terraces, of its redoubts, the bake-house with the white dome, again took on the look of the time of Charles V. The village suddenly found itself shrunk to the size of a hamlet while the castle seemed to loom larger. They could not quite say why, but suddenly the visitors and the town felt as though they had been forcefully ejected.

Lying on the low rampart, his cap pulled over his eyebrows, the gatekeeper, in spite of his nonchalant posture, looked like a sentinel. All day he stayed there, staring into the sky, a stick ready at hand. To those who tried to soften him up with "How is he getting on?" "People are worried about him," the fellow answered, from his languid position: "Very well. . . . Couldn't be better. He'll bury you all." His voice was resonant with a deep satisfaction. Some persisted: "We'd be so happy to see him again," and these were rewarded with the retort: "We aren't receiving anyone." These well-wishers promptly returned to their vehicles, leaving the gatekeeper on his wall very much pleased with himself, wearing that "we" like a crown.

Like the porter, the whole village identified with the Baron di

D., understood him, and shared the burden of his misfortune. In the tangle of alleyways which led to the castle like twisted spokes of a wheel, around the net shed whose tottering roof was supported from the ramparts, in the places where half-naked children played, in the little courts, on the terraces, on the doorsteps, on the roofs where tomatoes dried leaving trails like blood—everywhere the people of Sólanto felt that their happiness depended on the hermit, who was simultaneously present and absent, and whose existence haunted them.

To them, everything was interpreted as a sign, and they sought signs in everything. They thought they saw him. They *had* seen him. If there was a lamp shining across the terraces, it must be his. When it went out, all the fires of Sólanto were put out too. No sooner was it lit again, as it was each day at dawn, than the village awoke also. All of the sounds of that early hour, the footsteps of men heading for the boats, and those of the animals going to the fields, then rose up to the castle.

A sort of distant intimacy developed between the master of Sólanto, withdrawn to his rocky platform, and the little people in the hot streets, in the houses that lacked both pride and history. A mutual awareness resulted which transmitted perceptions back and forth, as if the village had seeped into the castle's hidden recesses, as if the castle had been absorbed into the village and become a part of it.

Knowing how closely he was watched, Baron di D. never gave way to the frenzies of solitude. The interest which he aroused had become, without his admitting it, one of his reasons for survival. The parlor kept him informed of the progress of his notoriety. Without that good man the Baron might never have known what the popular imagination had made of his misfortune, what legends were being built around him. Yes, a very odd notoriety. . . . Unknown hands had engraved the letters of his name on the wall of a chapel where people went once a year to pray to Saint Joseph. And under his name the same hands, the same fingers, had written on the wall where prayers were scribbled: "To have a child. . . ."

"To get well. . . ." "For a good harvest. . . ." A strange story
which made the Baron uneasy.

Once, when he went down into the garden to take his morning
walk, the porter pointed out to him, in the distance, a basket of
fruit under the porch and a lamb with its feet bound together.
Offerings! What did they want of him? The gatekeeper, always
tactful, nodded his head. His Lordship knew well enough how
their minds work around here. And, since Baron di D. said nothing, the porter added most naturally that in the fishermen's
houses, newspaper photos of the master of Sólanto could be seen
pinned up among various holy pictures over the great beds where
parents and children slept together. Although it wasn't customary,
the Baron could not help questioning him: "And what am I doing in such company, may I ask?" The porter raised his hands to
the sky. "They think you will intercede for them." A strange conversation. Among the saints, there also hung pictures of those
sentenced to death or to life imprisonment in the capital, some
who had been electrocuted in America or hanged in England.
Once again, the porter made his deferential gesture toward the
sky: "They too, you understand. . . ." The Baron di D. was afraid
that the porter had misunderstood his remark, and when the
porter told him that justice and society were always wrong and
that all those sentenced to death were martyrs, he replied: "And
if they're guilty?"

The porter hesitated, then grumbled, "Guilty? What does that
word mean? Jesus was judged guilty, wasn't he? So?"

His Lordship could not disagree.

Formerly he would perhaps have tried to tell this man that
he was an idiot. But now he hesitated to hurt him. And then
again, his whole life had been spent among such odd beliefs. He
had absorbed them completely. Often, when a drought made the
land crack and everything unbearable—the agony of the plants
white with dust, the flies buzzing against the closed blinds, the
constant wind, the misery of the panting cattle, the searing attacks of jealousy accompanied by an intense desire to flee, to leave

Sólanto, to disappear—on those days little girls with long black hair, dragging clownishly out-sized shoes, came to dance in circles under his balcony. He heard them singing: "Our dear little lord, make it rain, make it rain." Their voices were scratchy. It was both touching and laughable. Baron di D. attached no more importance to it than he did to the quarrels of the gulls on the rocks below. But he listened to them and thought of other music, other voices. Sólanto. . . . Perhaps it was, along with the name of his son, the only word that gave meaning to the long waking dream which was his life. That was what was left to him finally, Sólanto and Don Fofò, reserved, distant, a little too timid and withdrawn for his father's taste. No use speaking to him about any of this. And, to tell the truth, it was hardly surprising considering the education he had received. As a child, Don Fofò had for companions only those in whose eyes he was the master, the young Baron. Boys who were his subjects. At the age of love, what did he dream of? More inferior company. Don Fofò slept with those rare widows who, because of a government pension, were entirely dedicated to their widowhood. He sought women in black, living alone in the mountain hamlets, peasants, serfs who spoke only dialect.

Baron di D. looked upon his son with respect and pity. After all, he had only himself to blame. It was his obstinacy that sentenced the child to solitude. Raised in the manner befitting his background, Don Fofò would have turned out differently. Boarding schools in Palermo, and Rome. . . . But why brood over that now? Since the age of eleven the boy had been turned over to these hard, ignorant, superstitious peasants. The child had tried to oppose it; he struggled mightily against it. The child had tried. How he had wept, all those bitter-sweet childish tears. How he had pleaded with his father to allow him to study music. It was all that interested him. But the Baron di D. was evasive at first. "Let's talk about something else, shall we?" And when the boy persisted, rejecting the fields, the labor, the land, it became necessary to bully him a bit, the stubborn child. So Don Fofò had been thrust out, onto the country roads, forced to go to work, and then, to put an end to his reticence, and to silence his complaints, he was rewarded with a black chaise, a good horse, and a little gun. In other times an officer's commission would have been purchased for the sons of the family before sending them to take a hand on real battlefields. So why not a commission for Don Fofò? Why should anyone consider that cruel? The priests, the servants, all of them began with, "He's too young, your Excellency, much too young. . . ." And Baron di D. laughed in their faces. It made little difference to him that they thought him imprudent or crazy, but a few historical analogies were enough to convince them. Take the example of Maurice of Saxony. Was Maurice of Saxony too young when he became adjutant general at the age of twelve and had his horse killed under him? So? The story of this horse at the siege of Tournay had become a joke between Baron di D. and his son. When Don Fofò prepared to leave, as he did each morning, and the stable boy jumped down from the chaise handing him the reins, Baron di D. appeared on his balcony and in a happy voice shouted: "Bring the horse back alive, eh?" And Don Fofò would laugh too. In three or four years, he had grown accustomed to his life. But perhaps it was his relinquished dream of music that gave such a mournful cast to his face.

All this, Don Fofò's melancholy, the mysteries of Sólanto, the hellish memories: "Where are you now, my crazy darling? At whom are you making your big eyes? Why did you need to hurt me so?" All this and only this was left to Baron di D. With his son gone, the Baron pondered the sounds that rose from the streets. Neither laughter nor singing; only a silence, barely interrupted by the cries of birds; a silence stretched like a net against the blue sky, an oppressive silence, heavy with the desire to escape, thick with the dreams of flight shared by all the villagers of Sólanto held in bondage by the sea.

Baron di D. had nothing against adventure. He had nothing against either travel or freedom. But his mind withdrew in disgust from the idea that one might lose oneself in the universe.

And, to him, that was what emigration meant. To exchange one poverty for another equally tyrannical—he saw no sense in it.

So each time such a question arose, he called the guilty one to him, and predicted terrible consequences for him. Then, as final proof for his argument, he brandished before him an American review which had appeared in 1907. This contained a long article by a famous anthropologist attached to the Museum of Natural History demonstrating how the southern Italian, with his flattened occiput, had no right to the same civil liberties as a man of Germanic origin. There were frightful sentences in it which the Baron faithfully translated. According to the author, the cranial cavity of a Sicilian denoted an intellectual development barely equal to a monkey's. The article ended: "Why should we expose our race to the dangers of such miscegenation? Why should we open our borders to such an inferior stock? There are times when the country should be advised by its scholars." Then, without a pause, Baron di D. would begin to rage: "And you're absolutely determined to be treated as if you were mentally subnormal? You think you'll be happy if you leave everything you have to go live among those who talk about us in a way they wouldn't dare talk about a savage? So, you want to be a leper whom everyone mistrusts, a plague, a shameful disease! When you realize your mistake, you'll burn with shame. You'll be crushed by remorse. I'm warning you now, but then it will be too late. You won't be one of ours anymore. Your dignity will be gone. You'll be nothing but one of the oppressed, a poor bum. . . ." But nothing discouraged the dreamers. Nothing. Baron di D. pulled out his wallet, put a bill in their hands, and they went away, no one knew just where. Perhaps they crossed the ocean. The desire to leave had seized them like the tentacle of an octopus.

That was what Baron di D. pondered, high on his terrace, when he appeared to be following the flight of the swallows. He was thinking of that Alfio Bonavia, gone to New York with bare feet. An intractable boy. What had occurred between him and Don Fofò out in the fields? What insults had they exchanged? It is so

easy to become enemies, so easy for Sicilians to move abruptly
from friendship to hate. The version of the incident that he had
received was obviously abridged. All those precautions. One didn't
need second sight to see. . . . Baron di D. said to himself that a
misfortune like his lived long in memory. Then, inevitably, there
came the day of wrath when insult burst forth as though from an
unkempt package. How could anyone stop it? Was it for that
Don Fofò had threatened to kill his old playmate? If he had been
told the truth Baron di D. would have forgiven. Good God! Why
hold a grudge against a man because he called you a cuckold? And
now he was gone, that Alfio, lost to Sólanto, bound for New
York, they said. Would he live the same way over there, among
strangers? "Never, never will you be able to feel like a man among
them." How he would have liked to say that to Alfio Bonavia too.
But no. That one had proudly refused to appear at the castle. So
the little Alfio of other times had grown into this unmanageable
boy. You were fond of him, my Florentine, during that time when,
for one reason or another, the house had to be full of flowers.
How old had he been when *she* sent him to climb the big mag-
nolia and when everything was joyous? The child climbed up,
startling the wild birds. He disappeared into the foliage. How old
was he then? Six, maybe, and she laughed. The wax-colored flowers breathed a perfume that changed each hour: tender in the
morning, soft, hardly perceptible; sharp in the evening, violent as
living flesh that, full of the sun, breathes a new odor. To undress
in that odor, to sleep. To love it all, even to the fresh taste of the
water one drank on waking. To feel oneself the master of the
world because of that great love for her. God, how distant that
happiness was now! Even the naked bodies of the women servants
who offered themselves to him, even the pleasure he found in
them did not erase from Baron di D.'s memory the shadow of his
past life. That pleasure was nothing to him. No one could be deceived with that, not even those simple girls, so easily beguiled.
Because one cannot protect oneself from the poison of dreams.

II.

In all things, forgetting is the great defeat.
CELINE

The war came, the great one, which Baron di D. called an absurdity. He did nothing either to dissuade or to encourage the people of Sólanto to take part in a venture which, he said, was none of their business. A number of them chose the mountains instead.

In 1921, Naples held such a funeral for Caruso as no one had ever seen, attended by all kinds of people who had come from the remotest places. The city was crowded from Vesuvius to the Church of San Franceso da Paolo. It was a service to rival any pageant, and included soldiers in parade dress. It was rumored that the King himself had come from Rome to greet the coffin on the threshold of the basilica, but then there was no proof of this. The cortège was like a procession, making stops here and there, at Santa Lucia, for example, because Caruso had sung of her beauties; then also in front of the façade of San Carlo, with its brilliant gilded columns and bas-reliefs. That temple's doors had been left open in order to efface forever the memory of the frightful row which had taken place there in 1901 during the performance of *Elisire d'Amore* at which a few fanatics had wanted to prove, at any cost, that they were a more difficult audience than La Scala's in Milan. Besides, that was the first time Caruso had been heard in his native city. What a pity that there should have been such quarrels! There were so many of the clergy in the streets that it looked as if all the convents and churches of Naples must have been emptied. Preceding the hearse with its six horses were at least twenty ancient clerics in birettas and lace surplices, each carrying a candle, shuffling along in a row and sweating in the August sun, ready to drop dead themselves. It was on that day that Baron di D., in Sólanto, rediscovered his taste for music.

Two grand pianos arrived from Palermo and also a Victrola, a high mahogany box containing a talking machine, a great novelty. A whole afternoon was spent discussing the best place to put it. Between the windows, facing the sea? Or even, perhaps, right under the chandelier? The servants padded barefoot from room to room, and like wild creatures they circled in wonder around those fabulous objects. And each of them—the faithful gatekeeper, Don Fofò—was asked his preference. No matter where one put it, this round-bellied piece of furniture looked out of place. Finally it came to rest under the painted ceilings of the great salon, still sticking out like a sore thumb. But that was where the Victrola stayed, with its crank and its nasty little shutters which made it look like a night table. Something had to be decided once and for all; otherwise it would have been discussed for hours, and Baron di D. would have lost patience.

"Finish it up, then. . . ."

After that he would have preferred to be left alone. But Don Fofò, impetuous as always, had succeeded in starting the Victrola, and suddenly the violins of a double concerto filled the silence of the castle with their sound.

Baron di D. said a few private words to Don Fofò, who left. Then he sat down, his heart beating fiercely. He clutched the arms of the chair with his hands and looked about him fearfully. He seemed about to cry out. What could he do? Unable to struggle against images twenty years old which flooded over him like a cold sweat. . . .

"Your Lordship," one of the maidservants murmured in an anguished voice.

"Go. . . . Go quickly. . . . will you?"

She left him.

Then Baron di D. felt a sort of shame. . . . My Green-Eyes. . . . Great God! . . . My Green-Eyes. . . . Can it be that nothing is forgotten? Can I never hear another bit of music without calling out to you for help?

Then came the Fascist revolution, which the Baron di D. refused to call anything but "that funeral masquerade;" or, "that buffoonery." The growing resentment of the people of Sólanto toward those who supported the Blackshirts was equalled only by the undisguised hostility the Fascists aroused in the castle.

Don Fofò would never forget his father's look on the day when a militiaman whose task was to create goodwill towards the Fascist unions in the region presented himself at the castle. Baron di D., without uttering a word, fixed his eyes upon the man's polished boots and the black-tasseled fez which he twisted nervously in his fingers, and no one saw the terrible rage that began to grow in him. Instead of keeping the visitor for an hour as would have been expected, he asked him, with unbearable iciness, to go home scarcely five minutes after he had arrived.

If the march on Rome left them cold, they reacted quite differently to a piece of news which threw Sólanto into a panic: America was closing its door to Italians. The end of emigration. . . . It obsessed them. How could they believe such an incredible development? They saw it as an insult, a purposeful insult. There were many who did not believe it at all. They had to read the newspapers two or three times. That word no one had ever heard: *quota*. Who had invented such a thing? There were those who said it was the result of Sicily's uniting with Italy. Others said the King, or *Il Duce*, was responsible. In any case the people of Sólanto decided to hold it aginst the only American whose name they knew: Wilson, the President. His portraits, which up to that time had been hung in the little family oratories among the benevolent spirits and patron saints, began to be crumpled up and thrown away. The wind pitched in, blowing them around the town dump. One day someone found a bunch of them rolled in a ball at the bottom of a crate; another day several were hung on the hook in the public toilets. These fell into the hands of a tourist who carried them back to Palermo with protests. Baron di D. was the only one who rejoiced over this matter. America barred? He tried, without much success, to persuade those near to him that this was for the best. He regretted it not at all. Sicily would understand where her best interests lay at last, she would open herself to progress, and perhaps—who knows?—people would recover from their mania for expatriation.

Baron di D. listened to his Victrola present an incomparable voice. The chorus of the Hebrews had just fallen silent. There had been eight bars of the orchestra, accomplished well enough, upon my word! And a voice of copper struck across the salon of Sólanto "For the hour of forgiveness is here, . . ." when Don Fofò, who was returning from a distant part of the estate where his father owned some chestnut woods, placed a bundle wrapped in an apron on the sofa.

"Here's something I've brought you," he said.

But Baron di D. paid no attention. He was in Palestine, moving forward with Samson among the Hebrews. The Victrola was a truly wonderful instrument. Again he heard "*Sè la vua du Sègneur che parle par ma busce*" and the Baron was about to make his usual jokes about poor Caruso's wretched French accent, when the package, having been ignored for so long, began to protest. It buzzed like a cockchafer.

"What have you put there?" Baron di D. asked, with a shade of worry in his voice.

"My son," Don Fofò replied.

Baron di D. approached the sofa with infinite circumspection. He pushed back the edges of the apron: a little hand took hold of his fingers. A newborn baby! What a funny fellow he was with his crown of black hair and his way of looking around as if he were waiting for something.

"Good job!" the Baron remarked with warm approval.

Had a grandson fallen from the sky? There would be no greater joy to him than to have the child here always. He immediately made dozens of plans for this infant.

He would receive an education which would be quite unlike that given to his father. This one would be something else entirely. He would be sent to Palermo as soon as he was old enough. But not to be with the local aristocracy. What good was that? God knows what those worshippers of the Almanach de Gotha would tell him about his birth. No, no! He deserved better than that, this little fellow. He'd be sent to Palermo in the summer, when the duchesses would be away and the palaces closed. But anyway, wasn't he a darling? Green eyes, black hair, what better could one ask? The triumph of race. All of a sudden Baron di D. noticed a resemblance to the Garibaldian grandfather. It was perfectly clear, and this grandchild should be installed at once in his grandfather's bedroom, which had been closed so long. And his mother? What about her? Yes, what? Would anyone hold that against Don Fofò? Very well, understood, he didn't want to marry and she didn't either. In parenthesis, it seemed very natural to the Baron that Don Fofò had no taste for conjugal bliss, and this—this other, this peasant girl. . . . By the way, was she beautiful? Yes? Fine figure, breasts swollen with milk. . . . So much the better. It didn't surprise him a bit that she preferred her widow's pension to anything

else in the world. Obviously she had more faith in the resources
of the State than in those of the master of Sólanto. Very well. . . .
But that was no reason for separating mother and son, was it?
Well? How would this stubborn woman like a paid job near her
nursling? In any case, they would need a doctor. Men like us don't
know the first thing about newborn babies. Besides, according to
Don Fofò, it was also the seductress' first baby. She's about eighteen, you say? At that age she doesn't know any more than we do,
believe me. A widow at eighteen? That's odd. Whose? Ah, a *carabiniere*. Shot at the turn of the road. Hazards of the trade. So, a
doctor. It has to be a doctor who will agree to come to Sólanto
once a week, someone young, talented, and not one of those flunkeys you see attaching themselves to rich families. You give them
orders, you countermand them, you chide them, you haggle over
fees and they swallow all these indignities for the honor—on occasional Sundays—of sitting at the right of the lady of the house.
No! That sort of salaried journeyman can only be trusted to buckle
a truss on a hernia, and Baron di D. wouldn't have one of them
at any price. What was he looking for? A man of science whom
one would treat as a friend, a modern doctor of the kind they talk
about nowadays. You might even find one in Palermo. Meri. . . .
Somebody Meri. He'd seen the name printed somewhere. Immediately, he saw the article again. It was in a medical review. A
biographical note. . . . Meri. . . . Meri. . . . That was it, all right.
The review offered sympathy to this young scholar whose wife
had died, poor soul, a victim of dysentery only a few months before he had succeeded in perfecting a vaccine which was very
highly considered. Dysentery: for about twenty-five years a terrible
form of it had raged through all Sicily, spread by soldiers back
from the unfortunate expedition against Menelik. They had
brought it back from Adoua along with the memory of a crushing
defeat. Thousands of deaths and gastric upsets. That was why it
was called *Abyssinian*. Worse than the plague. This too the Baron
knew, and not just recently. He had heard people speak of it since
his childhood. Even if he was getting old, there are some things

one doesn't forget. That was why people boiled water ritually. And constantly the recurring question: "Have you washed the fruit well?" Behind these words you remembered the worried faces of another period: "He won't be sick, this little fellow?" Out of fear that it might be the *Abyssinian*, the whole family had begun to pray. They went to church. They promised novenas. No, that was a long time ago, but it was unbelievable how such things remained engraved on your mind.

In the days following, Baron di D. leafed fruitlessly through his library in order to find the review, then the article, and finally the name of the author. Meri, Paolo Meri. His house was serene, pink, and beautiful. He lived with a whole troop of children by the seashore at Palermo.

That was where they sought him.

He announced his visit after the siesta. That was the loveliest time of day on Sólanto. Shimmering vapors rose from the streets and at the foot of the castle you could hear the grumbling soliloquy of the sea, a circular melody restlessly turning and repeating itself.

Doctor Meri found the gate open and climbed the great staircase. The old servant, a little man sporting espadrilles who slid over the pavement with the discreet grace of a phantom, awaited him. He preceded the visitor, excusing himself at each door for being the first to enter, and one constantly heard him repeat, "You're expected. . . . expected. . . ." as if to persuade himself of the legitimacy of his errand.

At the threshold of a salon as vast as a ballroom, the doctor hesitated: two men were laughing loudly. One of them, the older, was bouncing a baby on his knee. It was agreed, then! The child *must* be called Antonio. The other was listening to him. Above them a huge crystal chandelier caught the red light of the setting sun and shone like the golden crowns which are held up during coronations. The scene, as it appeared at that instant, haunted Doctor Meri all his life. The jasmine from the garden breathed

its warm breath into the salon. But there were more subtle perfumes to breathe here. Something light, inexpressible, made up of
tenderness and regret. Here was a dwelling where love had gnawed
at the foundations.

"Please excuse me. I can't get up and shake hands with you.
Here, Fofò, take your little horseman off my hands. Have you
noticed, doctor, how when one is young one has an immediate
rapport with infancy, without giving it a thought? And then, all
at once, the rapport is lost, and one is old. I'm not an old man
yet, and still, sometimes, I don't know how to behave with this
scamp. . . . What the devil. . . ."

Antonio clutched his grandfather with all the strength in his
little hands. He thought he was laughing very loud and his lips
were parted, but what one heard was as weak as the hum of an
insect.

"You weren't expecting this, eh, Doctor? You must have heard
stories about us, Fofò and me, sinister madmen! Come now, no
use denying it. That's surely what they told you about us in Palermo. Instead of which, you see us here, Fofò laughing out loud,
and me with this rascal in my arms. You hear what they say about
you, rogue? It makes me laugh until I cry, too. . . . Oh the
devil. . . . The little wretch. . . . Wait a minute. . . ."

Don Fofò, amazed, looked at his father and saw him happy,
energetic, looking towards the future. He held Antonio on his
knees; he extended him towards the garland of the chandelier like
a playful offering; he invented a foreign language for him in which
the child bore all sorts of made-up names: "Ninuzzo my pretty,
my darling, my little African prince, my Arabian jasmine, who
told you you could sit here? Are you going to tell me this, my
heart, my paradise? Oh sweetness. . . . Sweetness," and Baron di
D.'s voice suddenly trembled a bit.

Here I am once again between pictures of the life that I loved
so much and the desire to flee from them. The endless night slips
by. Impossible to sleep. Feverish voices cry out the story of my

heart. I have suspected it for a long time: Sólanto calls me, holds me as tenaciously as the ivy that gripped its walls, its terraces where the setting sun leaves its long warmth; its humped porch, vaulted, faded, its bridge with uneven stones, its court decorated with pink laurel flowers upon which the eye hungrily feasts, Sólanto rises to my twentieth floor and breaks through the walls of the bedroom where the adolescent that I once was awaits it. I dare not move. I already suspected it in the street where I avoided new building fronts that might reflect a forbidden outline. I should never have enclosed myself in this prison of a bed: I should have gone on wandering along the river streets until I could no longer stand.

Yes, it's true, I went to Sólanto, but that was long ago. Life has been stronger than I. On the road that winds between two walls, a voice urges me to hurry and gardens turn their backs on our panting old jalopy. My father is at the wheel. Beside him, some of my brothers, only the oldest ones. In the back of the car, my grandmother says that we forgot to cover the canaries. But it's too late to go back now. Baron di D. is waiting for us: Antonio is fifteen today. Yes, I went to Sólanto. The first time was purely by chance. I had bronchitis and needed a change of air. A Wednesday. Baron di D. was waiting that day, as he did every week, for my father's visit—this time bringing me. We were sent to play in the garden, Antonio and I, and we hardly found three words to say to each other. But we sat inside a statue, a giant head set on the ground, whose open mouth sheltered a table and two benches. Then we cleaned out its ear. Asphodels grew there. It was an adventure, that first time. The second visit was several weeks later: Antonio had asked to see me again. Now that we had started to clean the giant, we must go on, he said. But it was no longer just a matter of asphodels. Damp branches of ivy hung down to the ground and gave the giant such funny stalactites in his nose that they had to be shown to Gianna—and many other wholly accidental marvels, a whole crazy vegetation stemming from a leak in the fountain, grass growing on our statue like hair, moss like down on its cheeks. But even in the midst of our laughter, Antonio had a serious air. Probably from living always with his father and the Baron. Or was it that he was troubled by something the gate-keeper had told him? Once upon a time, this statue and the grotto inside it were used for something that wasn't very nice at all. . . .

"I think it was used for serving lunch outdoors," said Antonio in a dry voice.

But the gatekeeper clung to his idea.

"They used to come here at night, believe me, Don Ninuzzo. At night. . . . Anyway, look at the ceiling. You can still see the soot from the torches."

And he added, mumbling between his teeth, that there had been a tunnel connecting the castle to the grotto "for conveni-ence," he said. We understood none of it. What could our play-room have been used for? I continued to think about it that eve-ning.

Finally that anniversary arrived and with it our departure from Palermo, through the noisy market crowds, then along walls touched with gold. I sat looking out the window. Strange women, dressed in sad dresses stood guard at the crossroads. What were they doing? I asked: "If they're soldiers, why don't they have a uniform and a sentry box?"

That seemed to have been the wrong thing to say. My brothers burst into wild stifled laughter.

"That Gianna can really be stupid! She thinks the whores are doing guard duty!"

"Disgusting neighborhood," said my grandmother in a tone in-tended to silence them.

But the scene had changed, and I let them laugh. Their sarcasm didn't bother me. Here were the last houses, the last churches before the loneliness of the beaches, the creeks, the landscape re-flected in the water. And then we began to wonder about the peasant and his cow, who could spoil our day by being absent or late. How children love such games. That cowherd obsessed us. We twisted our necks like tourists. Then we heard the wavering sound of a pipe: there he was, with his skipping step, his wild look. A slightly mad cowherd, but on time, he strode up the road pushing the hollow flanks of his cattle ahead of him. And he was as hollow and dusty as they. But women waited for their passing, and we waited for them. If they failed to appear it seemed to us an evil omen, or a kind of treason, or even as if in Germany there were a sudden breakdown, an abrupt halt by one of those carillon clocks from which, on the hour, a whole tribe of statues appears one after the other, holding out their arms and disappearing with a pirouette. Here things were simpler and we Meris would never know the complicated clocks that entertain children elsewhere. A nomad peasant who made his rounds of the town accompanied by the sound of a pipe was our entertainment. It was our music box, our dancing clock, our impatience. People said he was a shepherd in Argentina for a long time, watching huge flocks, but then he came back, because to live there was like death to him. Was it for this road that he came back, or for the women who waited for him, for the old bowls, for the cups, for the glasses which they held out to him, for their insistent matronly chatter—"I'm telling you I must have no more than a glass, Leonardo, not a drop more." "I can have as much as I want, can't I?"—for the laundry displayed like flags, for the circle of children who surrounded him every time he stopped, or for my grandmother? . . . Yes, no doubt about it. He had come back for her. Because in Argentina, no one listened to him play his pipe, no one stopped to look at him, and no one knew how to say as she did: "Bravo, bravo, Leonardo," in that deep singing voice which was hers alone.

At last the sea appeared, at last the ringing bell and the old train creaking into its station nearby, notifying me that Antonio was fifteen years old today, that we were going to his party, and that the trunk was full of sweets which smelled of caramel, full of preserves which Baron di D. doted on, full of oily plants produced by mysterious graftings, strange cuttings wrapped with strings. Different smells filled my nose, mixed in my head. There was the warm breath of the pastry shop, a confusion of odors from an old trunk. Then, I was no longer there. Here was the rock, here was the water, here was the shade where we sat, and here were the words which changed everything. In the night a cracking voice breathed to the stupid child that I was: "No, no, I promise you, you can't get a baby from kissing. I'm telling you, Gianna! And it doesn't come from the sky like a falling star, Gianna. It's not like that at all. Listen, listen, Gianna. A kiss is all right. Let's try it. Just one to see how it goes. . . ."

And suddenly I see Antonio again, as if through a mist. There he is with the coarse, embarrassing passion of his fifteen years. He frowns a little. What does he say? "I'm going to love you, you know. I'm going to love you very much and for always." And I believe him. And I feel his lips on mine.

Rocco Bonavia was four years old when his mother opened what she called "Home Cooked Meals," meaning that she was willing to welcome into her kitchen several men of different backgrounds who came to take their evening meal in her house. She was a passionate woman. She brought so much energy to this enterprise that very quickly all the immigrants of the neighborhood became her customers.

When Rocco entered the one room which served his parents as both lodging and work place, what he heard there, the questions discussed, always took him backward into the past of the people who met there—never into their present; as if the essential part of their lives was not what they would become, but the misfortunes from which they had escaped.

For Rocco, this world showed itself as in those primitive pictures where peaceful images from the childhood of a saint are side by side on the same canvas with the heartrending depiction of his martyrdom. He is seen all blond and babyish in his mother's arms, and then, *pfft*. . . . An inch away he has a white beard and his head is being broken with stones. What Rocco found comforting in his childhood was the present, the smoky, warm room smelling of soup, the lighted oven, his mother's movements.

The rest was made up of uneasy men whom chance had brought together, of their past struggles and the threats which, like a storm on the horizon, continued to hang over their future.

Listening to them, Rocco imagined Europe as an old molehill half demolished, whose inhabitants got out just before it caved in on their heads.

When the meal was over, when the kitchen was empty and Alfio helped his wife pull the mattresses out, Rocco would try to erase from his memory the natural enemies his mother's guests had fought against. Hunger. Prison. Injustice. They had left all that on the abandoned shore of a land they would see no more. Why go on talking about it? Couldn't one treat the past as snakes do their skins? As a remnant which dries in the sun, shrivels, and becomes dust? How could troubles left so far behind still weigh so constantly on their minds. And what language! The Polish Jews always talked among themselves about *pogroms*. Rocco believed for a long time that this was some shameful and incurable disease. And since so many of his mother's Jewish customers had found work with opticians in New York, he imagined it was some sickness of their trade. A disease reserved for spectacle merchants. Rocco would drop off to sleep murmuring to himself: "What a rotten place that Europe is!"

Alfio, his father, who went from one to another of the food stores all day long, and who also carted wood and charcoal, Alfio answered, "You can say that again, son, a nasty country. . . ."

Already crouching on her mattress, her legs folded under her buttocks, her belly and breasts tracing three sweet rounds under her night dress, the lovely Peppina hushed them.

"That's enough, Alfio. No more talk about all that. No buts! Time to forget those old stories."

Peppina had no patience with lost causes. Her people were from Genoa. And she knew how to make the two of them obey her.

"You, Rocco, go to sleep, quickly."

Then Rocco really went to sleep. But the things which drove Germans from Germany, which sent the Irish into exile, the harshness of living in Macedonia, the misfortune of being Armenian, the terror of the Balkans, and all the maladies of the earth, of plants and of cattle, theft, earthquake, the incompetence of veterinarians—charlatans, all of them, blood-suckers—unemployment, machines replacing men, strikes, mutinies and all the police who took over all the factories and the guards who attacked, and the children who were born of women who didn't want them, all these things weighed on his sleep like some great indigestible mass. Many times they had to wake Rocco, shake him to chase his nightmares. He had an infinite variety of them. Sometimes he was embarked in a boat which never arrived, or if he succeeded in disembarking a swindler robbed him as soon as he set foot on the ground, or else there was something he needed that he didn't have —he never knew just what—he was looking for it, struggling hard; he clung to the hope that if he could just name what was missing, the thing itself would come to him and he would only need to reach out his hand to grasp it. Then he could finally know rest, happiness, eternal holidays; but the thing remained vague, transparent, formless and colorless; he saw it disappearing down a sloping road, growing farther away, getting smaller. Then he made one last effort, he ran after it, and the word only came to his mind when he awoke with a start, when sitting up in bed, with sweat on his forehead. He cried: "The deposit!" in a frightened voice. "The deposit!"

Peppina sighed from her bed.

"Are you ever going to get over that? Rocco?"

Sometimes his father rose and went to him.

"I had the deposit all right, and you know. . . . And I had it in dollars, too. The little Baron thought of everything. I told you that a thousand times. Why are you worrying about those old stories? You weren't even born then. You were lucky. Go to sleep now, old man."

But there was something even worse. Nights when Rocco woke without crying out and watched his parents. Their sleep seemed so sad to him, like the sleep of travelers who slump on waiting room benches between trains. They lay against each other in an attitude more of anguish than abandon, a sort of collapse which, from a distance, in the darkness of the kitchen, looked like a fatal accident or the convulsion of some serious illness. Two bodies petrified as if by a bolt of lightning, dragging the burdens of the day into the unconsciousness of sleep. Alfio stretched out flat on the white sheet, stiff, with his head thrown back. Peppina, as if overcome, rolled up in a ball, her black hair sticking to her sweating cheeks and in the creases of her neck, hiding her face with one chapped hand which always hung over the side of the bed, palm up, imploring.

Rocco wondered if the rich were beautiful when they slept.

Twenty years later, when Rocco's political career was taking shape and it became easy to foresee that he would some day be an important man in New York, reporters, in whom he still had some confidence at that time, succeeded in drawing from him some memories of the day when he lived with his parents in that little room downtown. He told them about the mattress right on the floor on which Alfio and Peppina slept, and about the kitchen table under which Rocco's pallet was placed, because that was the only place where it would fit. But the way the press used his confidences filled him with a total disgust. *Life* had captioned the story: "His First Four Poster: A Kitchen Table," and the reader was encouraged to seek the secret of Rocco Bonavia's strengths and weaknesses under that table and on that mattress. Was he a bachelor? That was because he'd seen too much of his parents' night life. Good people, keep your children away from the marriage bed. And other whimsical sentences, arbitrary judgments beyond appeal. The world was just beginning to profit from the endless riches of psychoanalysis. That was in 1938. But not one of those subtle explorers of the human heart saw the drama of Rocco Bonavia as it had really been—in the disgrace and death of Peppina.

We do not choose our ways of escape. They choose us. I had not anticipated Rocco. I had not hoped for him. I moved towards him as children start into the night, drawn by dark wonders. In

Rocco's destiny there was a fascination completely absent from
the others I knew—Daisy Lee, Pam, Aunt Rosie. The editorial
offices, my hotel room, New York with its long petrified streets:
in these places I could no longer breathe. Rocco was an open door.
I passed through it as others embark on cruises.

Later, Aunt Rosie spoke of premeditation and even of a plot.
By becoming interested in Rocco, by delving into his life, by reading articles about him, I was poisoning Pam, I was influencing her.
In fact, I was only giving her a breath of air. And who can ever
guess what fresh air will do to someone who lives only by habit?
Give new curiosity? Make little cracks in the surface? For Pam
was changing, there was no doubt of that. It was a discreet change,
but no one who knew her could have missed it. She would whistle
at the table, or she would talk about going abroad for a holiday.
One day she announced that she would never wear a hat again, a
decision that frightened Aunt Rosie.

"Good grief, why? Why go around bareheaded?"

Pam's answer made her decision something less than revolu-
tionary. Princess Margaret, it seemed, went about with just a scarf
tied over her hair. Aunt Rosie breathed again. Margaret: a safe
model. Since Mrs. Simpson's marriage, since a king had stooped
to an American, Aunt Rosie had taken a liking to Buckingham
Palace. She talked about it the way old soldiers tell of their victories. But when Pam went on to say that she would give Ethel
the hats she no longer intended to wear, Aunt Rosie grew frightened again. To Ethel? Why to Ethel? Wouldn't it be better to
send them to Korea, to her brother the pastor, for the girls of his
mission? I made the remark that America was already sending
packages of old clothes to dealers in Southern Italy, why not hats
to Korea? Aunt Rosie was grateful for my contribution.

"You see, Pam, Gianna thinks so too. It would be so charitable.
Really, so. . . ."

But Pam replied rather rudely that her father was in Korea to
"convert the natives and not to give them bonnets." She added
that yellow people only had one hairstyle, the braid, and with such

an arrangement you could do without hats. The discussion stopped there. Such marks of generosity towards Ethel, such fraternization with the black servant, when a generous gesture to the little Koreans in the pastor's care would have been so much more noble, seemed ungracious to Aunt Rosie. She anticipated more disaffections in the future.

At *Fair*, nothing changed. A golden bath. We were there to know, better than they knew them themselves, millionaires' passions, their habits, their tastes. But none of us, even the most gifted, could equal the fervor which Daisy Lee brought to this cult. She conveyed a sense of all the luxury in the world. On the understanding that I was to be no more than suitably ironic, I sometimes laughed about it with Pam.

On certain days everything went on very quietly and Daisy Lee did not enter the editorial rooms. That was a good sign. It meant that our advertising was good and the curve of our sales was going up. At other times, a traffic of business men tracking towards Daisy's office warned us that something was amiss, and we prepared to put our imaginations to work until eight at night. It was going to be necessary to find an idea which would give *Fair* back its lost vitality. Daisy Lee made an entrance accompanied by tremors: tremors of the chains of her bracelets, the beads of her necklace, tremor of her voice which shook with worry, tremors of her silken skirts. She waited for certain members of the top brass to make a brief appearance in our open doorway. They would shake their heads with a funereal air and call encouragement to us which they always limited to the same phrase pronounced in sugar-daddy voices: "Good girls. . . . Good girls."

This gave the girls the green light. All that remained was to disconnect the telephones, forbid entrance to the office by hanging a placard on the door saying "Please don't disturb," and to get to work. Daisy Lee began by putting on a show of pitiful discouragement. She pretended to be a mere shadow of her former self, used up, empty of ideas, she went so far as to talk about retiring. Circulation was going down. Her voice broke: "*Non sum dignus.*" She lit a cigarette. The only thing left to do was quit. We listened—not too fearfully, knowing well that leaving *Fair* would have killed her: she wasn't even considering such an alternative. But it exhilarated her to frighten herself, to say she was finished. We soon witnessed her resurrection: spectacular! *Fair* was her life, her work, and we needed her. No weaknesses allowed. Then she leaned over the sales reports with the attention of a doctor reading a patient's temperature chart after major surgery. It was important that we should worry with her, and of course we did, without argument. We passed the reports among us reading them with broken-hearted groans. At this stage, it was unusual if Daisy Lee were not thirsty. She then gave us the key to what she called her "cellar": a cabinet concealed in the wall where full and empty bottles were piled in great disorder. While the glasses were being filled Daisy Lee let the married women, more anxious to get home than the rest of us, leave. She'd say: "My husband is used to waiting. . . . You'd better get yours used to it too." And you could feel how she detested them, those impatient husbands, stumbling blocks that they were to the magazine's circulation.

Then the rest of us stayed, the unmarried ones, lined up around Daisy Lee's desk as if around a workbench, listening to her voice getting louder with every glass, and her ideas unfolding. What to do? What to do to make women hungrier, thirstier; how to stuff more desires into their minds, more appetites into their hearts? What to do? For *Fair's* circulation depended neither on culture, nor on music, nor on art (which were Daisy Lee's pet hates) but only on those feminine hunger pangs which only magazines know how to assuage. Fashion, sexuality, travel, gastronomy—that was our formula. We would have been embarrassed to talk about anything else, and the "What to do?" soul-searching went on very late. A rich and greedy reader is more difficult to satisfy than any other.

It was at the end of one of these meetings and after Daisy Lee had begged us several times to come up with one simple idea, that one occurred to her and she passed it along to us. She had, it must be admitted, a deep understanding of the mechanism of human temptation.

"They have everything," she cried. "They can pay for wildly expensive cruises. They can rent steamers, buy islands. Let's tell them to economize. They'd never think of *that* themselves."

The following week *Fair* suggested to its readers: "Travel without leaving New York." That was the title of a new series of articles about foreign restaurants, "tested, judged, and recommended" by *Fair*. Pam and I were put in charge of the investigation. Pam was to supply the practical note. I went along to supply the exotic.

Memory's bitter mystery. The impossibility of foreseeing whence the attack will come. In the middle of the coffee break, the voice of Pam who touches the living wound without knowing it.

"Nothing ever happens to me," she said.

I turned on my stool, threw a dollar on the counter and moved towards the door.

"What's the matter?" she asked impatiently. "I didn't mean to offend you."

"You don't offend me."

"So what on earth is the matter? You really are impossible."

I left the restaurant and went out as if I were suddenly seeking the voice from the past, that lost voice which approached, then stopped, then retreated into the distance again, leaving me to stand on the sidewalk like a hunted animal, lost, like a beast at bay.

"Nothing ever happens to me, Signora Meri."

Antonio, at twenty, blotting out the rest of the world.

"Nothing," he said again. "Absolutely nothing ever happens to me."

Far away, the sea, and a cloud floating on the peaceful morning.

"Nothing—ever. I'm telling you."

Antonio turned over on his stomach and the skin of his back,

still wet, glistened. She laughed, but with a deep muffled laugh.
"What nonsense. . . ."

Circe in her grotto must have laughed like that at voyagers;
laughed at questions; a laughter that was earnest and intimate and
which was part scolding, part reprimanding at the same time.

That headstrong, impatient boy, who was complaining of being
twenty years old repeated: "Nothing, Signora Meri, really!"

"That's because you're happy, Antonio. Don't try to tell me
otherwise. I recognize happiness. The only people nothing happens to are the ones who are in love. Love is enough in itself.
Don't forget that."

The boy blushed with pleasure. He threw me a glance over one
shoulder and then smiled.

"You're never wrong, Signora Meri."

She looked up at the sky.

"How could anyone be wrong about such a thing! Anyone
could see you're in love just by the way you lie there in the sand
like a lizard, waiting for nothing, being impatient over nothing
and laughing at nothing. A man to whom nothing happens is like
a hunter lying in wait. He's watchful right down to his toes."

A swimmer still dripping from the sea caught the end of her
sentence.

"It's crazy how much you know about everything!"

"I know that nothing happens by accident."

Boats went by on the oil-smooth water carrying drowsy families.
The sun beat on the sand like a flaming sword. Songs from a local
taverna met and mingled in the sky with the bells of a late mass.
There was a little war between loudspeakers. We ran into the
water with the sound of a "Pater" in our ear, and when we were
through laughing, splashing each other, scaring each other, when
we returned to the sand, "*Ti voglio tanto bene*" was drowning
out the "*Ite, missa est.*" The cry of a vendor selling ices, his wet
tread along the foamless sea, pulled us out of our trance.

A boy with a lazy voice asked: "Sure you don't want me to
call him over, Signora Meri?"

"Don't move. It's too hot. . . . Give me my hat."

The man moved past us.

That summer on the hills which overlook Palermo artillery schools had been set up where soldiers crouched in the gravel and practiced shooting. Hearing them, she said: "Listen to those idiots. In such heat. . . . Really!"

When the firing continued and the cannons breached the calm of our siesta, she grew angry: "They're preparing for war, those criminals!"

The idea made the boys sit up.

"Are you serious, Signora Meri?"

Then she was silent, suddenly preoccupied, rapt in joyful contemplation of the summer day. And we stayed there at her feet, flattened in the sand, held there by her shadow, by her wisdom, by her presentiments.

We were only children on holiday. Everything was a game to us, or a subject for wonder. The cannons' grumbling, whose shots we counted; the sound between the mountains which echoed twice, three times; that makes four, no, only two real ricochets, really; the squadrons of planes over our heads tracing throbbing rainbows of sound. We watched them all day long, making a game of not closing our eyes, not blinking, braving the sun. The planes had an easy air which fascinated us. Where were they going? No one could tell us. And those soldiers in African dress? They sang: "Black skin, my Abyssinian beauty," a song we had never heard before. They spread across the beach like a sand storm. We saw them undressing, and on top of their trousers, their shirts, their carefully folded jackets, the colonial helmet. Then they threw themselves in the water with extravagant gestures, and their departure gave a funereal look to those little piles of clothes, so carefully arranged, as if they were the remains of a company which had disappeared into the sea. After that they would get dressed again to troop back to the city, or they would march two by two, dressed in khaki. What were they waiting for? From his balcony, Mussolini launched threatening statements: "War! A word which does not frighten us!" But we hardly heard him. Rome was far away. We lived with our heads in the clouds. Were we wrong to be so happy? We only lived as an adjunct to the sea, to the continual conflict between shadow and sun, between the warmth of our bodies and the cold of the water; we thought of nothing. We were prisoners of salt, of sand, of air, and of wind. Let an adult throw the first stone. Were we wrong? We were only children on holiday living through our last summer of peace.

There were no boys of twenty who would complain long about nothing ever happening to them.

Abyssinia! Why Abyssinia? Is it possible to go to war to win a few feet of sand from those people? Abyssinia! At the family meals at the Meri house that was all anyone talked about—and about the prisoners who had not come back. What had become of them? They were presumed dead. And the cruisers, which were becoming more and more numerous in the harbor, and of *Il Duce*, who was beginning to grow pudgy in his uniform and wore a white plume on the side of his helmet. Doctor Meri shrugged his shoulders. He was not a Fascist. How could he be when every day he was confronted with such poverty and corruption?

As for Baron di D., he hated the government with such violence that he was endangering himself. He could see no other reason for the war than *Il Duce*'s unacknowledged desire for a black honor guard.

"You'll see. You'll see I'm not mistaken. He's trying to dazzle la Petacci. He wants to offer her exotic flunkeys. He wants to bring back Abyssinian orderlies to stand outside la Camillucia's doors. Mistresses! She'll cost us dear, that woman."

Imprudent talk! The police were always watching, with their *agents provocateurs*, and their informers. But the secrecy so much in favor at that time, a code full of nicknames for the important officials, only made the Baron more ironic. He answered Doctor Meri's advice to be more prudent with irritable exclamations.

"Let the priests do the whispering. These black-shirted tyrants aren't going to make me change how I talk. And you know perfectly well that what I say is true, my dear Meri."

That was the time of forbidden music, cut films, censored mail, and letters surreptitiously opened and resealed; it was the time when the signs "Furnished Rooms" disappeared from house fronts because it was important to be anti-British, and besides, British tourists weren't coming anymore; the time of children in military uniforms carrying guns; the time of walls covered with inscriptions: "Mussolini is always right"; the time when propagandists arrived from the mainland to convert warm Sicily to Fascism. Ah, those films in which it was necessary to applaud the unmistakable Starace on his walking tours with his suite of ministers and generals, dragging along, running as fast as they could, an excess of spaghetti appearing as rolls of fat around their bellies. That was the time when muscle became a major preoccupation. There was going to be a war, and we must be ready.

What happened farther away—the growing appetites of the Germans, the guns paraded noisily in Munich, the governments of France which fell like autumn leaves—was never mentioned in Palermo. We had our own problems, and the intervention in Spain then being organized was enough to make us forget everything else. But in Sólanto, as in Palermo, several wonderful months were left to us during which Antonio and I managed to live beyond these things which made other people so angry. Wasn't existence becoming unbearable? Foreign publications were forbidden, which infuriated Baron di D. There was a shortage of certain medicines which no one protested, but which angered my father. Only Fascists could get jobs, and the gatekeeper complained because he could no longer buy silver polish from England! We ignored them. How would such irritations manage to reach us through the thick silence in which one finds first love? The grumbling world made no more impression on our ears than a falling feather.

I still knew almost nothing about love, but Antonio was conscious of it; he used great tact in letting me know that he was an experienced lover. I was amazed and tried to encourage his confidences, but we were never left alone. Sicilian families like to move in groups. Ours was like the rest. So, every time I went to the beach I was entrusted to the care of several younger brothers. On those days, Antonio and I nearly went crazy with awkward caresses, hasty embraces, kisses exchanged standing in the stifling heat of a cabana where, unknown to the others, we managed to be alone for a few seconds.

We needed an excuse to escape. Thanks to the complicity of a fisherman, Antonio managed to borrow a boat whose proprietor was given to long naps. We were able to set sail as soon as the wind rose, and we set off toward the horizon in the floating theater of our first experiments. But even there we were not alone, and our audacity was more dreamed than lived. Although vacation reading kept some of my brothers from giving up a whole afternoon to the whims of the wind, one of them, Riccardo—hardly more than a baby—was given the job of watching over us. Once at sea, Antonio, who was very fond of him, set out to keep him busy: "Sit in the prow, Riccardo, and let me know when there are rocks ahead."

The child assumed a solemn air. He was five years old. Believing that he was in the midst of a dangerous adventure, he squatted in the front of the boat, his eyes trained on the water, convinced that a single moment of inattention might be fatal to us. In the meantime, lying in the stern, Antonio steered the boat and caressed me.

Sometimes the wind dropped, abruptly interrupting our movements. Riccardo, when this happened, was revealed as a little companion of such innocent complicity that we were amazed. He took the supply of picture books we had brought for him and turning his back to us, plunged into the adventures of Tarzan. Without losing his casual air, his face impassive, Antonio lay down in the bottom of the boat and gently twined his legs with mine. We stayed there for a long time, drifting together, lips together, with the sea stretched under our bodies like an enormous sheet and the soft sound of the waves to soothe us. Far away, bordering the bay, Monte Pellegrino with its piled-up rocks rose

above us, sometimes like a great pipe organ against the sky, sometimes like the flaming silhouette of a god lying on the sea. We
said almost nothing, except for those monosyllables, those half
sentences which take the place of conversation in the hot sun.
"How simple it would be if I didn't love you so much," were the
only words Antonio spoke which remain in my memory along with
the memory of that boat.

But finally a wave of tenderness washed over us for the docile
child who had lent himself so readily to our game. Antonio called
to him: "Come here, Riccardo. Come take a nap with us."

The words were spoken so naturally that Riccardo came to join
us, quite happy, laughing at the prospect of sharing our sleep,
playing at taking a nap in the same way he had played at being
our pilot. I saw him nuzzling Antonio's neck, his shoulder, to find
a place to rest his head. Then Antonio's body looked different. In
a strange way he lost his hard brilliance, his mastery, his authority.
Not that he lost his charm: the change was becoming to him. I
no longer imagined him swimming or diving, looking as he often
did, violent, tense, but as a world of sweetness in which I would
have loved to lose myself.

I repeat, Antonio showed Riccardo a tenderness such as only a
young Italian could show a child of that age. Riccardo was nothing
to him, yet he always did things for him which would have made
a boy in another country blush. He took off his wet trousers, dried
him, changed him, and when it was time to leave the boat, he carried the child in his arms. But instead of diminishing him in my
eyes, the care he took of Riccardo made him seem more virile.

One day on the way back, Antonio wanted to stop at a *trattoria*.
The woman who greeted us, after congratulating me on Riccardo's
beauty, added with a friendly tone of worry: "Don't have another
one too soon. You're still very young, both of you." Then, looking
at my drawn features (we would return from these jaunts in a
pitiful condition), she suggested an eggnog to me, thinking I
needed at least that to make me feel better. I turned pale. When

we had not yet made free with one another, we were already taken for a married couple.

This life was draining us. The more intense our desire became, the vaguer our actions became, the more uncertain our behavior. We came, we went, making no contact with others, like people dropped from the moon; we were asleep on our feet.

Our parents were watching us. We were the subject of long consultations between Baron di D. and Doctor Meri. They thought: those children love each other. They repeated it to each other: "Of course, the children love each other, that's obvious." They still were saying it several weeks later. But we had decided to put an end to the lust which was devouring us. And they went on saying, "Those children love each other," when we were already lovers.

It was Antonio who suddenly became conscious of the drama being prepared for us: our life. It was he who was right about our timidity and it was his gloom which gave us courage.

Our adventure began on a September evening in Sólanto with three knocks at the door, and the entrance of a *carabiniere.*

Those three knocks, heavy, weighted, resounded in the great entrance hall and reached us with theatrical perfection. They were like the footsteps of the Commendatore and made one think of that terrible sound in the last act of *Don Giovanni.* Without his intending it, each of the *carabiniere*'s gestures was like a malediction. He stood still for a moment, he fumbled in his pocket and from his wallet drew a piece of paper, addressed to "the one that's named Antonio." His face was thin and greasy. He smiled. The visor of his cap was cracked in the middle. He did what was expected of him, he made simple movements: he came toward us awkwardly because of the nails in his shoes which slid on the marble, he searched out the interested party with his eyes, found Antonio, gave him the piece of paper, and the passage of that page from one hand to the other brought to all of us a moment of inexplicable lucidity. We were gripped by that lucidity. It overwhelmed us, submerged us with the brutality of an avalanche. No use reading that blue paper. We knew what was in it. An order. Antonio was expected at the School at Modena. The army needed staff: young student officers were invited to enlist before conscription. We knew it. Antonio put the envelope in his pocket without even opening it. The *carabiniere* opened his eyes wide. Such disinterest seemed abnormal to him: "Aren't you going to see what's inside?"

There was no trace of emotion on Antonio's face.

"I'm in no hurry. And it's not very interesting."

Then he smiled. His amused look, his slight haughtiness staggered the poor fellow who, confused, repeated: "What? You haven't opened it. You're not going to open it?"

Beside me Antonio's voice spoke softly to me: "Take him to the kitchen and have them give him a glass of Marsala. That'll make him feel better."

I saw in Antonio not just his attitude of the moment, but as he would be in the future, haunting my nights for years, as I have so often imagined him: shivering with cold, his fingers swollen, so ill-dressed and ill-fed that he was scarcely able to walk. I hate that picture of Antonio. His wretchedness makes me ashamed. He who was all manly grace, sharp and stirring beauty, had been transformed by all those defeats into one of those exhausted soldiers whom the world scorned. He had known fruitless dangers in battle, with limited arms and unworthy leaders; he had been led by those who stalled, those who balked, those who refused, he whose every gesture was fantastically precise, he who had mastered steel and motors. I did not wish to witness his destruction. I tried not to visualize him walking humbly among men with holes in their shoes, with bloody feet and sad songs: those tragic tramps, those broken soldiers, could not be his companions. He was young and strong and violent. He was audacity itself. He was that big tanned boy, that body which came to lie secretly near me in the bottom of a boat. I dare no longer think of the pleasure he gave me nor see myself loving him now that he has been made into that pale, broken shadow, that man who dies in a ditch, that missing person. But it's too soon to think of that. These few words, these sentences should only be like a tablet graven by chance and placed in the midst of my story to bear witness to the shining beauty of Antonio, and to his death, which I reject. Every detail of this decisive moment is remembered in the exile of my heart. Outwardly, what had just happened in the castle of Sólanto was nothing but the act of obedience of any twenty-year-old Sicilian. Military service. Nothing unusual about that. Nothing abnormal. Other men of his age were receiving the same order, at the same time. But in the light of later events this obedience takes on a new emphasis: Antonio acknowledged the right of a government he despised to dispose of his life. Let no one misunderstand the character of that obedience. Antonio was not a man to submit for simple reasons. He hadn't the deceptive docility of those who plan treason. Deserter? He could easily have chosen that solution. Nothing was easier in Sicily. And then, was it treason not to participate in that kind of war? Antonio was not one of those unconscious ones for whom war is a sensuous game, a superior form of orgasm. No. Antonio obeyed with a heroic casualness, a sovereign indifference. He went because he would have found it less than gentlemanly to do otherwise. He said he was going "to see" and also "because we have wasted our youth."

Because of those three knocks at the door and because of a *carabiniere* slipping in his hobnailed shoes, what had been innocence, young and secret love, became transfigured. Nothing was as it had been in the castle of Sólanto, nothing would ever be the same. The very essence of happiness had been taken from us: freedom from care. Because of that order and that blue piece of paper, Baron di D. wore a painful rictus, Don Fofò put his hand on his son's shoulder in an instinctive gesture of protection—"My boy, my boy, they never leave us alone."—and the garden grew dark, the servants ran aimlessly from room to room, the very frescoes on the ceiling in their plaster frames seemed suddenly unbearably heavy.

Then there was the incident of the volunteer, as if some tragic event were needed to fill the empty hours between us and his departure. Those short hours.

La Kalso and the adjoining streets was then a quarter for beggars, deserters, and whores, where poverty, like a kind of leprosy, became more obvious each day as the country plunged deeper into the war. A few families earned an honest living—fishermen, basket carriers, old clothes dealers, vegetable peddlers, cooks who sold food by the portion, or even by the mouthful to the passersby. But there was no way of telling a workman from a derelict or a prostitute from an honest matron. They shared the same filth.

The front of our house faced the wide spaces of the Marine Promenade, but on the other three sides it was plunged into the disorder of that fantastic district. An alleyway, hardly more than a meter and a half wide, separated the window of the "children's" room from another where, in the evening, a huge swarming family huddled together in the same bed. In spite of a shabby awning which the head of the family, before going to sleep, pulled modestly over the balcony, in spite of the screen formed by a line of scrawny plants, there was nothing we did not know about our neighbors' lives. From under that awning, through those plants, there drifted nocturnal communications, male cries of victory, the sighs and groans which took the place of sex education for me.

And it was in that room that the drama exploded. Antonio was staying with us that night. It could not have been more than ten o'clock, and we were together. Nothing more than that. We were spending the evening in conversation, having been allowed that much. Antonio seemed rather sad and downcast. He looked across the alley at the family opposite. Beneath the awning we could see that they were all there. But what was going on? The little ones had not yet gone to bed. They had just been thrust out on the balcony where they stayed, ragged and silent. Instead of fighting, as they often did, they were lifting a corner of the awning and peeping at their parents. The eldest girl was crying. Only the smallest seemed indifferent, sleeping soundly in his sister's arms. Inside

a stern voice seemed to be reading. Very unusual. Everyone there
was illiterate. So whose was this voice? A few words were clearer
than others. Cadiz. Franco. Spain. What connection had that
household with such things? Antonio went to the window and
called to the weeping girl. She must have been fourteen years old.
What was going on over there? Was someone sick? Was it the
doctor? No, it was only the public letter writer reading a work
contract which the father had signed the day before. But something was wrong. He had been promised land in Ethiopia. He was
already thinking of himself as a colonist, and now he was being
sent to Cadiz. He was being sent to Spain. Senseless.

Then all at once a cry arose, sharp as a roar, a grief. The man
understood. He howled: "Volunteer! I never volunteered!"

His voice broke somewhere between rage and a sob. Then the
lament began again, filled the street, rose, echoed from the buildings, swelled, rolled.

"Volunteer! Volunteer, but I'm not a volunteer!" That voice
was like a nightmare. It cried out to the wife, "You whore, you
whore, you made me sign! It's that King, that imbecile, that runt.
A King who sends Italians to fight in Spain against other Italians,
what kind of King is that?" There were cries: "Italians in Spain?
What Italians? What are you talking about?" The room was full
of people. Not just the couple, the children, the letter writer, but
other men, neighbors attracted by the noise. They jostled each
other to hear better what the man was saying, the man who beat
his head against the walls in a black rage. There were. . . . There
were. . . . There were what? Italians on the Republican side. Impossible to tell where the voice came from which cried, "That's
true. . . . That's true." Certain words rose above the din, returned
more often, burst forth more strongly: Madrid . . . Barcelona.
And there were others at which voices were lowered, hesitated, as
if making the kind of silence there is in grand opera. These were
names that were repeated. Who was Nenni? Who was Rosselli?
Who was Pacciardi? *Comrades, Italian brothers, listen give us a
hand.* . . . Why did those people make their appeals over the

Republican radio? *Italian brothers . . . Italian brothers.* It would sound from an open window, from a door, from a balcony, no one could explain how, *This is a soldier from the Garibaldi Battalion;* it invaded the terrace at the time when people were playing cards there. *Dictatorships are parentheses in the life of the people,* and always the boss, or else one of the waiters, very worried, ran to the set to silence that damned Freemason once and for all. . . . Jesus, Joseph and Mary, you couldn't ask your customers to stick their fingers in their ears! Well, was that story true? Were there really *Fuorusciti,* antifascists in the International Brigades? That's horrible, it's a trap. . . . How could anyone believe it? And the voice of grief, which never stopped, rose above the cries of indignation, of rage, above the children's cries, the howls of the wife who held her belly as if in labor, that voice of anguish repeated: "Volunteer. . . . But I'm no volunteer!"

Suddenly there was an outburst of shouts, a hurricane, a hubbub, something incomprehensible which pushed the children out of doors, a convulsive gesture of the mother which turned them into a weeping bunch piled on the balcony. The awning flapped. The inside of the room could be seen, a tragic den with a naked bulb hanging from the ceiling and the enormous bed on which the wife was kneeling, her thighs open, in hand-to-hand combat with her husband, who held a knife. No one could stop him. No one could cushion the blow he struck himself. He slipped from the bed and fell to the floor, his throat slashed. In a moment, the room was empty. No one wanted to be there when the police arrived. And nothing was left in the room except the woman, like a bundle of howling flesh, the children clinging to one another, and then the body at the foot of the bed, the body, its eyes rolled upward, emptying its blood on the floor.

Yes, my seashore queen, my silent one, my truth, you are so right: nothing ever happens by accident. Every instant of our lives makes ready for future events, each feeling, each idea opens the way for them. So it was for Antonio: the three knocks were struck on the door; the event had arrived. What pushed him first toward me and then toward his death was that terrible scene across the alleyway. It struck him with the deep certainty that nothing separated him from the wretchedness he had witnessed that night. Between that misery and himself there had only been the differences of birth, of fortune, of language. What did those matter? And could we, after that, go back to our long casual days, to our beaches, and to the magic indolence of an earlier time?

Abruptly, Antonio realized that he would never again be able to forget the misery of those people, nor their tragedy, and this distress gave a new twist to his thoughts. It was like the end of an enchantment, as if *before* had only been a useless garment which slipped from his body and was gone.

And this was what decided him, it was at that moment he decided to make me his. Yes, my sweet, my soft, my serious one, yes, my mourning dove, let us go alone through the streets, then through the roads which widen towards the dilapidated house hanging over emptiness on the top of the hill. Close your eyes and pretend you are the one who knew nothing, as you were that day, one who wished to know nothing.

If you had only asked us what that part of the country meant to us, you would have known what we had in mind and why we were going toward that isolated house, toward its high wall of uneven stones, enormous blocks placed one upon the other, piled up in disorder, built by or how no one quite knew, to become the support of a miraculous vegetation, cascades of bougainvilleas, jasmine, and plumbagos mixed together, the hidden pedestal, the hardly visible platform whence flourished, like flames, the cypress and aloes which crouched there; it would have seemed to you that there was nothing surprising about our decision and that without knowing that house, you could still have found it by the steep paths worn by shepherds and their flocks, the arch of a gateway, that pink of ochre, of earth, and of yellow, all colors which, had they been mixed elsewhere than in Sicily, would not have produced that final pink, that glorious pink, with—to each side of the arch and framing it like candlesticks—two palms, showing how once there had been a master here who had a taste for the grand, and a gardener, because palms do not grow by themselves on such heights. . . .

Even now, it does not seem believable that we were allowed to go alone to that faraway house. And yet, watching us leave, no voice sounded the least concerned.

"You'll have Zaira there to open the shutters for you and give you something for dinner."

Did you count on her to protect us from ourselves, or was Zaira only a fiction, an illusory presence which allowed your voice to stay calm? Silent Zaira. . . . We met her on the road, upright and solid, still young, with an enormous load on her head. She made a joyous gesture to us from afar, and hurrying, always upright, in order not to endanger the balance of her burden, came to meet us. She cut through the fields to join us faster without being troubled by the steep slope, the stones which rolled under her feet, and then, seeing a rock high enough to set down the fagots and bundles of rushes which she was bringing back to the mountain, she threw back her head, and with a movement of the spine she let them slide down her back. Then she approached her son whom she kissed gravely. When she spoke, she used to address him as "Don Antonio," and Baron di D. had had to admonish her many times to convince her to give up kissing his hand.

So, that strong and mysterious Zaira, guardian of the house, perhaps you imagined she would watch over us. On the contrary. She went out as soon as we came near through the vines of the garden and its flowers that no one cut. Perhaps she guessed by some telltale gesture, some look, that we were in love. Solitude had sharpened her perception.

"I have to go up to the sheepfold, Don Antonio. . . . There are some lambs due to be born."

"Forget about us, Mama Zaira."

Then she, a little upset, called him "Don Ninuzzo" as she had during the time at Sólanto when she was nursing him, and in her changed voice, so different from the one we knew, it all came back, the chestnut wood, the meeting with Don Fofò, the sense of insecurity. . . . Would she be abandoned? . . . Would they take her child from her? . . . And then the departure for Sólanto and the big bedroom looking out on the sea where the two of them had stayed, where she had raised him, the Garibaldi grandfather's bedroom, and the head of the baby which weighed on her breast, and his hungry lips. . . . How long ago? . . .

"I'll be back late, Don Ninuzzo. With animals, you never know. Maybe they'll keep me all night. . . . If you want to rest, your room is ready. The sheets are in the cupboard. Just air them a little after the sun is set. You'll find mozarella in a bowl that I put in the kitchen window so that the breeze would keep the water cool. The wine is in the well. All you have to do is pull up the bucket. But you'd better take the young lady out on the terrace before you eat so she can admire the view. And don't forget to decide about the tree. Because it's growing and growing, that tree, Don Ninuzzo. It must have been there more than a century and it sends its branches out every which way, that tree. You know it's true. So if you don't have the pruners up from Palermo, when you come back from the army, Don Ninuzzo, there won't be a house any more. The tree will push it over the top."

The tree! For years it had been simply enormous, and its shade, like a huge dome, stretched well beyond the terrace it was meant to protect. Leaning into the void, its branches spread wide over the abyss and also shot forth as if in an attack against the mountainside, invaded the garden, clasped the house with sinuous arms, knotted around it as if to stifle it, while its roots, sometimes visible above the earth and rearing up like enormous gray snakes, sometimes hanging down vertically like lianas, gave the view beyond a mysterious and gothic character. It grew, spread, contracted on itself, deepened; like a nave, like a transept in a cathedral, like a cloister the color of elephant skin, it was dark with spots of pale gray, it was a strange world looking out over a deep valley, a world of shadow hung high above the clouds, a place where we were alone, and young, without shame, not needing modesty.

But the house was the essential thing. There was a smoke, I remember it, which clung to it, a warm odor which held it. Brushwood? No, wood charcoal, look, there's a red spot down there that seems to pulse, a woodsman's kiln. The bedroom smelled of mint and lavender, of mountain and desire, of the fierce air that rushes down from the heights. Gianna, my Gianna, what if I don't come back? . . . It was the stars, that trap made us lose all sense of the day that is ending, of tomorrow, of ourselves; it was enormous hope, an oasis, a door banging in the night. It was that voice pronouncing familiar phrases, my love, my wife, the only ones remembered, the music of those nocturnal words, invented words: Zinna, my Zinounetta, you are my breath, my heart, my life; then the wondrous silence, sleep, the dawning light, the first sounds of day, the dog barking, the plants opening at dawn—my God, the Arabian jasmine, its perfume! And the swallows, what is stirring them up so? It was the footstep of the shepherd, his voice and his song which woke us, it was the scene of our nuptials.

III.

*The thing is that I'm not from these parts,
no, I'm not from here.*   ARAGON

One day Aunt Rosie had a big woman with too much make-up to
dinner, and the name of Peppina Bonavia was mentioned with
the soup, as if Mrs. MacMannox's guest had guessed that this was
a subject about which I needed more information. I didn't even
have to urge her. She chose this subject of conversation by her
own preference for it above all others. And the details flowing out
of that stranger's mouth were like an essential drug to me.

Actually, the drunks of the Bowery, that avenue that pitches and
rolls in the early hours of the morning, the neighborhood where
the passersby can see a wretched confusion of broken-down bodies
on the sidewalks; those men of the Bowery who will eat, suck, or
chew anything so long as it tastes of alcohol, my dear, do you

know that they get drunk on vinegar, on ether, on *eau de Cologne*, those people? Anyway, they are much more often German or Irish than Italian. Someone asked, "And the craziest of all are the Swedes, aren't they?"

"Really! That's enough!" cried Mrs. MacMannox, offended by this talk. "Crazy people. Drunks. Drug addicts. And we pay taxes to support such trash! The only place where they know how to drink without showing it is in England."

And with the clear authority bestowed upon her by a successful life, Mrs. MacMannox changed the subject.

"You're here for a change," she said to her guest, "and here we are talking shop. Shame on us. Shame on you. Come now, let's have a good time. Pam, put on a record, will you? Something new, something classical."

And she tried to discuss the arts.

But at the end of the evening, in spite of records, in spite of all the platitudes exchanged, in spite of boredom, I found that the whole story had been told of the beautiful Peppina's tragic end.

The lady with the big jewels, with the big nose, with the big voice, the big lady at Aunt Rosie's said Peppina had become "alcoholic out of idleness," and the word "alcoholic" in her voice took on an extraordinary resonance. Introducing me to her guest, Aunt Rosie had told how, only recently cured, this lady owed her recovery to Alcoholics Anonymous and what was more, being very rich, she had bequeathed her whole fortune to that organization. These converts are often found in New York, bowing under their new dignity, drafting reports, making lectures, sitting on committees. Converts to vegetarianism, to Hindu philosophy, to Civil Rights, to the rehabilitation of prostitutes. I listened religiously to this convert to water. It was because he drank brandy that Napoleon. . . . And Errol Flynn, too. . . . Each, in his way, victim to this scourge. . . . But none of this compared to the strange case of Peppina. A woman killed in the course of a fight between the police and vagrants in an old warehouse in the heart of the Bowery. The papers had made a big story of it, an unusual uproar.

What had the woman been doing there? She was said to frequent the place and to have spent the night there. And then, she was a woman whose needs were met. Her husband had a flourishing business. He had managed an Italian restaurant up to the time when he bought it. Casa Alfio on Mulberry Street. The best spaghetti in New York, and lobster *fra diavolo*. Really a delightful little place. Only twelve tables. Open night and day.

"When she was working, Peppina was sobriety itself," the woman went on in a pointed tone.

A dry voice. Authoritative.

"Her son, a good boy, was studying to be a lawyer. A glutton for work. That's Rocco Bonavia, you know."

"I know, I know," interrupted Aunt Rosie. "We all know him. Rather distressing, in my opinion. A dangerous demagogue. And how old was he when this happened?"

"Barely twenty."

The lady was in possession of all the facts, and ready to detail them. That was clear. But Aunt Rosie interrupted again.

"Well? One is a man at twenty, it seems to me."

Terrible Aunt Rosie, with that court forever in session deep inside her. Now all its judges woke up at once: "And not even capable of hiding her bottles. Come. Lack of parental authority. . . . Dangerous weakness. . . . You'll never persuade me otherwise. There are some backgrounds you simply can't overcome."

Rocco. Daisy Lee. I saw them again at Pam's house the day of the reception. "It's like a nightmare beginning again." His compassion. Now I understood. And also that phrase I had read in articles about him: "His studies were interrupted by his mother's death." What else could he have done after such a scandal. So, it was law he was studying?

Rocco, I learned, had hesitated a long time before choosing that path. He would have preferred to be an opera singer, or sometimes, when the women looked at him in the streets, a baseball player. A handsome gallant of eighteen. Athletic. But the relative prosperity of the Bonavias was not such that he needn't earn a living. He had found a job in an employment agency where his legal knowledge was useful. He drew up contracts. When his work was done, he gathered up his books and with an athlete's stride walked through several miles of dirty sidewalks, of tall brick houses, to catch a bit of an evening stroll on Canal Street.

Alfio took care of the restaurant alone, a little room painted Pompeiian red, where Peppina only appeared at meal time, the gracious hostess. A soft life, really. She no longer worked. Silk stockings, perfumes, buttered muffins in bed, she had a right to all that, and to her morning chat with Alfio—Alfio, who with soft footsteps brought her tray up to her each day, opened her windows, and left her to endless games of solitaire, the cards spread out on the sheet. It was Rocco who first smelled something wrong. Smelled, that is the word, for he wondered a long time about the odor that lingered in the corners of her room, rose from the warmth of the bed and hung over whatever she touched. She used clever tricks and Rocco was taken in by her deceits. That smell? Floor wax. A lotion. A disinfectant. No one knew better than she how to throw people off the track. But all the same, that smell, and that disorder. The playing cards, dirtier every day. The oddities. She refused to let anyone help her make her bed. She slept on the same sheets several months on end and often stayed in bed for whole days without moving, saying she was very tired, taking one nap after another, indifferent to everything, to the wrinkles in the dirtied linen, to the accumulated cigarette butts, to trails of ashes. And that distressed look when anyone came to disturb her. At the end of the day she would get up, dress quickly and come back much later, her eyes bleary, her speech slurred. I just, I only. . . . Peppina who had been so precise. All those lies, why? Rocco never suspected the truth. And then, abruptly, it all came out. She smelled of the saloon, by God, the sharp smell of drunkenness! In the morning she would leave her tea untouched, and if she tried, if she pretended to drink it to fool Alfio, the cup and saucer would rattle. Her hands trembled.

Several weeks passed during which Alfio and Rocco, conscious of what was happening, dared not speak of it. Peppina drank; it was one more trouble on top of the rest. It was the last straw.

But one evening Peppina returned in such a state that she could hardly put one foot in front of the other and Alfio, terrified, looked at her, the wife he had chosen, the one he had believed in, the one in whom he had hoped to believe until death, Peppina, babbling an incomprehensible story, her lips half paralyzed, her eyes mad. He burst out: "No woman of our country would dare to get into such a state!"

"From our country?" repeated Peppina. "What are you talking about? Which country?"

"You ought to be ashamed!"

". . . No more than a hole in my stocking."

Her voice, her attitude, everything about her was offensive to Alfio. It was possible to have crossed the ocean, to have forgotten one's life in furnished rooms and the misery of those first days. One could identify oneself with a new fatherland to the point of denying the land of one's birth. One could deny it in a thousand ways, that land, deny it to the point of feeling like a different man, and in spite of that remain incapable of tolerating the idea, yes, just the idea, the idea of a wife who drinks.

Peppina was an altogether demented woman; she had entirely succumbed to her dreams. When she became embarrassing, with those shameless enticements, sometimes addressed to the customers, sometimes to the waiters, with flirting airs and sudden disappearances into the kitchens to find a bottle, fill her glass, drink it down at a gulp, fill it again, and not return, when she began to go out around midnight and not come back before dawn, Alfio told himself: "She had no shame. She says it herself. And I who have hesitated. So many young girls in Sólanto who would have been happy to join me here. I worried about how much she knew, Peppina. . . . Too good at loving. She's known others before me." And revulsion became stronger than pain. While Rocco, who felt the same pain, who was present at the same scenes, who also saw the scornful clients laughing among themselves around the tables, in spite of that, in spite of the dirty reality, in spite of the disgrace, standing on street corners where he went in the middle of the night to look for her, in spite of the arguments on the way home and the blows exchanged—"No, not that, . . ." but sometimes it had to be—Rocco felt an indefinable tenderness rising out from the depth of his childhood, a measureless indulgence which engulfed him.

The police found him alone. Rocco was sitting at his table. An examination the next day.

"Are you Bonavia?"

"What do you want?"

"Have you a Giuseppina Bonavia in your family?"

"My mother. . . ."

"Sorry, young man."

"Why?"

"She's dead."

The last sentence pronounced with a rough certainty which could also mean: No point in beating around the bush with the likes of these.

There was a crowd around the warehouse where they took him and Alfio to identify the body. Other police were on guard. There too, no one made any effort to soften the horror of the scene. They were pushed like prisoners as they were led to the dead woman. "This way. . . . Move along. . . . Police." They gave in easily, resigned like so many Bonavias before them, pushed, humiliated, eternal wanderers expecting the worst. "All right, move along. Just one bullet. The wound is hardly visible. Under the hair, probably." "Probably—Hey, there's old what-his-name!" And the police gave resounding slaps on the backs of comrades they recognized in passing.

When Rocco, blinking his eyes in the half dark, saw Peppina lying in the moist dust, her skirts pushed halfway up her thighs, her blouse open, the word "Assassin" rose to his lips. He chewed the word and spit it out, from a resentment too bitter to hold back. An indignant policeman grasped his arm.

"Cool down, boy. It's not our fault. You let a woman run around like that. ... ."

"I didn't ask you anything. Let go of me."

He went straight to her where she lay, gray, open-mouthed, one arm raised in the corner of a wall plastered with posters, as if she were showing how the deluxe refrigerator can improve your home.

Alfio stayed behind, his hat in his hand, his blood running cold. "Peppina. Peppina, great God. You had everything." He saw Rocco bending to close her blouse and pull her skirt over her knees. Her color. A priest in a corner murmured something, then a woman came out of the shadow. Why was she talking to Rocco, that slut?

"Are you one of the family? I knew her well, you know. She came here often."

A terrible odor of urine rose from the woman's skirts. A reporter went over to her.

"You say she came here often?"

A policeman got rid of him. The woman stayed behind. A night-watchman, perhaps. Like a bat, living on darkness and filth. And authoritative in spite of that, pointing a severe finger at Peppina.

"Don't they close the eyes of the dead in your country? I can do that for her, you know. We knew each other pretty well, she and I. That is, if you don't mind."

Rocco nodded his head.

With her eyes closed Peppina didn't look much different. Rocco saw her as she once had been, sleeping amid the black mass of her hair, her hand open, the palm imploring, so tired. Why, when she had got away from all that, was free finally, why had she come to this. He had believed in her. He could not explain it to himself. What was she running from? The goad of poverty? Was that all that had given her strength? Outside that, nothing. . . . Was he, Rocco, nothing to her? With that thought everything seemed to be lost, and it seemed to him he could never live as he

had before. Rocco leaned his head against the wall to cry, discreetly, he thought, but a despairing sigh escaped him, then another, and he began to sob like a child. "It's my fault!" It was a
thought he could not escape. Something too obvious. "I ought to
have told her that she was superb, unique, strong, that we owed
her everything—I ought to have found words for it, told her often
—beautiful, strong, we owe you everything. Hugged her to me.
Look, look. There's nothing to worry about any more. It's like
heaven on earth. We have everything we want." But there were
those blows when he was trying to make her come home at night,
the splashing mud and the cries he could not forget. That was not
the way he wanted to remember her. No. To remember her, good
God, to remember her when she used to laugh, to see her again
when she had a reason for living. . . .

He looked at her for the last time, then made his way towards
the exit.

Alfio, leaning over Peppina, tried to pray. No words came. All
he could do was stare at the floor, hearing in his head the sound
of wedding bells and glasses clinking. Poverty! And his father-in-
law dressed in velvet with his damn Genoese accent, working for
Nelson Lee, the Chinese photographer on Mott Street. He earned
barely enough to support her. In the place of a dowry all she had
was a blue blouse. "Blue for luck," she said.

And it was true. How pretty she was in it. In the street men
looked after her. The first night, Peppina. The frail structure of
her hair collapsing, one pin after another, like a black river spreading on the white sheets. He would never forget it. But it was his
secret.

Two men came in, carrying a stretcher.

Certainly Alfio opposed his decision. But Rocco was immovable.
He could not be moved by his father's reasoning nor even by the
letter which Alfio sent him every day—although they were living
under the same roof—in the hope that by "the written word" the
boy would see how . . . The public letter writer, in consideration
of a free meal, might succeed in convincing him of the ridiculous-

ness of his "brainstorm." Nonsense. The end of his studies and
that far-off career planned for him! Never would he be heard
speaking those triumphant words, gesturing with his arms, solemnly clasping his hands before a rapt audience. To be like that?
Never, Intriguers. Climbers. Rocco refused suddenly to see himself
in that image which had for years seemed to him his probable
future. An ironic image now. He could only feel sick when he
spoke of it: "Making elocution out of other people's misery.
Wouldn't that drive anyone crazy? Talk, talk, talk, make pretty
words, well-rounded phrases, be brilliant at the expense of someone who trembles, already diminished, cut off from the world,
reduced to silence, weak, engulfed in fear. They've tried to convince me that it's a legitimate trade and I've gone along with it.
But that's over. Now I know what to think of it. Pretentiousness."
Peppina's death suddenly loosed in him unsuspected feelings of
discontent, of revolt. Everything was in upheaval inside him. It
was obvious that he had changed: his chin, his forehead, his
mouth, everything about Rocco became more drawn, more melancholy, more distant and with a sort of insolence—his mouth, especially, and even his smile.

Rocco believed he could now live without ambition. He would
take over from his father some day, and like him would be con-
tented with a small world made up of faithful customers who returned every evening at the same time, sat at the same table and
argued about how long to cook pasta, the inconveniences of modern ovens, and the cost of living. But could any man at twenty
live with the idea that nothing ever was going to change? Rocco
believed he could!

He had figured without Patrick O'Brady, an unextraordinary
Irishman. How could anyone have imagined that a meeting with
such a congenial idiot would change his life? All the same, one
often left those meetings with a sense of something new, unpredictable, which one could not explain to himself afterward. Thus,
from Patrick O'Brady, Rocco received new strength.

*   *   *

Patrick O'Brady came from a line of immigrants who were already worn out and who continued to vegetate through habit. But he was called "the Battler," as if he had inherited the violence of his ancestors. They had a heavy hand on them, his ancestors. The newcomers knew something about that. They had been received with kicks, blows, terrorized, pursued. Understandable, wasn't it? Shelter, work forbidden them. And what a mob! They came in all colors. Hindus, Malays, Filipinos. Enough to poison the race. The worst were the Chinese who had been run out of California by discriminatory laws. They took all the rights away from these people on the Pacific coast. To tell the truth, the arrival there of unexpected manpower which permitted itself to be treated like animals without making much fuss had made others quite happy. They put them to work at once: a railway to build. They were puny, these Chinese, but they had no equals in carting rails, ties, with nothing but a bowl of rice in their stomachs. And then, suddenly, around '73, there was a threat of depression in California, a financial crisis, unemployment. Who was to blame? The Chinese, to begin with. They were driven out. So they poured into New York. A bad business. Cockroaches like them, nobody had ever seen anything like them. You couldn't tell one from another, and a language like nothing at all, and bowing all over the place like they were up to something, schemers who got into the country nobody knew just how, probably through the Mexican frontier, and illegally, endless talkers, false as three-dollar bills, with their heads full of secret societies to protect their rights—the rights of Chinese-American citizens. Imagine! Or else exaggerated pretensions like selling their cheapjack goods, outlandish baubles, real dust catchers, and setting up laundries all over the place, as if cleanliness were their speciality. If you'd let them, they'd have got a real foothold in the neighborhood. Mulberry Street, a Chinese street. What next? Luckily, confronted with strong Ireland, those buggers were outweighed and more than one had been knocked down as he tried to get in.

Patrick O'Brady reminded one of those glorious fist fights. And that was not all. The Battler laid claim to other soubriquets. He was also called "Brad III" by his old customers, in particular, the ones who had known his father and his grandfather. For the saloon where he was marinating like a herring had been the property of his family for three generations. It was almost an heirloom, that license, and perfectly legal, authorizing the sale of beer, spirits, and all the rest.

By its simplicity, its dry cleanliness, its modest size, Pat O'Brady's bar was reminiscent of the old life of the neighborhood. Around that slightly sloping bar gathered a community in search of asylum, youngest sons from Ireland, farmers without farms, settlers without land, rogues who were deaf to the arguments of the very honorable recruiting officers of her Britannic Majesty—they said, My ass to the Queen, those Irish conscripts—rebellious men who had sailed too close to the wind. It could not be forgotten. It was as if that heroic epoch had left a sort of halo around Pat O'Brady's enterprise, but a very pale halo, very dim, for finally order reigned. A half century had been enough for all of them to settle down in neighborhoods which were no longer challenged. The Chinese were permanently entrenched around Mott Street, and there they stayed. There were no difficulties with the Italians. Room was made for them at one end of the neighborhood, not out of kindness—it wasn't Italian custom to act from that—but from religious solidarity. With Catholics, some agreement can always be reached. As for settling old accounts, that happened rarely. Faraway Ireland was free. It was no longer necessary to fear the incursions of certain patriots who, so they said, to support the nation of the Finians used to break open the cash register, threatening you with a pistol. No, that era was all over. Now Pat O'Brady drank more than he battled.

You could see him through the window, standing in his stocking feet, leaning on his bar, waiting for the sirens to announce the closing time of factories, docks, warehouses, customs houses which would send the crowd of drinkers to his door. He was blond, somewhat stooped, too tall, too thin, a man who didn't know what to do with his arms. Rocco acquired the habit of stopping at his place because it was convenient and because that champion, drowsing between his smoky walls, aroused a mournful curiosity in him. Go to the good neighborhoods, to the bars where the teenagers discussed cool jazz? Sometimes he hesitated. Escape the squalor? Jump Canal Street like a moat beyond which no one was Italian, Irish, Jewish, or Carpathian? Canal Street, like a finish line which separated the winners from those who were still running. A huge eraser to remove accents. But what was the use, because the music of Harry James, jazz, swing, and all the rest left him cold. Better to stay here, just a step from his work, in this anonymous crowd. Rocco looked vaguely at these men, mostly Irish, vigorous drinkers who consumed beer in incredible quantity, belched, swore at the top of their lungs, sang loudly: "Glory to Christopher Columbus, son of Holy Ireland!" their favorite song, and grew moustaches of brown or blond foam that went from nose to chops. What was Rocco looking for? Nothing very definite. The warmth of that room and its disorder was enough to make life tolerable to him. Almost gay. He had reasons.

One evening Patrick O'Brady, no doubt curious about this silent customer, asked him: "Are you a Democrat?"

Rocco said he wasn't anything.

"Fine, fine. Here's your lemonade. It's on me. We'll talk about this again."

That was the beginning. Just a few months after Peppina's death, Rocco scarcely knew what he was doing, and he ignored the whole incident. But it had broken the thread of silence, for soon after O'Brady asked once again, "Where do you work?"

"At the employment agency."

"The one next door?"

"Yes, I'm the one who draws up the contracts."

"What else?"

"What do you mean?"

"Why do you come here?"

"It's the closest place."

"Do you like it here?"

"I don't know. . . ."

"Make up your mind, yes or no?"

Where was he going with his questions? People nudged each other. The drinkers, that was clear, were interested in him, but Rocco paid them no attention. When O'Brady realized that his silence was final and that he would leave, as he did every evening, without explaining anything more, he went up to Rocco and took hold of his lapels.

"Do you know where you are?"

Rocco hadn't the least idea. And when the audience—twenty regulars in all—threw back their heads and laughed, Pat O'Brady added for their benefit: "Eh? This is not an ordinary place. Another damned Dago. They're all alike."

And shaking Rocco again, as if to waken him, he cried in his face: "Democrat, understand? This is the Democratic Club of your district and I'm the boss. . . ."

Pat O'Brady's voice reached Rocco, rough with that edge of violence that years of easy living had not erased.

More laughter, mockery, enormous belches, outbursts like the coughs a motor makes from all those mouths, from all those cheeks with hair bristling on them, from all those faces similarly worn by a past full of weariness and sweat. Open hilarity.

Cornered at the bar, Rocco thought: "It's me they're looking at. It's me they're laughing at," but at the same time he felt something like pleasure in it. For the space of a moment, the desire to stand before the mass of humanity made up by those bodies seated side by side crossed his mind. Insanely. He was twenty years old and this audience of revelers filled him with scorn. To sow confusion there, to get a rise out of them. . . . To preach. . . . To join his hands and say, "Brethren. . . ." To pull a newspaper from his pocket and intone the obituary column. . . . Or else. . . . Or else make their eyes pop and start a fight by saying: "Columbus was from Genoa, you stupid bastards, Genoa, understand? So take your damned song and stuff it!" But instead, Rocco asked in a serious tone: "Do you need a Democrat? Another one? Is that what you're looking for?"

What you could do. . . . What you could do with a voice like that! Why did that sentence come to his mind? He tried to think of something else to throw at that gray mass of faces. Behind the ranks of listening spectators he saw in the bar mirror his own silhouette, hard and dark, isolated. He saw that he was straighter, stronger than the people he spoke to. It was obvious that they were waiting for something. Not anything new. But some cliché. Again he hesitated. . . . There was still time. Afterwards, it would be simple. He raised his glass.

"A Democrat who only drinks lemonade, doesn't that scare you?"

They laughed and laughed; the clamor of a delighted audience. All that was left was for him to sign up. In a moment it was done. They gave him a form—date of birth, residence, profession. He wrote his whole name: Rocco Bonavia.

Rocco's was truly a dazzling success, a rise by leaps and bounds. Nothing went fast enough for him. He was driven by that desire to get ahead which raised him above the rest. He did not even give himself time to fall in love.

Having joined the Democratic Party by chance, and because deep within him something demanded that he go beyond his origins, fifteen years were enough to make Rocco into this powerful figure, this man whose decisions had become so weighty that they could influence voters in their choice of state governor or of mayor of New York, my friend Rocco, with whom I succeeded so well in worrying Aunt Rosie—"You'll see, one day he'll be president of the United States." She answered, "Please, please, Gianna, stop joking," in a pained voice, and we parted in anger. Fifteen years of uninterrupted work except for mass on Sunday, fifteen years of propriety, of well-cut suits, manicured hands, English spoken with a New York accent, fifteen years of culture so thoroughly acquired in any way possible and divulged discreetly, fifteen years of sobriety in gestures, because Rocco wasn't one of those gesturing Italians. The Italian disappeared, completely hidden. A real American. That was what Alfio thought: that was what never ceased to amaze him about this son of his who was always in motion, this dependable boy who came through the kitchens at God knew what time, sniffed a casserole on the way, swallowed something, dropped exhausted, and reappeared the next day at dawn, impeccable, close shaven—Rocco, his son, a real American who would revenge his father against the Letter from Palermo, against the poverty of his youth, the insults of Don Fofò, and even the weakness of Peppina. Yes, an American, that was also what had struck Pat O'Brady from their first meeting. Where did he get such assurance, that Rocco Bonavia? Moderate in everything, yet so influential with his compatriots that he could get their approval for whatever he wanted. "With what you have in your head. . . . With what you have in there," the Battler never stopped telling him. It was told how he had hired him only a few days after he signed up. And that was likely. For people knew a lot about Rocco's beginnings on Mulberry Street, and all agreed Pat O'Brady could not possibly have let a man like him get away. After all, he was only an obscure district chief, pretty much of a drunk, this Battler, and he had no importance beyond the votes he could bring in for the party. Bonavia, who represented youth, action, movement, could be useful to him. "Call me boss, will you?" He made Rocco his secretary.

No one had a right to sleep in 1938 with what was boiling up in Europe, those rumors of war, and anyone was crazy who said that if a fight broke out, if France and Germany really began to make fools of themselves, that America would intervene. What did she need that kind of trouble for, America? As if ten million unemployed weren't causing her enough misery. . . .

When Rocco Bonavia proposed "his idea" O'Brady could only open his mouth.

"How did you think of such an idea?"

"I don't really know. . . . I haven't thought about it. I have a lot of plans like that in my head."

"Genius! The boy's a genius. To think of such a think one night with his hands in his pockets, without raising his voice, like it's nothing at all." The idea went the rounds of the district. Rocco suggested putting pressure on certain workers at the employment office, his old comrades, not to help, not to look for work, not to do anything except for the unemployed who would agree to vote Democratic. Several members of the club wanted to know what kind of pressure this was to be. You wouldn't get what you wanted just by offering them a couple of free drinks. Money then? Little envelopes from time to time? Who was talking about that? Rocco declared that persuasion and well-chosen arguments would be enough. "Think of that!" O'Brady had exulted. After genius, honesty was the least expected thing among the followers of the Battler. Not that honesty wasn't appreciated, but. . . . Well, it was a good habit to get into. Funny fellow, Bonavia. . . . Hadn't he tried to convince Brad III that they'd have to be careful about their methods of putting on the pressure. Careful. . . . What did he mean exactly? He acted like he owned the world, this new secretary of theirs. Wasn't it very odd to use such language to Pat O'Brady, the picture of a shady operator, still efficient enough, in spite of alcohol, so that no leader in the city would have dared to displace him. And that was the man to whom Rocco said: "Twenty years ago, I could understand it. That was a time when a party could afford the luxury of being dishonest. Those methods don't work anymore. A party has to offer its members something more than a job and a goose on Christmas. It has to have an ideal, a program. Hope of new laws. It's time we got rid of that habit of free drinks. Money spent that way is pure loss, boss, believe me." Wasn't that crazy? That greenhorn, newborn Democrat, talking morality to old Brad. And in his own bailiwick, where he had been uncontested chief for so many years. Pat O'Brady's henchmen were amazed. At the end of a year all those people would begin to look sidewise at Bonavia, and the fact that the political chiefs were giving the new secretary of the district a close look changed nothing. Too hot-headed, with his crazy ideas. So Rocco had taken advantage of the visits of one of the influential members of the party to talk about consulting a public relations expert—a man named MacMannox—who was popular at that time. O'Brady had opposed that suggestion, and he was supported by the members of the club: "Mealy mouth!" "Hypocrite!" His photograph had often appeared in the papers. "A jumping jack, just about good enough to advertise canned peas. But a Party!"

But the influential member said: "I don't share your opinion, gentlemen. The idea is worth pursuing. . . ." It was an order. So much so that Rocco went to consult MacMannox the next day.

The interview began with a piece of personal advice: "It's necessary to be photogenic in your profession."

And, thinking it over, Rocco believed he was right.

Certainly Mr. MacMannox was not lacking in authority: he could not commit himself until he had visited the district offices. Good. If that was all it took to make him happy. "And then I'll let you know, Mr. Bonavia. . . ." And moving on with Rocco toward what he pompously called "your general area," MacMannox enthusiastically developed the idea of photography as an essential tool for political success.

Ah, if Rocco could have foreseen! Would he have accepted MacMannox' proposition? The assembly district. . . . But where the devil were they? In a vacant hotel on Bayard Street? That was where they'd set up their offices? What a mistake! Never in his life had Mr. MacMannox been inside such a place. Never. He was so upset that the tips of his moustache bristled, making little gestures of indignation around his mouth. "I beg of you, Mr. Bonavia, intervene with your leaders to give a new look to their activities. It's essential! Look at these corridors! They must be forbidden to beggars! Who are these people waiting for? You'd think it was a soup kitchen. And would you please tell me what's going on behind all those doors? Closed doors! Well, it's not too serious. Just have all this painted a light color, a very light color.

And have glass doors put in, yes, frosted glass. This effect of transparency gives confidence to the visitor and gives him the illusion of being part of the life of your offices. You'll never make a convert of a man you treat as an intruder. And don't pretend you feel comfortable here yourself. I feel as if I'd stumbled into the middle of a conspiracy. Nobody can persuade me that behind those doors people aren't talking in low seditious tones. Where can I be? Please understand. I'm not telling you to be as luxurious as the Chrysler Building. I'm just advising you to try to look like a bank, one of those nice little branches, open and bright and functional, where people of modest means put their money. You follow me? I don't think I can tell you much more, Mr. Bonavia. You have a long, long way to go if you want to seem respectable. Try to feel good, to feel honest, and you'll achieve it. Even if you have only ambition, pretend you only thirst after esteem. Esteem smells good. After that, you must buy some brains. That's necessary too. These days people set great stock in culture. If you can't get writers, university professors will do just as well. And then try to attract some well-known women. Look at these corridors. They really look sinister. What was I saying? Oh yes, women. You need a few women, Bonavia, that's absolutely necessary. Begin with newswomen. The others will follow."

Then Mr. MacMannox went slowly back toward his limousine, cautiously, one foot after the other as if there were really piles of filth to avoid in those corridors.

Rocco was of a reflective nature. He knew how to make use of advice which at first sounded disagreeable to him. That old tomcat MacMannox! Odd, Rocco said to himself, that it would have been necessary to consult him in order to see how wrong it all was. Of course everything needed changing. And not just the exterior of the Party; the interior as well. It must be purified, cleansed. What an adventure! Rocco's head was full of it. But that was for the future. For the moment, he must only listen and keep silent. Above all keep silent.

For three years Rocco reined his impatience. At least it was not
discernible to those who did not know him. With a circumspection rare in one of his years, he understood the extent of his powers
without ever putting them to use. One had to see him as he was
then—dark, hard, silent, and nevertheless clever at rousing interest
and sympathy. Very quickly all the Italians who lived in the district trusted him. At the same time no one knew them better than
he. Seated in Casa Alfio facing the street, Rocco could accurately
name one passerby out of every four. At work, he also knew who
his friends were, and how many children each had. Old Bonavia
couldn't get over it. He would stay and listen to him the whole
afternoon, his son, Peppina's baby, this *personage* whom people
stopped in the street? Sometimes by twos, by threes, in groups!
You know the head of the hospital. . . . And the principal of the
school. . . . My mother's still poorly. . . . My daughter, she's a
lovely slip of a girl who should have lessons. . . . Mr. Bonavia, if
you'd be so kind? Rocco omnipotent. It almost made Alfio laugh.
And the old woman, the one who waited for Rocco on Sundays
when mass let out, just to take his hand, softly, affectionately, calling him "*Roccucio mio.*" After her death, she left him her savings.
People had gossiped about it, of course. Then Rocco had made
a gift of the legacy to the parish priest so that he could put a new
statue in the church, and maybe a mosaic. The tongues of the
neighborhood were silenced, but those of Pat O'Brady's political
following were loosed. What a fellow that Bonavia was. Money
came into his hands and instead of giving it to "the organization"
he offered it to the first fellow that came along, to the priest at
the Church of the Transfiguration, another Italian, who would
spend it on baubles. And what did that church need with a mosaic? Bonavia was the only one who said it was cold, ugly, and
looked like a station waiting room, like the subway corridors. No
respect, these Italians. What a gang! In the face of this outcry,
Rocco had made a judgment of Solomon, an acrobatic feat which
left his audience panting. No hesitation: a little imagination and

a short visit to the priest of the Transfiguration assured him the final victory.

So. It was quite simple: Rocco no longer wished to offer that statue of Saint Rosalie which the priest said he needed, and he'd decided against the mosaic too. Had he changed his mind? the priest worried. Of course not. That was ridiculous and the good father could depend on his gift as before, but Rocco advised him to make a gesture towards his parishioners of the yellow race. He had some, didn't he? And, among the six thousand Chinese in the neighborhood, there must be some Catholics? What was he doing for them, what was he doing for the innumerable visitors who came to Chinatown each Sunday to see the sights? There were forty thousand Chinese spread through the city. Well? Well, why did the priest only buy statues of Saint Gennaro, Saint Lucia, and Saint Cataldo? What the hell did any of these statues mean to the Chinese? True, true, the priest agreed. But that was no reason to speak to him in such a way. What could have changed Rocco so? It hadn't been so long since the priest had given this boy a good kick in the behind. Terrible in catechism, always daydreaming. And here he was, with an astounding assurance, rebuking him about which statues he chose or didn't choose. How quick they were to turn into Americans in this country! "But my dear child, you don't understand at all. . . . Do you know that except for the Madonna, they recognize no one, my Chinese parishioners. You say they're Catholics. . . . Well, I wish it were true, but don't examine them too closely. Because with Catholics like that you can't go very far." Good. Well, a Madonna for them alone, and painted according to their ideas. All that was left was to find an artist. That wasn't asking for the moon, was it? Among the shopkeepers of Mott Street there was bound to be one who knew how to paint.

The priest went from hawker to hawker, pretending to be interested in the wares spread out on their trays. No, no, he wasn't interested in pajamas, no kimonos: he was looking for a painter, a Chinese painter. There were all sorts of craftsmen there, all

kinds of workers with a dizzying sense of lightness, of fragility, of
the transparent, the friable, of the weightless, of whatever hardly
exists, threads of silk, delicately folded rice paper; there were all
sorts of specialists in fans, in lanterns, incredibly complex wicker-
work, little miracles in straw, more twisted, more elaborate than
Spanish embroidery; there were lace makers who made buttons in
the shape of flowers and old men who carved signs, but no one
who knew of a painter. At the undertaker's, perhaps? Many families wanted to have a memento, something tangible, like a portrait. Let's try it. So the priest went to ring the doorbell of Lan
Hong Yin, the shabby undertaker, at whose place the dead were
left as in a morgue between faded screens and tattered partitions.
Lan Hong Yin hesitated. A painter, a painter! He had known
many in Peking, but were they still alive? So sorry, so sorry. . . .
The quavering voice of an old eunuch. . . . The visitor would do
better to talk to Wah Weng Sang, his competitor, who was a
young fellow. . . . And rich, too. So sorry, so sorry.

In front of Wah Weng Sang's place, the priest of the Transfiguration felt a ray of hope. The façade had recently been restored.
How could Wah Weng Sang not know a painter, he who put up a
luxurious pagoda and offered his clients as a consolation red-
lacquered vistas, soft continuous music, a regular movie set, and,
for the corpse, a sumptuous couch covered with crushed ice and
colored pink, because pink, so Wah Weng Sang believed, "pink
is the color for a happy death." Well? But Wah Weng Sang did
not know a painter. It was his countryman and neighbor, the
photographer Nelson Lee he usually went to. Fourteen dollars for
a black and white portrait, seventy-five for color, and no complaints from the family about the resemblance. A painter, a
painter! There was no one left but Shun Ying, the tattooer, who
did a little business with old clothes and also acted as a post office,
he was the only one in the neighborhood who knew how to handle
a brush. A former miniaturist, wasn't that just what the priest
needed? Lost his touch? Why should he? Why should Shun Ying
lose his touch? He wasn't one of those no-good fellows who used

an electric needle. He was a serious tattoo artist, who drew his
design without tracing, directly on the skin, with something like
a razor, and who then injected the coloring, saffron or Chinese
ink, with a needle which he used with a firm hand, piercing the
skin at an angle; in short, he was an artist. Did the Father know
that in Bangkok they said that an S tattooed between thumb and
forefinger would make a man invulnerable? And about the pearl
fishers? Did he know that they too said they were protected by
their tattoos? No doubt these stories of tattooing did not interest
him. . . . Well then. . . . The pleasure had been Wah Weng
Sang's. Indeed. . . . Wah Weng Sang among his red-lacquered
screens, Wah Weng Sang, the rich dealer in funerals, who bowed
to the reverend priest of the Church of the Transfiguration . . .
and bowed . . . and bowed.

To have studied Latin for fifteen years at the Seminary of Noto
and to come to such an end; to have worn, from the age of reason,
the soutane, and the round hat, the little cape, and the buckled
shoes, only to fail in such a parish. That was really a sad end. So
many things learned for nothing at the school. With no commit-
ment for the future. Head shaving optional. At twenty, military
service, after which they could change their minds, because a vo-
cation is not something you get on command. But the priest of the
Transfiguration had persevered, and he had never taken off his
soutane. For whom? For what? To do the bidding of this Mr.
Bonavia. A painter! How he carried on, that Rocco, and how he
had changed! Once he was so tender and affectionate, like the
children in Sicily. You acted like a nanny with those little fellows.
You wiped their noses, their behinds. And candy on the sly. To
think that Rocco had turned into an efficient American! A painter!
That's not so easy to find, you know. But since Shun Ying had
not yet refused, why not have faith in the tattooer? Why wait?
The command had been issued. . . .

Several months later—it was just when Rocco had decided to
run against Pat O'Brady in the district elections—Shun Ying's
canvas, finished at last, was hung over one of the altars of the

Transfiguration, with much ceremony. It scandalized the Irish parishioners. But they were well-known for their bias. They found it hard to tolerate that for the first time in the history of the district there was an Italian candidate in the elections, and the antipathy they felt for Rocco extended to all his projects. So, if he was the donor, he could go to the devil, him and his Virgin, now that he'd doublecrossed his boss.

From the Chinese Rocco received only praise. They all found that idol-like Madonna in the best of taste and they came in great numbers to admire her. She was the incarnation of their subtlest nostalgias: Shun Ying had painted the Virgin on a rather classic throne, decorated with precious stones and jasper, but he had seated her with the right leg folded under like a Buddha's, which was a little surprising, and made the other leg, the left, look rather lascivious under her blue skirt. Jesus was only able to sit on one of her knees, where he kept his balance as best he could. He was a bambini with a long pigtail, very yellow skinned, and oddly dressed in a robe embroidered with suns. To be sure, he was making a charming gesture with his little hands which played in the beard of a sort of bronze, who was wrinkled as a beggar's palm, and who, in a pinch, could pass for Joseph, but it was hard to get used to the third eye which each of these figures wore in his forehead. "In order to see beyond time and space," explained Shun Ying, who had drawn from Buddhist and Hindu sources to do this job.

When they admired their Virgin, the Chinese of Mott Street remembered her donor with gratitude. And Rocco Bonavia benefited from her glory, as the halo which she wore also encircled the new Democratic candidate's head with gold.

Then Alfio raised his arms to the sky: "You fool, where are your brains? Run for district chief against the Battler? You can't be thinking of it! Try to think what will happen if you lose: your political career compromised, me boycotted, you without work, the restaurant empty, no business, all of us in trouble. . . ." But his complaints went unheeded. Rocco, however, was not a man to ignore the fact that the voters of Italian origin made up half the district. "You hear me? To split half the votes in two, and not even. . . . Because even you can't believe they'll all vote for you, without exception. What then? Where's your majority? Where do you think you'll get your majority?" Obviously not from the Irish because they felt Rocco's treachery the most. "Well then? You damned idiot. . . . Well? The balance of votes, that indispensable majority, you think it will fall from the sky?" Alfio hadn't believed he could speak so well. But Rocco laughed in his face.

"Everything is possible. How do we know?"

Alfio gave his son a look of stupefaction. Wasn't he going to church a bit too often lately, or was he involved with a woman? With an appetite like his, he must be having an affair of some kind. But it was impossible to get anything out of him on this subject. Rocco's mouth was sealed. So what was the good of getting into such a state just because Rocco wouldn't listen to him any more.

"You're not yourself, my boy. Your mind is wandering."

Rocco's mind was hardly a step away, in the long street of the Chinese, the street of fan sellers and craftsmen, among the pushcarts, the merchants and the sailors looking for souvenirs. He knew very well that it was out of this disorder, those cries, those disputed prices, that a landslide would come to him such as no one dreamed of. Pat O'Brady's men could shout until their throats were sore, it would not stop the Chinese voting for Rocco Bonavia; he knew it.

So Rocco got the majority that Alfio had such doubts about. He became the district chief in the course of a day during which nothing terrible happened, but in which people sensed that at any moment things could have turned out badly.

Like sliding shadows, the Chinese came out of Mott Street, pouring out of the low houses, out of the shops with complicated signs and dragons, out of the narrow streets and dark alleyways and joined silently with the Italians going toward the polling place.

At the crossing, the policeman directing traffic watched them pass with a mixture of concern and disdain.

Nothing could stop those creatures who moved forward in a huddle, that was clear. Of a different race, they had a certain unity, they looked alike. The same strange sadness; the same tendency to stare into space, or air, or silence; the same taste for crowding together; the same olive color; the same hair, blacker than a crow's wing; and they all had in common that sense of inferiority which comes from being short in stature. It was obvious that they would all vote for the same man, it was so obvious that there were no scuffles. The partisans of Pat O'Brady went to the booths knowing they were losers, and the police might as well go back to the station house, several blocks from the Bowery, where they watched over the downtown area. For them, nothing much had happened, and Rocco wasn't particularly surprised either; he had taken his victory for granted.

It wasn't until later, much later, that he understood the importance of that day.

IV.

Oh America! If only you would send me uncles from your deep forests. FLAUBERT

"Finding work is harder than peeling skin off your back," said the letter.

Alfio had it reread three times. Calò also gave some news of Sicily. Rather gloomy news. The police will send you to the cooler for a yes or a no. And Calò had decided to marry a sixteen-year-old girl. Strange, that. . . . Sixteen! Alfio couldn't get over it. Sixteen, that was the age Calò had been when he'd left him at the gate of Civitavecchia with Baron di D.'s flock. . . . That was twenty-five years ago. Was there anything left today of that little Calò of those other days, anything of the fever burning in his eyes, of his hoarse, violent voice? Nothing, probably nothing to recall the child who had herded his flock and watched Alfio depart, biting his lips to keep from crying. What a kid that Calò was! No one to help him, nothing but the dogs, those great barkers whom Alfio could remember perfectly. Faded yellow skin, as if the sun and the dust had stuck to it. Pale eyes. Two starved mastiffs. "Historic dogs," Baron di D. said, who had traveled clear across Sicily to Montalbano di Elicona to get them. And he added, "They even frighten the Jesuits." Why historic? And what Jesuits? A very old story which Alfio couldn't quite remember. But the rest of his memories came back with a gripping clarity. He saw again the bag of oats brought to feed the animals on the trip, the balls of forage piled in a corner of the dark hold, the wild lamb, the one that would not let itself be led—hadn't she a crooked udder?—Calò's thinness, his way of sleeping on his stomach, his head in his arms, with a funny wrinkle at the corners of his lips; he even remembered the names—memory! How strange, really—even the names which he had always refused to call his dogs by. *Period* and *Comma!* He had to admit that Baron di D. was a funny man! What an idea. . . .

When Alfio had lost his temper saying "Nobody even knows what that means!" the Baron had suggested: *Here Boy* and *Help*. Another one of his crazy ideas! Imagine a shepherd crying *"Help"* to call his dogs! Finally, after one thing and another, Alfio kept on whistling for them as he always had, whether it pleased the Baron or not. Don Fofò had given him to understand that those were only jokes and shouldn't be taken literally. Which had confirmed Alfio in his opinion: funny fellows these D.'s, odd people, all eccentrics.

Humor inspired a holy horror in him.

He needed Calò's letter to make him remember his past. Sicily, Mr. Bonavia, Sicily comes back to you, Sicily denied, Sicily disgraced. Alfio felt only displeasure. He was doing his best never to think of Sicily. How could he succeed now that a letter had brought it all back to mind? "We are two, now, and we can no longer. . . ." How that brought back scenes of gruelling poverty, days without work, children in rags. "Living here is enough to suck the marrow from your bones, and for nothing, for less than nothing. . . ." Yes, that poverty, how well he knew it. It had been his own, and the horror that it had inspired in him never died. But the picture that he had of his past had changed little by little. A phenomenon he could not explain to himself. And all that was needed were a few lines written in an awkward hand to awaken his nostalgia? Alfio's country was composed of scarce jobs, long waiting, injustices, hard life, but it was also in Calò's language, his way of expressing himself, those sentences which stirred up all sorts of warm images, tender, cruel ones, it was in a tone which pierced his heart: "If you will get the necessary papers for us, if you can bring us over, Agata and I, you will be as the living hand of God placed upon our hearts. . . ." wrote Calò.

And then the letter no longer aroused animosity and rancor in Alfio's heart. On the contrary. It made him happy. It inspired in him an irrepressible desire to talk, and even to talk with his hands a little, to confide, to tell the news, to say to someone: "You know I have a brother, Calò. A brother who wants to emigrate. . . ." A sensuous wellbeing, a comfort. From the most distant, the most forgotten places ambitions awoke which he had thought dead forever, Sicilian hungers, something despotic, something dominating, a spirit of family. Abruptly he saw, as if in a dream, a Bonavia behind every counter on Mulberry Street: Calò was running the Italian drygoods store, the one whose proprietor wanted to retire; Calò was selling machines for making ravioli, gnocchi, spaghetti; he became the exclusive distributor of coffee mills, cheese graters, lasagna rollers which the housewives of the district used so much. Everything could be found in Calò's store: portraits of Mother Cabrini, paintings of Vesuvius, and biographies of the saints in the Paradise Edition. He was a wonder, that Calò. . . .

Oh, that letter! It was like oxygen in his blood! Alfio's features expanded: he trembled with joy. That sixteen-year-old Agata, that child bride! A woman with deep eyes, smooth hair, a woman wearing her hair as they did in Sólanto with a neat knot, very round, set low on her neck! What a blessing! Little Agata! Couldn't she take care of the Italian grocery? It was just a few steps from Alfio's place and only Italian products were sold there. If he helped her a little, she'd do very well, that child, and the position of the Bonavias would become even better. We. . . . He must bring them over. Which he hadn't even considered earlier.

It was Rocco who brought it all to pass, with a wave—a real wave, this time—of his hand. Immigration had never been more restricted than in the year 1939. But how could anyone resist Rocco's persistence, his obstinancy? He wore his most agreeable manner. He pushed through doors with a calm gesture, looking polite and elegant. Harsh voices greeted him: "Why can't these God-damned Italians stay home, why do they always want to come to the United States?" Their peasant skills wouldn't be any good to them in New York, that much was clear enough. And Rocco agreed. He repeated: "Very clear, very clear. . . ." with an air of conviction.

He was a past master in the art of getting what he wanted while seeming to agree.

Several months later, Mulberry Street threw itself into welcoming two more Bonavias, brought over quite legally.

But it must be admitted: three of them arrived. Agata had given birth to a boy on the crossing. Unexpectedly. . . .

To hide her advanced pregnancy had not been an easy task, and she had not accomplished it painlessly. This child, this belly which threatened to compromise her departure, to spoil everything—she had decided not to mention it to anyone, even her husband. Suppose he'd refused to take her with him? And if he'd left her there to wait, as had happened to so many women of Sólanto, solitary souls more to be pitied than widows, poor creatures living on hopes, rare letters, money orders which arrived or did not arrive, abandoned women. . . . Why take such chances?

In Palermo she found such a corset as she would not have found in any other city in the world. A pitiless vise. An armor so complex that it defies description with its laces, its hooks, enough to frighten a torturer from the Inquisition. Agata buckled it on without the least concern. The effect she obtained made the almost unbearable discomfort worthwhile. She could neither sit nor stoop, but her thickening waist passed unnoticed. Calò himself suspected nothing. The fact that she had never been willing to undress in front of him made it all much easier.

So they sailed; Calò very sincere and without the least suspicion of his imminent paternity. Agata very stiff, bearing the weight of her secret as best she could. Once on board, she could hardly last three days. She thought she was going to give birth at any moment. But Agata was the sort who once she made up her mind nothing could alter it. It was necessary to hold out; hold out she did. Is it any surprise that the child seemed in such a hurry to be born? What was the matter with him? Did he want to come into the world while they were still in sight of land? In mid-ocean would be the right time to tell the ship's doctor, to tell Calò and let the devil take the hindmost. There would be no more risk. But while they were near a port? Would they reverse their course? She was afraid so. So she must eat little, barely move, and keep cool.

Three women shared Agata's cabin, three Germans who did not tempt her to drop her disguise. One was very old and stayed quietly in her corner. Had she been the only one, Agata might have risked a confidence. But the others! She could hardly believe her eyes. Two women who wore tight trousers, never stopped smoking, eating spice biscuits, boastfully comparing and admiring the flatness of their breasts, all things which filled Agata with unsurmountable disgust and the ladies with immoderate thirst. They passed their nights drinking from bottles they kept in their suitcase.

Agata sought refuge in her berth, where she closed the curtains modestly. There, she set upon the hooks and laces of her corset in silence, she let them out with a deep sigh, then she lay unmoving, contemplating this bewildering thing, this swelling, this strange mountain which had pushed itself up in the middle of her body.

One evening, when there was more noise than usual in the cabin because the two Germans were practicing shameless dance steps together, there was no longer any possible doubt: the child was going to be born. She longed not to believe it, she turned and turned again, tried to sleep, repeating to herself, "blue as the night, as the night, as the night." But just as the phrase was beginning to take effect, a pain made her sit up with a start, as if two blades had pierced her from either side.

Then, restraining herself no longer, she opened the curtains of her berth, held her hand up for silence, and said simply, "Would you please help me to give birth, Signora?"

She hardly noticed the flabbergasted expression of the others who, interrupted in their dance, hurriedly fled from the cabin. As one hesitated, the other pulled her away: "Go on—come on. People who get in to such situations—it's their own fault. She made her bed—let her lie in it!"

This adolescent who asked in a schoolgirl's voice: "Would you help me to give birth?" as if she were asking for some jam, shocked them inordinately.

The door slammed after them.

Happily, the third passenger was calm and competent. When she saw her approaching with a decided step, Agata suddenly thought of Celestina, the old woman with the leeches, who also acted as midwife sometimes in Sólanto. She too walked with such a step—the stride of a good sister—when you met her with her jar under her arm, always worrying about changes in the weather and speaking of her leeches as one speaks of investments. What would she have said, Celestina, what would she have done had she been here? Agata imagined herself back in Sicily between her mother, saying Hail Marys as she always did on important occasions, and the mother of Calò, the one stroking her hair, the other holding her hand.

But they were not there, and Agata was in terrible pain. Then she really began to cry, unable to stop herself.

It was all over by the time Calò arrived. A son? He didn't understand. He had been wakened with a start, shaken. The ship's doctor. "Who's in labor?" They said it was Agata. The other men, his cabin mates, were bent double with laughter. "They were crazy!"

And Agata was crazy, too. She began to cry when she saw him, to beg him not to be angry, not to scold her, that she had done what she had to do.

The old German woman looked as if she understood it all and was very much amused.

She smiled at him. The baby had been washed in a basin intended for vomiting passengers. He had been wrapped in a napkin from the dining room. So his first initials were those of a steamship company: the happiest of omens.

When the first moments of joy and surprise were over, the troubles began. The next day the Captain came to say that it would be necessary to make the legal arrangements and to baptize the child as soon as possible. That was how things were done on shipboard. As he wished to show his gratitude to that leader of his new country, Calò decreed that his son should be called Theodore. "Theodore, you know, like Roosevelt." He only realized his mistake after the ceremony was over. The Roosevelt these days was not Theodore, he was told. "Foul mouths," thought Calò, who believed they were mocking him. But they insisted, "The President's name is Franklin, Franklin D. Roosevelt. The other one, Theodore, has been dead for twenty years."

"Are you sure?"

The captain looked at him and laughed.

"There's no doubt of it. Come come. Don't look so miserable. Theodore's a good name. You'll get used to it, you'll see. Anyway, it's too late to change. But didn't you know that the President's name was Franklin?"

"And who would have told me?" Calò answered furiously. "Your kind learns by traveling. We Sicilians, we live with animals until we get to be like them: halfwits, cattle. . . . I know it. I know I'm a halfwit."

That evening Calò was sorry he had said that the Sicilians were cattle. But the harm was done. He had a bitter taste in his mouth.

Agata said: "You're not going to make yourself sick over a silly thing like that, are you?"

"True," Calò sighed. "No one can know everything."

And they finally began to laugh together; to laugh over the child named Theodore, to laugh at the Germans who came with a bottle of cognac to pay them a visit in the infirmary, and to laugh at the song, "Ach, ach, Theodore" which the girls sang to cheer them up.

To these two who stayed snuggled together, belly to belly, Calò made some slightly lewd jokes: "At least we can be sure you aren't pregnant. My, my, look who I would have had to travel with!"

"Let's celebrate, let's celebrate," they said, their voices vague.

Agata in her bed pulled at her first cigarette. She rubbed her eyes and laughed as she blew out the smoke.

She was only a little tired, a little drunk.

Calò's arrival, his establishment in Mulberry Street marked a pause in Alfio Bonavia's patient work of self-denial. It was like a sentimental journey into the past.

Seeing his brother again, hearing him, living in close quarters with him was like finding the past again, burying himself in it and measuring just how precarious, how cold and how irremediably foreign the present was.

For Rocco, it was a more complicated venture. He was confronted with a way of life he had never known before. Agata's candor, her enthusiasm delighted him. She saw paradise in a bread crumb. And when she said: "But you have everything here, everything!" she put such fervor into it that one hung on her words. She had only to mention the most ordinary object for her words and her particular language to invest the forms of a chair, a table, no matter what, with warmth, with sunlight.

How had Sicily, the black island, the accursed island which in his father's oft told tales, appeared to Rocco as a shame glued to his skin, how had Sicily produced this child, wondering and wise as a Minerva? To hear her, she seemed to have crossed the ocean only to reinvent daily life and snap her fingers at what America had taught him of convention and good manners.

The Agata who settled down in New York was very careful to lose none of her old habits. The ease, the comfort that lay at everyone's fingertips, the hairdressers, the electric dryers, the stores full of elevators, the movie theaters lit up like altars before which Calò stood gaping with admiration, the great sparkling city spread out there beyond the neighborhood of low houses and narrow streets, the abundance, all that was self-evident.

But nevertheless, around her mirror she arrayed the thirty-two pictures of Saint Rosalie which she had been collecting since childhood—Saint Rosalie in her grotto, Saint Rosalie in a golden gown, Saint Rosalie chin in hand, thoughtful; in engraving, in photos, in black and white, in color, bordered with lace—another half dozen of Agatha, the saint of Catania, an amputated breast in each hand, and then, in silver paper, a beautiful Lucia, very erect and moving forward victoriously in spite of the knife thrust through her throat.

So much paper seriously frightened Alfio, the more so because Calò, a great smoker, threw matches everywhere.

"Your saints will set the house on fire!" he said without malice. "You'd better get rid of some of them."

But, Agata replied, "That is no way to talk," and there was such severity in her voice that poor Alfio was transfixed with shame. What had he done? She wasn't a fanatic. She never talked about prayers, orisons, litanies. No. And that mirror with its garland of pictures was no oratory before which she communed with herself. No. The relationship which existed between Agata and her pinned-up saints was much more complicated. It was a constant exchange, secret, composed of love and unexplained quarrels.

When, for some reason she never explained, she had a grudge against one of her protectresses, she turned the guilty one's face to the wall. One day, in a rage, she made St. Lucia do penance under the night table.

A cleaning woman went and asked Alfio what she should do about it. Should she throw the picture out or leave it there? Very cautiously, Alfio Bonavia asked his sister-in-law: "Why is Saint Lucia in the chamber pot?"

"She doesn't deserve any better."

That was Agata's answer. When All Saint's Day came, she turned the house upside down. Theo, her little Theo, her wonderful boy, her dream, her heavenly reward must wake up in a bed covered with gifts. And everyone must believe that these toys were sent to him by distant uncles, cousins, aunts one scarcely knew, all dead for a long time, who had sent him these gifts from Heaven. Yes, so it must be. And everyone must believe it so that the child would be convinced. And not just Calò. Alfio and Rocco too. "What uncles? What aunts?" they asked themselves, bewildered, the two New York Bonavias who had almost forgotten the names and surnames of the relatives left behind in Sicily. But how could anyone resist that white skin, that stern profile, those two deep passionate eyes, those volcanoes, those blue grottoes? Surprising Agata. See how she even raised up the Dead.

Christmas day was something else again. She wanted to make a crèche. Stooping over every drawer in the house, over the trunks in the attic, opening and despoiling the cupboards, she declared she could find none of the things she needed. Fascinated, bothered, then distressed and annoyed, Alfio and Rocco followed her search. What was missing? Everything. What everything? In spite of Rocco's offer, his assurance that *everything* could be bought in New York, Agata went on insisting that "What is missing can be found but not bought." She said she couldn't possibly make a crèche with nothing but things bought in stores.

Alfio, deeply insulted, went to ask his brother what all this meant. Calò explained. In Sicily, the Infant Jesus for the crèche is kept from year to year. How could Alfio have forgotten? Superstition forbids throwing them away or not using them. But what was the matter with a new one? Even when they were poor, even on the dole, they had gone in a body, the whole family, to buy the best there was for this. They had paid for their trip, left for Palermo. Had Alfio forgotten the shops of the via Bambinai?

Didn't he remember going there, himself, looking for the waxen Jesus? That was the specialty of the craftsmen who worked in the via Bambinai. Well then? Faced with such a wide selection, decorating a crèche became a complicated affair where a family's past and present met face to face. A mysterious and unpredictable occasion.

That year's Jesus, the most recently purchased, was plainly the only one worthy of being placed in plain view between the ox and the ass. The other Jesuses, those of earlier Christmases, were collected and buried under a mountain of moss-colored paper or even of earth—that varied each year—which served as material for the foundation and the scaffolding. The way in which they were placed indicated the esteem in which they were held. Had the year been a good one? The little sugar Jesus whom one could only praise got only a bit of straw, a shrub, a little angel for his burden, nothing, or next to nothing. But the Jesuses of the dark years which had been rampant with bitterness, rage, hunger, long nights of empty hopes, those Jesuses, alas, Christmas after Christmas bore the whole crèche on their shoulders.

Alfio shrugged, but what was to be done? Agata refused to melt into the New York landscape. She must have her past, her customs, her dialect, like a snail its shell. She carried them everywhere with her. Nothing in the world could make her renounce them. Eat differently, why? Change one's hair? Not be herself any more? Why? Why? She didn't understand.

Rocco was the only one to encourage her. He admired her vitality, her frankness. Hiding their origins had been the preoccupation of his father and all the emigrants he had known. Hiding in talk, in selling. Hiding. Deception with every breath. Become American no matter what. But Agata, she refused to hide, or to deceive. She continued to wear her villager's knot braided into a bun and pinned to the back of her head, her thick stockings which she preferred to fine ones, and she had to have a warm kitchen with a smell of tomato sauce to make her happy. She was the death knell, the antithesis to all deception. And then, what a worker. . . . In the Italian grocery, the work she got through. . . . The clients argued over her, adoring her. They wouldn't have anyone but her. But Agata didn't let it go to her head. She turned up her nose at triumph as she turned up her nose at New York, impersonally, without explanations. She sniffed at success, she prodded it with a prudent paw like a cat whom he rain has made mistrustful. And that too pleased Rocco. That prudence, that mistrust. He said so to everybody. "She's my aunt. . . ." he repeated, amused by people's startled looks.

His aunt? That little girl? Then he insisted: "Yes, my aunt. Isn't she fantastic?"

He brooded about her. He carried her in his heart like the truth. He could have loved her. Madly. But his work protected him, and chopping a path through the New York jungle was a job that kept him busy enough to protect him from such dangers. And then, who needs that kind of a drama in the family? He allowed himself neither enchantment nor tenderness. He had a great need to succeed.

In Europe, war had just broken out.

PART
THREE

I.

Remember how mournful I am and it will soften your heart. PAUL CLAUDEL

No, sorrow is not shipwreck. It does not engulf, it unfolds and it strikes. In a flash it makes one feel emptied of blood and breath, legs amputated, a gnawing in the stomach—that's sorrow. That's it, and it is prayer that bursts forth without one's knowing why, like the cry that answers the rockfall, the avalanche, the nightmare. "My God, what have I done to you? Why do you take from me that which was part of you? . . . Why?

Again I see the clear sky of a December morning. I see it all: the moment of exaltation caused by the brilliant light of the sun, by the sharp cold, by the transparency of the air encouraging a deceptive calm, a blind confidence, followed almost immediately by a brutal foreboding caused by nothing at all, but expressed by this phrase repeated ten times, twenty times between Palermo and Sólanto: "Wherever you are from now on" that phrase which came from some secret chamber, "Wherever you are from now on, you, my life, my strength," repeated and amplified by the rolling of the train, "Wherever you are from now on, remember what we have been, have been, have been," repeated ceaselessly until I was on the station platform of Santa Flavia, where a peasant's brutal "Hey!" stopped me as I was about to walk in front of his cart.

At Sólanto, though there had been neither cold nor frost, winter had nevertheless stiffened the garden, given it a haughty immobility and spread a crystalline hardness over the earth which roused my forebodings again.

It was almost three o'clock, and we were on the terrace listening to the slap of the waves when the man came toward us. We saw him far away. He made conscientious zigzags along the path, then climbed the worn steps cautiously, being careful not to slip, and we watched him, fascinated by the methodical manner with which he performed this simple task. We remained standing on the terrace, a little numbed by the wind and the sound from the sea.

When he arrived at our level the man hesitated. He was a *cara-biniere*, looking like all the rest with his cap with the cracked visor, his dirty skin, and the wavering step of a comedian seeking a pose to strike. He did not know what gesture to make as he said "Dead. . . ."

I did not understand. Dead? Who was dead and what did that voice want, droning on about the Greek Front, cardboard shoes, an error in firing: "An army of wretchedness, Your Lordship. . . . The men landed without arms." Antonio? Was he talking about Antonio? Antonio cheated, betrayed? Impossible! It's a lie. I repeat it in my thoughts, I say it aloud, again. It's just a mistake, a terrible joke. The sweat runs down my arms. I look at Baron di D. who has turned up the collar of his coat and suddenly in a strangled voice cries: "Get out of here, soldier. Please, get out of here!" But the man continues. Nothing can stop him and I can't stop looking at his lips which are bent upon wounding us; his mouth seems smugly conscious of its own importance. His voice unwinds, it is a rope around our necks. His manner is as determined as a firing squad. He is killing us. He feels powerful as lightning. For once he is the one who is listened to, and another is the victim, the young man who stopped a bullet down there in the Greek mountains. "We must be resigned. . . ." The words strike me, cold and round. They hammer at me. I hear bells in my ears. "Cardboard shoes. . . . Cardboard shoes." Where can I sit down? Baron di D. walks up and down. You would think that a squall was blowing him from one side of the terrace to the other. Is he going to fall? He can be heard repeating "Bastards . . . bastards. . . ." while the *carabiniere* continues to deliver his message with great patience: "No ammunition. . . . An oversight. The fault of the higher command." It is absurd, unbearable. How can words hurt so much? Never will I forget that stumbling methodical voice. "One of our units was bombarded by Savoia Marchettis. . . . A mistake, Your Excellency. . . . A real mess. . . ."

To be rid of that voice, of its slackness, its murderous indifference. I wait for it to give out. And if it was possible after all? If the words which leave a wound, if the irremediable could be wiped out like the sounds on a tape recorder?

A crazy hope is born in a moment of silence, during a second of hesitation that trumpets more loudly than a fanfare. The man is silent. I pounce on that absence of words, I thrust myself into it, I beg. Voice, I beg of you, spare me. . . . Say no more. Let me find once more the pictures of another time, our beaches, our solitudes, the violences of our bodies, our musical sunlight. Three insistent notes rose to my ears, enveloped me, ran inside me, scraps of a tune I loved. Antonio appeared before me, his body, so long and slender. But what has he come here for? The truth is in the faces that surround me. It is in the sadness I see in them. Antonio is dead. My sorrow tells me and the broken cry of the gulls repeats it over the sea: he is dead. These words will become my secret dwelling place. They will rise with me each morning. I will put them on like an old garment. They will be wherever I go. Wherever. I will see them in the folds of a blanket, in the unbearable fluttering of a curtain in the wind, in everything which falls and rises like a body breathing, in all that struggles and beats like a heart. I am afraid. I will never be free of this.

The man leaves. It is too simple. Something is going to happen that no one has thought of. A cataclysm. The sun will open and swallow him. Not just him. All of us. Yes, all of us. But nothing. Gone. Fled, leaving on the table the notice, folded neatly. How slow I still am at understanding: Antonio will not come back. I am alone. I give myself to those words, to their faultless emptiness. They welcome and enclose me. They weigh as much as an arm around my shoulders: I will never know an embrace as lasting.

That was my last visit to Sólanto. But before closing forever this chapter of my life, I must mention again the desolating horror at the thought of Antonio in his final state, exhausted, staggering, defeated, caught in the trap set by his own country which sent him to the battlefield shod in cardboard. How different from the memory of him in his strength, with his awareness of it and also his supreme indifference, with his slightly dragging walk, his bantering air and the coquetry with which he chose clothes that were a little too big for him as if he were afraid to show off the length of his muscles, of his legs, the sharp angle of his shoulders, to the point where everything he wore hung loose, slipped, and gave the impression of barely staying on his body. His companions, they tell me, were young boys.

There had been, in the midst of the battle, the son of a coachman in Potenza, a boy whose harmonica had been taken away from him because he played it ceaselessly and because he could not understand that his pleasure was dangerous in these circumstances; a Sardinian shepherd; two from the Piana dei Greci who claimed to know the enemy's tongue and probably did; two more boys from Lucania, three farmers, a young traveling salesman (the only survivor) who said to Antonio, "I know you, I sold you a bag of figs one day on the Piazza Bellini,"—taken altogether then, there were no more than about a dozen from the south who for the most part had no notion of the military craft.

But even if they had known more it would have done them little good, for there was so little ammunition that they could only shoot after specific authorization from Antonio. And I have often found that detail consoling as if the somber ceremonial demanded that these young men, with death at their heels, ask their officer for permission to defend themselves. "Sir, may I fire, please?" made it easy to imagine how a battle conducted in these terms is stripped of flourish—deprived of their status as warriors, of the conquered, making of them a troop of lost children, deserted, cut off on the top of a mountain, deciding to resist to their last bullet so as not to risk a punishment, and going thus to their death.

Perhaps Antonio was aware of the unusual character of that drama, of its scope. Perhaps at the moment of death, this very poverty had appeared to him as a privilege.

He was such a strange boy.

With Antonio gone, the Baron di D. was almost unrecognizable; his coloring turned leaden, his eye hardened and his voice became cruel and cold.

He was invaded and swollen by an infernal hatred. Some of his actions—such as refusing to have the name of his grandson inscribed on the Monument to the War Dead—marked him for reprisals. For everything was known, everything was repeated, and Sicily too had its informers.

It was madness to behave so. Did he do it on purpose? From the windows of the castle, at certain hours, broadcasts of Radio London could be heard. And his pianos? He had got rid of them. That's what sorrow does, unable to stand anything that recalls the past. But why burn them? And why in the garden? From afar the coast guard had taken those bonfires for signals and made inquiry about them. Seen from the sea the flames which rose to the door of the castle looked frightening, terrible. It had been talked about as far as Palermo.

In short, Baron di D.'s indignation was such that he seemed to be inviting punishment, as if he had only one fixed goal, to finish his days in Ustica or in some other island prison where enemies of the government were sent, chained four by four, *schiavettoni* on their wrists.

Deportation. That was what Don Fofò dreaded. And his despair, which was great—after all, Antonio's death had been a crushing blow for him too—grew worse from the fear that his father's vehemence inspired in him. Fofò was not afraid of the risk to himself. At the first warning—the mountain, its caves, its secret ways. He would escape; he would find refuge in some cabin where he would not even have to fear solitude. A number of outcasts, outlaws, lived up there in rock hollows, in the beds of dried up streams, so intimately dug into the desert landscapes that no force could get them out. And all his life Don Fofò had been the outcasts' friend. He protected them, employed them, and sometimes welcomed them to Sólanto, where he hid them. The mountain had always been Don Fofò's habitat. He knew every stone of it, every spring, every well, every woman: he felt at home there. But his father? Could he be exposed to such a life?

There was the Baron di D.'s age, his sorrow which withered him like a terrible wound, the insomnia he battled against night after night. And if that had been all! But there was always a greater obsession eating the old man, a desire to outrage those whom he considered responsible for Antonio's death, to provoke them, to throw his hatred straight in their teeth, that demoniac hatred inspired in him by the representatives of order, of the law, of the government. What was the good of deluding oneself? Nobody would stand for the Baron di D. up there. The Mafia would never tolerate among them the presence of a man who had lost control of himself to the point where the blood rushed to his face at the mere sight of a *carabiniere*.

The Mafia (one hardly dares to write that dishonored, lugubrious word—all blood and thunder—but how can one avoid it?), the Mafia, it must be accepted, held the mountain and everything depended on them. Silence, prudence, pretending, simulation, these were what they demanded of those whom they protected. And it was just those strategies which the Baron wanted no more part of. All the strength that remained to him he put into his opposition. It made little difference to him what came of it. Dangers? Risks? He didn't care. The future no longer existed. Antonio had been killed. A man of his blood had died, the victim of incompetence, of the murderous madness of this government. It was an assassination. The time had come to say so. He would arouse the people.

Yes, Baron di D. was no longer the same. A torrent of vengeance had engulfed him.

And once more the inhabitants of Sólanto participated in the drama being staged in their master's heart, identified with him. All, without exception, went into mourning for Antonio.

Incidents multiplied. Some were cruel, like the kidnapping of a young official of the government who had come to the region to rest for a few days and who disappeared without trace. Others were frankly comic. Such was the experience of an old man of Sólanto at the opening of a road which the people of the countryside would have been happy to do without. What did they want with it? The government continually talked up "panoramic highways" as the cure for all ills, and the newspapers made a great noise about the road which was opened that day at Sólanto, with many speeches, to a traffic made hypothetical by gasoline rationing and the absence of tourists. But a car full of officials came from Palermo for the occasion. They exuded an extreme joviality. They had to shake gold-laced sleeves and tasseled hats to make people forget strikes, mutinies, and a lost empire.

They had taken a devilish lot of trouble, those people. They must be repaid, no? The past year had brought only unhappy surprises and 1943 didn't look much better. An expeditionary force of Italians on the Don. More than a hundred thousand men, they said. Well, the emphasis placed on this inauguration, the excessive oratory, the forced smiles seemed like a kind of penitence. Italian workers were leaving for Germany by the trainful. When they failed to please their employers, dogs were set on them. Everyone knew it. Everyone! Guns with only one shot in them, old cannons left from the campaigns of 1896 which had been recalled into service, ministers who trafficked in equipment, generals who were money-lenders or else practical jokers like that Soddu who composed music for a film more capably than he commanded his men on the Greek front—not to mention the superior minds, the government financiers who worked for their own interests and through all the lands of the Empire held properties to dream of, hoards, fortunes! Yes, everyone knew it; one had only to listen. The people of Sólanto watched these officials from Palermo in their black boots with astonishment. There were tall ones, fat ones, all that under a molten sun, and not knowing what to do to produce an air of glory. Long faces. How out of place and ill at ease they were before the silent ranks of mourning peasants. What could they do? What could they expect from such an audience? An ugly look about them. The muteness of the crowd increased the nervousness of the functionaries.

The least embarrassed, a young man who had a good opinion of himself and his functions in the Department of Bridges and Highways, felt that—according to the directives from Rome—to establish direct contact with these people it was only necessary to gain the sympathies of an old man who stood there among the onlookers. The young bureaucrat went to get him. The old one looked at him coming like someone who does not understand very well what is expected of him. Why this friendliness? He heard himself addressed as "ancestor" and "forefather" and "grandpa," and this familiarity displeased him. Then he was pulled by the sleeve to the platform and asked to sit down. The peasant continued chewing in silence on a piece of bread he had pulled from his pocket.

This was indeed a very old man—tanned, wrinkled; his head was constantly tilting, sometimes to the right, sometimes to the left, as if his enormous cap weighed too much or he were listening to

the noises of the earth. He was questioned. This road represented
real progress. What did he think of it? The peasant listened,
smiled, showing a few yellow teeth, but it was plain that his inter-
viewer's enthusiasm left him cold. Come, come, wasn't this like a
miracle to a man who must remember the paths of the old days,
the mule tracks and the torment of the dust. The old man nodded
approval. Dust? Yes. He remembered that. The man in the black
shirt continued his tirade, repeated several times the words "ve-
hicle-worthy," rolling the words in his mouth as if to linger over
them; then going on, he added that there was much to be said
for Fascism, and the oldest peasant in the countryside, the wise
old man whom he had seated beside him, would certainly agree to
telling into the microphone all the good things he had found in it.
"Come, now, grandpa, don't we have a happy life here in Italy?"

Grandpa let himself be coaxed for a long time. He repeated,
"Italy. . . . Italy," still chewing his bread. His hesitations were at-
tributed to his age. Here was a man almost one hundred years old.
Through half-closed eyelids the peasant looked at the officials,
then at the microphone, then at the officials again. He moved his
lips, he was going to speak, everyone was sure of it. But something
still held him back. Foreboding? A fear? What? He was bombarded with questions. "Is the whole world really listening?" he
asked solemnly. "Are people listening, even in America, even in
England?" "Yes indeed, yes, my good fellow. You'll be heard clear
to the ranks of the enemy! Come now, say what you have to say."

The old peasant rose and everyone was silent.

He pulled his cap clear down to his eyes, made the sign of the
cross, squared off in front of the microphone which he grasped in
both hands, and cried in an anguished voice: "America! America!
Are you listening to me?" There was a silence during which the
young man from Bridges and Highways began desperately to regret
his initiative. In the first row, in their beautiful uniforms the big-
wigs were alert. Then the old man howled as loud as he could:
"This is Sicily! Help!" And he cried again: "Help! . . . Help! . . .

Help! . . ." Three times. Then he climbed down from the platform with a satisfied grunt. A real scandal.

Outrage, irony, it was all so alien to the mood of the time that
with the help of witnesses they succeeded in passing him off as
mad. They also mentioned a high fever. But in high places the incidents in Sólanto became the subject of discussion. A connection
was quickly made between the poor morale and the influence of
Baron di D. It must be cut short. An underling was sent to make
an inquiry on the spot.

He was treated as an intruder.

Sólanto appeared to him like a deserted fortress, like a dead city
with its alleyways empty, its doors closed, its narrow dark stair-
ways seeming to harbor cutthroats. What a country! Where were
the people? Furtive shadows disappeared as soon as you caught
sight of them. And then it was sinister that a whole town should
be in mourning. Why those cards on the doors? "For our son."—
"For our beloved child." What had happened here? Were the inhabitants all gone, all killed? Senseless. The sudden irrefutable
appearance of Death on every doorstep. Death, death, as far as the
eye could see. Could he have imagined, that underling, that the
mourning in which the whole village was joined was for Antonio?
How could anyone understand who was not a Sicilian? And why
should it be surprising that the underling was not? A recent decree
forbade any functionary born on the island to work there. That
was in order to put a stop to a growing discontent. An idea of Mussolini's. He was beginning to have enough of those southerners
who were always underfoot.

So law and order were in the hands of newcomers for whom the
local customs were as troublesome as deviltry, bewildered visitors
like the underling who sweated before the door of the castle of
Sólanto. But was that really the entrance to the castle? Everything
looked alike in this maze, everything was confused in the same
hostility. And then the poorest houses sometimes had doors like
citadels. The underling did not know what to think. Sweat beaded
his forehead. Suddenly a woman passed, a mute shadow, as if

masked in lead. Was this the home of the Baron di D.? She acted
as if she did not understand. Sicilians! Brutish goats!

The earth, the walls, every stone of Sólanto exhaled a heat
which increased his discomfort, increased the anguished indecision
of the man who waited in a torrid square in black shirt and boots.
What a country, good God, what an end-of-the-world sort of place!
And what a fiery wind blew here! He wiped his forehead. At that
moment, as if by enchantment, a man appeared, lying on a wall
in irritating immobility: the gatekeeper. What was that fellow
doing there and why hadn't he made himself known sooner? You'd
hardly leave a dog outside in such heat. But even after he had
hailed this odd fellow and had asked him to announce him to the
Baron di D. the gate remained closed, and the official remained
outside waiting to be received.

When he returned to Palermo he reported on his mission. He
told about the castle, with its endless corridors, its paved vesti-
bule, cool as a grotto; he told of the study and the high book-
shelves, he told especially about the large round tables where publications of all kinds were piled up, even reviews of British origin.
He repeated the word "British" several times as if to show his
superiors that nothing has escaped him.

Then he reported on the case of the gatekeeper who didn't seem
to know how to give the Roman salute—a very suspicious fellow!—
and about his own decision, the underling's, to give an example to
that tribe of degenerates. He entered the salon with a brisk step,
his hand raised. He recited from memory the phrase with which
Baron di D. welcomed him: "Spare me your buffoonery. . . ." A
man who was apparently unable to speak without some outbreak
of bad temper. His whole attitude had suggested that there would
be some sort of incident. No cross questioning was possible. No
notebook either. Baron di D. had snatched it from his hands. "I
have every intention of speaking freely in my own home." A mad-
man. Sick.

Then, in several well chosen words, the underling had extolled
the sublime sentiment which must dwell in the hearts of a family

which had given a son to the Fatherland. And the Baron had cried "Louder! . . . I'm deaf." He held a hand to his ear. But none of the previous reports had referred to his deafness. They even spoke of him as a music lover. Well? Was he being mocked? Useless. . . . "I am deaf." Those were his words. Suddenly the door opened. His son, no doubt. The same stern look. He too wore no party insignia.

The underling's report represented Don Fofò as being at least as suspect as Baron di D. He also might be held responsible for what went on in Sólanto. And as for the Monument to the War Dead. The underling was quite proud of the question he had asked point blank: "How can the father of an officer who died on the field of honor refuse to have his sacrifice perpetuated, engraved in stone?" The answer was not long in coming: "I don't want to serve as an example."

Horrible people. Trash. Oh, you wanted to put gloves on before handling them! Should be horsewhipped, yes!

The underling did his best, the report went on and on, but he found little response. It was the federal secretary who worried him most. He hardly listened. What more did he want? To have someone else die like that other one who was sent to Sólanto on the pretense of taking his vacation and was shot down like a rabbit there? What did those ironical looks mean, those undertones, those asides, those low voices? Badly informed! He! The model functionary! Nothing had escaped him. Literally nothing. What then?

He hoped for an explanation.

It came in the evening papers. Regrettable incidents. Three plastic bombs, three explosions at Sólanto.

The Monument to the War Dead had been blown up an hour after his departure.

This took place in May, on a calm day. So a decision was necessary. But it cost Baron di D. what separations always cost: hours of anguish over what one must leave behind.

It was, however, necessary to go. With the police reinforced, the

crossroads guarded, continual house searches, there could be no
other outcome. And horrors, like the pregnant woman who was
beaten to make her speak the name of the bomb maker who was
never identified. Who was he? An anarchist? Or else one of the
Separatists? What was his object? To serve the interests of Baron
di D.? He did them disservice. To act out his own desires, as the
police said? At least, if it had not been the police themselves who
had stirred up the attempt.

It was necessary to go. Baron di D. repeated in vain that perhaps
he would return, it was no use. He had no illusions. To leave was
to leave what cruelly, unbearably, even mortally had become as
necessary to him as the air he breathed: the story of a love without
equal inscribed on the walls of a Sicilian castle, his home. To go
was also to leave behind the ghosts who roamed there. Happiness.
Its perfume in each room and the picture of that woman whose
memory still woke him in the night; she whose presence he never
stopped feeling, in spite of the years, with the music between her
and him, music between them like longing. And it was all strangely
mixed, almost confused with the memory of Antonio who had
saved him from empty hours, from waiting without end, from the
fits of hatred which had fed on his betrayed love, from a stifled
heart. Antonio had cured him.

And then there was worse: losing the desire to return. He knew
himself well. He knew just how far, once roused, his will to detachment and silence could go. Beyond that, emptiness. Yes. To
begin to long for emptiness, for the rejection of life. To appreciate
it. This fear was only a confused idea in him. He did his best to
keep it vague. He tried to concentrate on the tail ends of phrases,
crumbs of ideas, of words. Peace, who knows? Perhaps one must
depend on it so that life could again become like a strong new
dawn, bursting with hope. But how could one believe in it? All
wars end badly and peace was going to bring more deceptions
than anyone could guess. That was plain. A radical change. The
horrible contradiction between what one had wished, and what
one got.

From all that, Baron di D. retained only the fear that after months of being far away, years perhaps, he would no longer even be able to desire to live in Sicily or be strong enough to return there.

Don Fofò was not an enterprising man. Nor was he sentimental. What he excelled in was rather a mixture of sensuality and impulsiveness. He took after his mother. And yet the Baron di D. woke in him a deep, permanent emotion, one of those feelings of uneasiness such as are roused by sentiments unequally shared. Nothing, he knew, could fill the emptiness of that heart. Not even he, Don Fofò, though his father loved him a great deal. This certainty established an unexpected bond between the two which made them indispensable to each other: the impossibility of lying to themselves.

And then Don Fofò had always lived marginally. His father was the perfect borderland of that society to which he belonged from a distance, of that closed, mysterious world, like a dim entity to which he was attached without knowing anything about it. The less he understood him, the more Don Fofò loved him. And this was the man whom the police were persecuting. To save him from the beastly tyranny which became more hateful every day, to convince him to escape, was a task to which Don Fofò had devoted himself to the point of tears, surprising himself with his intensity of feeling. He was attached to his father's style, to the things he loved, to his way of being, he who had passed his life running free among the fields, the farms, the peasant women. What could he do?

It took weeks. When Baron di D. had finally given his assent, the battle of Tunisia was in progress and things were going so badly for him in Sólanto that there was not a moment to lose. But Don Fofò knew exactly to whom to go. On that ground he was unbeatable.

He alerted several of his friends.

"To become expatriate without a passport," or "to join the people outside" were the expressions they used. A word was enough to make him understood. And his haste, his anxiety. Forced departures were not unusual. It was of primary importance to get the approval of the Mafia. By saying that it was under orders from America, one tells by and large the whole truth about what was happening during that period in Sicily.

In Tunisia, Italian troops were still resisting. But it was only a matter of weeks before the Mareth line was broken. Also a landing seemed imminent. For more than a year the American secret services and their Sicilian counterparts had been working together. The Mafia insured the silence of the former, the support of the latter, putting dependable men here and there, feeling the pulse of the troops, encouraging desertions, and also, as was natural, making all sorts of promises to the Separatists in the name of democracy. The Mafia controlled the country.

It was important to see that this landing should cost the fewest lives possible. That was the essential, wasn't it, and one needn't be too particular about the means of insuring it? Obviously. But the Mafia, after all. . . . An odd ally of the major powers? The Mafia responsible for the fate of an army? Nothing to rejoice about. It was a bad period.

Thus was established between the Italian convicts in the United States and their Sicilian counterparts an exchange of information, a traffic which could only have been conceived by American idealism in its naïve candor. What a strange undertaking! With fifty-two convictions, a history of pandering almost unequaled in the annals of crime, thirty years of hard labor, and still no one doubted the good faith of a gangster, Lucky Luciano, whom honorable gentlemen and top security officers consulted more than twenty times, it was said, behind the bars of his model prison on the best way to run the war.

The time was right. Lucky Luciano did his best. He was able to call up from his memory, as if by magic, a complete list of old associates whom the Seventh Army could trust absolutely.

It cut through Sicily like butter. When it was all over, very quickly and without losses—while the poor English, not so well informed, sweated blood and water and lost thousands of men— from the depths of his prison the obliging designer of this victory had the greatest difficulties in making his rights known. Nobody remembered what had been promised to Luciano any more. Just what was promised? His liberty?

He needed two lawyers and a great deal of patience to win his suit.

He was deported to Italy.

But that happened several years later, when the war was over. If the name of Lucky Luciano is introduced at this moment, it is because he was no stranger to what is to follow.

Don Fofò's friends lacked neither relatives nor means. To listen to them, the clandestine departure of the Baron di D. would cause not the slightest difficulty. On the contrary. "Distinguished interpreters," that was the most immediate need of the Americans. They had to have them at any cost. Evidently so many contacts with the illiterate were beginning to worry them a little.

To teach Sicilian, strange as it might seem, is not a task for an unlettered man. Much training was needed in this area. While all the Sicilians available in America would be used in the invasion force, it would be necessary to refresh these boys' memories. Born in the United States they had lost all notion of the island dialect. Yes, much help would be needed in this area and the knowledge of Baron di D. could be useful. But would that be enough to earn a living? They'd like very much to use him, but as for supporting himself from that to the end of his days? . . .

Questioned on this point, Don Fofò made use of a sister of his father's, American by marriage, and a distant cousin of the Vanderbilts to boot. She had gone down with the Lusitania, leaving a sum of money which Baron di D. had never touched.

Such resources were all to the good. But it was the cousinship with the Vanderbilts that made the most difference.

It then was necessary to investigate his past. Politically doubtful people were the pet aversion of the period. A discreet inquiry went on among the Sicilians in New York. Were there no immigrants from Sólanto on Mulberry Street? Perhaps they could give the necessary assurances.

Alfio Bonavia's restaurant acquired some new customers who had an intense interest in the Baron's past, his activities, and his friendships. They came often. Funny people. Did they know Baron di D.? No. Not exactly. But they had heard of him. All the same it was odd, these strangers who worried between the fruit and the cheese about the Baron and his opinions. Alfio wondered about them.

Rocco didn't take long to understand. He set everything in motion to facilitate the Baron di D.'s arrival in the United States. Rocco's political enemies tried to use some of his activities against him. They said he owed his political career to disreputable supporters. Luciano in particular. Rocco swore by the gods it was untrue, as it certainly was. Nothing but lies and calumnies. He only knew Lucky from having met him in the barber shop.

Luciano always knew about everything. Who were his informers? Sicilian sources, no doubt. He learned that he could, if he was willing, help a very worthy man to come to New York. A few words would be enough. . . . Those words were spoken. Now nothing stood in the way of Baron di D.'s departure. A launch which had been stolen was put to good use. Tunisia was only a few miles away.

Baron di D. no doubt would have been very much surprised if anyone had told him what he owed to the son of Bonavia, his former peasant, and more astonished still if he had imagined that scum like Luciano had intervened for him. He never suspected it.

When the hour approached he took Fofò by the shoulders and showed him the mountain over which the setting sun was casting long purple rays.

"Look," he said to him, "look how beautiful those bits of sky are. Like a red tide. . . . It was just such an evening when you brought Antonio to me. Do you remember?

Then he added: "You must, Fofò. . . . You must begin again. Do you understand?"

"I understand," said Fofò.

And he burst into tears.

"If I talk to you this way, it's because of all that. . . ."

The Baron made a vague movement of his head indicating the castle, the rosy clouds, and the distant olive trees. And as Fofò continued to cry, he said to him in an uncertain voice: "Don't cry, my boy. It hurts me. We may not be leaving each other forever, you know."

And he went to get his coat.

The launch arrived, paused briefly beside the rocks which rose from the sea like a platform, and removed Baron di D. from the sight and knowledge of Sólanto.

The shore watch was occupied elsewhere.

In the village, the evening promenade was proceeding as usual, and, as always, those men who still remained walked on one side of the quai while the women and girls walked together on the other. So there were more than fifty people who saw a launch draw up to a landing and two pairs of arms stretch out for the tall, slightly stooped man who stood on the rocks with a bag at his feet.

But no one mentioned it afterwards.

In Palermo, among Baron di D.'s few intimates, it was said that the castle was shut up once more, and the gatekeeper was posted like a silent sentinel on the garden wall. Nothing new about that. Circumstances had obliged Baron di D. and Don Fofò to go away for a while. To the mountains, no doubt. Not a word was spoken suggesting a departure to a more distant place. A secret revealed by no one.

On board the launch, three men talked together in low voices. They spoke of their younger days. The helmsman said that before he had become a *mafioso*, he had lived in Tunis in the quarter called Little Sicily, and it was plain that the thought of going back there gave him much pleasure. He had the wrinkles of an old major domo, a devoted manner and always addressed the Baron as "Your Lordship."

Then there was a discussion on the subject of Marettimo, "the last Italian landfall before the open sea," said the helmsman. And he added: "That's an island it's better to stay away from." It was surrounded by coast guard vessels.

In spite of speed and distance, Marettimo—but was it an illusion, a mirage?—seemed no more than arm's length away for a long time.

Baron di D. felt his heart beating in great blows and his lips trembling. "The last Italian landfall. . . ." He had never believed that he would hear those words. He had never even thought them. Images flooded his mind—voices, sounds, colors. Hanging in the sky he saw the red necktie of the schoolboys of Gefalu, and children in black walking in line. Then the grave and solemn tolling of the bells of Syracuse filled his brain suddenly, and he put his hands to his ears as if he felt his head bursting. He wanted to escape that noise by fixing his thoughts on some practical idea, something banal like his beret, forgotten in Sólanto, which he would need. But the storm of images would not stop. He was without defense against them. An orchard, all sparkling with dew, caught his attention; then a slow line of columns with dismantled capitals, a caravan which vanished just as it stood—motionless and threatening—silhouetted against the horizon. Then the sea offered him only a desolate landscape, fields of lava as far as the eye could see, a moonlike chaos, a black dream, and he closed his eyes.

When he recovered a voice was saying: "We've left it behind."

And since the Baron di D. did not answer, the same voice repeated more loudly, "We've left it behind, Your Lordship. . . . We're safe."

Baron di D. did not weep. He stared sightlessly at the moon rising in the sky. He listened to the regular hum of the motor, but did he hear it? Everything seemed to him illusory, uncertain: his thoughts, his sensations, his body itself no longer seemed his own. Far away Marettimo was only a blue shadow in the blue night.

A thousand unknown faces. A whole neighborhood standing at the windows. How had this come about? There was a feast day crowd on Mulberry Street. Full of noise, full of movement. In his only decent suit, the Baron was being given a hero's reception.

Rocco Bonavia had organized this show, but he played only a secondary part in it. For once it was Alfio, his father, who occupied the place of honor, walking to the right of the Baron with ceremonial step.

Everything worked together for the success of the reception: dry weather, a summer wind—quite cool for July—blowing in from the sea, the street hung with bunting, the women in sheer dresses, shop windows enshrined, vacationing children chasing each other from one sidewalk to the other like a swarm of maddened hornets, joyously floating banners carrying "Welcome" in giant letters, and also "Long Live the Man Who Said No," a sentence whose last words ". . . to Fascism" had been suppressed so as not to offend those who were still faithful to *Il Duce.*

The meeting had taken place in a customs house which by the whiteness of its walls, the comfort of its metal seats and by something aseptic in the air was reminiscent of the waiting room of a clinic. There were green plants everywhere. Not just any plants: exotic ones. And background music discreetly provided sentimental melodies. There at the airfield, in a white room where costly vegetation and bad music attested to the generosity of American hospitality, Alfio, who had come to meet the Baron, paced up and down wearing a straw hat, sports shirt and flowered tie—his Sunday outfit.

The travelers disembarked in waves. They crowded into the narrow corridor which separated the two ranks of offices where functionaries, squeezed into their chairs, waited for them. The movement was slow. Papers passed from hand to hand, were examined, leafed through, stamped. Sometimes something was in doubt, and everything came to a halt. The line stood still, then moved again in short jerks. It was like a tremendous caterpillar.

From the barrier he leaned on, Alfio saw all kinds of human specimens passing. Young girls with tangled hair carrying many cameras, large women very much perfumed and hung with furs, a little boy whose distress was so plain that it hurt to watch him. He walked in silence with no luggage except a tiny suitcase. Alfio saw that the child's clothing was too large, and had first belonged to someone else; the band of adhesive tape which held his suitcase closed and bore his name written in inked capitals: SOLO (but was that his name or his condition, a solitary child?); he saw the hair cropped as if the child recently had typhoid; and also his undernourished features. Where did he come from? The inspection of his suitcase gave Alfio a shiver of emotion, almost of indignation. It was like an operation without anesthesia. The adhesive tape had to be stripped off. A country smell leaked out into the aseptic customs house. The child looked at the uniformed man who was listing the remnants of his past: a goat cheese, a salami, a bouquet of thyme, and a pair of socks. Then, under the socks, three little packets which when opened dropped a shower of dried herbs.

After that, there was nothing more for Alfio but uneasy waiting. He watched an old man pass . . . then another man also old but taller, thinner, whom he recognized at once. Was it the very white, very bushy hair, was it the thinness which the black suit accentuated? The Baron was beginning to look like an old scholar.

He saw him moving farther away, going around in circles, pushed from one office to another with the bewildered look of someone who does not know what to expect. Alfio waved his arms, then rushed towards him. The Baron was baffled for a few moments. What a strange outfit. . . . What did that man want? He left his passport in the hands of a customs officer who was greatly distraught by the Baron's classification as a probationary traveler from an enemy country. When he reached the barrier where Alfio was standing, the Baron at first stood petrified with surprise, then gave a kind of cry of joy: "Alfio! It can't be!"

They threw their arms about each other. And this gesture had two opposite effects. In closing his arms about Alfio's body, Baron di D. became his natural self once more. He found his assurance, his dignity, composed in equal parts of malice and distance, as if he had caught his breath after a long time of breathlessness. Alfio received that accolade like a rough wave which tossed him back into the past. The Baron di D.! It was the Baron standing before him! The same man who had dominated his childhood and who lived in his mind like a myth for more than forty years—he was there, in flesh and blood. Alfio stood still, dumbfounded, suddenly conscious of the power which this exile whom he had just welcomed still held over him.

Nothing was happening as he had expected. He would have liked to be simple and natural. But he forgot everything—his acquired ease, his smooth conversation, his tone of "I fear no one. . . . I am at home everywhere" of which he was so proud. . . . He tried to speak the sentences of welcome which he had practiced with Rocco, but the words would not come out. And in his hand, the formula of a forgotten politeness quickly rose, quickly spilled over, drowned him. What a struggle! The Baron did nothing to provoke Alfio's odd condition. On the contrary. He spoke softly to him, asked news of his Rocco before Alfio had even asked about Don Fofò.

"Alfio, Alfio," he kept repeating, "is it really you? I always thought you'd succeed. . . ."

Then why must a litany of words, scraps of phrases arise from Alfio's memory, mount to his lips, carry him away almost to the point of crushing him? He said to himself: You aren't the same any more. Stop sounding submissive. And don't start talking to him in the third person. But scarcely had he said all that to himself than the most unforseen instincts took hold of him, like seizing the Baron's hand, kissing it, pressing it to his heart, a desire which he repressed immediately. But he could not keep himself from saying just to himself, Your Excellency. . . . Your Excellency, in order to find the right rhythm, and as he did so he improvised a sort of little ballet around the Baron, intended only to take his bag from him and oblige him to move forward.

Thus, without being aware of it, Alfio forced Baron di D. to recognize in him, in spite of his elegance as a successful man, in spite of his growing corpulence, his former peasant, his shepherd.

A river where boats hurried to reach port, a metallic bridge which straddled this river in one audacious stride, the deep canyon of the straight streets, too straight, the dizzying flight of the apartment houses towards the sky, and here and there—in good neighborhoods—the canopies stretched over the sidewalks so that people could enter their homes with dry feet. . . . Elsewhere, another surprise, geysers of steam spouting underfoot, a sea wind raising whirlwinds of dust, and the lighted signs which never went out forming incoherent messages on the fronts of buildings. All that to astonish Baron di D. between LaGuardia airport and New York, all that to give at one moment a sensation of youth, at another of being crushed; sometimes the sense that he was going toward a new life, sometimes that he was walking toward death; all that, and Alfio beside him, his shirt flapping, his sleeves rolled up, his muscles bulging, Alfio at the wheel, his hat pushed back on the nape of his neck, driving American style with studied nonchalance.

Suddenly Baron di D. had the impression that he had left New York, and every turn of the wheel confirmed his surprise. A radical change. A metamorphosis. With bulging eyes he saw the houses grow smaller, lose twenty stories at a time, then thirty as if by magic. The façades changed color and shape. There, they had been sharp, cold, severe like tall uninhabited ramparts. Here they were smeared with pink or beige and hung with laundry which moved in the wind. Most remarkably the straight streets vanished into a tangle of holes, hiding places; they began to curve and zigzag quite naturally. The sidewalks whose flat surfaces had seemed so vast to the Baron, as naked as a runway, suddenly disappeared under an inexplicable human swarm and were covered with market stalls.

He suddenly found himself again in the midst of ferment, in the midst of life, as if the substance which filled New York, hitherto invisible and secret, was suddenly poured out on the ground and vegetables and fruits had suddenly grown by the roadside.

"Where are we now, Alfio?" asked the Baron.

"In the Italian quarter, Excellency."

"And these people? Have they all come to see me?"

"All of them, yes," said Alfio.

Then they got out of the car and went down Mulberry Street.

Rocco, in his role of district leader, was in the middle of a delegation composed of several representatives of the Central Committee of Tammany Hall and of the top Democrats of the neighborhood. Old antagonisms seemed forgotten and Patrick O'Brady, his dreams of supremacy temporarily suspended, represented Ireland along with the most faithful customers of his saloon, all slightly tipsy. At the moment of introductions the Battler, in an excess of tenderness, clasped the Baron to his heart, calling him "brother" and "fellow sufferer" and could not refrain from shedding a tear.

Shun Ying the tattooer, Wah Weng Sang the undertaker, and Nelson Lee the photographer, led the Chinese contingent. There were about a dozen of them standing quietly in their corner and looking at the sky where the sun blazed. One would have said that nothing here concerned them very much. They remained silent while the head of their group went to honor the Baron with a deep bow.

Agata, Calò and their son, Theo, wearing his first long trousers, were there in the first row, as they had been in the parade. At the moment when the Baron, seeing them, stopped and they carried on a long conversation with him in dialect, without cries, without gestures (never gestures) but with a rising tone which culminated in the word "Sólanto" pronounced in a deeply pathetic tone, in that instant they were surrounded by the pack of photographers.

"Hug the child," they cried.

"Take the woman in your arms!"

The Baron did nothing. But, as they insisted, Rocco gave a nod indicating that they must hurry. An imperious nod. With shouts, with furious gestures, the photographers pounced on the Baron like wild animals. Flash bulbs exploded. Then they left without thanking him.

Baron di D. continued on his way, somewhat frightened by these people, these sidewalks, these streets, this crowd. He did not even know clearly what was expected of him. A visit to the neighborhood, then a toast at Casa Alfio after which he would be taken to his lodging, three rooms found by Rocco not far from where he himself lived. The Baron forced himself to keep walking, to let himself go along without trying too hard to understand the reason for these stares, this excitement. A curious adventure which sent a kind of fog to his brain, paralyzed his brain, emptied him of the slightest thought. Forgotten was the uphill path which led to the sea, the departure, the farewell to Sólanto. Not the least memory of the crossing. All that no longer had the slightest importance. He was in New York and he must march. Walk with Alfio. Walk with Rocco. One was at his right, the other at his left. If one had looked more deeply into his heart, one would doubtless have found at the bottom a profound satisfaction in not being alone.

So Baron di D. passed before a series of shops which had been decorated in his honor by expert hands with garlands, with bouquets, escutcheons in every shade of red, in every pink—with scarlet trophies, with rose windows with friezes—so that sometimes one seemed to be in front of a miniature theater, sometimes before a street altar on the eve of a feast day.

It was as they were passing the shop of Nazareno Baci, the accordian seller—*Established in 1908. Open daily from 10 A. M. to 6 P. M. Sunday and holidays by appointment only*—that a tune broadcast over the loudspeaker struck Alfio like a whip, then unfurled over Baron di D. in a great profusion of colors. A *Traditor* sung in C major by sepulchral voices, then another and another, drum rolls as if for an execution, the prolonged plaint of the violins, sharp tremolos, then a single beautiful voice, a man's voice, sang *sol, fa,-sol, re, sol*, "O Terra Addio" in a tone of unbearable sadness.

"It's a clearance sale," Alfio explained with an embarrassed look.

Beside the Baron a poster stretched across the door of Baci's shop announced, "If God the Father had vocal chords, he would have sung like Caruso." Rocco walked faster. But the sudden speed did not keep the blatant structure of Verdi's great aria from lingering for some time over the procession.

"O Terra Addio" rose to the depths of the sky like a magnificat.

At the end of the street was Dionisio Caccopardo's grocery. A terrible chatterbox. He stood on his doorstep, a smile on his lips, ready to welcome the hero of the day. The visit to his store was written into the program of the festivities: he was waiting for it as his due. They must go in. The racket of his conversation suddenly provided an unexpected defense against the faraway Caruso. Rocco heaved a sigh of relief.

The grocery was an odd place and well worth seeing. It was a cave, a grotto full of fantasy, the ceiling in particular. It seemed to be alive. The fans gave everything a fluttering motion and everything knocked together: vegetables artistically arranged in nets, jars of Santa Lucia olives, cans of oil decorated with a chromo in which the Sovereign Pontiff smiled his blessing, boxes of candy whose covers bore reproductions of the many residences of the late Queen Margaret, *provoletti* tied in bunches, herbs wrapped in envelopes, marinated eels decorated with full moons, salamis, panettones in their packages like hatboxes. Everything hung from hooks, everything swung back and forth, everything mingled with everything else in a sort of joyous abandon except for the provolones, which were more than six feet long and which hung side by side stiff as telephone poles, forming a deep tall forest. In this shadowy region, Dionisio Caccopardo did the honors, explaining that no store in New York could boast such a munificent stock.

It was then that the great jaw which jutted over a huge heap of hams appeared first, then the childish dimple, round and tiny, which dented the enormous chin. The bust of Caruso? Was it possible? Alfio repressed a start as best he could, thus rousing Rocco's suspicions. Why was Alfio staring so insistently at the darkest corner of the room? The head was there. Gilded plaster. It was there, massive and topped by a vulgar forelock. No question about it, it was Caruso's bust, his brows knit, straining in superhuman effort as if the great pipe organ of his voice was about to burst forth anew and his breath would blow like a tornado through the forest of provalone. Alfio, with a sort of fury, tried to make a path through the obstacles in his way: he must get the Baron out of here, push him towards the light, the air, the door, the street; he must at any cost distract him from this spectacle. In his haste he upset a pile of calendars adorned with the rivers of Colorado and with Niagara Falls, piles of soap flakes, religious objects electrically lighted, Saint Roch and his dog as a night light and luminous statues of Our Lady of Fatima—all merchandise which sold well in this neighborhood. And as he dragged the Baron after him, Alfio swept away brooms and brushes with a gesture of his arm as he might have held back branches. Nothing could stop him.

That was how things were when Dionisio Caccopardo, stubborn, talker that he was, made his visitors retrace their steps. There was no use in Rocco's interrupting him, he was determined that everyone must admire his stock of hams. All was lost. . . .

"I carry the best you can buy," he said.

And he separated each syllable of the magic word: "Ca-ru-so! They're Caruso Brand, made in the U.S.A. Ever heard of it?"

Then he began to lecture.

"There he is," he said, pointing at the bust. "There's our great man! Our Titan! Look at him! He's wearing an English style suit, God bless him! A king, sir, a real sovereign!"

The bust of Caruso was offered for contemplation like the Holy Sacrament. He was there to watch over the pounds of hams which bore his name, there for the devotees of success to feed upon. "Sacred Heart of Caruso, feed me. . . ." A shoddy, ridiculous bust: Caruso in a coat of gilded plaster and dust, like an old crumbling totem; Caruso in a frock coat, wearing his decorations, his whole display of ribbons, Belgian, Spanish, and French; all his medals lined up one after the other, the sculptor had omitted none of them.

"Ten, eleven. . . . There are thirteen counting the ribbons."

Dionisio Caccopardo seemed determined to describe them all. As he told it, the honorary police medal given by the City of New York was the tenor's favorite of all the decorations he had received. A burst of wild laughter rose in the Baron's throat and shook him from head to foot. A frightening silent laugh, something like an inner hurricane, a monstrous surge. The change that came over him was so painful that, in the same hesitating voice, Alfio and then Rocco asked, "Are you all right?"

They spoke as if he were a sick man. "Are you all right?"

"Why shouldn't I be?" he demanded, as if the question hurt his feelings. "Because of that? You're joking! If only I could find the least jealousy, the least little feeling of resentment in myself. . . . No, I feel nothing. Not the least twinge. Nothing which would make one say: Life. . . . Nothing. My heart is dead."

He felt a rush of rage whose real root neither Alfio nor Rocco could guess. It was because there was nothing the Baron di D. feared more than making a spectacle of himself. But it was apparent that he was battered, torn by a feeling of unusual violence, as if some voice inside the hermetically sealed cage of his body was desperately trying to make itself heard. When he managed to calm himself, his tone changed at once. A burst of gaiety came into his eyes.

"Betrayal? What could be more ordinary," he said in a mocking tone. "Try to tell me it isn't. Just try. You'd be wasting your time. There's nothing more commonplace and that's what is sickening about it. Let's understand each other: I'm not speaking of crime, or of desertion, or of betrayal by provocation. No. That betrayal brings its own punishment. That's why it takes courage. No. I'm speaking of deception as it is practiced in our civilized society and in our drawing rooms. The backstairs play an essential part in it.

Watch out for them. They are abject. It's the soft betrayal of our well-meaning circles with their parade of accessory friendships, of mutual acceptance, of friendly separations. That betrayal, you see, finds self-justifications and offers itself up with contrite airs. Oh my friends! If I had given such a woman the least opportunity to explain why she was deceiving me, if I had let her tell me how she was going to behave in the future, if I had let her propose that we be friends, if I had given her the chance to complain to me, or explain how sorry she was, scorn and pride would have driven me to kill her."

He stopped and stood for a moment before the bust which he looked at with disgust.

"What a farce," he said in a new burst of rage. "The vulgarity. . . . That's the worst invention of man. . . ."

And he added: "Poor Caruso! It's his turn to be made a fool of, by ham!"

"The best of all hams in its cellophane wrapping," cried Dionisio Caccopardo, who had caught the word "ham" and wanted to talk more than ever. He referred to some customers who thought the wrapping on the Caruso Brand so handsome they wanted to frame it.

And Dionisio Caccopardo began to take down a ham.

"Wonderful, sir. Look at it," he said, spreading paper carefully, as if it were an embroidery.

The operas in which the singer had excelled formed an odd structure around his head: rather glorious and heavy like a pediment made up of all the characters together. An inscription read: WE PRESENT HERE SCENES OF FAMOUS OPERAS, MANY OF WHICH ARE CLOSELY ASSOCIATED WITH THE NAME OF ENRICO CARUSO KNOWN THROUGH THE WORLD AS THE MOST FAMOUS TENOR OF ALL TIME.

And below, in small letters: PREPARED BY THE CUDAHY PACKING COMPANY, U.S.A., GENERAL OFFICES. . . . Dionisio Caccopardo recited the inscription from beginning to end with much emphasis. He repeated, "Of all time . . . of all time" twice, as if he were speaking to deaf men, or imbeciles. But the Baron hardly paid any attention to him. The paper which Dionisio Caccopardo was smoothing out with such care, its clumsy engravings, its helmeted victories, its badly costumed characters seemed to open an adventure to him: he allowed himself to be carried away by the crazy hope of rediscovering old emotions. Each fold of the paper was an old song found again, each mark was a sound; from each feature a forgotten melody rose and sounded in his head like a joyful hymn.

Caruso satiated and swollen with applause, with receptions, with dinner parties and rich food wore for a crown a scene from the second act of *Romeo and Juliet* and for a halo the arrival of the traveling players in Act I of *Pagliacci*. He had the Barber beside his ear, while Aïda knelt to invoke Isis over his vaselined hair. As in the past, Baron di D. confronted his phantoms. Nadir, when recognized, was singing "I think I hear it still. . . ." and Baron di D., as always, had to smile as he remembered what an abominable French accent Caruso had.

The Baron di D. left the complicated network of the hair, threaded his way between masses of human architecture, passed quickly over the tired eyes, the heavy jaw, traced the outline of the powerful neck still humming something like *"Je croa antandre anchor. . . ."* and a new burst of laughter rose in him, startling Alfio and Rocco. He lingered a long time over the double chin, nearly lost himself there. He crossed some scenes which he did not recognize, scaled balconies, made strange encounters: A Bohemian girl, three geishas, smugglers, a hunchback, some corsairs; at the heart of this disorder he met Lucia, her dress whipped by a hellish wind. Poor soul! Quite mad! Then in the turn of an alleyway, Marguerite. A bore! The Baron passed over her. And also over Dona Anna, in black as usual, always frustrated by the rape which never happened, always desirable. The Baron would gladly have lingered over her but he was torn by contradictory desires: to continue his journey, or to stop. That paper was like some labyrinth in which he did not want to lose his way. Suddenly he recognized a garden, then a tunnel under thick trees lit by the moon: *The Marriage* in a setting he had never forgotten. A mesh of black branches against a sky, present but invisible. And the wind in that forest was music. He climbed a few steps and, panting, entered the Countess's rooms in the middle of Act II. Figaro was singing. He scarcely listened. The Countess came forward toward the footlights, her arms crossed on her breast. She alone interested him. Never had she seemed more moving than on that evening. Each sound, each note vibrated, pierced him; her breath, her voice, everything that she was became *his* and stayed with him long after she was silent. He answered her quite naturally and left, drunk with joy, finally dispossessed of himself, of that thorn he had borne in his heart.

Baron di D. tried to make that moment last as long as he could. Then he again took his place between Alfio and Rocco and the procession continued along its way.

II.

Nobody becomes European overnight.
HENRY MILLER

Pam had chosen my anniversary at *Fair* to visit the Italian restaurants on Mulberry Street. A touching gesture. I had told her: "Don't expect them to be anything but bars, and very modest ones at that." "That doesn't matter," she answered. I was always making things complicated, and it had already been decided. That was where we were to celebrate our first year of work together and at the same time finish our research into exotic restaurants for our readers.

This was what Pam called a *celebration,* a word she used a good deal. In her engagement book it was confounded with many signs and dates through which only she could find her way. A day of *celebration* must begin with appropriate preparations. Pam put on

a mask and lay down with her feet in the air, her head low. She
remained in that position until she had belched, which was a driving necessity with her. She brought gravity and extraordinary con-
centration to this enterprise. She seemed to be praying. Then
bouquets had to be sent, or baskets of fruit; or cards, or letters, or
calls made, or telegrams, or candy—depending on the occasion.
For example, if a friend was celebrating the anniversary of a new
apartment, or a model kitchen, she only got a card of congratula-
tions; Aunt Rosie's big friend received a bouquet to commemorate
twenty sober years. And one must not forget the reader whom Pam
telephoned regularly, once a year, on the day when she had com-
pleted adding an inch to her bust, thanks to advice received from
Fair; nor those powerful Greek shipowners to whom Pam would
send a telegram on the anniversary of an auction in the course of
which they snatched a Cézanne from under the nose of the
Louvre: a story Pam loved to tell. She had been there when it happened. The words: Cézanne, apples, Louvre, Greek millions took
on a particular value in her mouth; she relished all of it at once.
Each time I waited impatiently for the moment when, out of excitement, she would blink her eyes to a faster rhythm, squirm in
her chair as if she were trying to be seductive, then suddenly reveal her teeth in a smile in which a world of hope existed, of
dreams, of wonder.

The research we were conducting together remains in my collection of strange memories. Sometimes I think of it tenderly.
That exploration had kept us busy for almost a year, like a long
carnival. There was the photographer who followed us everywhere,
a jaunty Englishman who had his nose fixed. And I see again the
young men, met by chance at parties, who recognized Pam and
enjoyed her. For the most part they were playboys, completely
ignorant, total zeros, but cordial and excellent gossips. Pam
skipped breathlessly from one subject to another. Always the same
slang, the same stories, the same desperate curiosity. Me, I listened.
Pam often irritated me, to be sure, but I was nonetheless fond of
her. Without her what would have become of me? In the long

run, what better counter-irritant could I have found? But sometimes her company opened a yawning void. The emptiness of the
tomb. I see myself again in New York, the rope of solicitude
around my neck. New York for a year: the hollowness, if I wasn't
careful, would devour me. For nothing is more deceptive than
false reasons for existing. It is as if you were on a moving express,
you are carried away by it. By the time you struggle, it is already
too late: you are caught.

But I was getting along well. *Fair* for me was only a door I had
passed through temporarily, an emergency entrance, so to speak.
When I felt I was smothering, when Daisy Lee's business of elegance was too much for me, I returned to the obsession which
dwelt in me; I found my island once more. It was my refuge. Suddenly I heard its raucous shouts, its racket, its buzzing, its fever;
children tormented me, tamers of lizards and fireflies, pickers of
wild marjoram; my universe revived. I heard its meager voices
speak to me in the bitter tongue of poverty; high voices, thin,
which whistled, bubbled, and pierced the air like a call to prayer in
Arabia: "I live by you," I told them. "From you I get my hatreds
and my strength. You are what sets me right and feeds me; you
are the only mirror of my dreams, do not leave me!"

In this way I kept my distance. Not without trouble, for it is
never easy to lead a double life.

Pam suspected it a little, but she never quite understood it. She
said, "You'll never be one of us." How could she understand? But
still, now we had things in common: where we lived, where we
worked, our jobs, the memories of this year, and that long collaboration we had undertaken to research the city from end to end,
those ferreting months, that series of noisy entrances into the
high temples of foreign gastronomy, bringing with us all the glit-
ter of the big women's magazines. Pam managed beautifully.

One day, fed up with all this swank, with the manager hurrying
over to our table, with the orchestra—Hungarian, Viennese, or
Mexican, it didn't matter—our first mouthful setting in motion the
maitre d'hotel who watched over our least gestures, disconcerted

by the elaborate attention our presence attracted, I remember telling her: "Pam, you are more feared than some pagan divinity. It wouldn't take much to make these people crown us with flowers; they'll offer us jewels and who knows what else. Maybe cars and fountain pens? Let's try it, want to? Let it be known that if they want to be in *Fair*'s good graces, the ice cubes in our long drinks will have to be rose diamonds. Real ones. Huge diamonds cut in facets. Let's try. . . ."

And I remember Pam joining her hands, smiling, sparkling. I was finally admitting her importance. Nothing could have pleased her more. If I had told her all I was thinking, if I had said to her: "These people act like the village whore. If we asked them, they'd take their clothes off," she would have blazed. With such small acts of cowardice I competently performed my role of *Fair* editor. And I did not even have to worry about sudden bursts of honesty: dissimulation always came most readily to mind. . . .

But back to our world tour, to that series of crazy evenings of which Pam was absolute master. Sometimes we ate in Mexico, sometimes in Turkey; each evening we changed hemispheres, changed capitals. The streets, the endless streets and the reflections of neon on the asphalt of the pavement took the place of sanity for us. For in order to start out on what Pam called our international eating tour we needed the phantasmagoria of New York spread at our feet like a multicolored carpet. Sometimes I felt dizzy. I cried for mercy. But always, in some out-of-the-way street—Pam knew them by heart—a Swedish specialty or a Hindu one had been prepared just for us and we must go there. I was living a bizarre adventure, but Pam seemed to find it quite natural. She went from one country to another with her notebook in her hand, serene and not at all self-conscious, like those heroes in the ballets of great spectacles whose entrechats carry them elegantly from the snows of Koubane to the sands of the Orient.

During these curious jaunts, Pam was forever bemused by *Fair*, its readers, its power. The magazine covered her like a second skin. At times it was frightening. She had a way of expressing her ideas which permitted no argument. What an extraordinary way she had of asking: "Are you a real French restaurant or are you only 'in the French manner?'" To convince her of his authenticity, the maitre d'hotel had to speak English with a Charles Boyer accent and the menu must include snails and frogs in the *plat du jour*. Otherwise she would get up and leave.

On certain evenings I had tried to make her admit that her secretaries were too zealous. Invisible trumpets announced our arrival wherever we met. "It takes all the interest out of our project," I said, "and we frighten away the subject. . . ." She listened to me in her polite way, then answered, "I hate anonymity. . . ."

When she ventured into a place where she did not know what the specialties were, she limited herself to saying: "Serve me something typical. . . ." Then she waited stoically. In this way I have seen her swallow eggplants with jam in an Israeli restaurant and terrifying spits full of lambs' intestines in a basement on Fifty-first Street, where the cook called himself a Greek.

Sometimes we necessarily repeated our experiences, since our articles depended on the contrast in our points of view. But I always let Pam begin. Her work was more delicate than mine. I only had to judge the decoration, the lighting, and the orchestra; Pam had to talk about food and service. The main responsibility was on her. Leaning over her notebook, she recited litanies of goulash, jellied calves' feet, roast suckling pigs, Galician stews, Wiener schnitzels, shish kebabs . . . all with brief dietetic comments such as "terrible for the figure" or "thoroughly intoxicating."

After several weeks, Pam had made up her mind. There were only two ways of eating. One was rational, distinguished, international: steak, roast chicken, salad, coffee with cream. The other, much more adventurous, consisted of adopting out of curiosity the culinary tastes of unusual and often disadvantaged peoples. "Exactly. Disadvantaged. The native cuisine is almost always the cooking of the poor. These people praise the merits of chick pea soup because green peas are beyond their means. And if they put

sauce on everything, it's because they have to. You'll never convince me of anything else. The trick is to drown everything in
pimento so that you can forget it's a cheap cut of meat, and play
the violin as loud as possible to encourage the customers to swallow it—and it's chile in Mexico and paprika in Hungary. . . ."

Sometimes I took it into my head to disagree with these dog-
mas, her mania for putting everything in its place. When it was
only about the Liechtenstein restaurant judged "absolutely fascinating" from the first glance (the word fascinating was accompanied by a smile like a bow in honor of the little principality and
its sovereigns), I could let it pass. I also accepted that a bistro
named "Jacqueline's *le petit veau*" or "Joseph's *pomme soufflée*"
were designated by her "more French than camembert" or "really
Parisian." But I was beginning to have my fill of the boned roast
venison that she had eaten "au Hapsburg" and of which she never
stopped talking. Certain words had incredible power over her, and
simply pronouncing them—as if they were not only sounds but
something you could taste as well—amounted to a favorable judgment on her part.

So, in the case of the boned roast, it was not the venison which
took on a mouth-watering sound on her tongue but the word
"Hapsburg." Why? To hear her, you would have believed she had
eaten with Charles V. It irritated me, but contradiction always
brought tears to Pam's eyes. So I was silent.

I was waiting for Italy's turn to come. . . .

When I saw him in that doorway, I hardly recognized him.
Rocco, sitting astride a chair, his hat pushed back, obstructed the
passage into a restaurant. He was smoking. I hardly expected to
meet him there. I was about to express surprise when he asked:
"What are you doing here? It's a long time since we've seen each
other."

I began to explain. I told him about our research and why I
was on Mulberry Street.

"And your friend?" he asked me.

"She'll meet me this evening. I wanted to be alone. To spend the day here, anyway."

As for him, he told me that it was chance that he was sitting there in his black suit.

"It's never happened before. Never."

He told me about an old gentleman who had just been buried. They'd wanted to have things as nice as possible so he wore his black suit.

"It isn't customary here. But for him, it's something different. You've come on a dark day."

"A relative of yours?"

"No."

He changed the subject, asking me how I had planned to spend my day.

"Taking notes," I said. "And I'll take also a look at the Chinese quarter."

And I told him in detail how I had to describe the restaurants and the neighborhoods that I visited with Pam, the atmosphere, what should I call it . . . the "exotic note" as Daisy Lee would say.

"With a woman like her it can't all be smooth going," he said in a calm voice.

He spoke to me leaning on the back of his chair, as if on a balustrade.

"It's just that the day you saw her she was in a filthy mood," I said. "But that was an accident. At work, I can tell you, she's a good deal more astute. God knows how many people wish they had her capacities."

"That may be," said Rocco. "But what difference does that make? You begin like that and you end in the ditch. A woman who drinks is a woman who drinks. I go crazy when I see one. It's a thing I can't feel indifferent about."

I told him I understood. He seemed amazed, frowned, and looked at me as if he were seeing me for the first time.

"Life. . . ." he said sadly.

I would have liked to tell him that I knew a good deal about him, about his beginnings, about his career, and perhaps ask him some questions, but it was unthinkable. Rocco had already lit another cigarette and was smiling like someone thinking of other things.

"Have you ever been here before?"

"No, never. Daisy Lee doesn't leave me much free time, you know."

"Would you like to sit down?"

I nodded and he called: "Cesarino! Bring a chair."

An old man appeared in a white jacket, wearing slippers. He asked if he should fix lunch for Rocco. The boss wanted to know. Then Rocco explained to me that the boss was his father and this restaurant we were sitting in front of was called "Casa Alfio." Then he repeated: "Alfio. That's my father's name."

Once more I would have liked to say to him, "I know that too!" but I was afraid of being tactless.

Then, changing the subject, he asked me: "Have you been in America a long time?"

"Sometimes I think it's been a century. Sometimes that it's only been a few days and that Daisy Lee, Pam, and the magazine are only dreams. If I had any reason to go back to Palermo, I would go. But I haven't anymore."

"How is that?"

Then I tried to explain to him. But I did not mention Antonio's name. I told him only of our house which faced the sea, the pink house that today was in ruins, and about my father who died a prisoner in Libya.

"He went as an auxiliary doctor. During that time we were living under bombs, my brothers and I. Without water, without gas, without wood. My grandmother had disappeared during a bombardment. She had gone to the Ministry of Food. They took the dead and the wounded in old coaches that broke down at every street corner. At the hospital a nurse barred me from the morgue. I was too young. And then she told me it was impossible to recognize anyone there. One of those confusions. . . . Then you know, there are days when I ask myself what I am doing on earth."

He nodded, then said: "I was born here, an American. But the war, I've always thought it was barbaric. And the people who felt easy in their conscience knowing that girls of your age were present at such massacres, they're filth or half-witted. The bad thing is that the world is full of them. . . ."

Rocco suddenly laid his hand on mine and asked me if I hadn't sat there long enough. He called into the restaurant, "We're leaving," and said to me: "Come on, let's take a walk. I'll keep you company for a while."

The best things in Mulberry Street were the smells, all blending from the displays of fruit and vegetables, from the fried foods which were being prepared almost everywhere behind the open windows. "It's lovely here," I said to Rocco. "You wouldn't believe you were in New York." But he muttered that no, it was horrible, a shame, and that he hoped to live long enough to see these old barracks pulled down and replaced by apartments as beautiful as the ones on Fifth Avenue.

"Winter's the time when you should see this quarter, not on a beautiful day like today," said Rocco. "You're talking like a tourist. With the snow and slush it isn't quite so pretty here, believe me, nor quite so gay."

"If I'm talking like a tourist, you're talking like a man who's so sure he's right that he no longer asks himself any questions. It doesn't even occur to you that two opposite truths can exist at the same time, be superimposed on each other to the point where you can't tell them apart. So these people whose houses you want to tear down, are you so sure of their happiness once you've put them in your glass prisons? What I think is that they'll be both happier and unhappier at the same time. But you don't understand that. You want to have things just the way you've decided they must be. Period, that's all. Oh, it makes me furious."

"So I make you furious?"

"Yes, when you talk like a bishop, you make me furious."

"That's because you don't understand."

"Understand what?"

"That I'd need a different father and mother to be a different man. . . ."

"What has your family to do with it?"

"In order to pay for the luxury of doubting, you have to start out by not being the son of an immigrant and a drunkard. Do you understand that? Haven't you ever noticed that the people here are ready to walk all over each other? Has that escaped you? So there's only one way to survive: always seem to know more than your neighbor. Never show any hesitation. Be positive. Show assurance even in the way you put your hat on. If you don't, you're dead, eaten alive."

I stopped, then he added, nodding his head at the street scene ahead: "You call that civilization?"

We moved forward with a whole swarm of urchins tagging at our heels. Rocco stopped every three steps. He spoke to this one and that one, always finding something nice to say: "So, Grandpa, bigger and better than ever. . . ." to the old man bent in two who ran the bakery, La Ferrarese; and friendly words or teasing ones for the young girls at the snackbar counter who were lunching on Italian hero sandwiches, several of which were laid out in the window to attract passersby.

We ended at a bar where Rocco suggested we have a drink. We went in. Three men got up and Rocco exchanged greetings with them. Then the boss ushered him to a table where we sat down. "You aren't giving me the cold shoulder?" he asked me in a worried voice, as if our conversation might have made me angry. Rocco put his hand on mine once more, saying: "Listen, I'll tell you something; we're living in a country where there's no reality."

"What do you mean?"

"That everybody thinks he's master of his fate here, but it's only an illusion. We're prisoners of many doors, always watched even if in the open. If we stick to the rules, O.K. But at the first sign of individuality, or worse, independence, we become suspect.

You'll hear it said that people are warm and welcoming here. It's true. They are. But they're also very suspicious and they never forgive us for being different. It's no use succeeding, being dependable, proving one's ability. That doesn't change anything. You're still different."

I would have preferred Rocco be quiet for a while so that something more intimate could happen. But he wasn't in the mood for personal confidences: "Listen, I'll tell you a story. It will show you why you have to be on guard here, even if it is a big country. There should be room for everyone. But that's not the way it is. Anyone who says 'Italian' here means 'schemer,' or 'crook.' You can't beat that; there's nothing you can do. It's a state of mind, like an invisible wall. For example, early this year I graduated from district leader to the position of boss, of manager—call it what you want, the title isn't important. I became the chief, if you prefer, chief of the Democratic Party for the state of New York. A huge stride forward. Unquestionably. A clear win by election. Not everyone objected to it, but you can guess that if you want to live without enemies, you'd better go into another trade than mine. I had known about traps that were laid to trip me up at the slightest occasion. One of them seemed particularly imminent. It was to make me look as if I were the candidate of the gangsters, the racketeers. From there it was only one step to say that I owed my election to their money and influence.

"One day I found out that a member of the Kefauver Crime Committee investigating Frank Costello—New York's underworld czar—had the nerve to ask that crook, 'Do you know Rocco Bonavia?' And Costello answered, 'Yes, for four or five years.' Maybe you think there weren't good souls eager to spread that news! There was no use in my collecting witnesses and proving it was all a lie. I became known as Costello's intimate friend, his straw man. For months, understand, months I had to live down that reputation. No use my living quietly, paying a little extra when I had to, struggling against corruption in all forms and cleaning up Tammany Hall from cellar to attic. Nothing I could do. People went on saying that I owed my career to New York gangsters. Sometimes, when people went too far, I lost my patience. You may have heard that I knocked a reporter down? Well, it's true. During an interview he had the nerve to say to me: 'You always work behind closed doors. That's pretty shady, isn't it? An office where the doors are always closed? And it proves you must have something to hide. Is it really true you're Costello's friend?' That's when I hit him."

"Why are you so bitter? Politics is the same everywhere, you know."

Rocco lowered his head. Perhaps he agreed with me. With all his anxieties and struggles, he revealed no more than a deep line between his eyebrows, a somber voice, and that odd smile, careful, with lips closed as if he were trying to hide his teeth.

"Excuse me, Gianna," he said gravely. "I don't really understand why I've talked to you so long. I must have spoiled your day."

"If you really want to find reasons for apologizing, you'd better look elsewhere, because you haven't spoiled anything."

"All the same you have better things to do than listen to me. There are a lot of interesting things to see in this neighborhood."

"And who said you weren't interesting?"

"Are you serious? It's a rare woman who likes to listen. I've never known one. There's Agata, of course. I don't know why it is, but when I talk to women I never feel that they're listening to me. There's something untamed about women . . . like animals."

I said, "You like them, don't you?" He answered that he knew nothing about them. Then he added: "Anyway, I think of them often, and I always think of them as a paradise I'll never find."

"We need that in our lives. It's the only thing we dream of for any length of time."

"Do you really believe that?" asked Rocco.

"If Agata weren't that wild animal, you would never think of her again. She'd be like all the others."

He seemed perplexed, staring out the window at the people

passing. Around us everything seemed to have stopped, as if time weren't moving. "What a neighborhood, God in heaven, what a neighborhood." He sighed.

Then a waiter approached and asked us if we wanted something to eat. He added: "When people talk to each other the way you're doing, it's a sign they've either made love or they're going to."

"Enough of that," Rocco growled.

"Don't get mad, boss. It's only a saying to give you luck," he said, leaving to get us a pizza.

Rocco couldn't help smiling. "Gianna," he murmured, "I could talk to you all day." And for a long time that voice, abrupt and a little vulgar, lingered in my ears.

What happened then was as final as one word too many, as sudden as snow giving way beneath one's feet, direct as a fall. When Rocco put his arm around my shoulders and held me against him for a long time, I had the feeling that he was taking possession of neither my arms nor my shoulders but of my past or at least of a part of me which could not belong to him. Why? I didn't know at all. I looked at his hand. What was there in common between that hand and mine, I asked myself with astonishment. Quickly, I must find something to say. So I spoke of Antonio. There. The name was enough. That name was a wall against which Rocco could hit his head. He stopped short. It was as if whatever attracted each of us to the other was forgotten, and already incredible. He sat there with knitted brows, without opening his lips. Then, defiantly, I asked him if it was the idea that I had gone to Sólanto and that I knew the village where his father had lived for so many years, if that was what made him silent. He shook his head.

"Don't joke, Gianna. You know very well it's not true. Sólanto, Antonio, Sicily, Baron di D., his son, your whole existence before coming here, for me those are words, nothing but words. What do you expect them to do to me? I was born in this country. You're the one who still thinks about all that. Come on, don't tell me it isn't so. You'll think about it till the end of your days. Wherever

you go, whatever you do, your childhood will always be pulling at
your sleeve. You're like Agata. Me, I had the kind of childhood
you want to forget."

There was nothing I could say to that. Rocco understood things
as well as I did and maybe even better. I could only repeat to myself: "You're like Agata. . . . You're another Agata," and it became
clear to me that we would never know each other better than this
day.

Rocco was wearing his distracted look again. It may have been
his eyes, very clear with a great deal of white around the iris—one
never knew what he was looking at.

"By the way," he asked, "do you know where the Baron went
after he left Sólanto?"

I shook my head that I did not: "That was Don Fofò's secret,"
I told him. "And, to tell the truth, nobody cared. There was no
time for people to be curious. After three years of war the only
thing that concerned us was survival." But as I spoke, I could see
that Rocco didn't believe me. So I repeated, "I promise you. . . .
That's the truth," and that seemed to convince him.

When he lowered his voice to say "We buried him this morning.
He was living here," I stammered: "It's impossible, Rocco. . . ."
and I let him see my grief.

"There are deaths one can't become resigned to," he said.

I would have liked him to keep on talking to me, but he was
already looking elsewhere. Then he called the waiter, who arrived
exclaiming: "Well, lovers, are you leaving?" He refused to let us
leave "like that." There was a customer who wanted to talk to
Rocco, and he, the waiter, wanted to offer us a dessert, a coffee,
something, anything. They had a drink. They chatted. "He'll tell
me later what happened," I thought, listening to them talk.

A little later, walking back, when we were passing through the
little streets, arms linked like good friends, Rocco told me about
Baron di D.'s last years. He let himself go, talked with his hands
and stopped between sentences.

"He never wanted for anything!" he said. "The whole quarter

was devoted to him. My father said it was like Sólanto: he ruled
us all. He wanted to get along on his own and not be dependent
on anyone. He gave Italian lessons. Most of his pupils were singers.
He always used to tease my father. 'I'm an immigrant who's succeeded, too. You see, we're even.' And they laughed.

"Every evening he'd have dinner with us. Old Cesarino had the
idea of serving him in white gloves. But when a customer called
him, he took them off. White gloves were something only the
Baron had a right to.

"Sometimes his pupils got an opera ticket for the Baron. He
always came back in an exalted state. Music was really a passion
with him. When Italy asked for peace, he told us he didn't want
to go back. 'It's not worth it,' he told me. 'I'd burst with rage. It
will take years for the country to get back on its feet, if it ever
does. A people who have seen so much necessarily become de-
based.' I was the only one he talked to seriously.

"The morning of his fall, when the doctor came to tell us that
he had bled so much that no one could see how he could recover,
I went to his house. The Baron was lying down, his forehead
bandaged. He seemed very weak. I suggested that we ought to let
his son know. He still found the strength to get angry: 'Neither
son nor priest. I've enough trouble without them.' Then he softened: 'But send me Agata. Do that for me. That will be enough.
. . . In any case, I reproach myself for nothing. . . .'

"When I came back it was evening and the Baron was dead.
Agata was crying. In his last moments he had asked her to take
him in her arms. She had lifted him as one takes a child and he
had stayed there as long as consciousness lasted, his head pressing
against her breast, his forehead against her cheek until the end. He
had tried to joke at first. 'Don't snivel, Agata. There are only the
two of us here. . . . I have only you to listen to. . . . My father,
poor soul, had nineteen people around his bed. . . . His room was
like a public square. . . .' But he grew continually weaker. Agata
was so upset that she took his hand to kiss it. He thanked her.
He told her she smelled of Sicily. 'There! You see. . . . As I

breathe, I think you are Sólanto. Let it be a sacrament between us.' Then she felt his breath no more. . . ."

As I listened to Rocco I was remembering again summers with Antonio when the war was only a faraway cloud, and when life without Antonio was not to be imagined. From that farthest distant happiness, sentences surged up, shreds of blue days, phrases between caresses, phrases carried away by the sea. . . "Gianna, time no longer exists." And others, still other phrases. . . . Sentences spoken afterwards, their sound, their taste of tears: "Get out, soldier, get out. . . ." Zaira's wail, which seemed to come up from her belly, and the cries of the women which rose from the kitchen.

The betrayals of memory. How to stop them. I could do no more. Thinking, for me, was always a journey to grief.

Pam was waiting for me at Casa Alfio.

It's no use telling myself how things happened, impossible. "Another of your hodgepodges!" Aunt Rosie cried at me before slamming the door in my face. She was beside herself. I could hear her in her room, talking aloud, blaming me for everything. It was my fault, I was the one who got Pam into this. "If it hadn't been for you, the idea would never have occurred to her." I threatened to leave her and go to a hotel. After that she reappeared, put on a hurt look, played the martyr, said over and over that no one loved her, that she had a right to some consideration, and I stayed. It was impossible to hold a grudge against her.

As for Rocco and Pam, that could be explained. To marry Pam was to increase Rocco's respectability and his chances of success. Didn't they have all the elements of a happy marriage? Did he love Pam? She believed he did and said so on every occasion. The fact is that she had been waiting for several years for something to happen which would make her unique. That something was here. Rocco, though American, was like no one else. Aunt Rosie said it was only his hair. "If he'd been blond she'd never have looked at him." She also mentioned how photogenic Rocco was, his dark skin, his broad shoulders. "She's already imagining the effect they'll make side by side in magazine pictures. Believe me, Gianna, she's marrying him out of professional shortsightedness."

During that period Pam and I lunched together every day. I listened to her confidences. Everything was confused in her, immodesty and reserve. Up to that time I had considered Pam a sort of backward student with borrowed opinions, a blonde with empty eyes feeding on the principles of beauty creams, so ineluctably devoted to her work that one could not imagine her surrendering to a man and even less to love one. I did not like to admit that I had been mistaken.

She began by telling me that she had no secrets from me, and that everything must be clear between us: she was marrying Rocco for the right reasons and to start a family. I congratulated her. Encouraged by my attentiveness, she swore to me that Rocco was taking no precautions when they made love and she hastened to add, as if this information were more important than all the rest: "It isn't because of laziness." At that point she stopped.

"Since you take them yourself, there's nothing to worry about, is there?" I answered.

"He's a healthy man," she said in a didactic voice.

Another time, when she was feeling very confidential, she said to me: "Up to now I've only known men who were petrified with fear, like college boys, or else terribly ashamed and vaguely homosexual. Or else indifferent, bored men who were only looking for company." I grew impatient: "Look, Pam, you're not going to make me believe you've only had spoiled children who have just let go of their mother's apron strings, fashion photographers, or lazy hypochondriacs. You must at least have met some others. . . ."

"A businessman," she said, her voice sulky, sullen.

"And then?"

"He'd been the husband of a college friend, a terribly rich Jewish girl. She'd left him."

Pam frowned. "I've never known anyone with such big flat

feet," she said. "When I saw them under the table beside mine, they gave me the shivers."

After that she began to explain to me that this man wasn't *comme il faut*, nor *like other people*, and besides, he was always looking at his knees when he talked to her.

"You mean he was abnormal?" I asked her.

And Pam, in her precise, efficient voice—what I called her telephone voice—told me about the flowers he sent her, superb flowers, expensive, enough to fill her studio. Aunt Rosie was in heaven! But there was a card with them on which the sender had written the sum they had cost. "He was really sick," said Pam, shaking her head. "He thought that he had to keep the woman informed about what he was spending on her." She told me also of dinners when he talked endlessly, and about the tables reserved a long time in advance in one of the best restaurants in town and about the long discussion over the menu. Nothing Pam wanted was good enough or rare enough. Once he came to get her in an old rented Bentley. But he changed his mind and they dined at his house on biscuits and orange juice. "He was depending on me to cure him. He used me," said Pam disgustedly. "In bed he had to have a little Japanese radio turned on in his pajama pocket all the time. He called it *a third voice*. Finally he had a nervous breakdown and everything ended."

I told her that her college friend might have warned her. Pam laughed. Her friend's case was different: he had never touched her. Besides that girl was an idiot and Pam never trusted her opinions.

At that point she looked at me and said: "Rocco, he's natural. . . ."

Then she added some thoughts on his career, on what his future would be like with her beside him, widening his circle of acquaintances—it wouldn't have taken much to make her give me a list of them—a whole program, told in a hurried voice as if she were afraid I would contradict her.

There was a silence during which Pam did a few ankle exercises, took one or two deep breaths and powdered her nose. She was uneasy. She opened her mouth as if about to start a sentence, blinked her lashes, shook her bracelets and remained silent. Finally she spoke of the life Rocco had led before knowing her and how sad it was, this man who spent his vacations in hotels because he had no friends: "Imagine, in hotels. I think that's awful." He should have visited rich worldly friends with large houses or even yachts, like the ones Pam knew. She waited for my reaction but I said nothing.

"Well," she asked me, "am I right? Doesn't Rocco deserve a life, well, a more brilliant life? Because after all, life is made up of the friends one makes, the people one sees. . . ."

"If you say so. . . ."

No one could have mistaken it; my voice was cool. Pam talked, explained, repeated herself, and I felt no enthusiasm listening to her. Abruptly, she put her face in her hands. "Gianna," she cried, "I beg of you, don't make things more difficult. What's happened to me is so unexpected. . . ."

Pam!

Even in the midst of her honest trouble she bore the stigmata of her profession. Even seeing her on the verge of tears, one could still be mistaken, believe she was getting ready to weep for some invisible photographer. Did I really speak to her? No. I had not yet won Pam's trust. But perhaps I should have put her on guard against the surprises which were easy to foresee. "Open her eyes for her," said Aunt Rosie. I did nothing. If I had said, "Pam, this man whom you find natural is your opposite," would she have believed me? If I had said: "He is as far from you as a desert. . . ." If I had shaken her until she listened to me and agreed. . . . But what was the use? She would have answered that she wasn't taking lessons from a foreigner. That was it. I was still a foreigner to her. She knew how to be pitiless when she felt like it. Rocco was much too simple, much too natural for me and besides I didn't understand anything about America. She certainly wouldn't have missed the chance to tell me so and all her phrases would have begun with *we*. *We* sometimes meant "Rocco and me" and sometimes "We Americans."

And so we would have left it at that. Everything would have ended as usual in empty looks, cigarettes we lighted, shrugs of the shoulders, and smoke. And silence.

A strange wedding. Pam played no more than a decorative part. The excitement was elsewhere. It was in Rocco's cold eyes, in the pallor of his look, in his silence which cloaked him in a disturbing dignity. It was he who received. He took over with such an aggressive pleasantness, as if he was determined that everyone should know that he was the absolute master of this ceremony.

Everything went as one would have wished. The day before, at Mrs. MacMannox's, a reception in honor of the couple had brought together the entire family of *Fair*. It was all laughter, chirpings, little stifled cries and flash bulbs going off. On hand were the most popular cover girls, photographers as handsome as dancers, some well-known painters. Rocco never unclenched his teeth while Pam never ceased to smile broadly. Daisy Lee had arrived unexpectedly. She made a dazzling entrance, mouth thrust forward, her feet in buskins—a fashion she was launching. She was dressed that evening in a violet shift around which she had wound multicolored scarves. With her flat cheeks, her big nose, her geisha's hair, she looked like a clairvoyant about to reveal her secrets.

"Let's forget, let's forget. . . ." Saying these words, she threw herself into Rocco's arms. He returned her kisses.

The religious ceremony took place the next day, in private, in the Catholic Church. That was what Rocco wanted. Neither Pam nor Aunt Rosie had objected. This was to prove their wisdom. Any other solution would have cost Rocco most of his voters. Would they have forgiven him for marrying anywhere except the Church of the Transfiguration? Surely not. So a Dominican had expedited Pam's religious education in less than a month. As for Pam's father, he was left to his missions. No one thought of consulting him, or even informing him. "A political conversion, my dear," said Aunt Rosie, who found it an opportunity to use theatrical phrases. She also spoke of "reasons of state, my dear," her voice full of tremolos, as if Rocco had already attained the highest summits of importance. She began to praise his seriousness, his reflective air. When she looked at him, her eyes softened. "He is dark," she said, "but thank God, it's only Latin." In short, her hostility ceased.

In the church the priest officiated with the solemnity due great occasions, as he had been taught in the seminary at Noto. He raised the ciborium as high as his hands could reach, with a slight hesitation before the culminating point, like a weight lifter; he bowed over the altar longer than usual, forcing the children in the choir to remain for long anguished minutes with their arms outstretched raising his chasuble; and at each genuflexion he bent right down to the ground, resolutely hitting his knee on the hollow step without minding its muffled resonance. "But they're athletes!" Mrs. MacMannox murmured, impressed by the ceremony.

Agata was in charge of the decorations in the church, a task she performed with joy. As if to flout the banality of the surroundings, she overflowed with imagination. Each of her discoveries was based on her unconscious memory of the time when the mass and the processions were the only feast days. Pam, when she entered the church, caught her breath at the sight. It looked like the banners of a celebrating city, a forest on a frosty day, or the palace of Sleeping Beauty on the evening she awoke.

A profusion of bright blue bulbs made a halo around the statues which were all crowned with flowers. To see them glistening with light, one would hardly have guessed how ugly they could be. And God knows they were! But one could scarcely recognize Santa Lucia who seemed to have been plunged into a bath of blue and gold. As for Saint Roch's sad dog, he had become beautiful as a unicorn.

Everything had been done and well done. Two necklaces had been added to the neck of Shun Ying's Virgin. Agata believed in that Madonna with all her heart. She was not put off by her slanted eyes, or by her yellow child. On the contrary, she called her "the Goddess" and spoke of offering her a dress. That day

Shun Ying's Virgin had a right, in addition to her necklaces, to a shower of scarlet stars.

Like the moorings or the rigging of a ship, paper garlands hung from the vaults, so many that once seated, Rocco and Pam—she was wearing a short white dress which Agata, at first glance, thought too simple (she would have liked a thousand pleats, drapery, something special)—felt as if they were in a ship at anchor.

Finally—and this was not the least of her successes—Agata had succeeded in getting rid of those candles in glass tumblers whose presence in New York churches can only be explained by a public phobia about fire. "Empty those milk bottles for me," she ordered the beadle. And there had been a long discussion between them about why she had used this expression which the beadle thought insulting. But Agata maintained that the wax seen through the glass really looked like milk. It was horrible. And she repeated, "Get rid of them," in a curt tone. Then she cried, "Some real candles, that isn't asking for the moon!" And she was ready to heap invective on his head if he refused.

Real candles, then, shone in the church, which seemed as strange to some as an ermine carpet.

Then came the luncheon, which Daisy Lee considered one of gothic elegance, drawling out the "gothic" at such length that she made a sound shaped like a noodle, a noise which prolonged itself indefinitely and held her lips pursed as if she were whistling. Why that word? Who knows? Perhaps she considered the frame of this repast gothic—a bare white room, the banquet room at Casa Alfio. Calò was seated beside his wife and held her hand under the table, while Theodore with the solemnity of his seventeen years, his quiet deep look, his face like an archangel, played his part of equerry to his Uncle Rocco from whose side he never moved. He poured drinks for him, lit his cigar, had eyes and ears, it seemed, only for him. Or was it Agata, dressed in black, who seemed gothic to Daisy Lee? "Gothic stiffness. . . ." murmured Daisy Lee looking at her. Anyway, for these reasons or for others, "Gothic" was what the editor-in-chief of *Fair* continued to proclaim. Everyone agreed with her that there was nothing more medieval than an oil bottle placed on a table or a napkin folded into a bishop's hat—"the linen has the candor and delicacy of the Middle Ages"—and that the bread in its basket had "incomparable vitality, extraordinary unity. . . ." Daisy Lee, carried away, called on Carpaccio, gave the address of the best baker in Bavaria, cited the name of a collector who was a friend of hers who possessed a grain of wheat from the time of the pharaohs. Whom did she not know, that day? Such a profusion of wines was not served for nothing. . . .

Aunt Rosie was beginning to feel ill at ease. She wore a baby pink dress and a hat made of flowers. "Am I in key?" she asked herself, and she began to regret that Mister Mac was not there to guide her. But Alfio, sitting near her, gallantly compared her head-dress with a nest of dreams, and everything was immediately all right. A nest of dreams. . . . What a charming man. Mrs. Mac-Mannox and Alfio Bonavia bantered over their plates. No doubt the conversation was a little confused, but never mind! There was a Broglio on the table, stirring the imagination. Charming man, this Bonavia. . . . And the two bronzes as centerpiece: one represented Fortune, the other William Tell in his father's arms. What taste! They exchanged anecdotes and then Alfio promised to come to visit her, to teach her to make that macaroni and eggplant dish she had two helpings of. Of course, he would come. That was a promise.

"May I call you Alfio?"

Mrs. MacMannox often felt a pressing need to make friends. That day she was succeeding marvelously. Mr. Bonavia was a man whom she'd be very pleased to receive in her home. Meanwhile, Alfio was thinking: America is a paradise! That little Pam had chosen well. After all, his family was perfect.

Alfio was living his hour of glory. This choice of Rocco's suited him beyond his wildest hopes. A modern girl, this Pam, efficient and making a mint in that magazine where she worked. How lovely it was that she was going to make Rocco happy. Alfio kept turning toward her to get the full impact of her calm blondness.

He was almost afraid to imagine the *afterwards*. To think of Pam in anyone's arms, in a bed, in his son's life? No. There was a danger that she would be spirited away, would suddenly disappear. Alfio was superstitious. And not only that: he always imagined the worst. He knew his hereditary tendency toward pessimism and he was ashamed of it as if it were a sickness. Black thoughts, one knew where they began, but who could tell where they would end? Suddenly he felt a sort of dizziness. What did that mean? Everything seemed confused. At this moment, neither Pam's blondness nor Daisy Lee's convincing voice kept from him an image which would return to haunt him. He felt weighed down, overcome by a phantasmagoria. . . . Peppina's face. . . . It was she on the day of their marriage. She, in her blue blouse. There was their lodging—what could you call that awful blind alley?—the laundry was drying in their wedding chamber and they were so hungry they could not sleep. How he loved her! She laughed at everything: at Alfio, at hunger, at the half dried laundry which dripped "tock, tock, tock!" on the floor with the regularity of a clock. How beautiful she was! For years she was the only one he desired, on the mattress on the floor, desire for her hair which attracted him like a black torrent, desire for her breasts which were so comically far apart, pointing out as if they didn't know one another, desire for the hollow of her thighs, for the divine outline of that hollow. Oh, Peppina! And Alfio was surprised by the prayer on his lips: "Almighty God, watch over her. She's only a little girl. Make her laugh the way she used to laugh in the night. . . ." A sharp pain. Like a rending of the soul.

When old Cesarino crossed the room with a new batch of bottles, he gave Alfio a startled look. They had known each other for more than forty years, since the Bonavias first came to the neighborhood, since the period of the home-cooked meals. He went towards him, dragging his feet in his new shoes as he dragged them in slippers. A dialogue in low voices went on between them. "What's biting you?" asked Cesarino in a reproving voice.

"It's a matter of the next world."

Cesarino shrugged his shoulders.

"You picked a fine time for it. . . ."

"You can't pick and choose," said Alfio in a weary voice.

"All right, drink up then, for heaven's sake. . . ."

He went to get a bottle.

Alfio filled a glass to the top. And with the third bumper his success again seemed undeniable to him, and Pam was just the daughter-in-law for him. Yes, Rocco would be a happy man. . . .

Calò said nothing. Talking was too hard for him. A fatal mishap he couldn't explain to himself. Why he? He was the only one in the family who spoke English with that horrible accent. But there was nothing to do about it. It was agonizing. In his mouth "u" became "ou," tearful, drawling, it made conversation impossible. Nobody understood him. So he was silent. But every so often Calò pressed Agata's hand under the tablecloth to comfort himself. And he murmured sweet things to her in dialect. That was his whole pleasure, to talk with Agata, unknown to the rest, in a tongue which was not that vile English, that chalice of bitterness from which he had to drink each day to the dregs.

"I hope I looked more in love than he does," he said, indicating Rocco with his eyes.

"How would I know. . . ."

Agata shook her head and closed her eyes, one of her gestures. Then she repeated: "How would I know," shrugging her shoulders. As if she really didn't know.

Both of them had the same distaste for definite commitments, flat "yesses," "no" with no recourse, all that deadly absence of mystery that abounded in the talk around them. They needed this haziness, this vagueness, half truths which fooled no one and gave conversations the unforeseeable character of dreams. And Calò pretended to believe her.

"So you don't know? You really don't know?"

"I know you chose with your heart. Rocco has acted with his head."

"My Agata, you know everything. You're a real genius, a seer, and I love you."

Calò smiled and said that the tablecloth over their united hands looked to him like a sheet.

Agata put her head on his shoulder.

Pam paid scarcely any attention to Rocco and he acted as if he had no time for her. Not a shadow of affectation between them. Rocco, like a man attracted by the difficult, was making a conquest of Daisy Lee. Pam seemed to believe that both their lives depended on the efficiency of her smiles. Their mutual understanding was clear, but there was something frightening about it. They made one think of two trains entering a station, two trains which had chanced to arrive at the same time on neighboring tracks.

Nevertheless everyone agreed that Pam and Rocco made a well-matched couple. A certainty which each expressed in his own way. "They have their whole life for kissing," remarked Alfio. "She can make him whatever she wishes," Daisy Lee answered, she who could only imagine this aspect of conjugal life. "He's going to love her, but he'll love me nearly as much," said Aunt Rosie, adding: "We're going to be friends, he and I, such friends." The idea of a mistake or a failure could not enter Theodore's mind. "Everything my Uncle Rocco does is well done," he thought. And "When the moment comes, I hope I'm as happy as he is." For Agata, "to speak of such things" seemed both shocking and pointless. The mere fact of alluding to it constituted an invasion of the private life of Pam and Rocco. "They have chosen one another," she said, and her comments stopped there. As for imagining indifference or "lack of love," that was inviting misery; she would not dream of it. Such ideas were foreign to her.

Cesarino was the only one to express some reservations. When he went back to the kitchen, when the chef asked him: "Well, how's it going out there?" Cesarino answered: "They're not cut from the same cloth."

*　*　*

Alfio was indignant. "You must be joking," he said to him. But Rocco was not joking. Their passage was reserved.

"Have you consulted with her, at least?"

"Why should I?" replied Rocco.

Then Alfio felt real rage, a rage such as only Italians from Italy feel, the rage of a man of the people, with gestures, threats and cries.

"You know what you're going to find over there? A starving country. Rocco, I'm ashamed of you, ashamed, ashamed, ashamed. . . . As if Sicily could interest anybody! Why not go to Saudi Arabia while you're at it? There are at least as many pebbles there as in Sicily, as little water, and for dirt, it's about the same. An island at the end of the world. That's where you're going to hole up. All you'll see is paupers, wretches, the handicapped, people with crippled thoughts. And what about her? What will she think of you, of us? . . . And what about me! You work and slave all your life to put down roots somewhere and to build some kind of reputation and what does your son do? He decides to take his honeymoon among the same filthy creatures you didn't want to have for relatives."

Rocco was annoyed. He had never seen his father in such a state. "Lord!" he thought, "how peaceful we were before. . . ." But he went on, thinking that he must be patient, that Alfio was getting old.

For the third time his father cried at him: "All right then, do whatever you please," in a furious voice.

What does it have to do with him, thought Rocco. And in fact, why am I going there? He didn't know. His head swam. Fatigue, maybe, the preparations for departure. This trip seemed more and more useless. He almost wished it were over. Suddenly Rocco realized that the future was no longer his alone but also Pam's. While he had lived among Alfio, Calò and Agata, with here and there a discreetly managed affair, it was easy for him to lead his own life. And that freedom was just what made the Bonavias happy. Love, Rocco told himself, must be what I've known here. The feeling that things are as they are because heaven wills them so. But now? Could it ever be the same?

This argument with his father affected Rocco like a cold shower. He left in a daze, full of black forebodings and a stranger to himself.

At the door he found Agata waiting for him. She approached him, took him by surprise as she grasped his shoulders and began to smother him with kisses. They fell on his eyelashes, his forehead, his mouth, his chin; she shook him, caressed him, embraced him as if Rocco were a child again. He laughed: "Stop Agata. . . . I'm not twelve years old any more, you know. And anyway, I'm the one who should hug you that way." She whispered in his ear in a voice that trembled a little. "I know where you're going. I saw your tickets. You're doing the right thing. What I wouldn't give to go with you."

When he put his hand on her cheek, Rocco realized Agata was crying.

"Agata! Calm down, I beg of you. Or else you'll make me cry too."

Agata struggled, did her best, but the tears still escaped, ran down her cheeks onto her dress. Rocco hugged her against him. This was really Agata, his pride, his wild little Agata. It was really she he was holding in his arms. For a moment he was conscious of nothing else.

The next day Rocco left.

III.

Innocent crimes? Who has not committed them?   PIRANDELLO

A superb festival, but Palermo was short of water and it was too bad that so many palaces, so many churches were still in ruins. A superb festival, everybody was there. The streets had been lighted for several kilometers, but this year the firecrackers were still dangerous: they exploded too loudly and as usual there were victims. A pork butcher had avenged his honor by murdering three men in the same family. His knife was forty centimeters long, but the inquest proved that the murderer's suspicions were unjustified: his wife was not deceiving him. And then a *carabiniere* had been hit in the head while the procession was passing. He left seven orphans. The police hadn't found the guilty party. A few incidents in all. That's how the local press expressed it: several incidents.

But the people were satisfied: the Municipality had spent hugely. Not those usual expenditures which left the public feeling discontented and cheated. Exceptional expenditures. The kind that made everybody happy. Such was the news the evening that Rocco and Pam arrived in Palermo. It was July 14th, the feast day of Saint Rosalie.

An illustrious visitor had honored the hotel where they lodged with his presence: Wagner. A white marble plaque explained that he had written *Parsifal* there, and it clearly implied that had it been written elsewhere the work would have been less beautiful. The Gothico-Mauresque decorations of the hall, the potted palms in the corner of the staircase, a mixture of luxury and bad taste, too many statues, all that added luster to Wagner's memory, a tourist of genius who had left some of his "soul" in Palermo. It all pleased Pam enormously. Aside from that, she made scarcely any differentiation between *Parsifal* and those imposing groups of Psyches, of dancing Cupids. For her, anything serious must be large and imposing.

That night the wind came from Africa. It twisted the curtains, made the doors slam and brought with it a searing heat. It had just begun, the porter told them. Toward noon it could be seen rising, pouring a thick dust over the city like a wave of wheat until one could hardly breathe. The porter apologized for it like a mother excusing her child's whims. "Nature always has to add her grain of salt. Too bad, really too bad," he repeated, mopping his brow. No, the air conditioning wasn't working. The motor had broken down. Minor damage. A replacement part had left Rome a week ago but it still hadn't arrived. At least so the station master said, although the porter seemed convinced of the opposite. The piece was there for sure, but certain people found it to their advantage to delay packages as long as possible. "Know what I mean?" And he made the gesture of feeling money.

A long exchange of ideas with foreigners who had scarcely disembarked seemed to this fellow the best way of making them welcome. "Funny man," thought Rocco, "and how obliging he is."

While he talked, the porter directed an army of adolescents in white jackets, their hair stiff with grease, who simultaneously had to manage baggage, keys, evening papers, fruit, a bottle of cold water, all this to be arranged in the travelers' apartments. The porter returned to that miserable piece of machinery which now, when most needed, failed to supply cool air. He cast his eyes to the frescoes on the ceiling: "Man can no longer control his inventions," he sighed, as if this conclusion had been dictated to him by the gods and goddesses who frolicked above among pink clouds. Then he began again to tell what he'd gone through to correct this miserable situation, about the specialist he had consulted—"A young Palerman," he explained, with a dubious grimace. A bad beginning. Really disastrous! The specialist had messed up everything: the electric wires, the telephone, the cool air, so thoroughly that in the kitchen you could hear noises in the refrigerator every time the elevator started. A miserable fellow, that specialist, who hadn't slept for three nights. Women were too much on his mind, probably. Well, one thing or another, you had to be understanding and excuse him. Saint Rosalie had only one feast day a year, and then the wind had to be stupefying. . . .

Pam observed that to her knowledge only the Carnival in Rio created such confusion. But this remark was not to her interlocutor's taste, and he shot her a reproving look.

"The Carnival in Rio, I know about that," said he. "I lived down there for ten years. It's a village fete compared with Saint Rosalie, a celebration for the poor. Think, Signora, how we have a regular triumphal procession. The illuminations can be seen for nine kilometers. As for the fireworks, a Rothschild couldn't pay for them. They last more than an hour. Yes, Signora. More than an hour of explosions that shake the ground under you—flashes, thunder, volcanic eruptions so big that clouds of powder hang suspended in the sky until the day after."

While accompanying Pam and Rocco to their room, the porter still had time to mention other guests almost as famous as Wagner. The hotel once had the honor to welcome the kaiser, who didn't know how to put his shoes on by himself, several grand dukes, a German countess whose name he regretfully could not mention although she had left a deep impression on the hotel, and finally, Anatole France. With his magnificent head, his Olympian forehead and his gray jacket which made him look rather military, the porter knew well how to bring back the pageantry of the past; with each name he pronounced, one expected to see his heroes appear in flesh and blood.

When they reached their room, he surveyed the furniture and walls with an inquisitorial look, wished the couple good night, then, passing the bed, stopped: "Matrimonial," he said, turning towards Pam. "A matrimonial couch." And when he pushed his thumb into the mattress as if to check its softness, repeating the gesture three times, Pam felt herself blushing to the roots of her hair.

This was a man who enjoyed a high reputation in Palermo.

Rocco went out to explore the city after nightfall. He expected to wander silently, to have a long nocturnal ramble. But nothing of the sort. Palermo glittered with lights. Thousands of bulbs tore the fragile fabric of the night. They lit up pediments, outlined statues with a single fiery line or, hanging from wires, turned the streets into sparkling tunnels. The city looked like an immense ballroom invaded by a dazzled and exhausted crowd. No music and even fewer dancers. Whole families emerged from one same fiacre, poured over the squares, spread out, flowed slowly through the streets. Never fewer than four people on one motor scooter. Three generations piled into carts where the crowding, the heat, and the discomfort lent a tragic look to the sleeping children. Lying across their parents' knees, shaken by the horse's gait, thrown forward, caught back, handled, pale, limp, their mouths open and heads thrown back, they slept like innocent victims destined for some horrible sacrifice.

What sense has a pilgrimage with no end? How could it be justified? Why pack into the stifling alleys? Why should several thousand women, children, adults and old men form such a dark and sticky mass during an entire night? Was that the only way to perpetuate the memory of a virgin whose bones, found on Mount Pellegrino, had saved the city from plague? As if four centuries of these festivals should allow them to better appreciate the fasts and penances she had undergone. . . And must they perspire that way to go on deserving her protection? Or was this fete only a pretext for showing off, to give public testimony by the number of children gathered of the family's sexual prowess?

Dancing, yes, on a cool night. Orchestras on the street corners, flower-decked carts, a carnival, that's gay. But how could one justify that absurd milling about under waves of light?

Pam felt irritated. In the end, that continual buzzing was exhausting! And that fairground activity, those pointless shouts, all those faces in a meaningless ballet; children smeared with candy, their noisy games, the squeaking little boxes they squeezed imitating a rooster's crow so exactly that one believed it real, and those strange foods offered on the huge stalls! The adults ate whole cones full of dry seeds which any place else would have been bird food.

"The fact is . . ." began Pam in a plaintive voice. But Rocco's face stopped her. Was there any doubt that he loved this night, this noise, this crowd and that he was finding beauty here, where she could see none?

"Narrow streets, roofs touching each other, what a blessing!" he sighed. "Look, Pam, the houses seem to lean against one another, they rub together, they seem to love one another, these houses."

Then he began to stare at the stars as if he were seeing them for the first time.

He wore a blue jacket with white stripes, one of those light jackets men wear in New York on very hot days, light trousers, and canvas tennis shoes. Children stood still when he passed, young people, men and women, a hundred heads turned to Rocco and his happy elegance, a hundred faces turned towards Pam's blondness.

"*Americani. . . . Americani. . . .*"

A persistent whispering gave testimony to the admiration this people in black felt for the daring costume in which they recognized the signs of a fantasy which would never be theirs. "Americani. ... Americani. ..." they murmured in their raucous voices, their sad voices, wherever the two of them went.

"I'm thirsty," Pam complained.

"Let's sit down," said Rocco in a resigned voice.

They hesitated a long time between the big coffee room of the Hotel Jolly, a reassuringly American oasis, and a restaurant perched on the top of a palace, glowing with a profusion of milky globes. Finally they decided on the terrace of a bar set in the shadows of the Marine Promenade. It was a temporary shelter where everything seemed confused and improvised. One could rent a single chair, or several at once, and a table, without being committed to anything by sitting there. Some customers limited themselves to bread which they pulled from their pockets. Others called a food vendor in a white jacket and ordered ices from him. Still others paid for a chair and sat there without uttering a word.

As soon as he sat down Rocco withdrew into silent meditation. He only had eyes for the movements of the vendor in the spotted jacket, the mass suicide of the gnats in the naked flame of a gas jet, and a young woman seated not far from him, wearing a very low cut dress, a creature the likes of which he'd never seen. She succeeded, without departing from a statue's impassivity and by no more than a few casual glances, to attract the attention of a well-dressed man who was also alone and who only seemed interested in feeding the dog which he held on a leash. Sometimes she asked for water, sometimes for matches which he held out mechanically, still feeding almonds to his dog who barked and caught them in the air. Then she dropped her handkerchief, which he did not pick up. She was certainly an odd character with impossibly black hair, a great deal of pink in her cheeks and mascara drawn in long lines around her eyes. Her face looked as if it were painted with poster paints. In the movement he made taking the handkerchief off the ground and holding it out to her, Rocco touched her hand: If I were alone, he told himself, I would talk to her and perhaps I would be tempted to go with her wherever

she liked. . . ." The lady gave him a sooty glance. Rocco turned
his head for fear the upset he felt would be visible. And he said
to himself, How odd. . . . It was not so much that his response
surprised him as the impossibility of explaining it to himself.

Suddenly beyond the tables a cry was heard. A young boy was
running, his sleeves rolled up. A flower seller. His mouth open
wide, he shouted, and his voice spurted forth, sometimes strident,
sometimes thin as the cry of the gulls. He brandished his flowers
over the diners, white shapes which looked like branches covered
with snow. He played with them like a kite, and Pam wondered
just what they were. One had to be a Sicilian to call these things
bouquets, these corollas stripped of their stems and leaves, these
naked corollas stuck on thin rings, these nuptial flowers which,
bunched together, formed a dishevelled torch. Their perfume was
stronger than the odor of the festive city, the stale smell of the
café, of frying, of warm fritters. It was stronger than all these
odors, good or bad. It was a living perfume, a solid perfume which
defied the warm air of summer.

"Jasmine," said Rocco, as if jasmine were an old friend who
had appeared to him suddenly in the midst of a crowd of strangers.
His eyes shone, he smiled. Jasmine. . . . He looked as if he were
really happy. Pam noticed that he kept on moving his lips and
murmuring "jasmine," as if he were speaking to an invisible person.

"Jasmine?" she asked. "How do you know?"

"Agata told me, and when she talked to us about those bouquets, you'd have thought, to listen to her, that she was telling us
about China or Persia. The children go out at daybreak. They go
to the gardens between the city and the mountains. And there
they pick climbing jasmine from the walls. It's not forbidden; the
jasmine doesn't belong to anyone. They pick it from trees, from
rocks, they dig holes in the black earth and bring it back. Their
mothers, their sisters pin the flowers one by one on dried reeds.
Then they send the children to sell the bouquets wherever there's
a crowd: at the bus stops, on the café terraces, in the public gar-

dens, at the door of the city hall, or even in front of hospitals on visiting days."

"They'd do better to send them to school," said Pam in a sulky voice.

"They haven't the money," answered Rocco.

"What kind of story is that!" cried Pam.

Then she shrugged her shoulders and said, "What a country. . . ."

"*Gelsomino . . . gelsomino*," cried the harsh voice, the shrill voice of a gull.

He approached. He seemed now to speak to Rocco. How old can he be? At that age one is neither man nor child. At what age is it that one still has trust in life but already fears it? That anxious look and the shoulder blades which thrust so strongly under his shirt. . . . Fifteen? Rocco wondered. Maybe sixteen? . . . And the voice of a starveling. . . .

What attracted one's attention was that obvious anxiety but also something in the boy's eyes which contrasted oddly with the childish delicacy of the face. A rough sketch of a man, thought Rocco. . . . And a single job: to run through the streets. . . . But there was something else: that cry which irritated to the point of pain, that long cry charged with urgency. Anywhere else such behavior would have hurt his business. People would have thought the boy crazy and made him be quiet. But in Palermo it was otherwise, since he was called from one table to another: "Here, Gigino. Bring the jasmine here."

And Gigino ran. He took a bouquet and held it out with a proud assurance and then with an impatient palm claimed his due. One hundred lire was collected according to a calculation so rapid that one scarcely had time to count, and Gigino left, shouting and brandishing his flowers over the diners.

But he also used a more surprising method to which Pam became victim: without any expressed desire on her part, a bouquet tossed in the air fell almost in her hands. Gigino followed at a bound.

"Try and see," he said in a voice of command.

And he stood planted in front of her. She favored him with a smile which she knew she could not help, the smile of a worldly woman, moistened lips, teeth exposed, tongue just barely showing. Perhaps she only wished to express her gratitude. But she did it so unnaturally that Rocco saw it and his face darkened. She has no dignity, he thought.

"Go ahead, be tempted," repeated Gigino without trying to hide his impatience.

Pam was going to take the flowers when Rocco pushed them aside with an abrupt gesture.

"I forgot my wallet," he said, feeling his pockets. "I must have left it at the hotel."

The incident was brief. With a supreme disinterest, Gigino put the bouquet in Pam's hands.

"I'm giving them to the Signora," he said.

And his voice betrayed a childish exuberance, a need to be proud.

"Take those flowers back," said Rocco.

"It's a gift," said Gigino with the same impatience.

"Go on. . . . Leave us alone. We'll buy your bouquet tomorrow."

Gigino looked scornful.

"Is that what you think? Suppose I don't want to sell it to-morrow."

He made a vague movement which could have indicated heaven or an uncertain future, then he turned on his heel, giving himself to a frenzy of running and shouting in the faces of the passersby.

The bouquet stayed in Pam's hands.

"What impudence," she stammered. "I know I shouldn't have smiled that way. It's probably my fault," and she was suddenly silent.

Rocco got up. "I'll be back," he said. He decided to go to the hotel and come back, determined to pay Gigino.

Seated on a stone opposite the table where Pam was waiting

alone, the jasmine seller seemed deep in his accounts when Rocco called him.

"Hey, here's your money," Rocco said to him.

But Gigino was not listening. He was making piles of money in his fingers: lire with lire, centesimi with centesimi.

"I said, here's your money," repeated Rocco.

"My money? What money?" asked Gigino without even looking at him.

Then, speaking with great haste as if he were afraid that Rocco would not let him say everything, he added, "Excuse me, sir, but everything is not for sale here. And you can't pay for gifts."

"That's not the point," Rocco said. "You talk to me as if I wanted to offend you, as if I were gloating over you by giving you this money. I'm only trying to give you what I owe you. Come on, take it. . . ."

And he held out a thousand lire. The bill impressed Gigino. He was silent and stared at the bill with frightened eyes.

"That's a lot of money," he said.

And Rocco said, "No, no. . . ." to quiet him.

Gigino took the bill and for a few moments seemed to hesitate, then he got up. He was not tall, and all one saw of his face were his frightened eyes.

"I'm going to show you," he said, "what I'll do with it. Look. . . ."

The last word was spoken with rage, with frenzy, then he repeated, "Look," raised his arms and approached Rocco who got the torn crumpled bill full in the face.

"That's what I do with your money," howled Gigino. "I didn't ask you for charity, did I? Leave me alone!"

Rocco felt an irresistible desire to thrash him, but Gigino gave him no time for it. He left on the run. Rocco looked after him as he disappeared around a corner, then he went back to the terrace where Pam was waiting for him.

"Let's get out of here," he said, "and fast."

She got up. Day was beginning to dawn.

"*Americani,*" muttered a voice at the next table.

Rocco walked faster. They passed in front of a row of men seated on a bench, then in front of other men smoking under a tree.

"*Americani,*" said a voice from the bench.

"*Americani,*" said a voice from under the tree.

If there was anything that Pam detested it was Rocco's tone, his hostile eyes, very bright (white with rage, she thought), his odd smile with clenched teeth, and she asked herself by what strange turn of events she was there beside a man who was beside himself with fury. I've chosen blindly, she told herself. Then she took hold of herself, began to think that Rocco's violence was caused by the fatigue of the day, its heat, by the incident with Gigino, and she went calmly into the bathroom.

Rocco heard her taking off her clothes, then her shoes. He heard her open and close the taps, the water running, the bottles she opened, her toothbrush grating, then the silence in which he imagined her choosing between two hair styles. In a few moments she would enter, perfectly beautiful, so well groomed, so blonde, and Rocco sighed. She works on a magazine even when she's undressed, and he thought that only a disorderly woman, an uncombed woman could have satisfied his sensuality. He lit a cigarette to give himself courage but a sort of panic made him put it out at once: he didn't want anything. Several of Pam's habits returned to his mind, all of them displeasing. Maybe she would still want to talk. Maybe he would have to listen to her questions. Maybe she would ask him to make love in the serious voice she used on such occasions.

A moment later, Pam came in. When she approached the bed, Rocco looked at her with a desperate glance, one of those mute appeals for silence. A wrong word or look and he would have got up and fled. He reproached himself. You're crazy, he told himself, completely crazy. But he needed to be in the street, in a crowd where the lights were and the noise and maybe he even needed the woman in the multicolored dress he'd seen in the bar on the Marine Promenade. Basically he'd only found happiness in brief affairs. He decided that he was made for women who came and went quickly—and only for them.

The next day Rocco went to a tailor on the via Ruggero Settimo. He came back dressed in white tussore with a tightwaisted jacket, a black tie, and a panama with a wide brim. He seemed perfectly at ease and sure of himself dressed that way. But Pam's surprise was such that she instinctively made a gesture to fend him off when he wanted to kiss her.

"What's wrong?" he asked her.

"Nothing, nothing," she replied.

What could she say to him? That she felt that he was becoming more and more foreign, more distant, more incomprehensible, and that this new costume strengthened this feeling? She was dumbfounded.

This singular transformation dated from his arrival in Palermo. But thinking carefully, she wondered if it all hadn't begun at the moment when the son of Alfio Bonavia had left the New York docks. He had taken to the sea the way a penitent retraces his steps to his church.

How quick he was to pick up Latin ways, this American who had always respected the value of time, who had been submissive to the power of work, of money, and so anxious to do well! Several days were enough for him to have adopted an Oriental passivity.

A fancy for siestas very quickly became whole days lived in nothing but torpor. Indifferent to the heat, the mosquitoes, the noise from the street, Rocco cultivated a routine that Pam considered fatal: barely awake, he lit a cigarette, ordered an espresso which he drank in silence, then went back to sleep. His sleep was interrupted by starts, kicks, and even by a fierce rattle in his throat when a dream brought him face to face with Gigino. For he obstinately continued to rehearse the memory of the affront he had received. Then he sometimes mumbled incomprehensibly and

went back to sleep with the expression of a man who has been insulted.

Meanwhile Pam, stretched out between the moist sheets,
quenched her thirst for artistic emotions in a Baedeker. Folded
plans, maps showed her the locations of those churches, those
temples which she would never see. The room smelled of coffee
and smoke. She told herself that this way of living was neither
healthy nor normal and that she would have nothing to tell about
when she got back. A sort of despair overcame her. I don't want
any more of this man, she told herself. There he is, sprawled out
for the day. I can't stand any more of him.

Sometimes Rocco got up for several hours at the beginning of
the morning. Then, almost always, he went to sit on the balcony
in his pajamas. There he peered into the darkness of the half open
windows of other rooms with the intensity of a birdwatcher.

A balcony shaded with canvas (according to a local custom
which made it possible to preserve the privacy of this airy space)
hypnotized him. An old man naked from the waist up was always
there. Did he get up before Rocco? Did he go to bed after him?
Whatever time it was, Rocco had never seen the balcony empty
of that carcass in ragged trousers. He tried to fool him by slipping
onto the balcony at dawn or in the middle of the night, but the
old man was always there.

"How strange!" said Rocco. "What can the man do there all
day and night?"

"Maybe he wonders the same thing about you," replied Pam in
an irritated voice.

One day the old man made a gesture which Rocco interpreted
as a salute. In any case, he returned it. Then they exchanged a few
generalities on the weather and friendly relations were established
above the noise of the street. The old man, who said he was a
prince and who was one, no doubt, never failed to ask after Pam.

"The Signora is well?" he asked.

"You're very kind," replied Rocco.

Pam looked at them suspiciously, and with a chill in her heart

thought that she was in the way. She was foolish enough to say so.
"You seem to lead just the life that suits you. I feel I'm in the
way."
Rocco thought she was right.

Others approach the night thinking of its shared response and
its happy disorder; Pam, she, followed a man in whom the end of
day inspired only one desire: to get up and go out. What Rocco
cared about was to find Gigino again. According to him, he just
had to find the jasmine seller and pay him. His evenings were
spent this way. In spite of her good intentions, Pam could not
accept what she did not understand. For there was evident dis-
proportion between the modest flowers which had fallen unexpectedly into her hands and Rocco's determination to treat the
donor of the gift as a guilty man. But how could she make him
listen to reason? When she tried, Rocco cried, "You can't understand!" with such anger, such explosiveness in his voice that Pam
felt nervous tears running down her cheeks.

On what terrace, in what square was Gigino crying his wares?
Not in the Bellini, or in the Dante, or in the Olympia, or in any of
the cafés where Rocco sat. But sometimes it happened that the
perfumes of summer, of flowers, of turned earth or else the clear
odor of jasmine arrived like a tide from no one knew where, making him suddenly think that Gigino was not far away.

Then Rocco questioned the waiters.

"You haven't seen Gigino by any chance?"

"Who, sir?"

"The jasmine seller."

"Oh, the jasmine Gigino! You're looking for him? He's not far,
let's see. . . ."

And a loud shout from a neighboring street showed that he was
right. It was his voice reaching clear to the table where Rocco sat,
his voice, elusive as the wind. It vibrated, was amplified from alleyway to alleyway, was lost, then flowed along the walls again,

shrill, sharp, and was lost again in an incomprehensible sound: "Aiini. . . . Aiini. . . ."

"Listen, sir, you hear that? I'm right. At this hour he's always in this neighborhood. You'll surely run into him. . . ."

But the terrace where Rocco sat was always the one Gigino did not pass. Pam grew impatient. They left. At once some mysterious instinct warned Gigino that the field was free. Arm extended, he appeared, tracing great white circles in the air. "Ah, there you are!" That was how he always was welcomed. "Ah, there you are. . . ." As if the whole town was keeping track of him and from the cries of the paper sellers to the call of the ice cream sellers, to the shrieking of brakes to the rumbling of motors, to all those familiar noises exclamations must be added which resounded wherever he went.

There are things one doesn't get used to. The day when after the usual "Ah, there you are," the waiter at a café where Gigino often came added, "Guess who was here. . . . Just five minutes ago: the Italian from America, the one who's always asking for you. He wants to give you money. My goodness, he's left. . . . That'll teach you. . . ." On that day Gigino shouted at the top of his lungs, "That'll teach me what?" with such violence that it made him tremble.

Then he had insulted the man in the white jacket, throwing in his face all the scorn that was in his heart for sedentary characters like him. "Old crow, get out. . . ." What could he teach him, that old fool with bruised knuckles who was condemned to run around a terrace like a squirrel in a cage? Nothing. And neither could that foreigner who thought he was so big and superior and who was so determined to be offensive. What did such people mean to him? What did he have to frig around with them for? They were the others, the privileged ones, and Gigino did not feel easy with such men. Flowers from bushes decided his fate. When a spring came that was poor in dew, or those droughts which discourage blooming, there he was, without hope, reduced to wretchedness. Did they understand that, those men? He was amazed, that American, he was amazed that a vagabond like Gigino could assume the right to make gifts. But giving didn't hurt anyone. And then the right to forget his own poverty, or even the right to cry . . . is that a right which belongs to some more than others?

The plate of milk that is given to stray cats; the "kitty, kitty" which is used to keep them near makes them bristle. . . . They shrink back. Their muscles stiff, they get ready to jump, then they look at the milk for a long time, ears flattened, back humped with shivers of rage running under the skin, ready to attack. But nothing happens and they run away. Gigino was of that kind. A stray cat trapped in the black gulf of the city.

He thought about the American. He saw him again with that air of profound conviction which spread through his whole body like an illness. A great laugh began, a laugh which split Gigino's face in two. He gave his strident cry as a farewell, then he darted forward and disappeared. But the water in the glasses and the spoons and the cloths and the tables and the whole terrace kept the sharp strong smell of the jasmine for a long time afterwards.

A bouquet left at the hotel marked the opening of hostilities.

"Is there a letter with these flowers, or a card?" asked Rocco.

There was nothing.

"And no one left them," cried Rocco. "They got here all by themselves!"

"I don't have any recollection of it, sir," the porter replied phlegmatically. "Maybe they were brought by a delivery man."

"A messenger!" Rocco burst out. "As if such bouquets were delivered by messenger!"

"Anything is possible," answered the porter in the same calm voice.

His face was unreadable and he seemed absorbed in sorting his messages.

Pam held the bouquet as casually as she would have handled a grenade with the pin pulled. "Take a look," said Rocco. She folded back the paper, which looked soiled to her, then saw, arranged in clusters in Gigino's way, white corollas of jasmine. A sure signature. She shrugged her shoulders.

"Maybe it wasn't he," she said.

"And who do you think it was?"

"Maybe someone in your family."

This lie deceived no one.

When Rocco announced that he had some cousins near Mondello and that he was going to pay them a visit, Pam imagined joyful games in the sun, sand, clear water and a distant buoy they could swim towards. That day Pam's courage returned. She put on a linen dress, let her hair hang loose and spoke of going swimming. But Rocco did not seem to be listening to her. Pam insisted. "Mondello is right on the seashore, isn't it?" And Rocco had laughed, saying that if half what he'd heard about Sicilians were true, the only time they went to sea was to catch something to eat.

Rocco's family spent its Sundays in a cabin built at the far end of the bay of Mondella above a massive cape which seemed to drowse over the water. To reach it, it was necessary to walk between rows of little buildings which were all alike with their broad verandas buried in tamaracks. The Bonavia cottage had the one distinguishing characteristic of being backed up to an olive wood with its terrace, propped up by pilings, sticking out over the sea. From all evidence this terrace was reserved for the men, who—in caps and shirt sleeves—were playing cards in absolute silence when Pam and Rocco arrived. The olive wood belonged to the women. They made a continual stir between a table placed under the trees and an unharnessed cart from which they were taking baskets of food. Some were dressed in black; these were the oldest. Others were dressed in the fashion of the day, bright colors and narrow buttocks in too-tight trousers. But whether men or women, they had a common enemy: the sun. Stretched from one tree to another, coverings made a shadow over the family table, while to protect the card players a tarpaulin had been stretched as well as possible over the terrace.

There were tears and cries from the women when they saw Rocco and then endless questions about Alfio, about Calò, about Agata, but one of the card players rose and shut them up. He was a large man who made more noise than they did. He made the introductions, spoke of a fish he had caught the day before, of the *frittatura* which they planned to eat. He came there every Sunday now that everyone lived in Palermo. Also there were his sons, his daughters-in-law, his nieces, his nephews, and "No reason to weep," he said. Then he added, "I'm your Uncle Anastasio. And this is Venerina, my wife. We were all born in Sólanto." But no one said anything about swimming.

The card players claimed Rocco. The women took over Pam. They made a circle around a baby, very new, which was giving ferocious yells. A pacifier and a bit of grape slipped into his mouth between two cries, wheedling, coaxing and still other caresses which Pam found repulsive (the women tickled the child's little sex with sounds of "grrr . . . grrr . . ." as if they were trying to persuade a canary to sing). Nothing did any good. His brow knit, his jaws clenched, already carrying within him all the desperation of his race, the baby cried. Then Pam thrust her hand with its freshly varnished nails in the direction of that wide open mouth. Abruptly, the child spit out the grape which had been swelling his cheek and began to suck avidly on that bunch of scarlet nails which were brighter than any sugar plum. His sobs abated. He slept. For Pam it was a huge success. She held the baby in her arms, listening distantly to the conversations which crossed over her, the noise of plates and silver, and farther, much farther away the music of a phonograph coming from the beach.

A difficult day. The sun was fearful. Pam did her best to forget her yearning for the sea, for its coolness, and for the sand down there where the little waves were breaking. Everything reeled within her. Distress rose in her throat like nausea. Educated by Aunt Rosie to a respect for the strictest hygiene, convinced that only masked and aseptic professionals should ever approach a new baby, Pam looked with amazement mixed with fear at the disorder and offhandedness with which Rocco's family lived. There were newborn babies everywhere: at the foot of the trees, in the shadows of carts, between parcels of food, two steps from the furious hand-to-hand struggles in which the bigger children were engaged. Frightened, Pam tried to dissuade two little girls who were throwing handfuls of sand in each other's faces. In vain. No one seemed to care about the dogs running in packs around the cradles or about the unharnessed horses which drove flies away with big switches of their tails. Nothing, neither cries nor arguments seemed to bother the closed circle of men.

Only once did Pam hear a male voice raised: "So when will lunch be ready?"

It was Uncle Anastasio who was hungry. He had called out without removing his eyes from the cards, without even turning.

Once, too, Rocco interrupted his game long enough to whisper in Pam's ear: "You know that bouquet yesterday?"

"Yes. . . . What about it?"

"They didn't send it."

He said this maliciously, as if it were her fault. She shrugged her shoulders. The whole business was stupid.

"I'm going swimming," she said.

The next day everything was spoiled for good. Pure and white as wax, a branch of jasmine found on the seat of a fiacre at the moment when he was getting in had a frightening effect on Rocco. His lips tight, a hard look in his eyes, he held the bouquet out to Pam without saying a single word. But he had a way of being silent which froze the blood.

The coachman's sleep prevented any suspicion of him. Had he seen anyone? No one.

"What do you mean no one?" protested Pam. "Do people put things in your fiacre without your knowledge?"

"Putting something down isn't stealing," answered the coachman who, suddenly cheering up, speeded his horse with a loud crack of his whip.

There was nothing to do but drive on. . . .

And the little girl who followed Pam, stumbling at every step, dragging shoes too big for her, nobody could say who had sent her. She offered Pam jasmine quickly as if she were getting rid of a compromising parcel. A little face made of wood, of stone, of silence. She beat a retreat, still stumbling, still dragging her shoes. "No, no one sent her," said a little boy whom Pam had asked because he seemed to know the other child. "She just wants to be nice," he added. The strange thing was that the scene took place in a nearly deserted alleyway.

Then there was jasmine which fell at Pam's feet, thrown from a window. There were those she saw one evening placed on the edge of her balcony. How did they get there? Still others were found in a taxi the day they went up to Montreal, and the bouquet left in the bottom of the boat which took them to Capo Gallo. Rare were the days without jasmine, and rare too those when Pam did not see in Rocco's face, in his eyes, a stubborn, unreadable look that she did not recognize. Oh, she was a long way from Aunt Rosie, far from New York and *Fair*, far from her dreams of success, of happiness. . . . The trip was turning into a hell. There was nothing about it that she liked: the odor of fish in the street, the smell of Parmesan at the table. Sicily upset her liver and the sickening food was one more betrayal. . . . And then these mysteries. . . . Rocco's abrupt departures each evening leaving her alone and humiliated in her room and not reappearing until dawn with heavy eyes, his suit rumpled and his cheeks black with beard. Where did he go? With whom? Had he begun to drink too? Because he had that mother, dead in a ditch like a derelict. Pam hadn't forgotten her. One morning she spoke her thoughts: "That's why you stay out all night. To drink." It was as if she were in a trance. But Rocco remained impassive. "You ought to go back to New York," he said. "That's the place for a nut like you." And he went to bed without saying another word. Indifference came with disgust. And fear, too, and a desire to end this trip.

Rocco visited a certain trattoria almost daily. Pam sometimes went with him there. One day they had discovered that terrace cut out of the side of a baroque façade and as if suspended above a night market: La Bocceria Grande. There was where Rocco passed his nights. Why? Pam asked him several times but he never answered. Actually he did not know himself. And it was so difficult to explain the intoxication which came over him when he was sitting up there. In what reminded him of a royal box, an observatory, life became unexpectedly interesting. He took his place there as if it were a theater.

It was not easy to get there. A staircase of ragged uneven steps first had to be negotiated. It was cool there. It was like a tomb or a mushroom bed. Stifled laughter, whispering, cries, scolding or pleading voices filtered from under doors. People passed. A man with an old American cape thrown over his pajamas went to the water closet on the landing. Then a woman in a flowered wrapper, carrying a bucket in her hand, went to empty her slops. Their silhouettes were outlined sharply in the half light. Pam recoiled. She could scarcely bear it.

Bits of stucco still clung to the walls of what had once been a vaulted gallery. From there, by three steep steps, one reached a patch on which was a sign: (or rather what was left of one: a quarter of a word: "Trat" written in neon capitals) shed a harsh light. The room was neat. An entire family, old men with wrinkled faces, mute women with huge haunches, children of every age busied themselves around the single oven. Before reaching the terrace it was necessary to step over sparse provisions, avoid tripping over the chickens which pecked freely, then lay claim to a table high enough to find oneself finally seated out of doors among the diners, all seafaring folk, fishers, sailors, fishmongers. They exchanged commonplaces which no one thought of arguing with. Their prayers were to the sirocco which promised them favorable currents and tuna in abundance. The migration of eels was also of great importance to them.

Pam looked, listened, waited and was silent. But the feeling of powerlessness crushed her. The sharp cries of the fishmongers rose

to her like an unknown barbaric sound. She would never understand, she could not. This strange people who at nightfall lost their
qualities of silence, clothed their poverty in waves of light, and
under her eyes gathered there to celebrate the living sea and its
gifts at the top of their lungs. . . . A mysterious ritual which went
on until dawn.

"Fresh, fresh catfish, beautiful catfish. . . . White as your mother's milk."

Herring mongers and cryers assaulted her ears with their eloquence. Whiting, bowed forcibly by a string binding the head to
the tail, octopus and squid artistically tied up, silver-varnished
eels, giant crabs, lewd and pearly rays, from that precious pile still
panting with life an odor of foam and algae rose and mixed with
the kitchen smells.

"Here's honey!" cried a child pointing at the bottom of a basket
where a gray gelatinous mass stirred.

Pam retched. She did not know where to look. Palermo was
killing her.

Rocco saw it all with wonder. Seven streets opened on the
square, the central stage where everything happened, seven narrow
and teeming streets in which he would have liked to disappear and
be lost. . . . Orange, green, or brown shades were spread over the
stalls, and seen from above they looked like vast carpets one could
not stop staring at. Shades? At night? Why? After all. . . . What
did it matter? Those inexplicable shades, those motorcyclists who
crossed the square for the sole purpose of startling strollers, those
men who walked slowly arm in arm, that mendicant Sister, black
as night, that cart from nowhere, the knife seller who, along with
his frighteningly sharp blades, hawked twice as many religious
objects as the neighboring stores, a matter of demonstrating his
piety—all this was happiness to Rocco; it was life as he loved it,
a high harmony. He soaked up the balconies, families hung at all
heights under all kinds of lights, families gray as the walls, families white as the linen that hung over the streets like a barrier,
linking the houses to each other. The image of Alfio crossed his

mind, then more thoughts, of his life in New York, of his ambitions, of his career. Enough, he thought. I hope I never hear another word about all that. And he suddenly had a sense of wellbeing such as he had never known. He tried to chat with his neighbor—a little old man who looked very respectable—and became very much interested in what he had to say about a certain seller of swordfish. The old man was delighted. It had been a long time, it seemed, since he had seen a merchant like this, such a gifted one. He gave every detail of the gigantic creature and at each slice he swore at the fish as if he were avenging some insult. He exhausted himself and wielded the knife with a disquieting dexterity. People crowded around him. The swordfish disappeared piece by piece. . . .

"Goodby, you dirty bastard! . . . Son of a bitch! . . . Thief!"

Little drops of blood ran along the trestles.

"By the skin of San Bartolomeo," cried Rocco's neighbor, "there's a man who can say he works like an artist." He raised his hands to applaud.

It was plain that he was feeling lyrical and anxious to awaken an enthusiasm equal to his own in someone else. But Rocco was no longer listening to him.

With arms raised, his head high and erect, his step supple, Gigino was slipping between the stalls with the lightness of a rope dancer. Six or ten quick steps carried him to a place where he stood still, then his cry "Gelsomino! Gelsomino!" shouted in a tone of insult, he took off again with a bound. Unexpected turns, moments of hesitation, short stops made him appear and disappear in the crowd like a boat in the hollow of the waves. A voice cried: "Hey, there's Gigino!"

Which surprised no one but Rocco, who for a moment did not know what to do. Then he got up with a jump. Was he drunk or crazy? His chair was upset. There was a knife on the table which he seized. The eyes of the diners focused on him. A long time afterward Pam remembered his face as he crossed the kitchen at a run between frightened children and chickens which flapped over the tables. She wanted to call to him, to hold him back, but a humiliating timidity paralyzed her. As for Rocco, if anyone had asked him why he had grabbed that knife, he would not have been able to answer. Why? He felt no hatred for Gigino, only a thirst for vengeance, an irresistible desire. Roused by a will to murder which surprised him, he went down the staircase at a run, missed a step, caught himself in flight, thought I'm flying, I'm flying, passed beneath the terrace, and disappeared into the crowd.

The rest was great confusion. A fury of howling brought the whole population of the crossroads to the windows. It was a woman's voice, tearing, almost immediately imitated by other voices like it. Roofs and terraces were peopled with unsuspected hordes. Women came from nowhere, appeared like a black froth rising to the surface of the houses, obstructing all the exits, making every balcony the support of a gigantic human swarm. Then the cries ceased and the crowd stood still.

Two men rolled on the ground. They tangled in frantic combat, met head on, crouched against one another in a paroxysm of violence. People stared at them. There was no longer the slightest cry in the square, not the least noise. The two kept on fighting and no one tried to come between them.

It might be a family matter.

On the terrace a voice said: "They'll kill each other." A peaceful voice which pronounced the sentence very slowly.

Pam looked. She saw a knife glint. She saw Gigino cornered, pushed up against a wall. She saw how he battled with his fists, with his hands, flung himself against Rocco. She cried out, or at least she thought she cried: "Separate them. . . ." But no one around her moved.

A low "ah," the sigh of a whole crowd marked the end of the fight, and the same peaceful voice could be heard: "They had no other way," it said, with a shade of satisfaction.

When the police patrol arrived, all that were left around the tables were impassive drinkers, and in the square a bunch of jasmine bathed in a brown puddle.

"It's blood," the *carabiniere* said.

And he pointed to other smaller spots at regular intervals. But the trail was lost between the paving stones.

"Hastily wiped up," the commissioner noted, examining the places for the tenth time since the morning.

He shrugged his shoulders. It seemed he was resigned to the mysteries of those Sicilian nights. Attacks without wounds, murders without victims were his fate. His part, rehearsed almost every day, forced him to question witnesses in the name of justice who were silent in the name of honor.

"What did you see?"

"Nothing."

"Was there a fight?"

"I don't know."

"So how did the blood get there?"

"There's no law against having a nose bleed."

"Who had a nose bleed?"

"Find out for yourself. . . ."

"What about those flowers?"

"They fell."

A simple formality which provoked no irritation on either side. That day the criminal weapon was missing and nothing was known of the aggressor nor of his victim. A riddle without an answer. Suddenly the commissioner stopped the swordfish seller. He had a great deal of blood on his shoes.

"Swordfish blood," the man affirmed categorically.

It may have been true. The commissioner decided to give up his inquiry but he left armed *carabinieri* in the square.

For several days, in the middle of the market, they mounted guard around a spot of blood and some flowers with soiled petals.

Pam waited. She waited one day, then two, then three; by the fourth, she had ceased to be aware of anything but that long wait. The world around her hardly seemed to exist. The old man sitting on the balcony opposite, with his hollow eyes and naked torso;

even the little chambermaid, who made signs out the window to the man waiting for her across the street in front of the café, or the days with their regular eruptions of violence. . . . What was the difference?

She stayed in her room. The floor waiter brought her meals. He set down the platter, complained of the heat in exaggerated terms (the heat for him was always *scandalous, intolerable, stifling*), offered Pam a few encouraging words, then dripping with sweat, poured the coffee and advised her to take a long nap. Pam stared out of the window, waited. She watched the bright day turn dark and the street lamps bloom in their long file, one after the other; she listened as the city awoke to the cool of the evening. The fifth day she could stand it no longer. She dressed and went out.

Mechanically, she followed the movement of the crowd along the via Maqueda and found herself once more (not really wanting to be there) in the hubbub of La Bocceria Grande: among jostling men, pregnant women who trailed troops of urchins after them, beggars squatting on the ground, bad smells, and young men who touched her, pressed against her every time the currents of the lurching crowd gave them the opportunity. One of them, seeing her wandering in her low-cut sleeveless dress with its skirt halfway up her thighs, treated her as if she were a whore. He repeated the word several times, whispering it with a kind of rage; when she outdistanced him, he stopped short with an exhausted sigh. Where was she going? She had no idea. The day faded. I must go on looking for him! she thought. But she hesitated. It seemed to her that the city, the houses, the piazzas, the streets, together with the crowd, formed a massive hostility which moved mysteriously by some unknown will; she had only to make the slightest false move to disappear as Rocco had disappeared; she had only to lean forward a little, to stumble on the sidewalk, to touch the ground with her fingers. And she would be swallowed up forever in the conglomeration of men, women, animals, and offal.

A few yards ahead of her a group of men stood waiting for her in silence. One man followed her slowly in his car. He drew up be-

side her and spoke to her through the open window: "Whore!"
He repeated the word tirelessly, as if by saying it he could achieve
some climax. "Whore!" The word echoed from doorways, sidewalks, bounced back from parked trucks, encompassed everything,
making an uninterrupted murmur, a deep, powerful river of sound.
. . . Pam sought refuge in the nearest café. But there a group of
adolescents, the oldest no more than fourteen, made a circle
around her. One of them tried to take her hand, then pulled her
dress. She heard one say, grinning, "Let's take her away with us. . . .
We'll see how long she holds out. . . ." She saw them staring at
her and laughing. She fought her desire to hit them, to kick them
like dogs.

When she finally understood how useless it was to walk the
streets looking for him, she went quickly back to the hotel room,
started when she heard the sound of a door opening, waited to
see what came after, then exhausted, went down again and took
up a post in the lobby.

Standing behind his counter, the porter watched her. He could
hardly believe she was the same one who had arrived with such a
sexy walk, such a ringing laugh, a laugh that seemed to take the
world by storm, such seductive poses—the crossed legs, knees showing—and none of that was left! Was it her voice that had gone
first? Or her stare? Foreigners come apart at the seams in this
country, he thought. It was a subject he liked to hold forth on.
The inevitable diarrhea of the English tourists. The doctor who
had to be called for them in the middle of the night. The fever
blisters of the French, their cracked lips. Not very pretty. And the
carelessness that came over them gradually in proportion to the
length of their stay! Not a single necktie in the dining room and
the inevitably rolled-up shirtsleeves. There was nothing more vulgar. And the Swedes' sunstrokes. What a plague! Sicily turned
them inside out, "as if our very touch did it. . . ." It might be the
air. From the time of the Allied landing in Italy, upset stomachs
and gastric disturbances vanquished them completely. With the
exception of the Moslem mercenaries, as if the poverty of Islam

felt at home with the poverty of southern Italy. In the night they could be heard dancing and playing the flute while their officers vomited in their reserved rooms. A curse. But what was the good of going over the past. The case of the American tourist, however, was of an entirely different order. Her disarray was visible and the porter watched her.

"Palermo affects the nerves," he said with the stiff sententiousness suited to his position.

Nothing in the tone or in the expression of this man indicated the least surprise at Rocco's absence, but Pam felt in some peculiar way that he had known about it for a long time. She asked, "Has my mail come?" in a timid voice, waiting for him to answer. Her anguish was written on her. Mail? No, there was none.

"Palermo affects one's nerves," repeated the porter in a mechanical voice.

And Pam walked away in a sort of stupor.

What nights those were! Staring at his empty pillow, she imagined the worst: Rocco assassinated, or Rocco as assassin. And the emotion she felt was neither sorrow nor worry but hatred. Yes, she hated that man and only wanted to be at home again among people she understood. Tears ran down her face like a storm breaking, a heavy rain full of all she had endured since her departure from New York, her successive disillusionments. Sicily, that steam room, that lost world in which all her certainties, her hopes, her happiness were swallowed up—all gone! Lost forever. Palermo, its stinking alleys, its women shriveled in their poverty as if it were a shroud, its ruins. The horror she felt at every step. The discovery of that other Rocco, a stranger to her, a man who spent his nights wandering and his days lying in bed ruminating on God knew what bad dream. Their arguments, his wounding denunciations. And then that scandal, those howling women, that outburst in a public square, blows exchanged, that fury, that knife. . . . And now Pam was alone. Alone because of that foreigner, that beast. Her dignity trembled: Rocco and Palermo, Palermo and Rocco together became synonyms for hell, for nightmare. What wrong turn had brought her to this place?

After a week of waiting among such thoughts, Pam lost patience. She had to cry her indignation to the first comer. Which she did.

At the word police the floor waiter turned pale.

"Don't do that!" he cried. "Everything can be arranged so long as the police don't get into it!"

Pam looked at him with the eyes of a madwoman.

"You ought to be ashamed," she cried. "Get out of here!"

Her hands were trembling. She had great difficulty in pushing him out.

"But, *Signora*, you asked my advice," he said, a groaning in his voice.

Pam had the porter called.

He came calm, smiling.

"Well?" she said to him.

He seemed shocked.

"I'm speaking to you," she said. "Answer me! My husband has disappeared. Disappeared! Do you understand?"

"Why talk about it?" he grumbled. "He must be in a safe place."

"How do you know?" Pam demanded.

The porter glanced around the room as if to be sure that no one was listening, then he looked at her and said: "Here, everyone knows. . . ."

According to him, La Bocceria Grande teemed with honest people always ready to perform a favor. Sometimes he referred to them as "fine fellows," sometimes as "dedicated people." What were those fine people doing? Nothing. But all you had to do was look at them to understand.

"Understand?" said Pam. "Understand what?"

"To understand."

Then he added, "Some of them are friends of mine." And he went through a complicated pantomime which Pam watched with astonishment. It began with a nodding of the head, "Fine people. . . ." Then his forehead wrinkled: "With no particular jobs." His eyelids blinked. "Some of them are friends of mine." For a fraction of a second the whole face radiated sincere joy, as if those "friends" were his sole reason for living. Then the corners of his mouth fell and his lips pushed forward, forming a sad grimace which expressed his regret at not being able to say more.

However, he had nothing good to say about the jasmine seller. "That Gigino! He came from bad seed, a nettle, crabgrass." Or else: "He was a *mascalzone*, born to be the despair of his mother." Or else: "He was a delinquent who deserved what he got." Rocco was unreservedly praised. The porter spoke of him in an entirely different voice. "There's a man," he repeated, "there's one that America hasn't spoiled." And he repeated it once more, and once again, until Pam cried: "That's enough!"

Pam expressed her disapproval only by a short movement of the corners of her lips. No more. But nothing escaped the porter.

"Ah yes," said the porter looking at her, "Palermo affects people's nerves. Just to judge by the way you've changed in such a short time, you'd say we were a sad people. Enough to make you believe we can never live like the rest of the world."

"It's because you like it that way," said Pam, and she tried to revive her laugh.

"It's nothing to laugh about, Signora," said the porter. "There really isn't anything. If we don't succeed in living like the rest of the world it's because we're all of mixed blood here and laws don't suit us. Sicily is not a happy land."

"So?" said Pam.

He raised his hand in a gesture of impotence.

"Well, there's nothing you can do," he said. "That's the way things are."

The next day he handed Pam a bill for "services rendered."

"Believe me," he said, "I've run myself ragged."

But he did not deem it necessary to say more about it, and Pam did nothing to make him explain. She was completely indifferent to "the peculiarities of the natives."

Finally she could look upon Sicily as something to leave. Reason had returned to her.

A cruise steamer which was returning to America via Naples and Villefranche touched at Palermo that day. Pam hesitated. But, the porter praised the luxuriousness of this steamer, the efficiency of a company which made offices and telephones available to "those passengers who needed to keep up their professional obligations." Pam was convinced. He also spoke to her about the stock market reports which were delivered each morning, knowing that this was such a telling and serious argument that she would not be able to resist it.

He was not mistaken.

On the way home she soon returned to her old self. The voyage was like a short convalescence. The ship's bartender had his specialties: Pam drank whatever he recommended. And then there were ventilators in the washrooms, mahogany woodwork in the dining room and syrupy jazz melodies which followed the passengers even into their cabins. Yes, this steamer had marvelous therapeutic effects on Pam. She had wanted Rocco and, having him, had seen that her choice risked compromising her public image. Then, with a perfectly good conscience, she had decided to forget that husband whose demeanor, conversation, and above all violence had covered her with shame. So an adventure was concluded —she would never have called it "an ordeal"—which left hardly more trace in her heart than a stone leaves on the surface of the water. Only a few ripples. And then nothing.

One day, at last, New York was sighted. What looked at first like a forest of stone became the harbor, the docks, the city and its massive splendor.

On the pier, Pam saw a silhouette dressed in pink which slowly grew larger: Aunt Rosie. Aunt Rosie, waving her arms, Aunt Rosie more and more visible with poppies fluttering around her hat. Pam called, took out her handkerchief and leaning on the rail, waved joyously.

Her first talk was about black hair which, in that heat, was never very clean.

"What did I tell you?" cried Aunt Rosie.

She was triumphant.

Then Pam spoke of Sicily and all her sentences included the word "Fabulous. . . ."

She was home, with a free heart.

IV.

He heard a movement. Two feet passed at the level of his head. He hastily closed his eyes so as not to show that he was still alive.

"Do you hear me?"

The voice seemed more confused than threatening. It repeated, "Do you hear me?" Out of surprise, Gigino opened his eyes. He slid a quick look around him, saw that he was lying on the ground, believed he was dead and fainted again.

Noises, steps, the voice came to him as if through a fog. He also thought he felt a hand on his shoulder and vaguely heard himself groan.

"He's fainted," the voice muttered.

And Gigino understood why he could see nothing.

The worst was that liquid which ran down his back, something like sweat. But sweat is not sticky. So it was blood.

"Sacred name of God, that's got to be staunched."

A compress came to stop the blood that flowed, while the voice continued its monologue.

My God, someone's taking care of me, Gigino said to himself.

Then he tried to keep his mind from drifting, tried to breathe, forced himself to it and succeeded in regaining consciousness.

He saw a basement. The light came weakly through a ventilator which also let the smells of the market filter through a mixture of water, sharp salt and moist baskets with algae lingering in the bottoms. The smell was familiar to him. He turned his head, stole a careful look at the ceiling and saw a man whose clothes looked incongruous in this dark cellar. He thought he must be mistaken. But the darkness was not so thick and it was no longer possible to doubt it: the American who had tried to kill him was there, looking at him and smiling.

It was not the smile of a self-confident man but a timid, almost a troubled smile.

"I'm sorry," said Rocco. "I'm really very sorry."

"Not as sorry as I am," said Gigino in a disagreeable voice.

But he quickly recovered himself. This was not the moment to be angry, he thought, and he added: "Well then, *ciao*," in a more conciliating tone. He said it softly, politely, like a young man paying a visit.

"*Ciao*," replied Rocco.

So contact was made between Gigino and the man who had stabbed him. And it was in an atmosphere of this kind of truce that they began to talk.

"What are we doing here?" asked Gigino.

"Some people hid us."

"The police came?"

"They came."

"I see," said Gigino.

"You see what?"

"I see these people are protecting themselves."

"Protecting themselves?"

"Protecting themselves."

"From what?"

"From everything. We must have chosen a very bad moment for fighting outside their door."

Gigino took a moment to think and then added: "Anyway, they did the right thing. I risked a lot."

Rocco bristled. "I was the one who risked the most, wasn't I?"

With his good arm, Gigino made a sign that it was nothing.

"But I was the one who had the knife," Rocco said.

"Oh, that! A little scuffle is nothing. You can always get out of that."

Gigino sighed. "For me it's really serious. I'm a flower seller without a license. That means I get caught five times out of ten. Life isn't easy here, I can tell you."

Rocco said no more. He wished he could look without tenderness at this adolescent leaning on one elbow like a wounded gladiator. To forget his serious look, his bitter mouth, to forget his arrogant voice, to forget his lost child's grace. To find again the fury he had once felt, that was what he needed to do.

"You really made me angry, you know," Rocco said.

But nothing happened. And the suffocating shadow of tenderness continued its slow progression.

Help came from the ceiling, made fast to the end of a rope. Each time the trap door squeaked to make way for the basket full of food, murmuring voices offered encouragement.

"All right down there?"

Or else: "All right, fellows?"

Sly faces appeared with hard shining eyes which blinked inside the frame of the trapdoor long enough to add: "They've posted four of them outside the door. But you'll see, *they'll* get discouraged. We'll let you know when *they're* gone." And the trap door closed again.

Judging by the cellar, the inhabitants of this house seemed to have no other occupation besides deceiving the police and out-witting their vigilance.

The trapdoor also issued forth a doctor. This gift from the sky let them know that being from the neighborhood, he couldn't be ignorant of what had gone on.

"But then," he said, "I go here, I go there, I'm used to it."

Gigino received his careful attention.

The knife had slipped under his shoulder blade. The damage was serious and the wound was deep.

"He's bled a great deal," said the doctor in a discouraged voice. Then he looked at his shoes as if he could make the necessary blood flow from them.

Rocco received his instructions with the obedience of a good nurse. He must check the dressing every hour and see that the wounded boy drank. The doctor also recommended complete im-mobility. Then he asked what he could do for them. Did they want him to notify their families? The doctor said that it was easy for him and that he could tell them something, he didn't know exactly what, but something.

"My wife is at the Palermo-Palace—" said Rocco.

"I know, I know," interrupted the doctor. "The porter is a friend of mine. We'll let her know. And you?"

Gigino shrugged his shoulders.

"Hurry up," insisted the doctor. "It's no good having your mother looking for you in every police station in the city. She'll put us on a spot and that won't do us any good."

Gigino gave a fierce sneer.

"No mother, no address," he said through clenched teeth.

Then the doctor made a gesture indicating, "That's good, that's all I want to know."

The trap door let him out. He left a whole arsenal of disinfect-ants.

Gigino took his attacker's good will as his due. He gave orders

and Rocco carried them out with the slightly penitential promptness of a man in the wrong.

When he was in pain Gigino rose on his elbow and raged:
"When are we going to get out of this morgue?"

But even when he fretted he addressed Rocco with a reserved
formality, using the third person.

"The gentleman knows that he's going a little strong on the
iodine?"

"Me?"

"Yes, that's who."

Rocco cut the smarting iodine with water. He crouched at the
wounded boy's feet. Gigino's apprehensive look hurt him. He tried
to disinfect the wound, but the bone showed under the skin.
Then he moved the hurt arm with infinite precautions, suffering
with each gesture, as if the living bone and the bleeding back were
his own.

How strange Gigino was, and what a singular power he exerted.
Rocco had never known anybody who was prouder in uncertainty,
freer in nakedness. Down in this cellar, Gigino could sniff the
gusts of wind and say: "They're really going to buy a lot of ices
today, the tourists."

The idea seemed to irritate him. He seemed to be furious, and
the words could scarcely be heard between his clenched teeth.

"How do you know?" asked Rocco.

And Gigino was silent, still unmoving, still leaning on one elbow, alert for those signs which only he could perceive.

"How do I know?"

He pointed to a moving shadow on the wall, or indicated the
distant banging of a shutter, or else he noticed that the evening
air grew no cooler and he said: "See how the wind is changing,"
as if this were something to be enthusiastic about, as if that
shadow, that banging could make him forget the blood that ran
down his back, as if it were necessary to know, in this cellar, from
which quarter the wind blew.

"The wind, sir, believe me, when it doesn't blow. . . ."

And Rocco believed him. Gigino was teaching him his courage, his secrets: crumbling enclosures, falling walls, hidden paths in gardens where the pomegranate ripens, the citron, the forgotten grapes offer themselves to satisfy the hunger of an adolescent. And Gigino always went back to the wind, sometimes saying that it was necessary, sometimes that it was the end of everything, speaking of the one that brought fever and the one which gave sleep, and how finally the wind was like poverty, you had to get used to it because there was nothing you could do about it.

To Gigino everything seemed simple. He had to eat as soon as he had declared: "Now I'm hungry. . . ."

In the same way his eyes closed after the first yawn. He drowsed, then he slipped sidewise and Rocco took the sleeping head on his knees. Seeing Gigino thus, so mournful, so curled up into himself like a child before birth, Rocco finally became aware of his own beginnings. It was like a revelation or like a sudden majesty. Gigino taught him who he was.

Here is my companion, my brother, he said to himself. Why didn't I guess it sooner?

And Rocco adjusted his support to the wounded shoulder. He worried about the blood which flowed or at the groan which escaped that proud sleeping mouth. From that sleeping body, loose and supple as a young dog's, a country odor rose which made Rocco puzzle a long time. Gigino smelled of the garden, musk, or else cinnamon. In any case it was a strong clean odor. Then Rocco saw that Gigino's pockets were full of jasmine petals and that his clothing was impregnated with the perfume. That was his odor.

In the depths of his fever, Gigino talked and Rocco did not always understand what he was saying. It happened that once Rocco thought he heard the word "hungry" and then he saw Gigino moving his thin bare feet as if trying to flee; that dark struggle between Gigino and his nightmare weighed on Rocco like remorse. Rocco felt responsible for all that he had been indifferent to up to now: to the suffering boy whose head was on his knees, to his sweat, to his childhood, to his mouth which had never learned to smile; but also to the glimmering light which filtered through the ventilator, to the great murmur which rose above the market as it began its nocturnal life with the noise of a snorting beast, and to that cellar which had joined them closer than a fatherland. Suddenly all the hate and rancor hoarded in his life inundated him. He saw New York again. He heard himself murmur: New York, my exile, my race denied. New York, I hate you. He was not surprised at himself; and this violence he felt did not distract him entirely from Gigino. The past seemed only a prolonged echo in him.

The squeaking trap door opened and the ritual whispers of the inhabitants above brought Rocco back to his strange situation.

"There are only two of *them* left."

Rocco started. These sudden appearances made his heart beat fast.

"What is it?" he asked.

"It's us. . . . It's us. . . . There are only two of *them* left outside the door. And only two at Saint Eulalia-of-the-Catalans. We have only to wait. They'll get discouraged, too. . . . And you have a letter."

Rocco thanked them.

Accompanied by a dish, the envelope came down from the ceiling attached to the end of a string. It was a message written in the third person announcing that in the interests of prudence it had been judged wise to "encourage the Signora to return to New York."

Gigino woke up.

"The porter?" he said pointing to the letter.

"How did you know?" asked Rocco.

"Who else could it be?"

"I didn't know. It could have been my wife."

"Oh no," replied Gigino. "It's the porter. Good hotels all have one like him."

"He advised my wife to leave."

"One way or other, she would have left."

"Why should she?" demanded Rocco.

"Because women don't forgive easily."

Rocco thought that Gigino spoke the truth. Men were more generous. More devoted. I've misplayed the social game. Pam will never forgive that. But at the same time he thought, why should that bother me, when I'm playing on a different side?

Then Gigino said again: "Women don't forgive easily," and when Rocco asked him: "Where did you learn that?" believing he must have repeated a sentence he had learned by heart, Gigino, without understanding the sense in which the question was asked, answered: "On the beaches, sir, I learned that on the beaches where they behave as if they're in mourning."

Then he looked at the cellar, the dish on the floor with the cooling soup in it. He also looked at his blood-spotted shirt and said: "You'd think the war had started again."

"The war?" exclaimed Rocco. "But you were scarcely born at the time of the war."

"I must have been born," he said, "since I remember. Anyway, do you think you have to have seen it to know? The war is never anything but noise and the smell of rotting. . . ."

"And Americans," asked Rocco. "Do you remember the Americans too, Gigino?"

Suddenly Rocco would have liked him to remember. It would have been something in common, a discovery that would have excited him, he wasn't sure just why, a little like having had the same friend or the same woman as Gigino.

"Tell me, Gigino. . . ."

"Would you believe," Gigino said in a thoughtful tone, "that all the Americans in my neighborhood were Negroes?"

And when Rocco laughed until he shook, Gigino said to him: "Look at what you're like! Yesterday you wanted to kill me and today I make you laugh. What's the use trying to understand? What's the use trying to understand what makes men enemies?"

But at that moment pain whipped through him and Gigino no longer wanted to talk about war, women, or the wind.

Death plays strange tricks. It hides its tracks and the warning signs of its victory can often be wrongly interpreted. Victim of such confusion, Rocco believed in an illusion. Crouched in a corner of the cellar, he seemed to read in Gigino's tired features the signs of healing. The flush in his cheeks, for instance, seemed to be the return of healthy color. And his deep voice, which sounded as raucous as it did when he was selling jasmine. Even more raucous, as Gigino complained from his choked throat. If he'd let himself go, if he'd cry out as he used to do, his voice would have resounded from the four corners of the town. And that itching sensation around the wound, wasn't that a sign that it was healing?

"You aren't bleeding any more," said Rocco.

It was true. The drops had stopped soaking through the dressings.

"What?" said Gigino, in a worried voice. "I'm not bleeding any more? That's not surprising. I feel like an empty bag."

But Rocco saw no danger, no threat, and the heavy presence of death walking straight towards Gigino was invisible to him.

To pass the time, Rocco told him about America. He tried to describe it with all possible eloquence, not for his own pleasure or satisfaction—he was beginning to feel a sort of attachment to his prison—but because he hoped by his description to waken hope in Gigino and perhaps even help his recovery.

Leaning weakly on one elbow, Gigino listened attentively. Rocco told him that as soon as he was able to walk and to go out without attracting attention, something new was going to happen, something better.

"Just a day or two, Gigino, and you'll see. We'll leave. I'll take you. You'll make your fortune."

"You really believe that?"

Gigino began to feel stabs of pain in his legs and in his shoulders. He felt a strange aching which ran like furrows in opposite directions. Sometimes the pain ran from his shoulder to his hand, sometimes it rose from the hand to the shoulder, setting up an unbearable tension.

"You really believe that? Well, we can hope. Because as long as I'm in this state, you can't leave either."

"Are you sure?"

"If I tell you so. . . . We are practically married, you and I. It's even worse than being married because I can't go out without you or you without me."

"Why?"

"They'd be afraid you'd give the alarm. 'Squealers' are what they're most afraid of here. Houses in this neighborhood all have something to hide. Understand? And each one opens into the next on the ground floor. . . . Yes, sir, you can go all around the square without setting foot out of doors. That's how it is. As soon as a policeman sticks his nose into one of these houses he's a threat to the whole neighborhood."

"And if I go out?"

"You wouldn't get twenty meters."

With an imaginary gun in his hand, Gigino clicked his tongue in imitation of the dry crack of a shot. "Your time would come," he said.

And when Rocco didn't seem to understand, he added: "There are guards in the windows, on the roofs, on the balconies. They're everywhere. They live up there, like angels, with machine guns between their legs. Women go up there with them. I tell you you wouldn't have a chance. They're good shots."

Gigino spoke with a slight regret, as if he realized how strange it all was and tried to excuse himself for it. Don't hold it against me, he seemed to say. Don't hold it against me that this is the way things are. But he didn't say it aloud.

There were always squeakings of the trapdoor, which opened like a big blind eye, and always voices from above whispering news, and always word of the threatening presence of *carabinieri*

who "aren't giving up," no one could understand why. The rest
of the time, there was only an immeasurable silence, thick, frightening, as if the hole where Rocco and Gigino had taken refuge
was a thousand leagues under the earth.

Suddenly Rocco could see the evidence before his eyes. He was
unable to look any place except at that sick body, each time with
a deeper sense of terror or despair. It was impossible to escape the
idea that each emotion he felt was for the last time. Rocco found
himself thinking that Gigino's hair was an unusual color, dark
and shining, smooth as the hair of a Hindu. Also he thought,
quite naturally, that death would dull the child's hair. From that
moment Rocco saw Gigino as he really was—collapsed, sunk into
the ground, his hair sticky with sweat, straining to breathe, panting.

Soon awareness of the inevitable spread outside the cellar, invaded the house, rose through it, finding secret means of commu-
nication, and everything changed. The trapdoor opened to admit
not only whisperings but also women of all ages who came down
the ladder like black beetles; moving quickly with the voices and
gestures of some mysterious brigade of mourners, they mounted
a guard around Gigino, whose significance could only dimly be
guessed. The doctor finally came. He saw that pain was breaking
Gigino down, making him lose consciousness. The child was
shaken by such horribly violent spasms that he could neither drink
nor speak and his lips were rimmed with pinkish foam. The doctor
repeated, "Too late, too late." And when Rocco shouted in his
ear: "To late for what?" the doctor answered: "Not the slightest
hope, understand?" He spoke first of a drug, something like a
serum which he ought to have thought of, then, with a sort of
broken resignation, he pronounced the word "tetanus," and Rocco
heard himself repeating "tetanus" as the doctor was leaving, as
he, Rocco, stood at the foot of the ladder, immobile and defense-
less.

It was the imminent death of Gigino which gave him the
strength to imagine his own end. The vision was brief. One mo-

ment of pure liberty which left him the choice of accepting or rejecting. He was astonished at the rapidity with which he moved towards Gigino. He looked at him curled up on the ground, shaken by tremors which grew more convulsive all the time. He pushed the women aside. Some of them were praying and making signs of the cross, others talked among themselves in hard voices. Rocco shut them up brutally.

"I'm going to take this child to the hospital," he shouted. "For the love of God be quiet!"

"Why to the hospital?" one of the women asked. "He's going to die anyway."

Rocco leaned over Gigino and took his pulse, which still beat. He tried to rouse him but couldn't. The huddled body had stiffened into itself and when Rocco touched it the boy started with pain. He said, "Listen to me, little one. . . ." but there was only despair in his voice. Then he called him, "Gigino, Gigino," in the tone one uses to the dying, and he heard himself with a kind of horror, as if this voice, as if this tone would be partly responsible for Gigino's death.

The child opened his eyes. He tried to speak, but what rose in his throat was only a rattle and froth which formed again at the corners of his lips. Rocco decided to act.

"Wait here for me. I'm going to get help."

Then Gigino, in his hoarse voice, distinctly pronounced Rocco's name, which seemed to be projected toward the ladder, thrown out as if the trapdoor inhaled it. Rocco saw himself making the movements which he would make several moments later. He saw himself climbing, he felt the rungs of the ladder under the soles of his shoes and his hands closing on the uprights. He repeated, "Wait here for me, little one, wait. . . ." and he carefully sponged the sweat running down Gigino's cheeks. Leaning over him, his heart full of a pain such as he had never felt before, he embraced him for a long moment, breathing the mysterious warm odor which the boy carried in his clothing and which still masked the terrible odor of death. Then he approached the ladder, slid through the trapdoor, was surprised to find the ground floor empty and, lowering his head a little like a man who is about to dive, moved across the threshold.

Beyond, the square too was almost empty. It was noon. In that square, at noon, he was alone. Far away, Rocco imagined he saw the man who was watching for him outlined against the sky and for a moment he felt that presence as if it were a crowd. There was the square, that man, and himself.

He turned his head, looking for the figure of the one who would defeat him and this search became the center of his thoughts. If I go out, he thought, if I succeed in getting to the opposite wall very quickly and from there into the alleyways, and then if I run. . . . He imagined the whistling of the bullet, he imagined the smooth round bullet which would set him free when it struck him.

To think I'm going to die for that boy, he thought.

To think I'm going to die in Palermo.

To think I'm going to die here, now.

Leaning against the door frame, Rocco looked at the square, at the emptiness of the pavement stretching before him, dazzling with sun. Like a pebble beach. The heat bore down on the town with all its weight. He must plunge head first into this gulf. Then Rocco shot forward and made several yards at a run. In the middle of the square, he stood still. It was there that the light, the heat, the noise became suddenly darkness, cold, and silence; there that Rocco had the time to say to himself with a kind of intense joy, I'm going to stay here; . . . there that he wheeled round and fell. Stretched out with his face against the pavement.

Around him, under the barbaric noon sun, men formed a circle.

He was dead when they took him away.

EPILOGUE

*We were a land which was spared at the time
of some very ancient engulfment, a sort of
Atlantis which had preserved a tongue taught
by the gods themselves—for I call gods those
prestigious powers, crude as the world of sailors, the world of prisons, the world of adventure, by whom all our life is ordered, whence
our life draws its very nourishment, its life.*

JEAN GENET

I cannot explain how it was I felt when the news of Rocco's death
was noised about New York. I say "noised" but the word is too
strong: it was barely a rumor, quickly smothered. It was considered
unseemly to talk about it, the execution in a public square of a
man we had known. The people at *Fair* saw it as a lapse of taste,
and to a certain extent, an affront.

"My instinct was right," sighed Aunt Rosie when she found herself alone with me and could speak freely. I can still see her, frightened, almost paralyzed with horror. But I knew too that with others her sense of drama got the upper hand, and alone with her old business acquaintances, Mrs. MacMannox let it be understood that Rocco was the victim of an assassin. In veiled words. This version seemed to her better suited to her niece's interests. If she had been able to put Rocco aboard a frigate and to invent a tale of mutiny, of pirates, she would have done so. But compared to what I heard elsewhere, Aunt Rosie's hypocrisy seemed attractive to me. I could hear the melody under her lies.

Pam, when she learned the news, was shaken with little tremors, but her sorrow seemed to stop there. That day she was obliged to confide the secrets of a complicated metamorphosis to her readers, and this absorbed her attention. And in the evening there was a party she had to attend, perhaps even two.

Leaving our editorial room, she held the newspaper out to me and with her usual grimace said to me: "Look at this. It's your friend, I think." I hadn't the strength to answer her. The others went on working without looking up.

In Daisy Lee's eyes, as in those of all who ran *Fair*, henceforth Pam was credited with the foresight to have known enough to leave Rocco in time, to have avoided finding herself in a loser's position. Better still: by having broken it off so quickly she achieved the reputation of being a levelheaded woman. Her hasty return took on the appearance of a premature accusation and Rocco's guilt thereby became more evident. I saw a portrait of Rocco take shape in which all suspicions were already formed. Rocco was finally revealed for what he was, a blackguard who was mixed up in all sorts of unmentionable dealings. His death could only be a balancing of accounts, or possibly a suicide. Rocco, who was for me a being of flesh and blood, whose fate haunted me, was only a prey to them. They set themselves to tear him apart according to the inexorable laws of a world which was mediocre, vain, cruel.

Rocco's death made it absolutely necessary for me to break finally with that world. But then, it had always been impossible for me to regard my work as a second exile, even though at times I found in it a sort of pleasure. The scorn I bore in my heart occupied me for a long time. Then too I understood now what Rocco had represented to me: Sicily rediscovered, more secret than it was possible for me to conceive it, because in him Sicily lived only behind a mask. I knew too what I had felt within myself when I had crossed his path; I had come to re-create through him that which was most threatened in me; it was for that I had loved him, for that and for the dreams that he was the only one to offer me.

Thus was Rocco's light extinguished on Mulberry Street, as the Baron di D.'s light had been extinguished for the village of Sólanto. Rocco dead. The Baron di D. dead. They had been expatriated in obedience to the irony of a fate which had ordained that each should die where the other had lived.

Nothing of Antonio was left me but the story of his last battle as it had appeared in a Sicilian daily, a newspaper clipping which never left me. The chronicle was written in the grandiloquent and familiar style of inscriptions—telling glorious stories of a knight, or about a royal visit—as one sees them on the façades of our churches. In order that the reader could judge what Antonio bore with him in death, and what that death had so totally erased, the article told the beads of a long ostentatious genealogy in which several heroes of antiquity and some saints figured. And so that none would read this story without emotion, it involved the memory of those children of the streets and young peasants who died with Antonio; the absurdity of their fate in that last hour had inspired that band of adolescents to create a series of blasphemous oaths which were faithfully reported by the writer as the last words of the dying. Everything in this account seemed to me to bear the mark of poetry, to be impregnated with a lyricism which delighted me. It seemed more satisfying than vengeance to me that Antonio's boys should have said goodby to life crying "Damned whoresons" or "Blood of a dog" to an invisible enemy beyond the mountains. It reminded me of the times of Sister Rita's paladins, of our Sundays drinking diluted syrup and flat Marsala, of the garden flaming with wisteria, of the noble names on our convent wall, of the happiness of our litanies and also of Antonio's long sunny naps, since all that was left of him was this printed scrap of paper, this modest memorial.

And now Agata, little Agata in her black dress. We lived, she and I, the only true witnesses of the past, two survivors of a drowned world. She was the wisdom of the earth, and in her mouth, words were more than just words. She understood everything quicker and better than others. She knew nothing. But in her heart she had enough to remake the world.

She made of Rocco one of the heroes in that oratory I have described, where were established the patron saints of our island. Thus Agata's sorrow took on the triumphant aspect of an act of love. She never said that Rocco was dead, but that he had "returned." Returned where, Agata? For the love of God, explain yourself. Returned to heaven? to paradise? She did not answer. Rocco had "returned." And since, when she spoke of herself, she also often said that when the moment came, when Theo was grown, she too would return, one could never be sure whether she was alluding to her death or to her return to Sicily.

Thus Rocco remained present among us, as if projected into the reality of our lives by an act of magic created by Agata. It was necessary to keep Alfio from growing morose, and miraculously, Agata succeeded. When the Gospel wasn't enough she called upon mythology. And I know well, I who knew her, that during nights when despair visited her and she imagined Rocco in the middle of the dark circle of his last watchers, she would waken Calò, shake him and ask him in an anguished voice: "Do you believe that a man can be changed into a bull?" Calò would search his memory and, to quiet her, affirm that he had seen that story sculptured someplace on a wall. Then Agata would go back to sleep, imagining Rocco with four feet wide apart, a tuft of hair on his forehead, tranquilly grazing in some field. . . .

She called herself a voluntary prisoner of forgetfulness, a system whose tricks she taught me each day. "You should forget, you too," she told me. She spoke of our past as a burden we carried attached to our feet. She said too, "Don't be drowned by it" when she could not make me share her enthusiasms, the enthusiasms of a little girl living in wonder, absorbed in daily life but who in her escape from misery was always trembling at the thought that her way of blotting things out might prove to be a mirage. So I also awoke to wonder. And I found, I too, that Theo was as beautiful as John the Baptist, handsome as a painted image, as a picture, as anything, and that the cariatyd at the entrance to the movie house was more golden than the Madonna of the Chair, and that the actress who came to eat pizza at Casa Alfio, that elegant new star had a body that could stop clocks, and that finally, it was miraculous when you thought how well God wishes us. But Agata's lips never formed the sounds of the word Palermo. If by accident one of us—Theo, Calò or I—allowed it to escape, Agata put her hands to her ears and cried: "Be quiet! You'll be the death of me. . . ."

Of the two of us she was the stronger, and I want the last image of this story to be the face of little Agata, who became my friend. Agata welcoming me at the door of Casa Alfio, where I ran to meet her every day, sometimes so quickly that it seemed to me that I was running barefoot across New York. "Sit down, girls. . . ." So Alfio addressed us. "Eh Gianna! We were waiting for you." So spoke Agata in her black dress, guardian of our thoughts, watching over our memories, Agata who circled round the table, ran to the kitchen, came back, went from one to the other with her handkerchief knotted around her head. She made us drunk on her discoveries, abandoned herself to her necessary joy, sometimes danced, in order that the word would never be pronounced which hovered over all of us and glowed in us like an eternal flame. . . .

Where could we leave the little we knew of Sólanto?

No more lights in the windows of the castle, over which the

gardener still watched from his shady corner, looking surly, his big cap pulled down over his eyes. Don Fofò only rarely went there. He lived now in the house on the mountain. A peasant woman whom he kept to distract him, a young girl—what they call *una giovanetta* in the countryside—had given him a son. So that Baron di D.'s wishes might be carried out, he was called Antonio.

And Zaira reared the child.

Moulin du Breuil 1961
Mondello 1964–1965
Morainville 1966

THIS BOOK WAS SET IN

ELECTRA AND TORINO TYPES,

PRINTED AND BOUND BY

AMERICAN BOOK-STRATFORD PRESS.

IT WAS DESIGNED BY

LARRY KAMP